©LOCKWOOD

The SUMMER DRAGON

TODD LOCKWOOD

The SUMMER DRAGON

FIRST BOOK OF THE EVERTIDE

DAW BOOKS, INC.

DONALD A. WOLLHEIM, FOUNDER

375 Hudson Street, New York, NY 10014

ELIZABETH R. WOLLHEIM
SHEILA E. GILBERT
PUBLISHERS

www.dawbooks.com

First Printing, May 2016
2   3   4   5   6   7   8   9

ACKNOWLEDGMENTS

My deep appreciation to all the following, for their time and advice and enthusiasm.

Betsy Wollheim, my editor and friend. Thanks for your interest in my world.

Eric Mona, my first mentor and teacher, and Anthony Waters, brilliant artist and creator; you were there at the very beginning. Gregory Frost, who opened my eyes to the craft of writing; Nancy Kress and Mary Rosenblum who helped me find my voice, and Marylou Capes-Platt who polished it. Scott Taylor and Shawn Speakman, who read early drafts and published me first. Lou Anders for invaluable input and friendship. Tony Green, willing to discuss plot until late into the night; Doug Wray, who's read my stuff since high school; and the entire rest of the gang in Colorado for uncountable weekends of inspired story-telling: Marty & Kate, Bill, Janet, Kathy, Lemuel, Kirk, Marv. All my willing beta-readers: Rich Howard, who gave me the first, most thorough critique, Henry Mayo, Caitlin Lockwood, Kipp Lockwood, April Moore, Jodi Lane, Karey Brown and Tyler Brown, Stacie Pitt, Elaura Lockwood Webb, Pierce Watters, Marie Brennan, R.A. Salvatore, Alan Dean Foster, and Terry Brooks. Your enthusiasm was my oxygen.

My biggest thanks goes to Leslie Howle, whose tireless support and passion kept me inspired. I would not be here without you. You're a writer's best friend.

Thank you all.

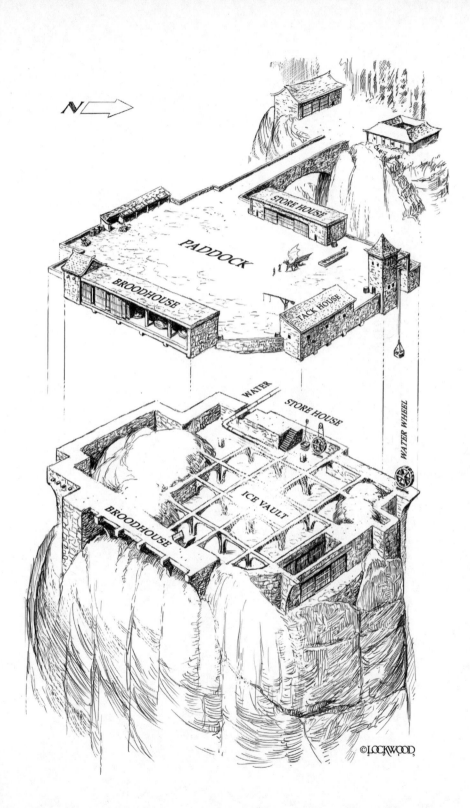

PART 1
The SUMMER DRAGON

They were feeding the babies when the slaughter began.

Graeden spotted the invaders first. Ragged shadows, dark and misshapen, descended from the twilight sky. He thrust his shovel into the cart of dried fish and left it there. Dragon qits in the nests complained when the delivery of food stopped. The adult dragons cooed to their broodlings to calm them, but they too looked out the big rolling doors to the sky. The long, narrow broodhouse, one of several stacked on the mountainside, opened on one side into the paddock; on the other it overlooked a high precipice. The roofs of Cuuloda clustered far below were bound by steep cliffs and dense forest stretching toward the distant plains.

The enemy had been testing the defenses of this high mountain aerie without success. The natural terrain provided substantial security, but these creatures had found a gap in the perimeter of Cuuloda's sawtooth peaks and mounted patrols.

Graeden squinted. They looked like dragons, but something was wrong. Emanations of green punctuated the tattered silhouettes. He felt a sudden chill and pulled his jacket more tightly closed. "Father—what are they?"

His father, Ardran, dropped his shovel, too. The breeze blowing in from the cliffside opening and through to the paddock smelled of ash and decay. "By the gods, Grae." His face lost all color. "The rumors are true. The Harodhi have found a way to corrupt dragons. They're Horrors. *Flying* Horrors."

Ardran called to his eldest, pumping water in the paddock. "Bahnam—raise the alarm. Alert your brothers. Then get the doors on the upper nests closed. Go!" Bahnam looked up to the sky over the broodhouse and his jaw fell. He dropped his bucket, dashed across the yard to the storehouse, shouting, *"Lem! Harien!"* Soon a bell rang from the yard. Shouts answered.

"Grae, help me close the aerie. *Move!*" Together Ardran and Grae heaved to the multiple big doors on the paddock side, rolling them on their tracks to close off the nests.

The qits began to squeal uncertainly, sensing the unfamiliar urgency. Their parents turned to the precipice-side with wings spread in threat display, shielding their babies from the approaching nightmares.

The bell stopped pealing, and Grae hazarded a final look out to the paddock. He saw Bahnam and two more of his brothers dashing up the long stair to the next broodhouse up the hill. Shadows chased them.

Something shook the roof. Plaster rained down. With a cry of frustration, Grae closed the last door and threw the latch, looked across the platform to the darkening sky. The twisted shapes descended in numbers impossible to count. They'd be here before he and his father could get the precipice doors closed.

Screams erupted from outside. A second boom on the ceiling above roused another chorus of fearful bleats.

"Grae," said his father. "Someone has to get word to the Dragonry in Haalden."

"What?" he said.

"Take Kiven and go."

"We've closed the paddock doors—I can't access the tack house—"

Bowshots snapped somewhere outside. A scream. Grae recognized the voice of his brother Harien, cut short by a chorus of rasping growls. His blood turned to ice.

"There's no time," said his father. "Mount up without saddle. Trust me, boy—you have to go. *Now.*"

Grae dashed to his favorite mount, his broodfather Kiven, and leapt up onto his neck. Just as quickly, the first of the Horrors landed on the lip of the platform two bays down. A monstrous winged shadow with a dark man-shape on its back surveyed the nests with eyes like green coals. Another alit next to it. Then another.

The broodparents charged the blackened monsters, hissing. Teeth met teeth. Claws slashed. Babies spilled out of the nests to dam up against the paddock-side doors. The monsters ripped their parents from the shelf, trailing blood off into the void. More of the things swept in to replace them.

Grae hesitated in shock as one of the dark riders dismounted and approached the bleating qits, a large bag in its hands.

"They mean to take the brood!" he called.

His father grabbed a machete off the wall. Stood uncertainly before his squalling qits. He met his son's eyes with fear. "Go! Save yourself!"

Graeden turned Kiven to the precipice. "Hai!" he shouted, clinging to the large scales on the back of his dragon's neck. They launched out into space. One of the Horror beasts snatched at him in passing. Missed. Continued on to the broodhouse floor, the scent of decay trailing after.

Grae looked back, even as he urged Kiven to greater speed. Their dragon sires and dams disappeared beneath a multitude of torn shapes. Roars became cries of pain as frenzied slashing began. More monsters massed on the roof and in the paddock beyond, the upper tiers of nests as well. Grae screamed in anguish. His home. His brothers. His parents. Everything he'd ever known.

The last he saw of Ardran, his father was backed into a corner, his brood behind him. Blackened things shaped like men approached, some with weapons, some with large canvas bags. Ardran turned to his babies. Raised his machete to deprive the enemy of as many as he could. The blade fell only twice.

The last thing Grae heard from his father was a howl of anger and despair as the hell things swarmed him.

O   N   E

A DRAGON HANDLER WITH *her head in the clouds is cursed.* Those were my mother's last words to me. Spoken in anger, they have haunted me ever since.

I paused on the stone bridge that connected the clifftop manor to the aeries. Was my head in the clouds if I dared to *hope*? I looked at the dragon silhouettes against the gray light ahead and shivered in the chill pre-dawn air.

Tomorrow was Brood Day. The Ministry buyers would come for our dragon babies. The season would end with feasting and spectacle. But this year might be better than ever. We had an extra-large clutch of dragonlings—our biggest ever—and Father had wanted a new breeding pair since forever ago. Surely the Ministry wouldn't need every qit. Father meant to petition them to let us keep two.

One for Darian. And one for me.

My ancestors, as far back as anyone could recount, had bred dragons, first for warlords, then for Kings. And after the Empire of Gurvaan subjugated our western province of Gadia, we bred dragons for the Dragonry of the Emperor. Our aeries weren't the biggest—that would be Cuuloda to the north, run by Ardran and his sons. They visited us from time to time to trade eggs or share news. But our qits were sought after. Father liked to boast that generals flew on our dragons. It was true.

Surely another breeding pair would be a good thing, wouldn't it?

"Maia!" Darian trotted back across the bridge with his lantern and plucked at my sleeve. "This is not the time to stand here daydreaming, girl. What's the matter with you?"

"Nothing." I turned and looked up at him. When did he get so tall? Together we continued on toward the paddock. "We've worked hard, Dare. We've earned it."

Darian didn't say anything. He had that look, the one that made me think of Father when his anger was brewing—hair black as a storm cloud, straight nose slightly wrinkled, dark eyes glinting. He wouldn't look at me. My stomach twisted. "It's the perfect year for it. We're both of age and we've got more qits than we ever had."

"I know, but—"

"But what? What aren't you telling me?"

His chin bunched up. "Not now, Maia."

"I know exactly which qit you've got your heart set on, Dare."

"Korruzon's mighty farts, Maia! We have work to do. Come on." He broke into a trot, leaving me alone in the dark.

I almost laughed—Darian had an irreverent curse for every occasion. He'd defamed Korruzon Himself, the mount of the Emperor Ahriman. Centuries old, Korruzon was one of the Avar—the High Dragons, mystical creatures of spirit and magic. Not like the mountain dragons we bred, mere animals by comparison. The High Dragons existed in a realm outside of the familiar natural world. Some claimed that High Dragons could even breathe fire. Korruzon had served every emperor since Gurvaan's beginning, as advisor, head of the Dragon Temple—de facto ruler, really. The Dragon Temple said He was older even than that—He was some sort of manifestation of the original creator of the universe. That was hard to understand, but the answers to my questions only made Him seem like something out of a story. Above reality. A God.

But something closer to home was wrong. What did Darian know that I didn't? I watched him disappear into the gloom. The war wasn't going well—we'd heard rumor enough to suspect it. I turned my back on the compound to see the first red light of dawn touch the waterfall to the north called the Roaring. Lights fluttered on in the village of Riat far below. Smoke in the chimneys spoke of renewal, the turning of the clock. Tomorrow, the Ministry's gold would flow into Riat through our aeries. Brood Day was a celebration for the villagers too. For all of us.

The clop of hooves and rattle of wheels turned my head. A wagon crossed the yard onto the bridge, pulled by a bay mare. A lantern swinging from a hook illuminated the driver.

"Fren!" I jogged to the wagon and climbed up. I'd known Fren all my life. He'd let me ride his horse when I could barely walk. We seldom saw him more than twice a year—in the winter when he brought us ice from the high lakes to replenish the vaults, and on Brood Day, when he brought us wood chips for the nests. Between times he might wander in with lumber or a deer for our dragons, or news from the forest.

The load of cedar chips in the wagon filled my nose with its spicy perfume. It would make a clean, pleasant presentation of the nests.

"How's your shadow, m'lady?" He looked down at me with a wide smile that deepened the laugh lines around his mouth and crinkled the corners of his eyes.

"My shadow is well. How's yours?"

"Well." He laughed. This was our usual greeting. Fren told me once that it meant something particular. A person has two shadows: the one made by the sun, and the one that follows each person after death, the aftereffects of every deed. "Allow light to balance the darkness," he'd explained, "for everything you do leaves a shadow—a ripple on the Evertide."

You were supposed to keep an eye on your shadow—the second kind. I didn't know what it meant, really. Something only Fren ever said.

"This is a new horse." He pointed. "I'll need to keep some distance today, cuz she's not used to dragons."

"I'm sure she'll be fine. We'll keep an eye out for you." I bounced down from his wagon and started toward the paddock.

"Happy Brood Day, Miss Maia!" he called after me. "I know your expectations are high this year. But don't forget you were born the day of a Morningtide. You're lucky!"

I laughed, but I didn't feel lucky. Not with my brother acting strange, and Mother's words echoing in my memory. I turned and hurried after Darian.

The sound of the Roaring swallowed the scuff of my boots on the bridge paving.

Beyond the tall stone walls of the storehouse, the paddock was a blur of action. Local farmers unloaded crates of melons and squawking chickens for the dragons' dinners, or shoveled out cartloads of straw or woodchips into holding bins. Extra hands hired from the farms swept and raked every inch of the compound. The tack house doors were open wide and the saddles already rolled out for the brood-parents' outing. The oiled leather and studs sparkled in the lamplight.

I turned the corner toward the still-closed broodhouse full of dragon qits and almost ran into Darian. He'd stopped to watch the show.

"Don't put that there!" Father waved off a sweating farmer's son backing a rickety cart up to one of the bins. "You! What are you doing? I told you to wait with that straw. It doesn't go there." The scrawny youth wrestled with the reins of his nervous horse, one eye on Father as he struggled to turn his cart out of the way. The poor boy looked ready to whip up his horse and bolt. I felt for him. On the day before Brood Day, Father's temper could be quick. He was a big man—his name, Magha, meant "mighty." Tattoos from his time in the Dragonry covered his arms. He had the bond mark, of course, and his insignias of rank, but also the strange filigree of the healing craft around his scars. He was imposing in any circumstance, but even more so with Shuja next to him.

Huge and jet-black, Shuja stepped eagerly into place under the saddle jib, his massive wings tucked in close, his long neck arched, the frill stretched taut and upright. "Han-t!" Shuja said happily. He was a good speaker, but that was the best a dragon-mouth could do with the word "hunt." Shuja loved the hunt. His eyes gleamed golden and happy. Father steered the crane's arm over Shuja's saddle, then climbed up to hook the saddle's rings to the jib, fore and aft, shouting orders over his shoulder. He turned our way and his eyes narrowed.

"Dare, where is your sister?"

"Right here." I stepped up beside Darian, noting the relief of the farmer's son now that Father's attention turned away from him.

"Good. The two of you draw water and bathe the broodlings. Clear the soiled straw out of the nests, wash them out, and refill them with wood chips. Sweep the platform and pick up any stray tools. Inspect the harnesses as you clean and oil them. I want everything sharp and spotless. Presentation affects sales!"

The Brood Day Lecture. I glanced at Darian. Hiding behind the glare of his lantern, he mouthed Father's words almost verbatim, his upper lip protruding comically. I punched him in the arm. *"Stop it,"* I whispered.

"Enough of the qit-play, Maia." Father's eyes took on that glint, like distant lightning. "Get to work. *Now!*" Typical. Darian starts something and I get blamed.

My older brother Tauman and his wife, Jhem, were leading out the other two sires. We hunted the parent dragons hard on the day before Brood Day. They loved it. The sires were first, and would be gone for several hours. Then the dams would get a turn, though after months of nesting they needed the hunt more than the fathers did. There'd be plenty of venison for the feast tomorrow, but more than that, an exhausting day in the skies offered freedom they'd not had in months, helping to blunt their anger and grief when the Ministry buyers carried off their babies.

"Let's go." Darian grabbed my elbow. "We've got a lot to do."

We started across the paddock toward the broodhouse opposite. "Look at them, Dare." I pointed at the three broodsires—they practically danced on the stones. A deep rumbling came from Shuja's chest, and the other broodparents repeated it. I could almost feel it in my bones. I tried to match the cadence and pitch, but it came out as more of a staccato grunt in my abdomen than a rumble, and it wouldn't carry across the compound like theirs did.

"You sound like you're about to throw up," said Darian.

"Very funny." I remembered Mother clucking and cooing at the qits. She told me more than once that dragons have a secret language of their own, and she was learning it. No one thought that possible, but she winked at me when Father laughed at her efforts. I'd been listening to the dragons ever since.

I understood their emotions, if not what they were saying. "They know their broods are about to be taken from them," I said to Dare, "but they're excited about the hunt. Listen to the change of rhythm, and the complexity . . . they're talking to each other. Mother used to think—"

"You're crazy," said Darian. "You can't speak dragon. No one can."

Mother's absence still affected Darian, I knew, even all these years later. But I treasured the memory of her chatting with the babies, her face alight. It balanced the other memory—better to think about that than her last words. "Maybe, maybe not," I said.

Shuja pranced sideways as the other sires were saddled, his wings half unfurled. The hired farm hands kept a wide distance, although they were perfectly safe with Father on his back. Shuja was our most magnificent dragon. His upright crest, massive jaws, and deep purple-black hide set him apart from the others. Of all our sires, only he had been born outside of the western mountains. He and Father bonded during their time in the Dragonry and had seen many battles together. Shuja's scales and smoky underbelly were covered with scars. He was the clear alpha among our broodsires and his golden eyes could be . . . chilling. You didn't take liberties with Shuja.

Tauman lowered the saddle onto his broodsire, Rannu, our second-oldest sire. Rannu was a classic specimen of the mountain breed with tan and stone-gray markings, stocky legs, and broad wings. He was the first bonded dragon of my older brother. As Tauman would one day be Broodmaster, Rannu was the future of our line. Not a beautiful dragon, but he threw qits that grew up to be strong and biddable. He had never mastered the word "hunt" to any degree, so he nodded his approval of this outing, nearly smacking Tauman on the head with his chin. I giggled as Tauman jumped back. My older brother was a bit too full of his place as heir and future Broodmaster.

Jhem, her bright red hair a beacon in the lantern light, struggled with her young broodsire Audax. Audax was wild, but he shouldn't have been that hard to control. He was one of a pair of cave-grays Father gave to Jhem as wedding gifts six years ago, mottled gray and white, with hints of silver in the hard plates on neck and legs. In spite of Jhem's scolding, Audax crowded Rannu, bumping the older dragon's wing. Rannu snarled a warning to the younger broodsire—*stay clear*. Audax returned a deep-throated rumble of annoyed defiance. *Jhem, hold him!* I took a step forward, but she instantly pulled his head down by an ear frill and spoke to him in low, firm tones, like a mother scolding a stubborn child in the marketplace.

I let out a sigh of relief. We'd never had a sire-fight in my lifetime. Jhem really needed to get him in hand.

Audax sat down petulantly, which allowed Rannu a few more inches without Audax actually having to remove himself. He looked like a big, winged, extremely dangerous puppy.

Father, just buckling his harness to Shuja's saddle, turned our way. Darian ducked quickly out of sight into the broodhouse.

"Maia! What did I tell you to do?" Father's face darkened.

I didn't need another lecture about doing things before I was told. Hurrying through the broodhouse door, I tripped over Darian's lantern where he had left it, just inside. It clattered off the wall. I yelled and dove for it, catching it before it could break and spill burning oil.

Outside, Audax snarled in surprise. The lantern burned my hands, and I dropped it. It shattered and flames erupted on the paving, just as Fren guided his new horse past the broodsires with his load of woodchips. Audax growled again and lurched backward. The horse squealed and bolted. The cart struck Audax's tail and tipped over. Fren catapulted out to land on Audax's tail frill, and Audax spun with a roar of pain, batting Fren the way a person might swat at a fly buzzing too near his face. The blow sent Fren flying twenty feet across the paddock to land in a crumple.

The panicked horse bolted through the crowded yard, dragging the sideways cart behind it. I heard Father shout and felt the blast of Shuja's wingbeats as I ran to the driver's side. Fren! I dropped to my knees beside him, sick to my stomach. He pushed up on one arm, clutched his chest, staring with glazed eyes at the paving stones beneath him. Blood was everywhere. Shuja had pinned the runaway cart, and Tauman struggled with the panicked horse. Jhem had Audax by the nostrils. Darian threw burlap sacks on the fire to smother it.

Fren looked up at me. "Don't hurt my horse!" he rasped and slumped forward.

I eased him onto his back, pulled his hands gently away, and opened his slashed shirt, swallowing my sickness. Audax had torn a gash from shoulder to hip with his talons. Blood welled from the wound, thick and warm as it ran over my hands and puddled on the stone. Avar! I yanked off my jacket, rolled it up, and pressed it as hard as I could against the gash. The fabric turned dark, and red started to seep from beneath it. It wouldn't stop. I pressed harder and Fren groaned. Suddenly Jhem was pressing on the fabric with me. Fren's eyes rolled back into his head, reappeared glazed and gray. Dying? I choked on a sob.

"Darian—get a rake and start cleaning up this mess." Father knelt beside me. "Let me see." He pushed my hands away, peeled the blood-soaked jacket from the gash. Whistled. "That's going to be an impressive set of marks."

"Will he be all right?"

Father said nothing as he eased Fren up so Jhem could bind my jacket to him with strips torn from his bloodied shirt. Then Father picked him up like a child and carried him to the saddle jib, whistling for Shuja. Tauman used the crane to lift Father and Fren onto Shuja's back.

"We're taking Fren to the Temple." Father spoke to Tauman, never once looking in my direction. "Get those broodsires out of here and work them hard. I'll join you when I can."

Finally, he turned an icy gaze on me. "Curse all, Maia, can't you keep your mind on your work?" He leaned forward, and Shuja launched into the air. With one downbeat of his wings they cleared the paddock wall and were out over the valley, a silhouette against the pre-dawn sky.

I stood frozen. Stunned. "I didn't mean to kick the lantern."

Jhem clasped my shoulder. Her face was pale, and she blinked back tears. "Don't worry. I'm in more trouble than you are."

The compound was silent—everybody was looking at me.

Curse all, Maia, can't you keep your mind on your work?

It felt like an omen, as if my mother stirred in her grave.

A dragon handler with her head in the clouds . . .

T W O

I FOUGHT BACK SOBS as Darian and I cleaned up the debris from the cart and raked the woodchips into a pile. Tauman and Jhem were deathly quiet as they stabled the poor horse. I could tell that Tauman was waiting to explode once they were alone—he couldn't be happy about Audax's behavior, and Jhem would get an earful. She hadn't been born to dragons like he had, though she'd always shown an aptitude—he wouldn't have married her otherwise. But it seemed that she never quite measured up to his standards, and this wouldn't help. He could be a bastard sometimes, but Audax shouldn't have snapped. I didn't know whether to feel sorry for her or angry that she didn't have Audax more under control.

When riders and dragons finally took to the sky for their pre-Brood Day hunt, I sighed and crumpled onto the stone sill of the watering trough. The silence was dense and scornful. A sniffle escaped. "Poor Fren!"

Darian put his arm around my shoulder, and let me weep for a few minutes. Some part of my mind noted the blood on my trousers, saw that despite several buckets of water, there was still blood on the paving.

"I didn't mean to kick the lamp. I didn't see it there." I groaned instead of adding *where you left it*. "Somehow I always end up in trouble."

"He won't stay mad—"

"It's just like the last time I saw Mother. I always get—"

"Don't, Maia."

"Blamed for whatever—"

"That wasn't . . . you didn't—"

"You and me were fussing over that sick qit instead of doing our chores. But you left right before Mother came around the corner, and I'm the one who got lectured."

"You were little." Darian fidgeted. "You don't remember it right."

We both fell silent. I wanted to say *that was your fault, too*, but fighting wouldn't fix anything. I shouldn't have brought up Mother's death. The memories chattered from that deep inner silence where they normally slept—her last words as she sat on Grus, scowling, and other specters better left in darkness. Father loved to tell of her bravery and skill when he met her during their time in the Dragonry, when the empire of Gurvaan annexed the small country of Ebrolin. I couldn't possibly measure up to her example.

I shrugged off Darian's arm and dried my eyes with a quick swipe of my sleeve. "We've got work to do." I entered the broodhouse and Darian followed.

The platform was long and wide enough to contain four gigantic nests in a row—boxes of wood crafted in octagonal shapes two feet high. Three of them were filled with straw as bedding for sleeping broods and their watchful mothers. The fourth was empty. In past years the aeries of Riat bred as many as four pairs of broodparents, though never in my lifetime. Father hoped to fill that fourth nest again. I tried not to look at it.

Eight enormous doors on either side of the nests could be rolled aside to open the broodhouse to the paddock or to the precipice overlooking the village, or both. The paddock-side doors were only rarely opened when qits filled the nests. But dragons love heights; the cliffside doors were open most days to inspire that instinct from the very beginning.

I unlatched the first of the cliffside doors, and Darian joined me. Together we rolled them open to let the sun warm the babies.

Bloody dawn spilled over the horizon. Long shadows streaked the farms on the plains eastward. Far below us, the village of Riat was puddled with lingering fog. The cliff faces to either side of the valley steamed in the early light, while the Roaring spilled off the heights to the north, sending its curtain of mist across the valley. Raptors circling in the warm light above punctuated the quiet with their calls: *keirr . . . keirr.* It was the beginning of what should have been a beautiful day.

We turned to the aerie, where qits already began to wrestle in the first light. Darian hunkered down in front of one of the nests. "Look at him, Maia. He's the biggest one. He's going to be magnificent someday." He'd said that at least once a day for weeks, but today his face was different.

The young dragon topped a pile of dragon babies, dark scales winking in the sun as he tugged on the ear frill of a littermate. His crest—the frill of spines and leather just behind his head—promised to be as impressive as that of his Father, Shuja. Coppery Grus, the broodmother, stretched her leathery wings wide—enjoying a rare moment when the aerie wasn't crowded with adult dragons. She purred a warning to Darian when he reached out a hand.

"Don't, Darian. We don't know if we'll keep any yet." Young dragons bonded quickly, and the bonds lasted a lifetime. Contact had to be brief and businesslike—that was one of the first, most basic rules of dragonlore. It was probably the hardest thing about raising qits—you couldn't touch them any more than was necessary.

Darian knew that. "I'm not going to pet him," he shot back. But he tucked his hands into his armpits and craned his neck that littlest bit closer. "I just want to look at him. He's gorgeous."

"You'll spoil them for the Dragonry if you—"

"I know! I know. Don't be a nag."

I directed a wicked scowl at the back of his head.

But I understood Darian's desire. In the next nest—that of Rannu and Athys, my brother Tauman's bonded pair—was a brown female qit with buff-colored markings who always seemed to perk up when I came by. While her littermates tussled, she sat alert in the corner of the nest and studied me with her amber eyes. I ached to touch her soft, dry skin. Her mother, Athys, watched me too, inscrutable brown eyes set deep in the stone-gray brow.

I couldn't caress her baby, but I couldn't help staring into those intelligent little eyes.

" 'The best ones in the nest raise the value of all the others,' "

Darian said, quoting Father. I felt his eyes on me and turned. His face was puckered in a scowl. I knew that he really meant *we shouldn't get our hopes up*. The Dragonry would want the best ones.

"I wish I'd seen the lantern . . ."

"I know. I'm sorry, Maia. I'm sorry you got yelled at. I won't let you take the blame alone. I promise."

For Darian to admit any part of the blame for anything was rare. He was like Father that way. My anger toward him softened. "Audax started it, really. He's so emotional."

"The youngest male in the aerie—he thinks he has to prove himself. He needs to be taught his place."

"Jhem is getting a lecture on that right now, you can bet. *High Ones*, but I hope Fren is going to be okay."

"Well, that was a disaster even if Fren survives. Jhem probably deserves it."

"She's trying. Audax is still young."

Neither of us spoke for the longest time.

"Nag," said Darian.

"Horror," I answered.

He grinned. "Come on, Maia. Back to work."

We moved through our chores quickly, paying extra attention to detail. After the babies had eaten a breakfast of melon rinds, ears of corn, and fish, they tumbled out of their nests to play on the platform. The broodmothers, Grus, Athys, and Coluver, policed the rambunctious qits while Darian and I removed all the soiled straw from the nests. Then we brought buckets of water to wash platform and qitlings simultaneously. This was something new and exciting for them. They splashed and played, with happy yips and mischievous kitten-like roars. With their antics, they practically cleaned each other. All Darian and I needed to do was occasional spot scrubbing with a mop, and then broom the water over the lip.

It was impossible not to be cheered by their play. I started to feel better, but when I thought of Fren crumpling in my arms, his blood everywhere, my stomach tightened into a knot. I still had his blood under my fingernails.

Later in the morning we fed the babies again—an extra-large meal of dried beef and smoked livers. It would fill their bellies and make them sleepy, but leave relatively little mess. Then the real labor began. We wheeled in mounds of wood chips to refill their nesting boxes. The inquisitive qits were in and out of our carts constantly, but we didn't mind. Their dry, shiny scales were surprisingly soft at this age—we were tempted to sneak a caress here and there as we fended them off. The little brown-and-buff female made an especially thorough investigation of my cart, as if she sensed my interest and approved of me.

At last we were done, and the broodmothers nudged the qits into their nests. As we checked and oiled the harnesses, we watched the qits scuffle with their littermates, converting the last of their excited energy into play. Then we swept the deck, and the shushing sound of broom on stone lulled them to sleep. We gave it a cadence, because dragons love music. The mothers purred to add a soothing counterpoint.

Soon they were curled in tight clusters of shiny leather, tiny snouts tucked under folded wings. With the bedding refreshed, their naturally clean, talcum scent filled the air. I sought out the little female in the nest of Rannu and Athys. Her back rose and fell under her mother's wing. I squatted down where I could see her better.

Darian patted me on the shoulder. "I just saw Father, heading north on Shuja to find Tauman and Jhem. I hope that's a good sign for Fren. They won't be back soon, and the broodlings are all asleep. Our work here is done. The help has all left . . ."

I looked up at him as his voice trailed off. His face was clouded again, and a shiver tickled my back. He seemed to be on the verge of saying something, but then his lips softened into a weak smile. "Let's go check the traps."

I was tempted. It was a daily duty anyway, though maybe not on the day before Brood Day. This particular afternoon it might be salve for our wounds, but it didn't feel right. "Dare, I don't think we ought to—"

"No, I think we should." He looked terribly serious. Before I could answer, he sauntered into the paddock, then crossed the bridge to the homestead atop the cliff and past the winter stables into the trees. Once out of sight of the compound, he darted between trunks and hurdled deadfalls, eager to be lost in the deep stillness.

I followed.

THREE

DARIAN OUTPACED ME, but I knew where he was going. I could hear him in the brush ahead. Eventually I stopped trying to catch up to him and slowed to a walk. The day was bright and warm, but the cool green shadows and the rich, damp smell of earth and leaves refreshed me. The underbrush whipped against my legs.

On a normal day, we'd have taken our time checking the snares. There were wild berries in season. Choice mushrooms in the shadows. Other treasures to be found—arrowheads or spear points, or ancient, rusted pieces of machinery. But Darian had gone straight to our most productive trap, the one near the ruins.

I couldn't stop thinking about Fren, or about Father's anger. The day felt wrong—a confused mix of sun and warmth, terror and guilt, joy and sorrow. I was frowning when I caught up to Darian at last.

The crumbling walls and pillars of an ancient temple compound broke up the trees. More light reached the understory so there were tender leaves in abundance, and a small rivulet of snowmelt from the higher peaks provided fresh water. It never failed to bring grazers into our snare. A small deer had been impaled on the spear and lifted up above the reach of groundling predators. Darian had lowered the catch, reset the trap, and now prepared to dress the little deer.

I plucked some berries from a nearby bush; I didn't want to see more blood. I sat on a block of marble with a pile of berries in my lap. I was often drawn to the ruins when Darian was busy with other tasks or when my own duties gave me an hour to myself. Riding on Grus, Mother used to bring me to the ruins for picnics when I was small. I felt a chill, as if her ghost were here and had brushed against me. I pushed the memories down and let the tumbled blocks and pillars distract me.

We didn't know their story completely. The dhalla—Mabir, our local Temple priest—talked about it often, but we didn't understand half of what he said. There was a name—Cinvat—an ancient city buried somewhere in the forest beyond the ridge that this temple once served. We knew the tales were important, of course, and that someone had put great effort into this ancient shrine. I liked to study the crumbling walls and the stumps of marble columns, all covered with remnants of carvings that suggested a story long lost. A statue made of two different colors of stone dominated the center of the patio. It showed two dragons, a black one carved out of dark stone below and a white one made of marble above, locked in combat. They didn't look like our dragons.

"I wonder who carved them." I wiped berry juice from my chin.

"You know—old dead people," said Darian.

I scowled at him.

We knew they were Avar—the dhalla said so—High Dragons like the emperor's mysterious Korruzon. The White Dragon was Menog, and the black one was Dahak—that much I remembered, and their struggle was the epic climax to an ancient tale. A cataclysmic war had ended here long ago, but somehow the details never stuck with me.

"Were they real?"

"Of course they were." Darian continued sawing with his knife.

I'd never before wondered if they represented something real. The ruins had only ever been inspiration for our imaginations. We summoned up armies of monsters to face and defeat in the course of a summer's afternoon, before we climbed the cliffs overlooking the Copper Sea to watch the kiting of the ocean birds, which became fleets of attacking dragons in our eyes. We knew those tales best, for they were *our* tales, not like those of the dhalla. *We* were the heroes, and the victories were ours.

"Do you suppose our games were like . . ." I frowned, considering how to phrase the question, "like the ghosts of these people, trying to tell us their story?"

Darian looked up at me with one eyebrow raised. "That's crazy-talk, Maia. I have no idea what you just said."

I let it go. I wasn't sure what I meant myself.

He finished dressing the deer and tossed the entrails into the bushes for smaller predators to find. Then he put the carcass out of the sun and washed his hands in the stream.

The perfect afternoon settled around me like a warm blanket. Perhaps Darian had been right to drag me out here after all. He could be a good friend when he wanted to be. I felt better.

But I knew we'd lingered long enough. "We need to get back, Dare."

"There's something I have to tell you, Maia." I saw that same expression of unresolved conflict on his face.

My breath caught in my throat. "What?"

Darian scowled and kicked some dirt over the bloodied earth at his feet. "You're not going to get a qit this year."

Oh no . . . "This was our largest brood ever, with lots of—"

"Listen to me."

He looked intensely uncomfortable, but finally managed to look me in the eyes again. "I overheard Father and Tauman talking last week, after the courier left. Something is going on . . . some new expedition or defense. The Ministry is grabbing up every baby it can. I don't know what happened, but Father told Tauman that it sounded bad, like the emperor is worried. Father said we may not keep any dragons this year or next."

"*Or next?*" My stomach sank.

"Which means I don't get a dragon either, Maia. If we can't keep two, we probably can't keep any. A breeding pair has to bond early, right? The Ministry asked for a lot of babies. We could buy a second qit from one of the other aeries. Cuuloda maybe. But the Ministry isn't leaving any to buy."

"You're certain?" I fought back anger.

"I'm sorry, Kidling." That was the nickname he used when he needed to be both an older superior and a friend. "Tauman tried to convince Father. But the choice isn't really theirs to make. It's just not going to happen." Darian sat down next to me and put an arm around my shoulder. I shrugged it off. His hands flopped resignedly into his lap. The silence swallowed me. Words would not come.

Father had to make decisions based on business, but this made no sense to me. Could the Ministry really need so many qits that we couldn't keep just two? Wouldn't another breeding pair give them even more qits in the future?

No dragon. The little brown and buff female wouldn't be mine, even though she and I both knew it was right—that we belonged to each other.

No dragon. I buried my head in my arms and remained that way for a long time. Darian was silent but stayed beside me. Finally, his arm tested my shoulders again. This time I allowed it. The events of this morning now felt like a prelude, a sure sign that things weren't going to go well.

I thought of my mother again. "Dare . . . do you believe in curses?"

"No. Why would you ask such a question?"

I looked up and swallowed. "Do you think it's possible for angry words and"—my voice caught—"bad deeds to create a curse, without meaning to?"

"You're not cursed, Maia, if that's what you're thinking. Sometimes bad things just happen." He hugged me a little tighter. "You have to learn to trust yourself."

The world around us seemed eerily aware of my sorrow. A dead calm settled. The air had grown perfectly still. Not a bird or insect stirred.

"Listen how quiet it is." Having made the observation, it suddenly struck me as unnatural, and Darian stiffened.

A soft *whoosh* of air rattled the leaves above us, and a shadow blotted the sun. Our heads snapped up, and the silhouette of a huge dragon passed above the treetops. As we gaped, the great beast sculled the air once, twice, with wings like the sails of a ship, and settled upon the tumble of ruins crowning the hill above.

It was the biggest thing I'd ever seen, colored like the sunset on a bronzed ocean horizon, with tinges of green at the edges of the wings and frill. It had horns like the twisted trunks of trees, and muscles that rippled with every least movement. Its scent wafted down the breeze toward us, rich with stone and earth, sap and spices, rain and lightning. It stretched upward and shook its mighty head so that the frill snapped like a flag. Then it looked lazily around, seemingly oblivious to our presence just down the hill. The air was charged with electricity.

I didn't feel Darian's hand on my arm until he shook me twice. "That's a High Dragon!" he whispered. "Maybe even Getig, the Summer Dragon!" I was too dumbstruck to speak. "Do you know what that means?" he asked, but I wasn't listening. I stood and started up the hill, drawn irresistibly to the magnificence of this animal. I disturbed a stone with my foot, and the great head turned our way. His gaze met my own briefly, and a chill shot down my spine, freezing my feet to the ground.

His eyes were molten copper orbs, the slits narrowed against the strong light. He fixed me with a look of stern evaluation, and I sensed an import, a sad urgency that I could not define. Time stopped as I tried to make meaning out of this strangely intimate gaze. My heart didn't beat, my breath caught in my chest. Then the magnificent head dipped slightly, as if in acknowledgment of something, and he launched into the sky with a loud crack of leather and rush of air. He disappeared beyond the crest of the hill.

I tried to follow, but Darian pulled me backward by the shirt. "Do you know what this means? It's a sign! The Summer Dragon! It's a sign of big changes!" Darian took my face in his hands and made me look right at him. "*I'm going to get my dragon!*" He laughed. "Come *on!*"

Then he was galloping down the hill toward the compound. I looked one more time at the hilltop, trying to see the beast again in my mind. As I turned, the statue of Menog and Dahak caught my eye. I knew in that instant that the sculptor had seen the Avar. He had *known* what they looked like. Before I'd always thought the sculpture exaggerated, but now I saw it was a subtle and realistic portrait. The arch of their necks, the breadth of their chests, the musculature of the wings—it was perfect.

The breeze stirred again at last, swirling some leaves about my ankles. Insects chirruped once more in the trees. A bird trilled lightly nearby. Darian's feet crashed through the distant forest, and one long, happy *whoohoo!* echoed through the valley.

The absence at the top of the hill drew me. Before I realized, I'd started the climb. I crawled over lichen-covered boulders and logs, leapt a rivulet, scrambled through some ferns and bracken, and found the foot trail to the crest. Soon I emerged into sunlight, on the very spot where the creature stood when his eyes met mine. His scent still lingered among the scattered ruins—a summer smell of orchards and grass and earth, but no other sign that he'd been here. I hopped onto the highest outcropping, my arms wrapped around the stump of a pillar, and scanned the landscape beyond.

The sky was empty but for a few scudding drifts of cloud. Cliffs shone on the far side of the valley. For a moment I expected to see him there—we knew that wild dragons sometimes nested among those steep crags where they could command a view of everything that moved in the woods below. On occasion Mother and Darian and I had picnicked right here, to watch them wheeling in the far-off currents.

But this wasn't one of the wildings, and I could see no dragons there now.

"Where did you go?" I could still smell him. Or was I simply more aware of the scents of summer? The birds' calls were bright, melodic notes playing above the rush and murmur of the wind. The trees danced in undulating waves. I could feel the entire mass of the world below and around me, its tumble toward night, the pull of the universe on my bones. I closed my eyes; it felt like flying and falling all at once.

Was that *him* making me feel this way? Was that Getig? I'd been on the verge of tears just a few minutes before, but now I couldn't help smiling as I viewed the valley. It seemed *more* than it was before, transformed in some indefinable way. Greener. More alive.

Sunlight flashed on something white in the trees below. My heightened awareness drew me to it. So out of place—a stark brightness in the deep shade. Intrigued, I gauged its direction from where I stood, climbed down from the outcropping, and slid my way down the scree slope below.

The trees below dwarfed any on our side of the hill, the undergrowth more lush and tangled. I fought my way through the dense border and into the open shade beneath the canopy. The air was cooler, rich with the smell of humus. The boles of the trees were straight and branchless, like pillars in a temple. Sunlight reduced to

thin shafts of gauzy green flickered in and out of sight. Moss made
the boulders and logs of the forest floor into a strangely smooth landscape of alien shapes. Frogs croaked nearby, but eerily, the moss dead-
ened all sound.

I considered my bearings, then headed into the still, green depths.
The terrain rose gently, and soon I saw sun flash on white ahead of me
once again. A slab of broken stone, like an altar, created a space
among the trees where sunbeams danced. Moss gave way to light-
starved saplings, ferns, and the occasional wildflower. In the center of
the table lay the corpse of a dragon.

It hadn't been dead long, but scavengers had already stripped
away most of the soft flesh. The white I'd seen was the skull, grinning
nakedly, with only a few remnants of skin on cheek and forehead. Its
remaining scales were a dusty stone color with patches of bronze,
fairly common among the local mountain breed. Its neck was arched
back in the contortions of death, the wings drawn in like crumpled
tents. The torso was hollowed out, leaving a shell of ribs that crawled
with ants and flies. The stench hit me all at once, and I moved to the
upwind side. It didn't help much, but I was both fascinated and re-
pulsed.

It couldn't have been very old—perhaps two or three years, judging by the size and what remained of the frill. I couldn't tell if it was
male or female, but it would have been saddle-trained long since had
it been one of ours. It might even have been old enough to breed, had
it found a mate. It wouldn't have been as healthy as our farm-fed
breeding stock, but would have been tough and smart. A serious injury might lead to starvation and death, but a dragon had no natural
enemies apart from other dragons and humans. Every two or three
years, a wilding would become a nuisance, and Father and Tauman
would be forced to bring it down. But the hides and meat, bones and
sinew were always salvaged. It would never be left to rot in the woods
this way.

A cruel wire noose bit deeply into the bones of its left rear leg. It
seemed that someone had tried to capture this animal, not kill it. But
it broke loose, came here, and bled to death.

Poachers. Father would want to know.

I squatted down, looking into the empty eye sockets. "Poor thing,"

I said. "I wish I could've seen you alive. Perhaps I have—perhaps Darian and I watched you from the hill."

It was almost too much: Fren's mauling, Darian's news, the Summer Dragon. And now this. Was there no end of portents and news today? I didn't know whether to laugh or cry. But then Darian's words finally struck me: *I'm going to get my dragon.* Why would he assume that?

The Summer Dragon was a sign of big changes, he had said. Perhaps because we had seen him, those big changes would be ours.

I'm going to get my dragon. Perhaps I would get my dragon, too.

I jumped up and ran back into the forest, crashed through the tangled margin, and scrambled up the slope. I was scratched and bruised by the time I reached the top of the hill again. I jumped up on the ruins for one last look back, just in case. And there he was.

Getig, the Summer Dragon, perched across the valley on a tall spire, his wings spread wide to warm in the sun, or perhaps to cool on a breeze. Then he leapt and snapped his huge wings downward, caught an updraft, beat his wings one more time, then turned and vanished beyond the line of cliffs. I watched for another few moments, but he didn't reappear. I shivered in the full heat of the day.

Though my legs felt like they might crumple beneath me, I dashed toward home.

F O U R

THE COMPOUND WAS EMPTY. The day help from the village was gone. Long shadows already crept across the paddock as the sun touched the mountaintops in the west. It was late. I would be in trouble again. Where was everybody? The compound should still be active, though the qits would be bedding down for their final night in the aeries. Something about the silence made my skin crawl.

Lantern light winked under the enormous, rolling doors of the broodhouse. Someone was there. I entered through the man-door on the end of the building.

The big cliffside doors had been rolled shut, too, and the nests were full. All three broodmothers plus Audax turned their heads when I entered. Shuja and Rannu were missing, though, which meant that Father and Tauman were gone as well. Jhem was at the far end of the row, her broom making the soft, shushing cadence that would ease the qits into sleep.

I started toward Rannu and Athys's nest for a peek at the babies, but Jhem held a finger to her lips and waved me back. I stopped, craning my neck, but I couldn't see the little brown-and-buff under her mother's wing. Reluctantly, I backed out of the broodhouse.

I sat on the parapet overlooking the plains below the aeries. Thunderheads boiled upward on the horizon, ablaze and menacing in the last ruddy light.

Jhem emerged from the brood platform, closing the man-door carefully behind her. "Where have you been? We were worried about you!"

"Father and Tauman aren't looking for me, I hope."

"No, no. Your father returned from Grus's hunt only long enough to switch mounts and head back to the Temple. Fren's injuries are serious, and your father is very concerned. We hadn't been back long when Darian returned with your remarkable story. Tauman took Darian to the Temple, too, to talk to Mabir."

"Oh," I said. Confused and exhausted by the avalanche of events, I was unable to find another word. What next?

"I should take you to the Temple, too, except that someone needs to be here. It's bad enough that you and Darian abandoned the brood-mothers for hours. What were you thinking?"

"The qits were sleeping! And we're supposed to check the tr—"

"That's a poor excuse and you know it. *Today* of all days."

I groaned and set my head on my knees. "I know. We just needed to have a moment to ourselves."

Jhem crossed her arms. "So tell me what happened." I couldn't tell if she was curious or angry. Probably both.

I took a deep breath, but then the familiar sound of Shuja's giant wings cracked on the air. Jhem and I looked at each other fearfully, buffeted by blasts of wind as Father and Shuja landed in the paddock. No one spoke as he dismounted and turned to the saddle jib.

Trembling, I started forward to help, but he held up a hand. "Wait there, both of you. We'll have words in a minute."

Tears glistened in Jhem's eyes as her hand sought mine. She squeezed my fingers hard enough to make me wince. Father climbed back onto Shuja to hook the saddle rings, then down again to swing the saddle into the tack house. Finally he rolled the center door on the brood platform open wide enough for Shuja to enter. The big male seemed to understand the mood in the compound and said nothing at all as he passed inside. Chirps and sleepy barks greeted him. Then Father rolled the door shut again.

Hands on hips, he stared at us, his dark eyes flickering. "Fren is alive, no thanks to either one of you. Mabir ministered to him the entire time we were gone. If I didn't have other important duties today I'd have stayed at the Temple." He pointed at Jhem. "*You* have got to get Audax under control. He's not your *pet*—he's a predator, the offspring of wildings. If you don't show strength to that animal you are going to lose him. *We* are going to lose him. I can't have that. I need to grow these aeries. The fact that our largest brood ever might not be sufficient for the Ministry is proof enough of that.

"And you . . ." His eyes locked onto mine. "Every time I turn around you're engaged in some sort of qit-play. You're not a little girl anymore. By Korruzon, you're old enough to be wed! I need you to pull your weight. I'd hoped you would show some of your mother's strength and passion by now. I'm disappointed, not only in the lack of focus and the tragedy that has come of it, but because afterward, you disappeared into the forest for hours. What in Gadia is the matter with you?"

"I . . . Darian and I—"

"No talking! Darian has received his earful from me, too. Mabir wants to hear your version of this story in the morning. In fact, he doesn't want you to tell your tale to anyone else until he can hear it. He wants it *unspoiled*." For an instant his face was questioning, but then it became overcast again. "So I stand here in the dark. I have no idea what is going on *in my own aeries*! All I know is that I have a community to hold together. People depend on us for their livelihoods. I can't do my job and yours, too." He crossed his arms, looking back and forth between Jhem and me. A distant rumble of thunder made me shiver.

"I'm sorry, Father." I was afraid to wipe the tears from my cheeks.

"And I am sorry, Magha." Jhem finally released my hand.

"*Sorry* won't knit Fren's wounds or calm a wilding broodsire! I don't want you to be sorry. I want you to be responsible."

I nodded weakly, blinking away tears.

Father's expression softened, if only a tiny bit. "Tomorrow is still a big day—perhaps now bigger than a Brood Day has ever been. I don't know what your experience means, Maia. I hope there's some good portent in it. We need it.

"Finish your work. Then get some sleep. We rise early." He turned and stalked across the bridge toward the manor.

I crumpled onto the parapet and stared at the ground. Jhem brushed hair out of my face. "You okay?"

I laughed once, more of a sputter than anything. "I actually thought that would be worse!" And then I didn't know whether to laugh or cry, so I did both.

Jhem sat next to me. "Maybe that's because of what you saw. Dare I ask what happened?"

"Apparently I'm not supposed to tell."

She shrugged. "You don't have to."

I don't know why—perhaps because she looked so sad, or because I desperately needed someone on my side—I told her. If I trusted anyone to keep a secret, it was Jhem. She was an outsider, adopted as an infant from the Temple orphanage by a local farmer. Even she didn't know where she was from. Somewhere north and east, most likely, judging by the light skin and unusual red hair that had set her apart all her life. Maybe that's why she withdrew from everyone. Teased, accused of tainted blood somehow, she gravitated to animals—they didn't care what color hair she had. She gained a reputation as a horse-handler as she grew older. Maybe that's what drew Tauman to her. When he started courting her she began to work with dragons, and she seemed like a natural. Eventually he asked for her hand.

He got a bride, and I got a big sister. I'd felt a kinship with her early on, even though I wasn't an outsider like her, really. But all our places were so well defined. Tauman: heir. Darian: next in line. Me? Kid sister. Jhem: Wife of heir. We were the afterthoughts.

She didn't like to talk about her past, and I didn't press. Our kinship was enough, though I sometimes wondered if Tauman only wanted a wife who would be grateful to him. He'd rescued her from her torment, after all. It wasn't clear. I always knew that his future as Broodmaster consumed him. Sometimes he seemed to adore her, other times he was such a shit. Dragons are not horses, so she had a lot to learn. I thought she did well, but Tauman pushed her hard.

In this moment, I needed her friendly ear. I sniffled, wiped my nose on my arm, then slowly recounted my version of events: the mauling of Fren, the news that I wouldn't receive a qit this year. But when I came to the sighting of Getig, the Summer Dragon, it all started to spill out of me, every detail. It felt good to let it out, better to have found a confidante in Jhem. But I didn't mention the sensations of a planet alive and moving beneath me, or the unfathomable scrutiny of the Summer Dragon. It was too new and too personal to put into words. The emotions defied translation. I kept to basic actions: I saw, I climbed, I ran, I followed.

By the time I'd finished, the plains east of the aeries were deep in shadow. Only the tops of the thunderheads remained in light, branded with the last of the sun.

I was surprised to see Jhem studying me with an intense look. "What do you suppose it means?" she asked.

I wiped my eyes. "Darian said that Getig is a sign of change, that we will . . . that we might get our dragons after all."

She smiled and patted my hand. "You are persistently optimistic, aren't you? I understand, Maia. It's in your blood. Your family has been breeding dragons for longer than anyone can remember. You were born to it. But don't get your expectations up."

"I want a dragon of my own. I want to fly! Despite what Father might think, I've worked hard, and I've earned a qit. It's my time."

She brushed something off my cheek. "Well, at least you know what you want. Listen to me: Everything is going to change, has changed already. Imagine—Getig, the Summer Dragon, in our mountains. Something tells me that this is the last normal night of your life, of all our lives. Everyone will have an opinion about what it means. The dhalla will throw his bones, and no doubt the Ministry priest will have a say tomorrow. And Father and Tauman, even Darian, will have questions and answers as different as earth and cloud. Maybe they'll figure it out. But things happen for their own reasons. Sometimes you can't make sense of them until much later. Or too late." The color drained from her face, and I realized that she was fighting back tears.

"Maia, just do this: Whatever happens, stay true to yourself. Don't stop being Maia. Trust your instincts. That's the only way you'll ever make sense of it. Okay? Promise me."

I must have been making a funny face, because Jhem started to laugh, even as a tear ran down her cheek.

"I . . . promise?" I said.

She wrapped her arms around me and kissed my forehead. "Don't stop being Maia."

I returned the hug, happy for this bit of comfort. "Did Tauman give you a hard time?"

She wiped her eyes and looked up. She seemed to be considering her words. "I messed up. I can't deny it. I . . . I don't want to speak ill of your brother."

"He can be a bastard sometimes."

"He's trying to live up to your father's example, and to his own expectations. That's not easy. So he tries too hard. He has good qualities, too."

"Not being a bastard would be a good quality."

She laughed out loud but squeezed my hand painfully.

A distant rumble turned our faces to the east. The thunderheads had faded into the purple darkness, but lightning within their bodies made them flicker like enormous, billowing lanterns. We watched for several minutes as flashes illuminated the cloudscape one column at a time. The centermost one had become an anvil-topped monster, stretching higher than even dragons could fly. Lightning occasionally arced outside the cloud or licked the prairie below. Every now and again a low roll of thunder reached our ears. It was spectacular, beautiful. A summer show worthy of the Summer Dragon.

Jhem whistled low. "Wow. Someone is getting pummeled. I hope the Ministry train escaped that."

Odd that Jhem saw a storm where I saw beauty.

She stood. "They'll be here tomorrow. Come on, let's finish the night's work."

F   I   V   E

FATHER SHOOK ME AWAKE. "Up! Maia! It's Brood Day. Work to do."

I sat up, looked around dizzily. The window was dark, but light burned my eyes—Darian with a lantern. Father threw my work clothes at me. "The Ministry wagons are just east of town. Let's go. Let's go!"

"Why aren't you yelling at me?" I asked, with sleep-deprived bluntness.

"Time enough for that later. Mabir forbid me to ask you questions, so I'll have to settle for working you like a dog. Come on!"

Then he was gone. Darian turned his back while I pulled my clothes on. "What happened, Dare? When did you get back? What did Mabir say? Is he coming today too? Did you—"

"Do you want me to answer one of those questions, or do you want to get them all asked at once?"

"Just tell me what's happening!" I fastened my last buckle and pushed Darian out the door. We trotted out into the chill dawn and started across the bridge to the paddock.

"I don't know how much trouble we're in. We might have caught a break when we saw the Summer Dragon. Mabir asked Father not to punish us. Yet. I'm still worried, though, because . . . now I've already said too much. Mabir told me I couldn't talk about it with you."

"Why not?"

"Because he wants your story *unspoiled*."

"What's that supposed to mean? Does he think we're *making it up*?"

"Maia, get off my—"

"What happened with you and Mabir?"

"He asked a lot of—Maia, I can't talk about it!"

He took off at a run and left me sputtering behind him.

When we arrived, Father had already rolled open one of the doors on the paddock side of the brood platform so the broodsires could step out to stretch their legs and wings.

"Come on," Father shouted. "Let's get this show started!" Something in the mood had changed overnight; the immediacy of the work, maybe, the comfort of familiar routine, or the excitement of the day. Brood Day was here! Father's face was focused, but open, unclouded. Tauman and Jhem opened the tack house doors together and readied the saddle jib. Tauman even gave Audax a comforting pat on the cheek. Our dragons had a cheerful bounce in their gaits and nodded excitedly. They would wear their best gear, brushed and polished— Rannu's shiny brown leather set with studs that sparkled in the lantern light, Audax in white leather with silver details, and Shuja in black, nearly invisible against his black scales. The adults wore harnesses and clothing to match—Tauman in brown and tan, Jhem in white with her striking red hair swept up into a bouncing horsetail. Father wore his black armor from their time long ago in the Dragonry. This was real pageantry—a show for the villagers and Ministry alike.

While Tauman and Father maneuvered Shuja's saddle into position, I came up beside Darian and punched him in the arm. "Why won't you tell me what's going on?"

When he didn't answer I punched him again. "Darian!"

He turned to me. "There's going to be some kind of meeting today between all of us—you, me, Father, Tauman and Jhem, Mabir, the Ministry merihem and buyers. Then they're going to decide what it all means and what to do. All right? Now I've told you more than I was supposed to, so stop hitting me and let's get to work."

He stalked into the broodhouse, his face troubled. It was unlike him to pass up the pomp and spectacle of the Brood Day flyover. He seemed scared, which stoked my worries again. What else did he know that he wasn't telling me? Why was I always the last to know?

I helped to harness the broodsires. When all three riders were strapped into their saddles, I stepped back to look with pride on my family and their dragons. Father was grinning. He actually looked relieved. Shuja was stepping proudly, tossing his head and making his frill snap. Tauman gave Jhem a thumbs-up when she smiled hopefully at him.

Audax stamped his feet. "Up!" he said, an easy word for a dragon's mouth to master. He knew what was next, and his clear anticipation made me laugh out loud. Father caught sight of me, but he laughed too, as if the burden of yesterday's events was forgotten. The brood was readied, the hard work done. Soon the Ministry's gold would flow into the village through our aerie. Brood Day was a release, the culmination of months of hard work. We all felt it. Even the cooks and servants from the manor house were crossing the bridge to watch the spectacle from the high vantage of the aeries. I felt a weight lift from my shoulders.

Father caught my eye. "Maia, let the babies out. It's time!" I started to roll the heavy paddock-side doors open. Suddenly Darian was there with me, unable in the end to resist the moment. Together we opened the broodhouse completely.

Dragonlings spilled past me and into the paddock, excited to see this open space for the first time. The broodmothers shepherded the tumbling horde deftly with the gentle touch of paw or wingtip. This outing served two purposes: the qits needed a good romp to wear them out, but they would also see adult dragons saddled for the first time and observe that humans rode on their backs.

"Preen!" Father commanded, and Shuja stood up on his back legs, wings stretched straight back, his neck arched and his chin down, forelimbs clawing the air in rampant pose. Rannu sat up straight as well, and even Audax made an attempt to mimic them. The babies huddled closer to their mothers, but barked and mewed in excitement. Father laughed aloud.

My chest swelled with pride and longing. Father had taken me on Shuja's back for many rides, but to fly on a bondmate of my own would be completely different. I tried to spot the little brown-and-buff, but there was too much movement and not enough light.

Father held a hand up. "The dawn is breaking. Any moment now."

A horn sounded in the village, then another and another. The sound echoed from the cliffs, multiplying. The wagons of the Ministry had arrived.

"That's it!" Father clenched his upraised hand into a fist. "Shuja! ROAR!"

And Shuja roared, a magnificent, rumbling bellow of power and authority that rattled the broodhouse doors and trembled in the stone beneath my feet. Rannu and Audax added their voices and found a harmonic that resonated off the cliffs and reverberated through the canyons. I cheered at the top of my lungs, unheard. The babies all retreated under their mothers' wings, but the broodmothers joined the song too. I faintly heard Darian's laughter beside me.

Then, before the echoes of that majestic symphony began to fade, Father shouted "HAI!" and all three broodsires leapt into the sky.

Darian and I ran to the parapets to watch. Far below, the Ministry wagons wound through the village streets, their white-painted roofs winking amber in the dawn light. The great, lumbering *taarku* that drew them seemed freshly washed—perhaps they had been caught in a downpour last night after all. The caps on their nosehorns and tusks gleamed gold. Cheering throngs lined the avenues in their best apparel. Children ran and skipped in front of the wagons. Soldiers in the van were shadowed by young boys bearing wooden swords and sticks for pikes. Above the rooftops elaborate kites flew, with long colorful tails.

Later, the best cooks in Riat would prepare delicacies on numerous outdoor grills, and the finest local wine and beer would pour freely. Trinkets would be sold, and gifts given out to the children: wooden dragons with flapping wings, ceramic eggs containing stones painted like hatchlings, dragon masks, soldier dolls, noisemakers, and sweets. Kites of all sizes. There would be bonfires, music, and dancing late into the evening. It was Brood Day!

"Look how many cages there are this year," Darian said. "More than last year."

He was right; I counted twenty-two. Each might hold as many as twelve qits. "Wow! I wonder how many are already full."

"Good question. Riat is the third or fourth stop on their tour, I think. It looks like we weren't the only aerie with a large brood."

Four Ministry dragons circled above the train, though still below our vantage on the clifftop aerie. We could clearly see the sigils painted on their wings—the marks that identified their place in the Dragonry. Three were nurse dragons—older females whose function was to calm the qits soon to be separated from their parents.

The fourth one stood out—a white behemoth with dark stripes on his neck and shoulders, wearing the armor of a Dragonry lancer. He would be the officer in charge of the acquisition.

"Look, Maia!" Darian said. "Who's that? Someone new?"

"I don't know. He's bigger than Shuja. Is he? I think he's bigger!"

The Ministry dragons climbed in a tight spiral, and we looked up, knowing what was next. Cheers arose from the crowds in the village. Shuja, Rannu, and Audax were high above and mounting higher still, circling. They unfurled silk banners from their saddle packs as they twisted upward—red for Rannu, white for Audax, black for Shuja— each banner two hundred feet long. Eight Brood Days ago, Mother and Grus had carried the third banner. It was the last time we'd put three banners in the sky. Grus moaned nearby, watching intently, poised as if she might leap to join them. It was a melancholy sound only Grus ever made.

Then they dived, slowly at first, but accelerating quickly with their wings pulled in tight. The banners streamed behind them, tracing their maneuvers in color on the sky—first a spiral to the left, then a spiral to the right, then a complex braid that made the crowds gasp in delight.

"Audax did it!" I shouted. "A perfect braid!" Jhem and the others had been working with him for weeks.

They dove straight through the ring of Ministry dragons, then pulled up and made a hair-raising pass just above the rooftops of the village. The banners cracked and snapped behind them. The people's roar of approval followed them back into the sky.

They made huge, vertical loops that spun in opposite directions, then linked them together in a chain, then interlocked the three, and finally took off in three different directions just as the nurse dragons and the lancer climbed to join them. When they assembled again they redrew their braid as a serpent crawling across the clouds.

More loops and exaggerated barrel rolls followed weaves and zig-zags. Shuja put on a solo display of swirls and coils and knots in the air, while Rannu and Audax framed him with a giant circle. They finished with all three banners interwoven into a knotwork, separated briefly, then dove one last time in an ever-tightening spiral that came apart at the last instant. Three dragons skimmed the rooftops in three directions, roaring, as the people waved their arms and cheered.

It was the best part of the Brood Day celebrations. Once again my heart soared to heights of longing and joy. It was so beautiful, and I wanted so badly to be a part of it. I looked for the little brown and buff but couldn't find her in the confused milling of excited baby dragons.

"They're coming in!" Darian started shooing qits back toward their mothers to clear space for landing. I joined him, and with the mothers using their wings as fences, we soon had all the dragonlings corralled. Shuja, Rannu, and Audax landed first, each rider stuffing the tail end of a banner back into the saddle pack. Behind them came the nurse dragons and the big, white-and-striped Dragonry lancer.

S I X

"**K**ORRUZON'S LEFT ASS-CHEEK, that thing is huge,"
Darian muttered next to my ear.

"Darian!" I couldn't help laughing. "Don't ever let Mabir hear
you say that."

"Well, look at him. Only the biggest and strongest dragons get to
be lancers."

With Shuja and the newcomer side-by-side in front of us, it was
clear which of the two was bigger. If I hadn't seen the Summer Dragon
only the day before, I might have been awestruck by his size. He was
a magnificent specimen, a cliff dragon from the ocean shores far to
the east, judging by his coloring and minimal frill.

The rider sliding down off the saddle was no less impressive. A big
man, though not as tall as Father, I was pleased to note. His gravings
surprised me. More than mere tattoos, gravings were the work of
Temple priests. Imbued with special properties, they enhanced skills,
strengthened muscles, assisted in healing, or created bonds. He was
covered with them, from the top of his shaven head, surrounding the
bond mark on the back of his neck, down his arms—practically engulfing the marks of rank—and even onto his hands. He walked with
the easy gait of a man accustomed to respect, the swagger of the Dragonry rider.

Father offered him a hand, quickly taken. I tried to sidle closer to
hear their exchange, but was swamped in a tide of baby dragons rushing forward to investigate.

"Darian! Maia!" Tauman waved us over. "Come help with these
saddles!" As Father greeted each of the visitors in turn, Shuja stepped

under the saddle jib, with Rannu and Audax lined up behind him. Darian climbed onto Shuja's back to hook the saddle while Tauman and I worked below.

"Is that a new officer?" I asked Tauman, indicating the lancer and his mount.

"So it would seem." Tauman squinted. "A tough character—look at all the gravings. The ones on his arms are for strength. I don't recognize the ones around his eyes. Those can't be cheap. He comes from money, I'd say." The swirling characters and strange patterns seemed to define the natural lines of the muscles and veins beneath. They wound under his jerkin, suggesting that his torso was covered, too.

"Four talons in his mark of rank. And four talons on his pennant." Tauman pointed at the banner waving from a slender, flexible staff mounted to the back of the saddle. "He's a captain, commissioned officer. Career Dragonry with political aspirations, no doubt. Could be a valuable ally. Riat will need friends in the capital."

"That dragon is enormous. Chalk cliffs?"

"That's right. From Gul. They're big, but they're a little wild. Look at the size of the rider's bond mark. It's been enhanced a couple of times."

"What does that mean?" Bond marks were important—the most important gravings of them all. They enhanced communication, intensified instinctive cooperation, nurtured the bond between a rider and his mount. Every dragon and rider had one, on the nape of his or her neck, a circular pattern of runes and other symbols. The captain's was large and densely written.

"Well . . . he needs more control over his mount for some reason. The dragon might be a bit unmanageable. It might be his second dragon, so the bond mark from the first had to be countered and overwritten. Injury to the dragon can sometimes weaken the bond. Or the rider could be abusive and so he needs more control."

"So why is he here and not off fighting in the war?"

"Good question."

"Aph!" said Shuja—*off*. We were neglecting our duties.

"Ha! Look who's in charge." Tauman winked at me.

Together we winched the saddle with Darian riding it off Shuja's back and into the tack house. Shuja bounced out from under the jib and Rannu stepped in place. I climbed onto Rannu's back and waited for Darian to return. We would trade places this way—one above, one beneath with Tauman—until all the dragons were unsaddled. It was a dance, an efficient choreography of machinery and muscle.

I hooked the saddle before my brothers finished below, and took the spare moments to study the lancer and his mount some more. The rider was younger than Father, but older than Tauman. Thirty-three or -four, perhaps. He wore a scowl, as if a great weight dwelled inside him, accentuated by the gravings around his eyes that wrapped over the top of his shaven head like intricate wings.

From my vantage point, I couldn't see the dragon's bond mark where his neck joined his head, but what I'd thought were stripes on his neck and shoulders were actually complex patterns and characters. They didn't have the same finish as the military symbols painted on his wings. They were gravings too. The beast had a particularly wicked scar on his upper lip, decorated with medical gravings to assist in healing, which gave the impression of a permanent sneer.

Tauman and Darian finished with the harness, and swung me into the tack house on Rannu's saddle. I unhooked it quickly and rejoined Tauman. Audax stepped under the jib and Darian climbed up.

I watched the riders of the nurse dragons dismount. Two looked to be military men by their dress, older retirees whose dragons, too old for combat, still proved their value to the Dragonry by comforting the babies in the cages. They were familiar. I'd probably seen them on previous Brood Days. The third was a merihem, or Ministry priest.

"That's a new merihem, isn't it?" I pointed with a nod of my head.

"Yes, you're right," said Tauman. "There seems to be a new one every couple of years."

The dhalla, like our Mabir, were priests whose primary duty was to teach and shepherd the commoners through their daily lives within the Dragon Temple. They were versed in essential graving skills, such as healing—and many, like Mabir, had to know how to administer the bond marks for dragons and their riders at the base of the skull.

But the merihem were elite priests, the healers and practitioners of Temple Science in the military hierarchy, especially in the Dragonry. They studied for long years in the capital city, Avigal, at the *Maktaa*—

the religious school of the Dragon Temple. Their understanding of the subtlety and range of Temple Science was unsurpassed. It would have been one of the merihem who drew the elaborate gravings on the lancer and his mount. I got the impression they were closer to the Temple's center wheels of power. Closer, at least, than our country priest would ever be.

This merihem looked to be younger than the Dragonry captain—twenty-eight perhaps—with long, black hair in multiple braids, wearing the black dress and cylindrical cap of the position. He surveyed the swarming dragonlings with interest and showed no alarm when they sniffed at his clothes or brushed against him in the course of rambunctious play.

"Done." Tauman slapped my back, bringing me back to what I was doing, and we hoisted Darian into the tack house on Audax's saddle.

As Darian climbed down to rejoin us, Father approached with the lancer and the merihem beside him. "Tauman, Jhem, Darian, Maia, I would like you to greet Captain Rov ad Reanag, commander of the acquisition this year."

The lancer bowed, crisply and very correctly. Tauman was right; he came from money.

"And this is Bellua ad Reitleh, merihem of the Rasaal." Priest of the Ministry's inner Temple. The Rasaal was the Temple authority, the Head of the religious structure.

The merihem also bowed, though with somewhat less formality. Up close, he was very handsome. He had a square jaw, straight nose, and dimples that winked in his cheeks when he smiled at me.

Father bowed in return. "Gentlemen, my eldest, Tauman and his wife Jhem, his brother Darian, and my daughter Maia. They are at your service. Do not hesitate to ask them for anything you might need. First order of business, of course, will be to unsaddle your mounts and feed them while you look over our fine brood of qitlings." Father smiled, gesturing toward us, palm up.

Tauman bowed—quite nicely—and then shook hands all around. Jhem did likewise. Darian bowed like a tangled marionette, then shook hands as well with a huge, beaming smile on his face.

I did my best to make a presentable bow, but the soldiers were already engaged with Father. The lancer, Rov, turned away to speak with Jhem and Tauman. Only Bellua took my offered hand. "A pleasure, my lady." He bowed. "Certainly you are the flower of this aerie—a wildflower in the wilderness."

I felt my cheeks flush and hoped he wouldn't notice. He bowed again, and then wandered into the sea of qits with his hands clasped behind his back.

Very quickly, Captain Rov had summoned his big white under the jib and boosted Darian up onto the saddle. Darian patted the animal's neck. "What's his name?"

"This is Cheien."

"He's gorgeous!" Darian examined the saddle with his fingers. "This is real lancer armor?"

"Yes, though we've removed the lance track, winch, and stop. Unnecessary for the task at hand." Why any of it was necessary for the job of buying and transporting baby dragons eluded me. Did people attack the acquisition train?

"How old is he?" Darian seemed oblivious to the officer's taciturn manner.

"He's twelve."

"Father was a lancer. Shuja is twenty-eight—that's Father's dragon." Darian pointed helpfully. "I hope to get one of these dragons for myself this year."

Rov's expression was impenetrable. "Is that a fact?"

Darian's mouth snapped shut. "Well, that was before."

"Pardon me." Tauman was under Cheien, casting a dubious eye at the straps of the lancer's armor. "May I trouble you for some help with this?" He gave me a surreptitious wink; he'd interrupted to save Darian further embarrassment. Yet something about his expression was guarded, as if there were more than Darian's honor at stake.

"Of course," said Rov. "Start with these straps."

Just then the bell on the gantry rang, indicating that someone at the base of the cliff desired a ride up. "That will be Mabir, the dhalla of our Temple." Father gave a courteous bow. "Gentlemen? If you'll excuse me."

Every emotion asserted itself at once: hope, fear, desire, anticipation, dread. Darian's refusal to speak to me earlier had alarmed me.

Would Mabir see the appearance of Getig as a sign that we would get our qits, as Darian thought? Or was I still in trouble over yesterday's events? I had no idea what to expect. I could still feel Fren's warm blood on my hands.

I looked for Jhem, but she was busy shepherding qits toward the nurse dragons. I swallowed, then joined Father on the gantry platform. "I'll help you."

Father set his jaw and put a reassuring hand on my shoulder. I wasn't out of trouble yet, but perhaps there would be no reckoning after all.

He released "the basket"—a railed platform ten feet square, suitable for moving goods and personnel up and down the cliff face. As it started to descend, I looked out over the parapet.

One road snaked up out of the village to the base of the pinnacle atop which the aeries were built. It crossed a bridge over the river Wilding where the mists of the Roaring wafted around it, before it arrived at the gantry landing. The mechanism was designed so that the cages could be attached to our winch. We would haul them one at a time to the clifftop to be filled with babies and then lowered again. The first wagons were crossing the bridge, the river tumbling beneath them and on toward the village.

But there was a small, black cart at the base of the pinnacle already. That would be Mabir. In years past, he'd had a dragon, as did all priests, and would have flown to the aerie with the others. But his ancient mount had died five summers ago. At his age, if he were to bond another, it would almost certainly outlive him and possibly need to be destroyed when he died. He chose instead to take a cart, to accept a ride on another's dragon, or to walk.

The basket landed at the bottom, and I could see Mabir's tiny form move onto it. Shortly, the bell rang again. I released the brake, and started to crank the basket back up.

"We can open the aqueduct, Maia—let the water wheel pull him up."

"Okay, but I'm going to get it started. I need to burn off these nerves. I don't want to be shaking like this when I talk to him." I smiled hopefully.

Father nodded and joined me at the wheel. We turned it together.

The axle creaked and groaned, and the ratchet clattered. It would take a few moments before the stream of water provided assistance.

I closed my eyes. From the village far below came music and sporadic cheering. Nearby, the babies made playful noises; the nurse dragons would be engaging them, while their mothers held back reluctantly. My little brown-and-buff would be among them. It was the first stage of separation, of their ultimate betrayal.

But she's going to be mine, I reassured myself.

The waterwheel took over. I stepped back and opened my eyes. Soon the basket arrived with a loud clank, locking automatically into grapples along the edge of the platform. Mabir had arrived.

HIS BLACK ROBES hung loose from bony shoulders. The cylindrical cap of his office topped a face like a withered potato. The wiry beard that clung to his chin sought escape in every direction at once. But his eyes had a bright twinkle that fit his humor better than the dark dress of his order. We all knew him as a patient man with a ready laugh who gave much of himself to his brood. I'd always liked him; he was the closest thing I had to a grandfather. In my mind he was ageless.

He wasn't smiling now, though. "Hello, Maia. You have had an adventure, I hear." Mabir ambled forward with some care. He refused to use a cane, and referred to staves with disdain as "props."

I nodded, unable to make my voice work.

He placed a comforting hand on my shoulder. "Well, we'll discuss it now. I'm sure you have been sitting on nettles while you waited for me. I am sorry about that." A hint of a smile touched his lips. "Magha, we should do this before any other haggling or discussion takes place."

"I agree, dhalla." Father nodded.

"The nurses and their riders can watch the qitlings while we talk. The officer and the merihem will join us in your manor?"

"Yes, dhalla."

"Good enough." Mabir extended an elbow for me to take. "My dear?" Now he did smile, and I felt better. As we started toward the bridge, Darian joined us and offered the dhalla another arm to lean on.

"Thank you, my boy. Not a word until everyone has gathered!"

By the time we crossed the bridge and entered the shade of the veranda, Father and the others caught up to us. Father summoned Kaisi, our cook and housekeeper, and told her to set breakfast for all.

Something was wrong. Father's face was pale, his brow furrowed. He avoided eye contact with us, but cast a furtive glance at Rov and the merihem. Both visitors looked grim.

Kaisi bowed, retied her apron a little tighter, and vanished.

"This way, gentlemen." Father led us through a hall to the inner courtyard, where tall bamboo shaded a patio of stone set with two heavy wooden tables and comfortable wicker chairs. Boulders around the perimeter peeked out from under ferns and hostas, with wildflowers and grasses at their feet.

Father immediately pulled up a chair for Mabir, then he and Tauman moved the tables together. Soon all were seated in tense, awkward silence. Darian and I sat opposite each other in the center of the joined tables. I caught his eyes. He was pale, too. I clamped my hands between my knees to prevent myself from fidgeting. Kaisi returned with earthenware cups and a pitcher of water. For our Brood Day guests, she had even included a chunk of ice from the vaults. Then she vanished again, off to the kitchen to assemble our meal.

Father cleared his throat before any casual conversation could be struck. "Friends . . ." He struggled to find words for a moment. "I confess that I have been withholding news the last few weeks, hoping it wouldn't prove to be a distraction as we prepared for this day."

Tauman's apprehension turned to shock. "Oh, High Ones . . . not Cuuloda."

Father nodded grimly. "The Harodhi have been probing the aeries at Cuuloda. We didn't think there was any real danger, as Cuuloda's high mountain ranges provide a natural defense. But now Captain Rov brings dire news."

Darian and I locked eyes again. He was ashen, and Mabir's mouth hung open.

Rov stood slowly and scanned the table. "It's true. I received word only this morning by courier. Cuuloda has been taken by Harodhi."

Mabir moaned softly, put a hand to his lips. "Cuuloda is . . . *was* Korruzon's most productive aerie. This is a bitter blow."

Tauman's hands trembled on the table. "Were there . . . Horrors?"

Rov nodded. "They drew us away with new Horrors in Ebrolin; spread the Dragonry thin. Then they overwhelmed Cuuloda with numbers. Refugees limp in from Haalden with horrible tales."

"What are they?" I asked. "The Horrors, I mean."

Rov glanced at Father, then fixed me with a grim look, his mouth a hard line. "Consider beasts made of mutilated men and animals sewn together, with helmets bolted to their skulls, weapons for arms. Walking carrion." He paused again, eyes downcast, as if fighting with his own words. "They came out of Harodh by way of Tammuz, in the hundreds, and there was no stopping them. They are unquestioning, tireless, and brutal. They don't sleep. They eat everything living and dead: the livestock, the grain stores, even the roots are dug out of the fields and consumed. They leave not a tree, not a bush, not a twig of grass, nor any living animal."

I'd never heard them described before. Not by anyone who'd ever actually seen one. Rov's words chilled me. "Where do they come from?"

"They're constructs. Creations," said Rov. "We don't know how they're made."

"Why don't they just eat each *other*?" I asked.

"They are in thrall to their creators," said Rov. "Some foul magic keeps them under control. But when they're turned loose, they're hard to bring down."

The courtyard fell silent. Father had told us stories by the fire on many a winter's night of his time in the Dragonry, but never anything like this. He sometimes wondered at the very fact of the Horrors; there had been no such monsters—only men and animals—when he fought in the war.

"What about Ebrolin?" Father asked.

"You're right to wonder, since that's the battlefront. Ebrolin is safe as far as the desert highlands of Tammuz. The only thing that slows them is a lack of something to consume. The homesteads are vulnerable because they bring life to the desert, though the refugees destroy all as they flee. But Ebrolin was a feint—Cuuloda was the prize they sought."

"Haalden?" asked Tauman.

"Overrun."

"How far have they pressed?" Father again.

"They were stopped at Chaaladan, but the bridge had to be burned to do it."

"What happened to the brigades there?"

"Unclear. But the Horrors must be held to the far side of the canyon. Cuuloda is surrounded by mountains, so they are somewhat contained. But the province is lost. The Horrors have been given a place to gather and consolidate their strength. They've burrowed in, where our Dragonry can't assault them. Worse, our forces in Ebrolin are divided, facing not only north but west now as well. I fear Harodh will press us hard in the coming year. Their use of the Horrors has grown."

Jhem leaned forward, her eyes wide. "What about the broodparents and the clutches at Cuuloda?"

"They were overrun so quickly, there was no chance to get any of the qits out. The broodmaster's son reported that when he saw his father last, he was putting the entire brood to death rather than let it fall into enemy hands. I know no more than that. The picture is still a sketch."

Father slumped in his chair. "Ardran didn't make it out?"

Rov only shook his head slowly, and Father hung his head.

Again, silence enveloped the courtyard but for the rustle of a breeze in the bamboo canes. Pallid faces looked one to another. Jhem wept openly. I was in a fog of disbelief. I knew Ardran and his sons. They visited from time to time. We had sold them a qit to refresh their stables just two years ago. Shuja's dam, Grus, had come from their aeries in a trade before I was born.

Mabir cleared his throat and rapped on the table with his knuckles. "Honored guests. Friends. Something amazing has happened here in Riat that we must discuss before we do anything else. Our two young friends here have had an experience that I now believe is related profoundly to this news and must impact the decisions being made today."

All faces turned our way. Father and Tauman frowned intently. Rov and Bellua looked mildly curious. Sweat tickled my back.

"I have already heard the story from young master Darian, and it is amazing. Circumstances kept me from hearing Maia's version of things until now. We will hear from her shortly. But I don't want to give this any more build-up. I think the best thing is to simply get started. So, Darian, if you would please, begin with the event here in the aeries and tell us what happened to you yesterday."

Bellua and Rov looked at each other again, and both leaned in closer as Darian gathered his words.

"Go ahead, my boy," Mabir prompted.

He started slowly, as I did when I told Jhem the night before. But once he found his rhythm, it spilled out of him. The merihem stiffened as the tale progressed, frowning down at his clasped hands. When Darian admitted to forgetting the small deer in the ruins, Bellua hitched his chair closer to the table. "That is an ill omen—"

Mabir held a finger to his lips. "Please, good merihem."

With a nod from Mabir, Darian finished. "And so, I remembered that the Summer Dragon was supposed to be a sign of change, or a bringer of change, and I thought—"

"What makes you think it was a High Dragon, and not just a wilding beast?" Bellua leaned in for the answer.

Darian didn't miss a beat. "Begging your pardon, sir, but I know dragons. This was not a wild dragon. It was huge. The biggest thing I have ever seen! It was to our dragons as the sun is to a lantern!"

Bellua's frown deepened. "This seems impossible. Exactly how big—"

"Good merihem, let us hold our questions." Mabir smiled uneasily. "We mustn't influence the tale to come. It's long past time that Maia was allowed to give her version of events."

He nodded toward me, and my stomach clenched.

Bellua looked surprised. "This *girl* has more to tell than that?"

Mabir turned and faced him directly. "Why don't we let her tell her story before we judge?"

Rov put a hand on Bellua's shoulder. "Let her speak."

Bellua sat back and crossed his arms. "Very well." His face was troubled—the handsome young man who had called me *the wildflower of the aerie* seemed long gone now. Why did he find this news so troubling?

Rov studied me with furrowed brow. Tauman and Father stared intently. Darian looked expectant. Jhem winked, and nodded ever so slightly. I cleared my throat and swallowed.

The first few, hoarse words eased the way for the rest. I took us into the forest, eyes closed to picture everything exactly as it had been, and tried to describe it all—the way the woods became still, heralding the Summer Dragon with silence more compelling than an army of trumpets, and the tremble of the trees at his passing. Wings like beaten copper, muscular shoulders that rippled like a net full of fish. His eyes that pierced like sharp summer lightning. When he lifted off again I could only follow, to the top of the ruins and into the valley beyond, as though a tether had been pinned to my heart. The colors, the smells, the earth turning beneath me, the living forest that swayed in time to some age-old but ever-present rhythm, the euphoria that gripped me even in my sadness. How it led me deep into the green sanctuary of the trees, where I discovered a dead dragon with a noose around its leg.

"And I knew that Father would want to hear about the poachers," I finished. "So I started home. When I climbed to the top of the ridge, and looked back, and I saw him one more time on the far cliffs. Then I came home as fast as I could because . . ." I opened my eyes. There were no more furrowed brows or angry grimaces around the table. Each face was blank, dumbstruck, completely rapt. I swallowed and took a deep breath. "I thought that perhaps there might yet be a baby. For me."

Complete silence.

At some point during my tale, Kaisi had set the table with two big bowls of rice-and-corn pilaf, hard-boiled eggs, fruit, cheese, and wine. She stood in the archway where my words had halted her, a strand of black hair hanging across her astonished face. No one had yet touched the food or wine.

Mabir spoke first, wide-eyed. "Remarkable." He looked around the table. "You see, good Bellua and Rov, we have many things to consider."

Bellua laid a finger against his cheek. "First and foremost is to ascertain whether this was, in fact, the Summer Dragon, or if it was a High Dragon at all."

"Oh, I think there can be no doubt that it was a visitation by one of the Avar," smiled Mabir. "You heard the descriptions, which came from two young adults with intimate knowledge of dragons. I doubt very much that they could be fooled into such depth of emotion by a wilding dragon."

Bellua folded his hands together on the tabletop.

Mabir continued. "So, the foremost task is to determine the relevance of this visitation. For whom was the message intended, and what was the message?"

"The answer to the first question is obvious." Father held his hands out to indicate Darian and me. "Whatever the meaning, it was intended for my children."

Mabir smiled benignly. "But because they are your children, and you are the broodmaster of the Riat aeries, it is also relevant to the aeries, and to Riat, which complicates the divination."

"Yes, I suppose. Of course. But you cannot disconnect that relevance from my children."

"No," Bellua corrected. "Assuming for the moment that it was an Avar, you cannot disconnect the relevance from our Lord *Korruzon*, as all the High Dragons are reflections of Him."

Mabir shook his head. "That is disputed by men more learned than you, good Bellua—"

"Korruzon is *Rasaa*—head of your Temple, Vizier to the Emperor, Overseer of the Empire. *All things* are relevant to Korruzon."

"Undoubtedly. But the Avar abound in lore and history, throughout Gurvaan. They predate Korruzon."

Bellua took a deep breath. "Korruzon is the living manifestation of the power that existed before all things, the Original Flame of a universe born from fire, whose writhings pushed up the mountains and hollowed out the seas, and who will continue on unto the end of time." His tone was that of a teacher lecturing a stubborn child. "All High Dragons past and future are manifestations of *Him*. So says the Dragon Temple, the Rasaal. So say the merihem. The truth of this is manifest in the breadth of the empire that Korruzon founded four hundred years ago and still oversees. That includes your province of Gadia. You should purge your quaint, provincial need to cling to the icons of your distant past. All Avar—all High Dragons—are reflections of Korruzon."

"The statue in our own ruins is evidence enough of the schism," said Mabir. "It predates Gurvaan and Korruzon alike. Why does it depict two Avar in combat if both are reflections of Korruzon?"

Bellua waved the comment off. "Clearly it is an ancient metaphor of struggle, not to be taken literally."

All fell silent, while Mabir and Bellua studied each other. I was surprised at this sudden confrontation. I'd been unaware that Gurvaan and its provinces disputed the finer points of Temple scripture, but I recognized a power play when I saw one. The stained glass in our own modest temple showed Korruzon as the Most High of all the Avar, but depicted other Avar, too, including Getig. It had never been made clear to me what Mabir meant when he called them the "guises" or "aspects" of Korruzon. Now Bellua spoke of "reflections." It confused me. I imagined a being that could send images of itself out into the world, to see and hear and maybe even communicate on His behalf—as if Getig was really Korruzon in disguise, but with a change of clothing. That seemed bizarre.

Before I could make sense of it, Mabir replied in measured tones. "Based on the descriptions given and the timing—the day before midsummer—we must accept that it was, in fact, the Summer Dragon, regardless of whether it was a unique individual or a reflection of Korruzon."

Bellua did not argue, but sat stone-faced.

Tauman sat a little taller. "So is it a good omen or a bad omen?" You could count on Tauman to stick to business.

Mabir considered before he answered. "The manifestation of the Summer Dragon is neither positive nor negative in itself, only a sign that a moment has arrived. It might be a long moment like an era, or a short one, like a season. Getig sometimes appears at the height of material well-being, which is why he is called Summer—after the Solstice, when all things are at their fullness. But the material world is transitory, and his coming might presage either the abundance of a good harvest-to-be . . . or the long decline of a drought-filled summer. Many things are possible. Darian is not wrong to describe him as a harbinger of change. More correct, perhaps, to call him an avatar of possibility. He is but one aspect of the Cycles.

"Context is everything. Location is part of the context, and in this case it is the village of Riat, specifically the children of Magha. Unfortunately, the context also includes the mauling of Fren and the discovery of a dead dragon, not to mention the accidental offering of a deer, discarded carelessly on an ancient altar. These are not coincidences, and, considering the timing of this dire news from Cuuloda, may be evil omens."

Bellua glanced at me, his eyes questioning. I bit my lip as he nodded at Mabir. "And so you lead yourself back to my point. There is no such thing as 'local context' where a High Dragon is concerned, as all are reflections of Korruzon. The sighting of a High Dragon necessarily reflects on the fate of our nation, not just this village. And certainly not merely on the fortunes of a pair of children." He emphasized that last word just enough to make me cringe. "If an omen can be stretched beyond the children to the aeries, and then again to the village of Riat, then you must extend it to all of Gurvaan and to Korruzon Himself. All Avar are reflections or guises or alternate representations of Korruzon—Korruzon who is the true one and the only. Your argument for the separateness of Getig from the Most High is pointless. Worse, it's selfish."

Mabir's gaze sharpened. "You cannot make an omen serve your desires. An omen obeys only itself."

Tauman intervened again. "But how do these other omens affect the context? Fren, and the dead dragon, and the deer—"

Father's fist struck the table. "Enough of 'context!' Apart from Getig, none of these are signs; they're just things that happened. I can appease any ill portent seen in the mauling of Fren by caring for him and giving him work in the aeries. That will be an expense, but it is the right thing to do and I would have done it regardless. There—I cancel one of your bad omens. As to the dead dragon, we will investigate, of course, but I suspect that dragon's home was on the far side of the mountains. We can appease that injustice by doing what we would do anyway: find and kill the poachers."

"I commend your pragmatism, Broodmaster." Bellua frowned deeply. "But though you may think you are canceling omens, you may find that you are merely ignoring their true meaning. How does this sighting serve Korruzon and the empire? I fear the worst."

Father shook his head. "You complicate things when you cast every little happening as a dangerous sign. I heard Shuja fart this morning; should I kill a chicken? Make an offering?"

"Burn some incense?" said Tauman. Darian stifled a laugh.

Bellua's lips became a hard, straight line. "Jest if you will. It's all interconnected." He turned to Mabir once again. "You said yourself, dhalla, that these were not coincidences. It is a tight knot of circumstances that cannot be disconnected. The mauling, the discarded deer, and the dead dragon sully your children's part in this. To disregard such evil signs might well invite a curse into your valley."

My skin prickled at that word, "curse," and at the second uncertain glance from Bellua.

"I'd planned to keep two qits this year," said Father. "It was a good brood, and the timing is right. But your requisition demands all the qits. If the Dragonry needs dragons, it should allow me the resources I need to expand. Why is that not the best plan? This makes no sense. Throw that at your 'context.'"

Bellua shook his head. "You can find breeding stock in older dragons—"

"It doesn't work that way, and you know it. Dragons bond young, and the bonds last a lifetime. Only in rare cases and with special handling can older dragons be taught to bond with a lifemate. I only managed it with Shuja because he was still young when we returned from the war, because Grus has a very gentle, patient nature, and because I am damned good with dragons!" Father crossed his arms. "Why don't you just tell us how your wings are aligned? What is it that you want?"

Bellua looked from Father to Mabir and back again. "First of all, this story must be contained until we can decipher its meaning."

"What is to contain?" said Father. "The news of the sighting escaped last night. Mabir heard it in the Temple infirmary, and the acolyte, Tulo, was there with villagers in prayer."

Mabir nodded. "I was ministering to the faithful. I'm afraid the word is already out, good Bellua."

"What is your need for silence?" said Father. "I would think you'd want the whole world to know."

Bellua shook his head slowly. "You may have spilled a barrel of snakes. This will take on a life of its own if we aren't careful. The message of this event must be carefully managed."

"Why?"

Before Bellua could answer, Captain Rov stood, his tattoos writhing eerily on his forehead as his scowl deepened. "Enough bickering. This didn't just happen on the day before midsummer, it was also the day before Brood Day. That makes it significant to the brood itself, and therefore to the Ministry of Defense and to the Dragonry. You want *context*? Let me remind you that we *just lost our most productive aerie.*"

Mabir swallowed nervously, while Bellua studied the faces around the table.

Rov glowered. "There is your *context*. The Ministry needs dragons, and it needs them now. We must retake Cuuloda then cross into Harodh and kill Horrors at their source. I have requisitions to fill, Magha Broodmaster, and arguing over signs doesn't change the fact. It will be a year before the qits are old enough to begin combat training. Combined with Bellua's analysis that all omens serve Korruzon, I believe that neither *child* should get a dragon, because I need them. I need them all."

My heart froze. I looked at Darian, and he looked back with ashen face.

"Please, good Rov." Mabir rose painfully. "This pulls two ways. If Korruzon forces the *context*, as we're calling it, to expand all the way to Cuuloda and the battle with Horrors, then Getig draws it back here again. You cannot ignore the smaller aspect any more than the greater one, no matter how dire. If Getig's appearance is related to the fall of Cuuloda, then why did he appear *here*?"

"Because the qits are here. They're clearly important. The Dragonry needs them."

Father thumped the table again with his fist. "*I* need them, and the Dragonry is best served if—"

"I'm sorry, Magha. You do not realize how desperate the need for them has become."

"Then listen to the dhalla! *Honor* the Summer Dragon. Leave me the qits that I need so that I can expand the aeries."

Rov looked exasperated. "I have my orders. The qits are ready now, and we need to get them to the training grounds and the recruits who will bond them. I won't debate this forever!"

No one spoke for several long seconds until Bellua cut through the silence, his voice as clear and sharp-edged as a shard of broken glass. "There is a bigger question we still have not answered. We don't know that the children saw anything at all."

My jaw dropped.

Darian sat straight. "What do you mean? Of course we did!"

"Hush, Darian," Father reprimanded, but he looked at Bellua as he said it.

Mabir's face stretched long with disbelief. "Why would the children invent such a tale?"

"They attend your sermons, do they not? And did they not tell that the old temple ruins were one of their favorite haunts? Ruins that include a statue of High Dragons. Why would fanciful imaginations *not* consider such a tale, with that as inspiration?"

"What are you suggesting?" said Mabir.

"Magha's children desperately want dragons of their own. By their own accounts, they knew they weren't going to receive them. What could change the calculation? What might generate favor for their cause? A cause their father shared. The favor of the Avar of Change?" He looked at me. "Perhaps they have concocted this story to create an illusion of divine acquiescence to their desire."

"You impugn me when you impugn the integrity of my children." Father's tone was low and icy.

Bellua raised a hand. "I don't mean to suggest that you coached them in this tale. That's an unfair accusation—"

"Now you put meaning in my words that I did not intend."

"I don't mean to impugn anyone but to determine the truth. I require proof."

I could take no more. "Then let's go find proof!" All faces turned to me as I swallowed. "A High Dragon stood on the ruins yesterday. I know it, and Darian knows it. So let's go see for ourselves." Darian nodded, color returning to his cheeks. I was suddenly aware that I'd been to the top of the ruins and found only a lingering scent.

Bellua also nodded, but his eyes were clouded. "If there is no evidence, then this whole exercise is a waste of time, and Rov should receive his dragons."

Mabir leaned on the table. "Then you would agree that, if we can ascertain that the sighting is a true event, some sort of tribute must be paid that rewards the children and expands the aeries?"

I held my breath. Mabir, our wise old dhalla, had neatly trapped the merihem in his own logical construction.

"Perhaps." Bellua nodded at last. "*If* we can so ascertain."

"And you, Captain Rov?" said Mabir, "You are the master of this acquisition."

Rov looked at Bellua, then back to Mabir. He locked eyes with Father, then Darian, and finally with me.

My skin shrank.

"I will defer to the decision of the dhalla and the merihem," Rov said.

Mabir nodded. "Very well, then. The mauling of Fren is a given, and Magha has already explained how he will counter that bad omen with a good deed. If there is a dragon corpse in the forest, we can find it and affirm the truth of it. Let us eat some of this food before it goes to waste, then visit the ruins and make our determination quickly."

E I G H T

WITH LITTLE FURTHER discussion, we returned to the compound and saddled dragons for a flight to the ruins. Father took
Mabir on Shuja, Darian rode with Tauman, and I shared Audax's saddle
with Jhem. Bellua and Rov followed the others to the temple ruins, while
Jhem and I flew beyond the ridge. The valley looked just as it had yesterday, with a warm sun, gentle wind, and birdsong. Yet it felt entirely different. Gone was the sense of wonder, the immersion into mystery.

It did not take us long to spot the dragon corpse from the air, and
we landed in the clearing. Jhem knelt beside the body as I had done,
her mouth downturned. "It's a female. Lighter-boned than a male.
Not even Coluver's age. I hope she didn't have babies."

Silently she used her knife to separate the last few dried ligaments
holding the skull to the neck. She took the rear leg bone with the wire
noose still imbedded in it as well, and gave them to me to hold as we
flew to the ruins. They were large and heavy, and difficult to hang on
to. In the end we had to wrap harness straps around them to keep
them in place.

I felt awful with the grisly remains of this wonderful creature in
my lap. It shouldn't have died that way. Suddenly it did feel like a bad
omen to me, as if a curse had awakened that would soon assert itself
in force. I started shaking. I couldn't stop.

Jhem wrapped her arms around me. "It's all going to be fine."

When we landed, everyone was gathered beyond the statue of
Menog and Dahak. Mabir looked up at our arrival and summoned us
over. He pointed at the bones that I carried, then to the block of marble I'd sat on yesterday. I set the remains down gently.

Bellua poked at something behind the statue with a branch. "And this is the deer you dressed? Lying here gnawed by vermin and covered with flies, in a holy place dedicated to the Most High?"

A look of horror swept Darian's face. "We"—he paused—"we were excited. We'd just seen the Summer Dragon."

This was the first time Darian had said we, not I—when he explained a failing.

"So you hid the offering where it would be found only by the foulest scavengers."

"It wasn't meant to be an offering. We just wanted it out of the sun. We were going to bring it home."

"But an offering it became, because of your negligence."

Darian shrank where he stood, then saw the dragon bones that had joined our bounty from the day before. His eyes met mine, then dropped to the remains of the deer on the temple floor.

"Here is proof of the other omen." Mabir indicated the skull and leg bone. "Noose and all."

Bellua did little more than glance at it. "I see only ominous signs, but no proof that a High Dragon visited anywhere near here."

"Can't you see, Bellua, that this alone is proof? Why would the young ones invent a tale so polluted with bad energy? If they were going to fabricate a story, wouldn't they make it as beneficial to their cause as they could?"

"Or did they take advantage of symbols that might lend authenticity to a lie?"

"We didn't—" Darian began, but silenced himself, glancing at Father.

"We should look up there." I pointed to the top of the ridge. "That's where he landed."

Mabir patted me on the shoulder. "Let us walk, shall we? It has become difficult for this old man to climb on and off of dragons."

Mabir leaned on my arm as we climbed the hill to the ruins. It took time to negotiate the steep terrain and undergrowth. It was hard work for the old dhalla. Once there, Mabir and Bellua began to inspect the site. Mabir needed aid, as the grounds were littered with cracked pillars, tumbled blocks, and deadfall. In silence, he turned rocks with his toe and bent occasionally to study the earth. It was almost all gravel and crumbled marble. There was little to see. Desperate for some evidence, I started to look, too.

I pictured Getig again in my mind. The image was still so clear. I could see exactly where each foot had rested: one forelimb there, on that fallen column, the other there, on that cracking block, and a rear foot . . . "Here!" I pointed at the spot, waving everyone over. By the time Mabir arrived, all the others, including Bellua, had joined me around a large patch of moss.

It contained most of a massive footprint, easily five feet across. Unmistakably, the pad and talons of a dragon's foot had crushed the moss into the damp earth beneath.

"By Korruzon," said Father and Jhem, almost in unison.

"See?" Darian grinned. Father failed to admonish him.

"So there you are, merihem Bellua ad Reitleh." Mabir held a hand toward the impression on the ground. "Proof that a High Dragon stood upon this spot."

I looked up hopefully.

The merihem nodded slowly, his brow fissured in thought. "We have heard at least six interpretations of its meaning already: Magha's, the dhalla's, Captain Rov's, mine, and each of the children. See how quickly an event like this can develop its own momentum? A thorough investigation is in order. I should take Darian and Maia with me to Avigal, to be examined by the Council before we go about inventing meanings or dispensing qits."

My heart stopped.

"No," said Father. "It's too long a journey, tied as it is to a wagon train. Even if you leave the wagons and fly, you would make me short-handed for weeks or months. Raising broods of dragons is laborious, as you well know."

"You can always hire help to do menial work like shoveling and—"

"It's not all menial work, merihem. Darian and Maia grew up with dragons. They understand them. They're comfortable around them. What happened to Fren was the result of unfamiliarity; he shouldn't have taken his cart so close behind a dragon. And I need those broodlings. The Dragonry needs for me to raise more dragons."

Mabir patted Father's arm. "The High One appeared *here*, Bellua.

And the signs at last show us the way." He spread his hands to indicate all the gathered evidence. "Magha has already resolved the problem of Fren's injury. Now we must honor the appearance of the Summer Dragon in Riat, whether he was Getig, and unique, or a reflection of the will of Korruzon." He nodded deferentially to Bellua. "It should be an offering of life, not of more death. And because of the Day, I would recommend that it come in the form of a qit, one for each of Magha's children."

"I agree," said Father.

Bellua stared at the footprint, studying it, as if the answer to his dilemma would leap from it and take wing.

He nodded to himself, then looked up. "I concede that Riat deserves acknowledgment. I agree that the disposition of the qits is the heart of the matter, and that we must reach an agreement that protects every interest. The boy will receive his dragon."

Darian clenched his fists together. I held my breath.

"But we must also appease an offering of flesh poorly tendered, and the death of one of the very creatures whose existence defines Riat and the aeries of Magha. The High One Himself showed us the rest of the answer when he led Maia to the dead dragon. She was being negligent of her duties when this occurred, by her own account. It is the one sign in all these portents that is hers alone. Maia will not receive a dragon."

The words tightened into a sharp knot of pain in my stomach. I collapsed to my knees. I could see the little brown-and-buff in my mind's eye every bit as clearly as the Summer Dragon.

Bellua continued. "Thus, Korruzon will be satisfied that we don't give away more than He would have us give, at least until we can seek His council. The blessing intended by the Most High will also be honored. Rov will get all the dragons he requires save one. And Magha will begin to grow his aerie in anticipation of future needs. Do you agree, gentlemen?"

Rov looked at Bellua, his face grim. "I defer to the wisdom of the merihem."

"This isn't fair," said Darian.

As tears began to sting my eyes, I looked to Father.

"I need two qits, not one. Don't unbalance my aeries. I need a second broodling. You've created a problem for me that you won't let me resolve out of my own clutch."

"The broods are not yours," said Rov. "They belong to Emperor, Ministry, and Korruzon."

"I will lose Darian's young one as a broodsire if he's too old to bond properly with a new mate, or if the chosen mate is too young. It depends on the qit's personality, but you can't predict personality or select for it if the pickings are thin. The only way to ensure that two dragons bond is to raise them together. Those bonds last a lifetime. A rogue male is not something you would wish upon me."

"You oversee wild stock, do you not? In the valleys beyond the cliffs? Why could you not steal a qit from a wilding nest?"

"No. I wouldn't even consider it. A wilding baby has no experience of human care. It wouldn't respond to a human." Father's voice had grown edgy. He was only barely maintaining his calm.

Bellua shook his head. "Be that as it may, the Rasaal Council must hear this tale directly. Lord Korruzon Himself should hear it—"

I interrupted. "I thought you said that was Korruzon we saw yesterday. Wouldn't He already know all about His own visit to Riat? Ask *Him* what it means."

Father gripped my shoulder. "Let me handle this, Maia."

Bellua barely restrained his anger. "Korruzon will want to hear directly how His message was received. He cannot think for you, nor interpret for you. We should appeal directly to His wisdom."

My anger finally burst out. "Why do you play these word games?" I shouted. "From the moment you heard our stories, you've done nothing but look for evil—"

Bellua turned his furious gaze to me. "I play no games, child. My motives are simple: to protect the interests of the empire, and above all to further the interests of the Rasaal, and those of Korruzon—"

"You weren't here yesterday! You have no idea—"

"And those of Korruzon, your Lord and Protector. This is an incident of potentially monumental importance. It cannot be judged only in light of your quaint, provincial routines or the desires of *children*. Nor can I let it be turned into a folktale, spreading and acquiring a narrative all its own. The Rasaal has a serious interest in ensuring that the truth be properly told, in its proper context."

Father put his hands on my shoulders and pulled me back. "The Ministry needs for me to grow my aeries. At the same time it's making it impossible for me to do so. I need my daughter's experience here every bit as much as Darian's, *and I need another qit.*"

Mabir's face pinched in concentration. "A yearling is not too old to bond with a mate." My ears burned. Was Mabir backing down?

Father shook his head. "Only if circumstances are right. I'd be a fool to count on that."

"Then perhaps you should wait until next year for *any* qits," said Bellua as he stepped up to Father, his face mere inches away. "I begin to understand why you spilled the story of the sighting to the village—to cement in the minds of your townsfolk that it was ordained, immutable, and tied to Riat. You thought you might use it to wring a pair of qits out of the requisition. But you are very mistaken." He glanced at each of us in turn. "It is my duty to ensure that this story maintains some semblance of accepted truth. I have allowed you one qit; as Captain Rov pointed out, the qits do not belong to you or to any broodmaster, except at the sufferance of the emperor. You may find it very difficult to acquire a qit if you insist on telling this story your way. If need be, a dam can be found for your new broodsire. Even if I have to arrange a marriage for your daughter in another aerie, which a year from now may be the only option you have left."

I felt my face go white. I looked to Jhem and Tauman, Father, Darian, and Mabir for some sign of dissent, but all were silent with shock on their faces.

"There are merihem as well who would happily marry a dark-eyed beauty so well versed in dragonlore."

Bellua glanced at me, and for an instant his gaze dropped to my breasts. He seemed to realize his indiscretion; his face flushed ever so slightly as he looked back quickly to my eyes. My throat tightened with anger and embarrassment. I folded my arms over my chest.

Father stood in stark silence, eyes wide. "You don't mean that," he said at last.

"Broodmaster, your stubbornness forces me to use whatever leverage I have." Bellua finally looked away from me. "But my purpose is not to steal your daughter. My purpose is to nail this incident down before it develops an unwholesome life of its own. This is for your own good. Darian will receive a qit, with the blessing of Korruzon. Maia will not."

All eyes pinned Father. His gaze might have killed Bellua where he stood.

I felt as though I'd swallowed a coal.

"Broodmaster?" said Bellua.

Father bristled. "This is less like a negotiation than it is extortion."

"This was never a negotiation, Broodmaster."

"Curse you. I'll take the one qit, then. Just leave my daughter out of it."

"I have explained why I cannot."

"We're not done here, not by a far—"

"Oh, we are. We're well and truly done." Bellua turned on his heel, mounted his dragon, paused to look down at us. "And Maia *will* leave with me when I go."

"*Bellua*—" Father began, but Bellua launched and didn't look back.

NINE

BY THE TIME we landed in the paddock, I'd found a tight, spiny knot of anger with which to fight back my tears. I was determined to show a brave front despite my pain. I clenched my jaw and set to the immediate business of unsaddling mounts and feeding the babies in the paddock. Father and the others were distracted by these simple tasks, or chose to be. No one spoke to me, which was fine. I avoided all eyes and made a point of not looking for my baby. I was certain I would lose my composure if I spotted her.

It became more and more clear to me: each of those present had interpreted my experience in a way that furthered his own agenda. Rov agreed only with those points that allowed him to demand babies and fill his requisition. Mabir protected his little bit of authority by ensuring that the *context* expanded enough to contain his flock. And just when it seemed that he might rise to my defense, he'd only agreed to a solution that met in the middle of all the conflicting interests.

Bellua worked to make sure that Mabir acknowledged his superior position, turning Getig into a mirror of Korruzon. Worse still, he'd threatened to haul me to Avigal, the capital city, to be interrogated by more of his ilk. When I thought of his eyes flashing to my breasts I grew more and more angry—and terrified.

Father had said the fight wasn't over, but the needs of the day swept him up. The aeries were certainly more important than I was. So what did that make me? Chattel? I swallowed tears. If Bellua took me away from Riat, anything was possible. He made it sound like an inquisition before Korruzon Himself, but it could be something entirely different. Bondage? Rape? How far would Bellua go to bury my story?

Even Darian had included me only when he needed to share the blame of an ugly omen with someone else.

There was but a single instant in the entire discussion that made sense to me: when Father offered to care for Fren. He would supplant injury with comfort, evil portent with good deed. "There," he had said, "I cancel one of your bad omens."

It was my introduction to the politics of business and religion. I felt betrayed. Worst of all, though, I felt betrayed by the Summer Dragon. It was as if he had summoned me to find the omen that damned me.

When the babies had been fed and the paddock swept, Father waded among the qits. "Darian! Show me which one is yours."

Darian looked at me briefly, his mouth downturned, but then he moved carefully through the brood to the little black-and-copper that he had chosen. He knelt down in front of the qitling and reached out a tentative hand. The baby stretched his neck forward to sniff at Darian's fingers.

"It's okay, son. You can touch him now."

Darian's hand cupped the baby's chin. Immediately, other qits crowded around, bumping against his leg and sniffing too, as if a barrier they'd never known existed had just crumbled. Darian smiled, then glanced at me and his smile vanished.

"Ignore the others, Darian. Only look at yours. Touch only him." Darian did as he was instructed, and soon the other babies wandered away to begin new games of chase and pounce.

"Speak to him, son."

"What do I say?"

"It doesn't matter. Tell him a story. Describe the weather. Babble like a lunatic."

I was unaware that I'd been backing up until I ran into one of the broodhouse doors. The weathered planks were rough on my hands, while the chin Darian caressed would be soft and smooth. Envy swarmed up inside me. I fought it. I didn't want envy. I wanted only my hard anger.

Father summoned the riders of the nurse dragons, Janno and Marit. "Gentlemen, I need your help. It's time to divert the babies away from their parents." The two old soldiers nodded and called

their mounts. This was everyday business for their experienced females, who proceeded to herd the qitlings with their wings and forefeet. I caught sight of the little brown-and-buff tumbling with another
baby, her brown eyes winking with delight.

No! Only anger.

Father whistled to his mount. "Shuja! Grus! Come with me. I have
a surprise for you." Shuja stepped over immediately, and his copper-
colored dam came behind. "Do you see? One of your babies will remain this year."

"Haa!" Shuja tossed his head. "Shoosha [purrrr]." Shuja was
happy.

"Qit," said Grus, more softly, and pressed her cheek against Shuja's neck.

"Tauman! Jhem! Call your parents. It's time to sequester them."

In short order, all six parents were gathered around the little
black-and-copper. I glimpsed him between their legs, crawling in and
out of Darian's lap. "Having one of the babies in the stable will be a
comfort to them," I heard Father say. The nurse dragons now instinctively began to separate the babies from their parents. Bellua's dragon
stood back from the proceedings, head high, aloof. The merihem
started to wander my way. I pressed back against the broodhouse
door as if I might merge with it, pass through, and come out the other
side. Broodlings surrounded me in a yipping tide of joy. The brown-
and-buff stopped once, right in front of me. Her eyes met mine, and I
trembled on the brink of indecision. But before I could reach down for
that illicit touch, she bounded off for a wrestling match or a game of
bite-me.

My family and our dragons headed toward the bridge to the
homestead. The dragons would stay in the winter stable, as we called
it—the permanent quarters for our breeding dragons in the clifftop
homestead. We were done now with the broodhouse until next spring,
when new clutches of eggs would be laid. I watched them go until the
nurse dragons stepped into my line of sight. Bellua waded among the
qits, hands behind his back. He looked up, directly at me, raised his
eyebrows in some false, conciliatory show of sympathy, and opened
his mouth to speak. But I fled through the man-door into the broodhouse, furious and confused, and choked back tears.

The brood platform was silent and empty. No massed tumbles of broodlings, no mew and yip, no scamper and tussle. Only muffled echoes from the other side of the doors.

The emptiness was large, and I was small.

———

I had all but one of the nests cleaned out when Jhem found me. The cliffside doors were open, so I could shovel the soiled wood chips over the precipice. She grabbed a broom and started sweeping the remnant dust at the far end of the row. She said nothing. I was numb, beyond anger or grief or any other emotion. Drained. We toiled in silence.

The sweeping went faster than the shoveling. We met at the final empty nest, Audax and Coluver's. I sat on it, elbows on my knees. Jhem leaned her broom against the wall and sat next to me, wrapped her arms around my shoulders, then rested her head on mine. "Your father is in a hard position, Maia. He will do what he can to protect you, but the Ministry dictates what the Ministry wants."

I stuck my hands under my armpits to stop their trembling. "Where's Darian?"

"In the winter stables. Your Father wanted him to begin the bonding immediately, before Rov or Bellua had a chance to reconsider. He's named him already: Nitac Aru: *A sign of victory*, to honor the Summer Dragon and put good energy on the day. Mabir will administer the first graving in their bond marks after the banquet."

I ought to have been in tears, but my eyes were dry. "Good energy on the day. That's hilarious."

"Darian asked me to tell you that he's sorry for what happened—"

"Oh yes, I feel very much better now."

"And that he's worried. Don't be angry with him, Maia. He's trying, in his way."

I brushed my hair out of my face. "What am I going to do?"

"Stay brave. You're Magha's daughter."

I wrapped my arms across hers. "But for the Summer Dragon, we would have kept no babies this year. Instead, we keep one, and I have become a problem." I groaned. "Bellua said I would bring a *curse* . . ." I choked on the word.

"Don't let your thoughts take you there, Maia. Getig did appear.

I don't care what Bellua or Mabir say, I take hope from that. Because of him there is also time, and a chance. Bellua won't be leaving right away; he and Mabir have to concoct their version of your story." Jhem cradled my head against her shoulder.

"I won't go. The way he looked at me . . ." Sizing up my worth as chattel. But he'd seemed embarrassed by his indiscretion too.

A tear ran down Jhem's cheek. She kissed my forehead. "It's not over."

Father and Tauman entered the broodhouse, spotted us, and joined us quietly. I sat up as my family gathered around me.

Father wiped his brow with the back of a hand. "High Ones, what a day."

Tauman crossed his arms. "Who among us, besides Maia, has seen a High One? I have not."

"Nor I." Jhem brushed hair back from my face.

Father sat on an empty nest. "I saw Korruzon from afar when I was in the Dragonry, during maneuvers in Avigal. He was unlike anything I'd ever seen. An undeniable presence. Huge, black, with wings the color of fire, red stripes like flames on His chest and legs. Eyes bright as the sun. If I hadn't seen Him with my own eyes, I would be inclined to dismiss talk of High Dragons entirely."

Tauman and Jhem looked at each other, then at me.

"But it happened. It's real," said Jhem. "The question is, why here? Why Maia, if it doesn't mean something?"

"You heard." Father looked at each of us, but his gaze lingered on me. "It was meant for Darian. Because Maia was there too, Korruzon had to arrange a 'not for you' omen, just for her, to break her heart and free her up for what amounts to an abduction."

I clenched Jhem's hand.

She squeezed it in return. "The man is a pig."

Tauman shook his head, as if to clear it of conflicting thoughts. "Mabir didn't refute Bellua's interpretat—"

"Of course he didn't!" said Father. "What else could he do? Bellua is his superior. More than that, Avigal holds our purse strings. The Ministry dictates according to its wants."

That was almost exactly what Jhem had said only a minute ago.

Father sighed. "Mabir and I did what we could, but it's recoiled on us. I'd return the qit if I thought it would save Maia, but then Bellua would be free to take Darian too if he so desired. Don't forget he wanted both of them to stand before Korruzon. Bellua has all the power he needs to get what he wants."

My voice sounded thin and quivery when I spoke. "I won't go."

Father put a hand on my shoulder. "I won't let him take you."

"I don't trust him. If he takes me away, he won't allow me to come home. I know it."

He nodded. "That is my fear, too. He has no interest in taking you to Council. That's only pretense. What he really wants is leverage."

"I think the word you want is *hostage*." Jhem's chin was outthrust.

"This isn't about me at all, really," I said. A statement, not a question. "He's using *me* to scare *us*. It's about the Rasaal and who gets to interpret the stories."

"It's about you all right," said Jhem. "If you were ugly he'd have thought of something else."

Father looked at me. Then he looked at Jhem, and the corners of his mouth drew downward even further. "Jhem is right: the man is a pig. But Maia is also right—he wants to bury this story. It can't be Getig; it can only be a guise or aspect of Korruzon."

"But at the expense of production?" Jhem crossed her arms. "We just lost our most productive aerie. Why in Gadia would that not be more important than his blasted authority? You would think that the Ministry would *need* for us to increase production."

Father shook his head, as if the only simple answer was unacceptable somehow. Then he looked down, frowning. "Bellua seemed to show doubt when he saw the footprint in the ruins. He doesn't know how to interpret it, but he could no longer deny that a High Dragon had stepped in our valley. He's confused or envious. Perhaps even scared. He gave away more than he wanted to. It rankles him to have his doctrine questioned, so he laid a trap baited with a single qit. And I stepped into it knowingly."

"We can't wait a whole year for another qit," said Jhem. "Bellua knows that. If Darian's dragon fails to bond with a mate . . ."

Father nodded. "Of course he knows it. He used his authority to drive wedges into our arguments. Allowing us one qit puts us at the Ministry's mercy. He gains control."

"But why?"

"There's something much bigger going on here. What would it mean to the faithful if any High Dragon other than Korruzon appeared in a distant province? Avigal is not about to cede authority to a province, least of all, religious authority. If Bellua can't bend the story to his version of truth, then he'll try to turn it into something dark. Or murder it entirely."

"What about Rov?" said Tauman. "Can we convince him to give us another qit? It's his decision ultimately."

Father shook his head. "He won't go against the Dragon Temple in matters of faith."

"Then who is in charge here? Rov? Or Bellua?" Tauman's voice was edgy now too.

"Any other year, Rov, of course. But the Summer Dragon introduced a factor outside of his reckoning. And besides, he wanted *all* the qits to begin with. I wouldn't give him a chance to reconsider the decision he's already made."

"What do we do?" Jhem's hand squeezed mine painfully. "We can't let that puffed up merihem take Maia to Avigal. Once she's out of our hands . . ."

I felt again Bellua's gaze touching my body, and I stood straight. "We have to fight them!"

"What would you propose we do?" said Tauman. "Start an insurrection? Go to war with the Rasaal?"

Jhem snorted. "We have a day, perhaps, to convince Rov or Mabir to . . ."

"It's not going to happen, Jhem. This is business. As Father said, the Ministry owns us. It's not just Bellua pinching us; Rov showed his muscle in negotiations already. We aren't going to get as much as we'd hoped. But Bellua is determined to tell this story his way."

"Jhem and Maia are right," said Father. "It can't end this way."

"We'll lose!" Tauman leaned forward. "This is the Ministry we're talking about. Rov is its voice here today, and Bellua has made up his mind for him. Would it be wrong to consider how we might take advantage of a marriage—"

"*What?*" snapped Jhem.

Tauman spoke slowly, as if to an imbecile. "We would do better to figure out what advantages we can still—"

"Are you talking about your sister as if she was a commodity to be traded?" Her voice was barely above a whisper.

"I already told you: I won't go."

Tauman could barely glance at me. "Will you let me finish? We need to be practical. We have an entire village—an entire province—to think of."

Jhem stiffened. "I don't believe what I'm hearing! Your own blood and kin . . ."

"I'm not talking about marrying her to a merihem, but one of the other aeries might—"

I hit him in the arm with a fist. "You self-serving pig-horror! I hate you!" My own brother was willing to trade me for some small measure of security. Was that all he thought I was good for? He recoiled, and I hit him again. It felt good.

"Back off, little girl, or—"

"Enough!" Father barked. "Enough."

I stared at Tauman, so angry my knuckles were white. He glanced at me again, but could not meet my gaze.

Jhem held me tightly. "Then what of Getig?" There was a note of scorn in her voice. "Why here? And why Maia?"

Father looked up with his face drawn and gray. I hadn't seen him look so sad since the death of Mother. He echoed, "What of Getig?" Then he looked at me, his eyes darting back and forth between mine. "What of Getig?" He hung his head. "Maia, I regret my harsh words yesterday. Your mother always warned me that my anger was too quick. I still prove it." He shook his head, seeking the right words. "You're like her, you know. She was a daydreamer too. I loved that about her. But I worry for you sometimes. The world is changing, and you need to have a clear eye."

Father never apologized. Never. It felt like preparation for my departure, a need to make amends before it was too late. My Father, the mighty Magha, bending under the pressure of the Ministry. It almost undid me. Despair tore at my anger.

No one said anything more. Not until Father stood and motioned to Tauman. "Come on. All of you. Guests from the village will be arriving soon." He took me by the shoulders. "Maia, I want you to put your brave face on. Can you do that?"

I nodded, fighting back a sudden rush of tears.

"Good girl. We'll figure something out. This isn't over, not as long as you're still here. But first we have a banquet to host, and then one final task to perform." He left the broodhouse, and Tauman followed.

In the paddock, somebody small and boisterous caromed off one of the dragon-doors with enough force to rattle it. Happy growls ensued.

Jhem and I rolled the cliffside doors shut. They wouldn't be opened again for months.

T E N

I MADE MY WAY to the manor house unnoticed, bathed quickly, and changed into my best silks and leathers. I started for the door but stopped in the shadow of the hall where I might observe unseen.

Kaisi's family came every Brood Day to help with the preparations and cooking. They had set a long table with dinnerware and flowers in the main yard, between the manor and the winter stable. The deer from yesterday's hunt would be the featured course, one dish among many.

I was late. The first course of seasonal greens was being removed. Rov was just sitting down. I could tell by the expressions at the table that news of Cuuloda had been the first order of business. There was Dren, the head of the fisher's guild, with his sun-scarred neck and scraggly beard. Beyond him were several of the local farmers and their wives, weeping or with faces buried in their hands. Bek the smith sat with his gigantic arms crossed, chin down. Carpenters and leatherworkers whose names I couldn't recall shook their heads in disbelief.

Father stood at the head of the table, dressed in his finest black and purple, to match Shuja's hide. My place was four seats to his left, after Tauman, Jhem, and Darian. There was an empty seat to his right, where Mother would have been seated. My last memories of her surged at the sight of her empty chair. What would she have said in this morning's inquiry? Would she have fought for me?

That train of thought summoned ghosts too near to my grief. I pushed it down. I composed my brave face.

The next seat was reserved for Mabir, as the spiritual leader of

Riat. To his right sat the most honored guest—Rov, the leader of the acquisition. Bellua sat to Rov's right, with Marit and Janno beyond. The rest of the table was peopled with locals and their families. I noted with distaste that this arrangement would have put me opposite Bellua. I took a step backward into deeper shadow.

Father raised his hands until the table was quiet. "Not all the news is dire. As some of you already know, an amazing thing has happened. Perhaps it's a good omen not only for Gurvaan, but also for Riat. I hope it will balance the bad news that Captain Rov brought us. My tongue is ill-equipped for this, so I turn to the good dhalla Mabir."

Murmurs chased down the length of the table as Mabir lifted his ancient frame to a standing position. "Friends! Shhh! Shhh! Attend!

"These are indeed auspicious times for Riat and for all of Gurvaan. Something has occurred which even I find hard to believe, except that I've seen the evidence with my own eyes. The young son of the broodmaster has been part of an amazing occurrence, the like of which is related only in song and scripture."

Mabir had already written me out of the instant legend. But why? To protect me? To quiet the story of my evil omen? In fear of the Ministry?

"Only once in many generations will the Most High visit the faithful. But yesterday, on an outing in the forest—indeed, while visiting the ancient temple of Cinvat—young Darian ad Magha saw Getig, the Summer Dragon, whose sign I observed with my own eyes this very morning in the ruins!"

Mabir had used the term "Most High," which could refer to Korruzon alone or to an entire older pantheon, carefully neither refuting nor confirming Bellua's view. But the merihem's face grew darker as the table erupted with questions. He jumped to his feet. "Good people! Please! We'll answer what questions we can. But this is what we know: Clothed in the colors and scents of summer, adorned as the Summer Dragon, the Most High and Benevolent Korruzon visited your valley. The sighting was brief but undeniable. The young master returned home immediately with the report, and today we have confirmed the truth of it from evidence in the temple ruins. There was no direct communication, but the appearance alone is a message to all of Gurvaan."

The table buzzed with amazement, but I stood in rekindled fury. My part in the day's events had been painted out entirely. *No direct communication?* Getig's eyes still pierced me to the core, even in memory. The event was scarcely one day old, but already it sounded like fiction.

The throbbing anger in my skull drowned out Bellua's voice. I clung to the wall as one of Kaisi's sisters hurried in with an empty tray. "You're late, miss, you'd best . . ." Her words followed her out of hearing into the kitchen. Duty demanded that I go to my seat at the table, but what I really wanted to do was throw Bellua off the cliff. I was trapped between duty to my family and duty to my Temple, between fury and fear. I couldn't move.

Bellua's voice made itself heard again, preparing the villagers for my departure before he dragged me to Avigal, to twist my words before the Council or Korruzon Himself. And after that, what?

I wouldn't go.

Kaisi's sister dodged me as I turned into the house, barely lifting a tray laden with meat out of my way. "Miss Maia! Where are you . . . ?"

I turned down a hall, into my sleeping chamber and grabbed a knapsack off the wall.

From outside came cheers and then a rumble like thunder as the villagers thumped the table with their fists. Applause. Mabir, or maybe Bellua, had just announced that Darian would receive a qit of his own. My cheeks grew hot, but I went to the window to peek out. I could see almost everyone.

It seemed as if the gathered neighbors and friends were looking for something hopeful and encouraging to grab hold of in the wake of Rov's awful news. Everyone was standing, and Darian's cheeks were visibly red even from here. It was surreal.

Mabir raised his arms until the ovation died down. "My friends, people of Riat, Broodmaster Magha and family, honored guests. Let us say a prayer of thanks."

All heads bowed as Mabir closed his eyes.

"Most High, we receive Your message with faith in Your benevolence, praise for Your wisdom, and fear of Your strength. Your mighty wings shield us. Your talons, like spears, defend us. Your eyes, like firebolts, regard us with love and grace. You are the Original Flame that flickers in our hearts. We are Your servants in this wicked world, and so we accept Your commandments with humility. Your ways are a mystery, not for us to question. From beyond the infinite You come, and from You come all things. So as You have commanded, let it be done."

The assembled voices repeated, "Let it be done."

I shook my head, my lips twisted. Who had so commanded? This was a sham, the first endorsement of a lie.

"A toast!" Tauman raised his goblet high. "To Korruzon and the Emperor, to country and village, to the aeries, and to Darian!"

I could take no more. I turned with my knapsack to start packing. Some things would be essential—extra clothes, food—which meant a raid on the kitchens at some point. A knife. I would want a crossbow from the armory in the front hall, too. I would have to wait until darkness.

And then what? I sat on my bed with a jacket stuffed halfway into the sack. I had no idea what I would do or where I would go. Not yet. I had only a memory of the Summer Dragon's fathomless gaze.

What I really needed was a plan. As the cheers and laughter continued outside, I sat with my head in my hands, thinking.

ELEVEN

DARIAN KNOCKED ON the door and pushed his head in.
"What?" I said, pushing my knapsack under the bed with a foot.

"Can I come in?"

I shrugged and waved him in.

He went to the window and looked out, his hands seeking his pockets, then each other, then his pockets again. He seemed unable to decide which emotion to feel, eyebrows and lips contending in mismatched confusion. "The banquet is over," he offered at last.

"Good."

"Aru is sleeping, so I slipped out for a minute. Aru is what I named—"

"I heard."

His face settled in an unhappy frown. "Are you all right? Are you going to be all right?"

I sat on the edge of the bed and studied my boots. "What do you care?"

"Maia, I'm as stunned as you are. I don't want you to go. I didn't know Bellua was going to be so . . . be such a . . . it all just happened so—"

"You promised me that I wouldn't take the blame alone. You promised! But you left me hanging in that inquisition this morning. And the only thing I did was find a dead dragon. I didn't kill it; I only found it. But all the reward goes to you. All the blame goes to me! It's *Mother's fall* all over again, and you don't care!" I stood and shoved him—hard—and he stumbled back.

I expected him to shout at me or return the shove, but he only stood, wiping his hands on his jerkin as if he might brush my anger off. "That's unfair, Maia."

"I took all the blame then, too."

"I told you, you don't remember it right, you—"

"She scolded me. She said, 'Maia, I'm disappointed in you. Get your feet on the ground, girl, and start pulling your weight. Don't be a burden.' And when I tried to apologize, she interrupted me and said, 'A dragon handler with her head in the clouds is *cursed*.'"

"That's an old Dragonry saying. I've heard Father say it. It doesn't mean any—"

"It was the last thing she ever said to me."

Darian shifted uncomfortably. "She didn't mean it. She was just angry. She scolded me too, just so you know. She told me, 'Maia is your little sister, and I need you to help keep her in line.' And that was the last thing she ever said to *me*."

"And now Bellua practically says the same thing."

"What?"

"You heard him. He said that giving me a dragon would be *inviting a curse* into Riat. Because I tripped on your lantern. And found a dead dragon in the forest."

His shoulders slumped, then shrugged.

I dropped onto the bed and buried my face in my hands. I'd raised the specter of Mother's death again. "Please leave me alone."

He touched my shoulder, but I slapped his hand away.

"You're right," he said. "I was supposed to look out for you, but I didn't. I got caught up in my own excitement, and I let you down. I'm sorry, Maia. I really am." For once he sounded sincere, and a glance at him confirmed it. His eyes were red like they were when he tried to hide unmanly tears. But I wasn't ready to give up my anger. I needed it still. "Will you go?"

Instead, he sat next to me. "You know what I think?" He stared at the floor. "I think the Summer Dragon came for you. Not for us and not for me, but for you. That's what I think." Then he stood and headed toward the door but paused and said over his shoulder, "Father wants me to tell you that it's time to deliver the qits, and yes he wants you there, with your 'brave face' on."

He left quietly.

———

The first of the Ministry cages clanked into the grapples on the gantry platform as I entered the paddock. The qits were milling happily, though I could see that they were weary from a long, napless day. They were excited to be out so late in the evening, with no comprehension of the reason the nurse dragons corralled them all in the gantry end of the paddock.

Our parent dragons were absent, secluded in the winter stables with Darian and his qit, where Mabir would be giving the new bondmates the first ring in their bond marks. Villagers surrounded the gantry, watching, giddy with drink and anticipation.

I looked for the little brown-and-buff, but couldn't find her. One of the nurse dragons ushered babies into the cage with deft, patient applications of wing and forefoot. It was Bellua's dragon. He was there. How appropriate. He saw me, held my gaze for a long moment, then turned back to his nurse at work.

My fury was gone. I didn't want to think about him anymore. Jhem spotted me and came to stand silently at my side.

The first cage was filled, and the door clanged shut. The little female wasn't among them. Father and Tauman manned the winch. They released the lock on the brake, and the cage started to descend. The gathered villagers cheered. Partway down the cliff face I heard the excited yips and mews of play turn to bleats of fear. I'd witnessed this part of Brood Day many times. It was the saddest, most emotional part of the day. But it had never been so personal before.

It hit me abruptly—they were going off to war. They would be turned into killing machines, for the Empire. For Korruzon. I'd always known that, but this time it felt different, and I shivered.

After a few minutes, the next empty cage rose to the top of the cable. The metallic clank of the closing locks echoed in my ears. It was happening too fast. Nurse dragons performed their careful shepherding act again, and another load of babies was directed into the cage. There were eight qits, mine not among them. That left eight babies in the paddock.

I looked again for the little brown-and-buff, and found her easily now. She looked unsure. The bounce was gone from her gait, her head and tail low, her wings drawn close. She and the remaining qits had been unnerved by the cries of the others and shrank together into a tight group when the villagers cheered the descent of the second cage. They crawled over one another, crying for their parents, only to be buffeted gently toward the gantry landing by the nurse dragons. I felt a lump rising in my throat and clutched my hands close to my chest.

The little brown-and-buff ran up to me, looked at me with her big, intelligent eyes. Despite myself, I reached down and cupped her chin in my hands. Her skin was soft and dry.

"No, Maia." Jhem's arms surrounded me from behind, pulling my hands away.

But it didn't matter. The little girl of my desires didn't respond to my touch the way Darian's baby had. She flinched and dashed off, bleating unhappily. There was fear in her call now as the wing of a nurse dragon blocked my view of her.

I knew in that moment that she was gone. That she would never be mine. Had never been mine. That all my hopes had been for nothing. A lump filled my throat.

The qits grew more and more alarmed at the clatter and rattle of the gantry mechanism, as if they understood that it was the sound of their betrayal. The third and final cage locked into the grapples with a loud *chank*. The nurse dragons performed their tender act of treachery for the last time. I saw my girl stumble into the cage amongst the press of little bodies. Jhem squeezed me tight.

"*I don't know what to do,*" I whispered.

"I know. I'm so sorry," said Jhem quietly.

The last baby was urged into the cage, and the door swung shut. The clatter of its closing educed a chorus of frightened cries.

I started to shake. Tears brimmed in my eyes as the brake released and the cage descended. The crowd cheered long and loud. I saw a glimpse of her before the cage fell below the level of the platform. The timbre of the babies' cries rose, as they finally understood that their world was forever changed. They no longer sounded concerned or lost, but terrified. I heard them above the noise of celebration and the clatter of the winch as they made the long descent down the cliff face.

At last the tears broke through my resolve. Jhem held me tight as sobs convulsed me, my face buried in her shoulder long after their terror had passed beyond hearing.

I LAY IN BED, exhausted, but I wasn't waiting for sleep. I was waiting for the manor to grow quiet.

My world was such a mess. If the Summer Dragon hadn't come to us, there would have been no controversy. The Ministry would have taken all the qitlings. Darian and I would have been disappointed, but life would have gone on as normal. Perhaps next year the timing would be better. Perhaps Father would have thought better of me.

But because Getig had come to us, we got to keep one dragon, and that unbalanced everything. And the simple accidents of tripping on a lantern and finding a dead dragon now gave Bellua reason to steal me from my home.

Images and feelings chased each other in my head, but of all the debated signs and portents, the little brown-and-buff flinching at my touch seemed like the ugliest omen of them all.

I kept coming back to Getig's eyes. Those eyes. They summoned me still. I shook my head angrily to dislodge the thoughts. I needed a plan, somewhere to go that made sense. I ran a hundred different rescue scenarios through my head, in which I stole the brown-and-buff from the train and hid with her in the wilderness, or in another province. But I knew those were fantasies. Even if I could find a way to steal a qit from the ministry train, raising dragons required structure and resources. I would be a fugitive.

She was lost to me. I wept for her again, convulsing in silent whispers until my neck and sides hurt. Finally a yawn broke my tears. I was exhausted, but I dared not sleep. I wiped my nose and cheeks on my sleeve, then realized that I hadn't changed out of my good clothes. I wiped my sleeve on my breeches, trying to gather my thoughts.

Half dreams intruded.

Mother sat upon Grus, scowling. "A dragon handler with her head in the clouds is cursed."

Dragon bones defiled the altar in the ruins. We shouldn't have left them there. "I didn't kill it," my dream self pleaded, "I only found it."

Bellua leered across the table at me. "First we must ascertain whether this was the Summer Dragon or some lie that you concocted."

"It's not a lie!"

I shook myself awake, alarmed that I'd spoken out loud.

I couldn't afford to sleep. I pulled my knapsack out from under the bed, went to the door and listened. The manor was quiet, but I hesitated at the threshold. In my gut I knew there was an answer in all of this, one that didn't rely on Father or Darian or anyone else.

The Summer Dragon's eyes kept calling me back.

"What am I supposed to do?" I closed my eyes and tried to reason out a plan.

I stumbled down the scree slope and into the forest. I found the spot where the dragon dam's corpse lay. It would be intact still but for the skull and leg bone we had left in the ruins.

"The High One Himself showed us the rest of the answer when he led Maia to the dead dragon," Bellua had said. "It is the one sign in all these portents that is hers alone."

Mine alone.

It couldn't have been very old—perhaps two or three years in age, old enough to wear a saddle. Old enough to—

My eyes snapped open.

I understood. A dragon dam can die and leave a brood behind. This was the answer. Suddenly I knew where I was going and what I had to do. I wouldn't sit and wait any longer for Mabir, or Bellua, or even Father to set things right.

I changed clothes quickly—my stout leathers, a warm shirt and jacket. I pulled the spare clothes out of my knapsack and stuffed a blanket in, then crept out to the corridor.

The manor was dark and silent. Brood Day generally ended in exhaustion for everyone, and this had been no ordinary Brood Day. I made my way to the kitchens. After considering a moment, I took all the venison, including a large haunch. I might need it all. I wrapped it in bread and cabbage leaves and then some of the kitchen towels to contain the juices.

Then I gathered new apples, raw potatoes, and some carrots. I folded it all up in the blanket and pushed it into the pack.

We kept most of the hunting gear in the main hall. I took a water-skin, a small bag containing flint and steel, and stuck a hunting knife in my belt. A coil of rope went into my pack. Our compound bows hung on the wall. I had some skill with the weapon but decided instead on the light crossbow Kaisi used to take raccoons out of the trees. I was a fair shot with a crossbow. I slung it over my shoulder, along with a quiver of bolts. I closed the door carefully, quietly, on my way out.

The round face of the moon cast its blue light from the southern sky. A thin line of orange lantern light peeked under the doors of the winter stable, where Darian spent his first night with his new charge. Gentle voices keened quietly inside—our dragon dams mourning the loss of yet another brood. But I had a different path now.

First I needed to create a false trail. I took the bridge to the compound, stepping as lightly as possible, then crossed to the gantry. I set the pack and weapons down, then released the hoisting platform—the "basket." The locks opened with a loud clank that I was sure would wake the entire village. I set the brake again quickly and waited.

When my heart had slowed again, I released the brake and let the empty basket fall. In the darkness, it was soon out of sight below me. It was risky but needed to be done. When everyone realized I was missing in the morning, I hoped this clue would lead in the wrong direction, into the village and onto the plains beyond, on the assumption that I was following the ministry train or simply running away. I needed as much of a head start as I could manufacture.

When the basket landed at the bottom, the pulley stopped turning. Creaks and squeaks gave way to the murmuring breeze. I crossed the bridge again, crept through the yard and into the trees. I paused once to look back at the compound, bright where the moonlight touched it, black in the shadows.

Bellua would haul me off to Avigal—and only the Avar knew what other fate. Without another qit, Father was forced to accept Bellua's terms and I became expendable. Worse, I was the leverage that Bellua used to wrap the story of Getig in Temple garb.

There was another way to interpret all the signs. Bellua had said it himself: The one sign that belonged to me alone was the dead dragon in the forest, an adult female cruelly trapped and killed at the height of breeding season.

Somewhere on those far cliffs where Getig had appeared to me last, on the cliffs where wilding dragons raised their broods, was there a baby dragon without a mother? I had to know.

The aeries of Riat needed another qit, and it had to be mine. Without another backward glance I headed into the forest.

Night transformed the statue of the High Ones. Dahak, made of some dark stone, disappeared into shadow. But white Menog hovered above like a ghost pinned on a shaft of moonlight. The breeze was its eerie voice. Windblown shadows gave a semblance of life to the perfectly sculpted wings. Beneath was the block of marble that had been an altar in my dream, where the skull and leg bone of the female dragon gleamed white in a puddle of moonlight. I might have been looking at the spirit of the dead dragon rising above its bier.

Thoughts of omens and signs filled my head. The skeleton had been the linchpin of Bellua's arguments. I couldn't leave it sundered. That would only add credence to his position. My sense of propriety and my dream together seemed to demand that I reunite the scattered pieces with the rest of the skeleton before I set out on my mission. I shivered, but set to the task.

Her skull would be difficult to move. I'd barely managed to hang on to it yesterday, while strapped onto Audax's saddle. It was half as long as I was tall, and easily weighed three stone. How odd that in my dream it had been light as a feather. I pulled the rope from my knapsack and considered my options, then laced the rope through the eye sockets and around her teeth, making loops I could stick my arms through. It would hang on my back, cushioned by the knapsack. I removed the wire noose from her leg bone, coiled it and stuck it in my pack. When I had the skull arranged on my back, I laid the leg bone across my shoulders too and started up the hill.

By the time I reached the ridge my legs and shoulders burned. I knelt on the outcropping, glad to take some weight off my neck and shoulders for a moment. Two days ago I'd looked for Getig while standing here, the earth and forest alive below me. Now all was silent and deep in shadow, with the bright face of a full moon floating above the far cliffs. Behind me, dawn outlined the trees. The sun would be up soon.

I took a long draught from my waterskin, then started cautiously down the slope, grateful that the moon illuminated the treacherous footing. Even so, the skull was awkward and heavy. Before I reached the bottom I had to remove it from my back and use the rope sling to lower it one step at a time before me, following as strength returned to my arms and legs.

The last of the moon vanished as I entered the dark forest. It was cooler in the trees, and the smell of damp earth mingled with the sharp spice of pine. Dew made the moss slippery, so I dragged the skull behind me rather than carry it. My eyes picked out a narrow track through the forest in the pre-dawn gloom, but it was slow going. Finally, when fingers of pale morning light filtered through the trees, I found my way to the table of stone where the dragon's bones lay.

I untied the skull, lowered it into its proper position with care, then laid the leg bone where it belonged.

I felt a need to make some sort of invocation, some small prayer for her departed spirit, but I didn't know what to say. Every approach sounded childish in my mind. The act of restoring her bones to their proper places would have to speak for me. I bent down and kissed the top of her skull, petted the smooth nose once, then left the clearing behind me.

———

The forest that had seemed so inviting two days ago was an obstacle now. I couldn't see the far cliffs that were my ultimate goal. There were no clear paths, only jumbled piles of boulders, tangled deadfall, and thorny undergrowth. My knife wasn't well suited to hacking through foliage, and I chided myself for not thinking to bring a machete. But I had to reach those far cliffs, and do it before Father and the rest divined my plan and came looking for me.

Wilding dragons built their nests in those crags; that's where Ge-

tig had perched the last time I saw him. If there was a baby, that's
where I would find it.

As the morning wore on, I stumbled upon a game trail that wound
to the west. Relieved, I settled into a better pace, and even started to
trot, with the knapsack bouncing on my back.

At noon I fished an apple and some carrots out of my pack to
munch on as I went. I wasn't hungry enough to eat an uncooked potato, and I was saving the meat; when I found my baby, I would need
to feed it. Though the trail climbed up and down over large blocks of
stone that had tumbled off the mountain face, I felt that I was making
excellent progress. The canopy had thinned, however, so I kept a constant eye on the sky for Father and the others. Ideally, I'd have scouted
my route before I ever climbed down from our own ridge. But it was
dark then, and I'd been determined to restore the skeleton of the
dragon dam. That detour had probably added several hours to my
journey.

As the sun passed its zenith, I came to a rise where the trees had
failed to clothe the granite foundation of the mountain. A round outcropping of stone capped the hill, offering an excellent vantage. After
scouting above for riders, I clambered up a skree slope and hopped up
the knobs to the dome.

I could see back the way I'd come, and forward to the cliffs where
the Summer Dragon had perched the last time I saw him. Getig had
crossed the valley in a few scant minutes' time, but I was barely a
third of the way there. I let out a groan—it would take me until nightfall to get even halfway there. If I had to, I would march through the
night, but I needed to reconsider my approach. Perhaps the straight
route through the forest wasn't the best path after all.

To the south lay an endless carpet of trees that ran all the way
down to the sea. Due west stood the cliffs in afternoon haze. I couldn't
climb those steep escarpments. To the north, the mountain stepped
up toward a high ridge. The trees were thin on that slope, but I could
see a number of game trails even from here. At least two of them
slanted up toward the cliffs where they thrust out from the mountain
itself. There was less cover than I liked, but was the most accessible
path to the cliffs where Getig had perched, to the nest I hoped to find.

Suddenly the silhouette of a dragon appeared above the cliffs. I scrambled backward down the escarpment to the cover of the trees. Was that Shuja? Rannu? With foliage in the way it was hard to be sure, but dragons have excellent eyesight, and I couldn't risk being spotted. My heart pounding, I backed into the deeper shadows under the canopy to wait. There was a flat, moss-carpeted boulder under the tree, so I sat down.

Whenever Darian and I had flown over the forest with Father or Tauman, all we saw were endless trees below and mountains above. But this was personal, intimate. I could touch the stone, breathe in the scent of bark and moss, and taste the clean, pungent air. I was struck by how square all the boulders were, and how flat this little hollow under the canopy was. The boulder across from me was almost cup-shaped. I stopped chewing, surprised. It *was* cup shaped, and full of mulch, with saplings growing in it. The stone was pitted and crumbling, and moss hid details, but the artifice was clear: it was once a fountain. Perched on the edge was a frog carved of the same stone, a cap of moss on his head, his lips pursed as if he should be spouting water into a pool. The boulders were the fallen walls of a long-ago building. I could see now that several trees stood within a ring of up-ended pavers, like jagged teeth. This had been a courtyard, and a forest had erupted through it. Now attuned, I looked further into the forest and saw straight ridges of wall surrounded by cracked blocks, all in mossy cloaks. Here a toppled pillar rested with its fluting still visible through a coat of green. There a tree had fallen, exposing a stairway of marble under its roots.

Cinvat. It was the city that our ruined temple had served, long, long ago. Father brought it up every time he attempted to teach us some history, and Mabir spoke of it in his sermons. What little we knew about Cinvat had been gleaned from the explorations of the dhallas from our local Temple. Father and Tauman had probably poked around in it. Perhaps Jhem had joined them a time or two. But the hard, time-consuming life of raising dragons for the Ministry had kept anyone from studying it deeply. It was far older than even our aeries, that much I remembered. Cinvat was part of the deep background of our lives. It even lurked in the subtext of the games Darian and I played when we were younger. We had spoken once of someday taking our very own dragons into the valley to look for it.

But here it was, all around me. Up the hill to the north where the sun fell bright on the mountainside, broken stairs and the stumps of columns peeked out from between sparser trees. Off the trail behind me, so obvious I don't know how I missed it, sat the outline of a building above a bowl so perfect it must have been an amphitheater. On the trail ahead was a round boulder with a human profile, the giant bust of a head sinking into the loam. Some king or ancient deity?

Once again, as in the minutes just before the Summer Dragon had rustled the leaves above our heads, I felt a chill ripple down my spine. I was overwhelmed with a sense of history and the presence of people long gone. This forest had ghosts in it. I tried to imagine how it had looked when it was new, when the courtyard bustled with human activity and the buildings stood tall in the sunlight. What did the people of Cinvat look like? How did they dress? What had happened to them? Mabir never said exactly what destroyed this beautiful city. Now I wished I'd pressed for answers. Seeing had made it real. What were the stories the people of Cinvat told each other about their distant past? Had my own ancestors lived in this city?

Nearby, a fallen tree had begun to decay. All along its spine grew saplings of future trees, some with roots that stretched eagerly down to the earth below. The ruins were like that log, but on a far grander time-scale. The ribs of an ancient city disappeared little by little into the natural landscape.

Cycles of death and rebirth. Cycles within cycles.

Next summer, Darian and I will bring our dragons here to explore . . . Goosebumps pebbled my arms. I packed my knapsack quickly and scanned the sky—no sign of the dragon. I started out again, heading north to find one of the game trails leading west along the mountain's toes.

The bottom of the slope proved to be a jumble of boulders ejected by the mountain and the trees they had knocked out of the ground. There was virtually no cover. I spent far longer than I'd hoped negotiating tangles of deadfall and gaps between boulders too wide to jump across. Twice I misjudged and took a tumble. Luckily, I broke no bones.

Finally, I reached the first of the game trails and the sparse cover of trees. My waterskin was getting low. Another mistake. I should have refilled it while I was in the forest, where there were streams and pools. I drank half and resolved to keep an eye out for a rivulet. The sun sat now on the brow of the cliffs, casting the valley I'd left behind into blue shadow. I was exhausted, dirty, scratched, and bruised. But I needed to cover ground. Twilight should provide me enough light until the moon rose, in about an hour. I would go as far as I could by moonlight, now that I had an actual path to follow.

My feet ate up the trail. Day passed, and night unfurled with a strange magic. As the moon emerged and then stole into the starry vault, shadows changed from purple to turquoise. Smells were less earthy and dank, more crisp and sweet. The owl-hoots and fox-howls of the early dark gave way to vague noises: distant snufflings, grunts, and screeches that I didn't recognize. I couldn't see more than shapes against the stars, so I had no way to tell how much terrain I'd covered. As the moon began to dip, I watched for places to hole up. I was sore. My eyes were dry and itchy. My tongue tasted like dirt. I needed to rest.

At last I came to a boulder field. Several large crags leaned together to make a sort of room that the trail passed through, with a dusty floor and a skinny window of stars for a roof. I shrugged out of my knapsack and leaned back against it, freed my knife and laid it beside me, then loaded and spanned Kaisi's little crossbow. It was bad to leave a crossbow cocked and under stress for a long period of time, but I wanted it ready if I needed it.

The night was cold. I pulled the blanket out of my knapsack. It was only a little damp in one spot from sitting atop the venison. I wrapped it around myself before I lay down.

I was almost at the cliffs. I should reach them early in the day tomorrow. An animal far away made a strange call, like the cry of a deep-throated hawk. Other animals screamed or croaked with voices almost human. How clever was I to consider sleep in the wilderness home of dragons, with a knapsack full of meat for my pillow? I should have planned better. It would be just my fate to run into some big wilding sire. No sleep. I'd catch a rest, then continue before dawn.

F O U R T E E N

SUNLIGHT STUNG MY EYES. I sat up abruptly in a daze. Rock walls and a dirt bed. Why? Remembrance flooded, and I rubbed my bleary eyes. I was still sore, but a little refreshed. I stretched, scratched an insect bite on my neck, ran my fingers through my hair. The morning was just underway—I might have had four hours' sleep. I chose a nook between two boulders to relieve my bladder, then folded up my blanket, drew down the crossbow, and stuck my knife back in my belt. I pulled an apple and a carrot out of my knapsack, looked dubiously at them, but resisted the temptation to tear off a hunk of venison. It would be a sparse breakfast, with not nearly enough water to wash it down. Though the apple was mushy, the juice was still sweet, and soon I was spitting out the last of the seeds.

I stopped chewing when I realized what I'd been staring at in sleepy disregard: a fire pit not eight feet away from me, a circle of blackened stones around a gray pile of ashes. I looked around, suddenly feeling the eyes of those who had made it. All was quiet and I was alone. I went to investigate.

The pit was cold and a bit windblown, so the fire in it hadn't been recent but it still smelled of smoke. Now I saw ominous stains on the rock wall behind it, brown streaks that ran down into dark, dry circles in the dirt. A tripod of blackened branches taller than me leaned against the wall, bound at the top with a coil of leather. There were discarded bits of rope scattered about, and the butt end of a broken arrow. A stack of firewood. And there were bones. Most were small, but there were some I recognized. Only the wings of a dragon contained long, slender, hollow bones like the broken few scattered on the hard-packed ground.

Situated along an easy path, this place would shield a small fire from the wind and screen the light from casual gaze. It really was the perfect redoubt. I'd spent the night in a poacher's hideaway. I could only imagine what Darian would make of that.

When times were hard, Father would overlook poachers who acted out of hunger and took only deer and other game. *Charity keeps a community healthy,* he would say. But there were others who took only dragons, knowing that dragon leather and bone and blood were valuable in the underground market.

Dragon poachers were opportunistic killers, only in it for the money. He showed them less mercy. They could upset the entire balance of our livelihood. All the emperor's aeries reserved land for wild dragon stock, to rejuvenate the bloodlines from time to time. Aeries traded eggs from their wild reserves when they could. Rannu and Athys had ancestors in these very mountains. Audax and his mate Coluver were the offspring of wild dragons. Father had taken their eggs from two separate nests in this valley as a wedding gift for Tauman and Jhem. It was in our interests to maintain this natural equilibrium.

I realized that I hadn't seen a wild dragon in weeks, apart from the Summer Dragon, Getig, and the dragon I'd hidden from yesterday.

How long had the poachers been here? How much damage had they done? Had they already killed my baby? My stomach clenched into a hard knot. They wouldn't hesitate to kill *me*. But I'd known they were here somewhere, that sooner or later I would find sign of them. It didn't change anything; there was no going back.

I studied the floor of the redoubt, looking for indication that someone had passed recently. Though I could see the hoof prints of a deer or antelope, I wasn't very good at trail-craft. I could barely make out my own footprints. Taking a deep, calming breath, I gathered up my knapsack and slung my crossbow, making sure my quiver of bolts was easily to hand. Then I looked cautiously out the exit to the west.

I was closer to the cliffs than I'd expected to be. They stood out in crisp detail, cracked and furrowed. There were almost no trees on those spires, fewer still on the short plateau where they met the mountain proper. The defiant remnants of a granite shelf overlay softer stone, much like our compound's pinnacle but barren and pitted—the perfect place for a wild dragon pair to hide a nest.

Hawks wheeled in the heat rising off a crag to my right, high above. Their cries of *keirr! keirr!* echoed in the upper canyons. There was nothing else in the sky, not even a wisp of cloud. Not a single dragon.

I took a deep, nervous breath and started out. My head was on a constant pivot, checking every direction below and above for movement. Whenever cover was good, I stopped to survey, but I made good time. The cliffs drew nearer and nearer and I gained altitude by degrees, until I found myself almost on a level with the plateau less than a mile away.

I heard the hawks again, ahead, beyond the point where the trail followed the curve of the mountain to the right and out of view. Something interested them; they had been there all morning.

I pulled my pack off and tied my jacket around it, to help keep the meat cool. As the juncture of clifftop to my left and mountain to my right drew near, I slowed to a more cautious pace, pausing at every tree or rock to scan the skies.

Then the deer track took a hard turn to the right, around a bend and down toward a dark chasm that loomed suddenly—a stark, vertical crack in the mountainside that hadn't been visible before. This is where the wheeling hawks were concentrated. I felt a damp rush of air at the same time that I heard the splash of water. A stream flowed out of the cave, and water fell somewhere within. My pace hurried momentarily, in anticipation of a cool drink of water, but I stopped short as the vista opened before me.

The trail forked suddenly—sharply down to the left, slightly upward to the right. Ahead of me the crack gaped open and revealed itself as a deep cavern in the side of the mountain, going back and back into darkness. The floor of the trail changed abruptly. Now even I could see that beyond the fork in either direction it received plenty of human foot traffic. I crouched, suddenly alert to every sound and smell. With cool air issuing out of the cave mouth, there shouldn't be an updraft of air here. The hawks had to be gathering for some other reason. With that to alert me, I recognized the thick, sour smell of carrion.

Slowly I pulled the crossbow off my shoulder, spanned it, and loaded a quarrel. Then I crept forward cautiously.

The left fork meandered down toward the cave floor. I chose to take the right, reasoning that it would be wise to take a look from above. The way opened up onto a broader ledge, with smaller trails rounding boulders or dipping between bushes or trees. I inched forward, listening intently, but now all I could hear was a stream of water around the bend and the calls of the raptors above, echoing. Smells shifted in the breeze, fresh blasts of moist air alternated with the foul, acrid stench of decaying meat. Sweat tickled between my shoulder blades. Finally I peeked over a rounded spike of stone onto the cave floor. My stomach lurched.

The carcass of a yearling dragon hung upside down from a tripod, the rib cage yawning open, head and legs missing. It had been flayed, gutted, stripped of all but the tendons holding the skeleton together. Two hawks worried tidbits of flesh out of the joints, while the surface of it crawled with ants and flies. A blackened half-keg sat beneath it, dark brown stains surrounding it on the sandy floor. My eyes wept from the stench, but I couldn't look away. A wagon a little further in bore two massive wooden kegs, streaked with black, surrounded by a collection of buckets and a copper funnel, stacks of claw traps, and wire nooses.

More hawks on the ground were squabbling over something. Three qits lay in the shadow of the stretched corpse, swarming with flies, hawks fighting for position on their little bodies. Their neck frills were cut off for some reason I could not fathom. An inexperienced fool had tried to cut the ports in their wings for the straps of saddles they might one day wear, but had missed and hit the alar veins. A foolish way to kill a little dragon.

I squeezed two fistfuls of hair in my hands and fought to stifle sobs. I wanted to lash out, hurt someone. I couldn't believe what I was seeing. Was the baby I sought one of these?

I bit back a moan of anguish. It couldn't be. Getig had perched on one of the spires south of this cave. Perhaps the baby was out there still. Perhaps it was not too late. I clung to the thought like a cinch strap. The only alternative was too horrible to consider—that the Summer Dragon might be so cruel as to lead me here, merely as a witness for this evil, knowing that the likes of Bellua would pin more foul omens to my name with no hope of redemption. A sign of Getig's trust, rewarded with pain and humiliation? I couldn't accept that.

Then I saw the human corpses, three of them, wrapped up in blankets beyond the charnel wagon. What had killed them? Dragons? I hoped so. I hoped that the parents of all these mutilated babies had exacted at least that much revenge before they were murdered, too.

Wheel tracks led back into the shadows, suggesting that more carnage waited deeper in the cave. I knew only one thing: I needed to find the baby before it was too late. I had little more than two hours of light left. I would head out to the plateau and search for the nest that the poachers hadn't found yet. If it wasn't there, I would gather my courage, figure out how to brave this ugly chasm, and . . .

Something struck me hard in the back, knocking me forward. My chin hit the boulder, and I rolled sideways to see what it was.

A figure swathed in dark cloth stood only a few paces away from me, lowering a crossbow. Fabric surrounding his head obscured all but his eyes, pale and strange. He muttered something unintelligible and drew a quarrel from his quiver.

I jumped to my feet, shaking badly, immediately aware that I had but a single shot in Kaisi's little crossbow. I dared not miss. He fumbled with the spanning mechanism on his crossbow. I raised my own and advanced. His eyes widened as he took a step back, dropped his crossbow, and snatched a thick, curved sword from a sheath on his hip. I let loose, and my quarrel thudded into his chest.

He lurched toward me. I stumbled backward and fell to the ground, raising my arm in feeble defense. But he crumpled to his knees in front of me, and his sword landed in the dirt. He wavered for a moment, staring, then toppled to his side. He stretched out weakly, clawing my left foot. I scrabbled backward out of his reach. After gasping for a few seconds, he moaned softly and deflated like an untended bellows. He was still, staring at his empty hand with shock in his colorless eyes.

Minutes passed before I could do more than stare back at him. The fall had pulled aside the fabric in front of his face. His skin was deathly white, translucent like milk. His eyes were the pale lavender of an oyster shell. A few strands of cobweb hair stuck out of his scarves. I'd never seen the like, but I'd heard tales.

He was Harodhi, one of the ghostly pale northerners who warred with Gurvaan. The people who used Horrors to fight their battles. Here, in the mountains of Gadia—my home province.

A sharp pain stung my ribs on the left side, under my arm. I reached down and was surprised to feel warmth and wetness. My fingers were bloody. I pulled off my knapsack painfully and turned it around.

A crossbow quarrel stuck out of the haunch of venison in my pack. It had emerged from the other side to slash me across the ribs, below the shoulder blade. Had it not been slowed by the meat and deflected by the bone in the middle, it would have been deep in the center of my back.

I started to tremble. My arms felt weak, my legs boneless. My head spun. I tried to remove the arrow from my knapsack, but the head became stuck in the meat. I left it, too dazed to think it through. My own quarrel was buried to the fletching in the Harodhi's chest. I looked at him again. Pink drool dribbled from the corner of his mouth. Already, body fluids had started to pool, causing the upper side of his face to collapse strangely. A fly crawled onto his eyeball. I shuddered and drew back, not wanting to go any nearer. But despite my revulsion, I found the wits to take his crossbow, larger than my own, and release the quiver from his belt.

He seemed young, perhaps two years older than me. Desperate, I backed away from him to the fork in the trail. With fumbling hands I cocked both bows and loaded them, slinging a strap over either shoulder. I felt ridiculous, guilty, elated, and horrified all at once. I descended slowly toward the cavern.

But for the sound of water falling and the hawks tearing at the carcass, all was still. I was alone again. A small stream cut through the sandy cave floor at my feet. I dropped to my knees, bows clattering beside me, and cupped water to my lips with my hands. It had happened so suddenly, but I was alive. As the rush of fear abated, images of what had just happened overwhelmed me—I'd killed a man. I couldn't stop seeing a fly crawl on an unblinking eye. I vomited into the stream until there was nothing left to vomit. Wiped my mouth with fresh water. Fought back the dry heaves that followed. Drank some more and vomited again.

I moved upstream a few feet and washed my face, rinsed my mouth with water and spat it out until the acid was gone. Sat for several long minutes, shivering and sobbing. Drank again and managed to keep it all down. Finally, I thought to fill my waterskin.

I was covered in a cold sweat, but the shaking had subsided even if the tears had not. There was more than mere poaching going on here. I was in over my head. I needed to go home and tell Father—this couldn't be allowed to continue. And yet I couldn't go home. There was nothing there for me. I would be linked to this abomination, too. Bellua would use it to force Father's hand. I would be taken against my will to Avigal and a fate only the Avar knew. I was trapped.

There was still only one answer: I had to find the qitling. I gathered my things and started toward the trail, when a sound caught my ear. In the valley, not terribly far away, subdued voices and a clattering, like wheels. Overhead, the screeching of the hawks grew louder. I inched to the lip of the valley and looked out.

There were wagon tracks leading down the slope, newly carved through the undergrowth. At the base of the cliffs was a contingent of men wrapped in the same loose, dark clothing as my Harodhi attacker. Some bore curved swords, others carried strange halberds with hooked blades. Behind them, two donkeys drew a two-wheeled cart. On it were human bodies, like those in the cave, wrapped in blankets or cloaks. I'd killed the man they left behind as guard.

I needed to get away as quickly and as quietly as I could. Fleeing into the cave was a poor choice. I had no light and no clue what I might find. The thought of passing all that carnage only made my stomach roil again. And if I was trapped here, if they found me . . .

A short way below, a game trail crossed the wagon track and wound toward the plateau. There was just enough cover to get there if they didn't look up at exactly the wrong moment. Crouching low and watching them, I crept forward, but another sound rooted me where I stood. I listened in fear. In another time and place, his shout might have been part of an innocent game, as simple a thing as a call to dinner. But here it was disaster. I ducked behind a rock, my heart sinking.

Somehow he had deduced my plan, followed me, and even passed me by at some point.

Again I heard him, to the south and west, somewhere on the plateau, loud and insistent.

"Maaaaiiiiaaaa!"

It was Darian.

THE HARODHI LOOKED up the cliff face in the direction of Darian's voice. I took advantage of the diversion and dashed for the foot trail, not waiting to see if they had spotted me. Once they were out of sight below the sharp edge of the plateau, I broke into an all-out sprint down the path.

I was terrified that they would hear my thudding footfalls and the clatter of my crossbows. But they had already heard my idiot brother shouting on the clifftop. It was too late for silence. Soon they would find their companion dead in the cave. I had to locate Darian, silence him, then find a place to hide.

The path quickly vanished as the last of the sparse trees gave way to the hard stone shelf of the plateau. There was no cover here at all.

I spotted him a couple hundred paces away, standing on the lip of the canyon in plain sight, looking back across the valley and raising his hands to his mouth to call my name again. How could he not see the poachers on the trail below him? I pushed harder, legs aching, lungs burning, sweat stinging the wound on my side.

"*Maaaiiiaaa!*"

Just beyond him was a crack in the floor of the plateau where we might find cover. As I closed, he heard me at last and turned my way, his face pinched in anger.

"There you are! What is the matter with you, you irresponsible, crazy—"

"Shut up. We have to hide!" I barely slowed as I reached him, but grabbed two fistfuls of sleeve and dragged him toward the crevice.

He wrested his arm from my grip. "Maia, what are you doing? Let go of m—"

I grabbed his shirtfront and pulled him close, looking over his shoulder at the juncture of cliff and mountain. "There are Harodhi at the base of the cliff. They heard you shouting, and now they are coming to find you. We have to hide before they see us. *Now*." I pulled him toward the crevice, hoping there was an immediate way down, short of falling into it. "Come *on*."

But Darian slapped my hands away again. "*Harodhi*? Are you insane?"

"Dare—please don't argue." I took his arm and pulled again. As I turned away he caught sight of the arrow still protruding from my knapsack.

"Why do you have an arrow sticking out of your pack?"

A glimmer of comprehension struck, and the color drained from his face. I tugged again, and finally some urgency came to him and he picked up his pace. As I paused at the rim of the crevice he muttered, "By the High Ones, Maia, what have you gotten me into?"

"Here," I said, hopping down to a ledge about five feet below. Darian sat on the edge of the crack to consider the drop, and I lost patience. "They're coming, Darian! Let's *go*!"

He kicked out and landed beside me as I considered our situation. The crevice dropped forty or more feet beyond our position, but another shallow ledge led westward to a crack that snaked back into the cliff face like a miniature cave or tunnel. I leapt across the narrow chasm, then again to the floor of the tunnel. Darian followed.

"What in the name of High Ones have you gotten yourself into?" he said.

"Did I ask you to come? Why are you here? You have a dragon to tend!" I pounded his chest. "Why did you follow me?"

"Why did I . . . ? What is wrong with you? Everyone is worried sick. Bellua is ranting like a lunatic. They're all looking—"

"Does Father know you're here?"

"No! Father and the rest took your bait and followed the acquisition train. They thought you were chasing one of the qits from our brood . . . which is pretty much what you intended, right? After they left, I started to wonder. So I went to the ruins to see if you were there. When I saw that the bones were gone, I put two and two together and came up with *crazy*."

"*Shhh*. Hold your voice down," I whispered.

"You think Getig was showing you something, don't you? You think he wanted you to march into the wilderness to find a *qit*." He whispered now too. "I figured I would catch up to you easily. I sure didn't think I would be gone this long." He rubbed the new bond mark on the back of his neck. "I have a qit to tend, but here I am in the middle of dragon country chasing my headstrong, foolish—"

"Then go *home*."

"I can't. Something about *Harodhi*, I think?"

I groaned in frustration. "We can't stand here and argue. They're coming."

The cave receded into darkness. I took a few tentative steps in.

"Gods, Maia. These tunnels could be full of dragons."

"I don't think so."

"Tauman told me about these; he said the whole south end of this plateau is honeycombed with little holes like this. That hard shelf makes a roof and the dragons have been digging out dens for eons."

"Then it's a perfect place to hide."

"Not if a dragon or three or *twelve* are living here!" He grabbed my pack straps and pulled me back. I spun about angrily and wrenched his hands away. "Darian, listen: the Harodhi have been poaching dragons. I haven't seen any wild dragons in weeks, have you?"

His mouth opened, but nothing came out.

Sand and stones suddenly chattered down from overhead, and a shadow moved on the far wall of the crevice, cast by something on the clifftop above us. I slapped a hand over Darian's mouth, and we froze in place, watching as the shadow moved slowly eastward. It paused once, clearly the shape of a man outlined by the lowering sun.

Darian's hand was a vice bruising my arm. Slowly I pried his thumb loose, and he let go. Then I signaled into the tunnel and he nodded, eyes wide. Carefully, quietly, we inched back into deeper darkness.

Soon a tangle of branches and bones blocked our retreat—the nest of a dragon. Ten or twelve feet across, it spanned the small cavern. We couldn't possibly cross over it without making noise. We were trapped. Darian gasped. We looked fearfully back toward the entrance to the tunnel. I held my breath.

The shadow was unmoving for several long minutes, then it squatted and I heard a scuffling. It disappeared as the figure that had cast it dropped onto the ledge outside our hiding place, not more than forty feet away.

Swathed in loose clothing, pale eyes peering out between the folds engulfing his head, a Harodhi warrior struggled against darkness to see into our tunnel. Darian was deathly quiet as the man knelt and took a crossbow off his shoulder, then pulled the lever that cocked it. He removed a bolt from a quiver on his belt and placed it in the groove, set the trigger, then slowly pointed it in our direction—and did nothing as he waited for his eyes to adjust to the darkness. My heart pounded out a short eternity in my ears. My lungs screamed for air, but I dared not breathe.

A voice somewhere else on the clifftop called, and the warrior answered sharply, his foreign tongue cracking like a whip against the silence. I almost bolted but kept my wits long enough to remain rooted to my spot. Darian made no sound.

The man raised his crossbow and loosed into the tunnel. The bolt passed between us and clattered into the dragon's nest, startling me again, but the Harodhi warrior gave no sign of following it in. He seemed fearful, and listened for another minute or so before he stood and backed cautiously out the way he had come. A new shadow appeared, and the man looked up. A low conversation followed, until finally the warrior gave an irritated outburst. The second shadow hunkered down. Was he going to join his fellow? But then the first man reached up to take an arm offered from above. He scrambled up out of the crevice, back onto the clifftop, and both departed.

Darian let his breath out, then hissed, "By the High Ones, Maia, if Father doesn't kill you, I will. What do you think you're doing?"

I wanted to hit him, but I flopped down onto my knees, laying my bows down and pulling the knapsack off my shoulders. "You know why I'm here. You did the math. Two plus two remember?"

"Yeah, you're crazy. How did you end up with an arrow in your back?" He hunkered down next to me, leaning closer. "Are you hurt?"

"Only a little bit."

"Let me see. Show me."

"It's too dark in here. I'm fine."

"I can see. Turn toward the light."

I turned toward him, pulling my shirt up to show him the cut below my shoulder blade. He touched it, making me flinch. Maybe I wasn't so fine.

"It's still bleeding," he said. "We have to bind that up. What have you got in here to work with?" He grabbed my knapsack but paused, looking at the arrow still imbedded in the haunch of venison. "Korruzon's ass, Maia. What happened to you?"

I wiped my cheeks on my sleeve. "There's a cave where the plateau meets the mountain, a big one . . ."

"Tauman told me about it. It's a dragon's lair."

"Well, now it's a poacher's hideout, except the poachers are Harodhi. You saw: white skin, white hair, pale eyes."

"Wait a minute. You went *in there*?"

"They're blooding and skinning dragons in the cave and leaving the carcasses for the hawks and ants to clean. Wheel tracks go back deeper into the cave. I don't know what else they're up to, but one of them—one of them surprised me. He shot me in the back, but the venison stopped his arrow."

He took my shoulders in his hands. "Where is he now?" There was desperate concern in his voice.

I looked him in the eyes. "I . . . shot him. With Kaisi's bow." I held it up, as if that would prove the tale.

Darian crouched in stunned silence, staring at the bow. Then, to my surprise, he pulled me close and put his arms around my shoulders, hugging me. He said nothing as I hugged him in return.

Eventually he spoke. "We have to tell Father. And Rov. We have to get out of here. We can't hide forever. As soon as it's dark, we're going back."

"I can't."

"We have to, Maia! They've shot you once already, and you were lucky. We can't—"

"No, Dare. *I can't go back.* Not without a qit."

"You most certainly can. This is insanity, Maia, even without poach—"

"You don't understand, Darian. If I go back without a qit—"

"Even without poachers to complicate things, how did you think you would steal a qit from a *wild dr*—"

"You aren't listening to me. I can't go back without—"

"Maia, Maia, *think*. We can't do this. We have to be reasonable—"

I twisted out of his grasp, grabbed my knapsack and my bows, and stood.

"Where are you going?"

I walked back toward the opening of the tunnel, heart racing, my mind barely keeping pace. "I have to find a qit."

Darian grabbed my elbow, but I yanked it out of his hand. "Don't try to stop me, Darian. Please." I turned away from him, suddenly overwhelmed with conflicting doubt, need, fear, and resolve. "I have to do this, Darian. I have to have a qit, or . . ."

"Or what? You're willing to die out here rather than go back? Is that it? You're way out of your depth here, Maia."

"You were there when Getig landed on the ruins. And you put two and two together. You even said that Getig had come for *me*. I know you understand. You're just scared."

His mouth was shaping a response when new sounds came up from the valley below.

"Shhh!"

Darian caught his breath and listened with me. Shouts. The braying of donkeys. And the terrified bleating of a small dragon.

"Avar, Dare. There it is."

From the mouth of the tunnel, we could see down through the crevice. Scree filled the gap, making a coarse stair of jumbled rock leading down to a slivered view of the valley floor below. Another contingent of Harodhi warriors worked their way up the slope toward the main cave, possibly two dozen men. In their midst was another cart drawn by a second pair of donkeys, but on this cart was a rectangular cage made of metal straps, large enough to hold a dozen qitlings or even a bear-sized juvenile. But in it was a single baby, bleating in fear.

My heart leapt, then sank. Then leapt again. I'd already lost one baby, but Getig had led me here. Hadn't he? *"That's the baby,"* I whispered.

Darian shook his head. "Oh, no. Oh no, Maia. Oh no no no . . ."

I jumped across the gap to the next ledge for a better view. The rock shelf ran to the far opening of the crevice, giving me an expanded view of the scene below. Darian came up behind me but stalled his protests as he looked over my shoulder.

The qit raced back and forth in the cage, squealing in terror. A tan-and-silver baby—classic mountain coloration. The donkeys brayed with discontent but struggled against the slope with determination. The warriors all looked backward, down the hill, toward something out of our sight.

"Gods, Maia, there are so many—"

"Something else is happening, Darian."

The shouts of the Harodhi warriors increased in volume, and they formed a line across the trail with crossbows raised. Then a roar shattered the late-day stillness, the unmistakable bellow of an angry adult dragon.

The pitch of the warriors' cries changed. A couple of them broke and fled in panic as a fully grown dragon galloped into view from the right. He was tan and silver, like the baby, a magnificent specimen of the Gadia mountain breed, like Audax or Coluver. Clearly male, with a tall top frill and muscular build, smaller than Shuja, but scrappier, leaner, hardened by a life in the wild. He seemed to be wounded, most notably because he did not attempt to fly at all. He clung to the ground as he charged, roaring defiance, and the qit in the cage screamed in answer.

Crossbows snapped at his charge. Bolts struck his natural armor with zings and thuds, and a great many bounced off entirely. He fought his way to the nearest line of archers and weighed in with claws and teeth. There were screams of pain, cries of anger, dragon bellows, and terrified bleating. Two of the Harodhi were flung spinning into the nearby trees, but the crossbows continued to sing in a furious, staccato chorus. The dragon crossed wings in front of himself to deflect some of the barrage, but he snarled in pain and anger and backed away.

My heart went out to him—the proud father defending his baby. Was the dragon I'd found in the forest two days ago his mate? Or was it three days already? He hesitated only an instant before charging

117

again, his wings crossed before him as a shield. Two more Harodhi warriors were launched into ruin before he retreated from another onslaught of crossbow bolts.

It hurt to watch. The little dragon in the cage screamed with terror unlike anything I'd ever heard—not even as our brood was lowered into the clutches of the Ministry. The father dragon circled briefly, then made one more assault on the line of archers. Bows snapped, arrows cracked, and the dragon sire fell back from the withering onslaught.

There came a sudden, croaking roar above and to our left. We both squatted down instinctively as a shadow swept over us from the west. A dragon glided past in stark silhouette against the bright sky.

Darian jumped up. "It's Father!" he cried, and began waving his arms.

But I grabbed Darian around the waist and dragged him back against the crevice wall. It wasn't Shuja, and it wasn't Father. It wasn't any dragon I recognized, not even one of the Ministry contingent. It was lanky and brown, with a pale, greenish underbelly and dappled skin above. I'd never seen such a pattern before. Billowing cloaks enveloped the rider, like the soldiers on the ground, but with a red sash around his waist. To my relief, neither dragon nor rider noticed us. They glided down to circle above the combat below. The dragon sire backed off, and the soldiers used the respite to reload their bows.

"By Korruzon! Since when do poachers have dragons?" Darian whispered.

"I told you; they're Harodhi."

Darian shrank against the stone wall. "Let's get out of sight."

I nodded, inching back toward the tunnel.

Suddenly another dragon and rider swept overhead from our left, a bigger blot against the sky. I recoiled, stunned by what I saw.

It was *wrong*. Its skin was black—not glossy and smooth like Shuja's, but with a texture and sheen like charred wood, pitted and cracked. The wings were tattered along the edges and riddled with holes. Light shining down through the membranes revealed not the reddish veins of a healthy animal, but a network of black lines. It had no top frill at all. Dark metal armor covered its neck and chest, and a helmet of black covered even the eyes. The rider was swathed in black robes, with a large black sword slung across his back.

A stench followed it—foul and corrupt, like burnt flesh.

Darian was past me in a shot, leaping into the tunnel out of sight. I lingered a moment longer, unable to get the image of mutilated baby dragons out of my head—of qits with their top frills removed. Was this what was intended for them? Transformation into whatever this was? A shadowy ruin, fetid and dark? Intense cold gripped me. I knew its name. *Horror.*

The rider of the first dragon, still circling above the skirmish, shouted something and the black monster dived straight for the father dragon. He keened unhappily, but folded his wings and fled into the trees, where the Horror could not follow without giving up the advantage of flight.

Smart father, I thought, but my heart ached for him.

The qit in the cage wailed in terror as its parent disappeared. Soldiers whipped the donkeys, but they didn't need encouragement to pull hard toward the cave. The contingent of men paused only long enough to gather their dead and wounded. Then the Harodhi dragon rider and his winged, black thrall followed them out of sight to the left.

A chill shook me, and I ran to the tunnel after Darian.

"**M**AIA, THAT WAS a *Horror.*"
Darian mouthed the word, as if there were danger in saying it aloud.

I sat beside him, shaking.

"Are you ready to go home now?" he whispered, derisively. "Do you think the odds against your little adventure are stacked high enough yet?"

I said nothing, but shrugged out of my knapsack again. My wound was starting to throb. I groaned and clutched my ribs, leaning back against the dragons' nest.

Darian moved closer. "We have to dress that, Maia. What have you got in here?"

"Food mostly. And a blanket."

"You've got half a deer in here. What were you going to do with that?"

"I have to feed the baby—"

"We have to stay hidden until Father and the others come looking for us. It's only a matter of time."

He pushed the arrow through the haunch of venison, studied it for a moment, and set it aside. Then he pulled a chunk of meat out of the pack and handed it to me. "Eat this."

"I'm saving that."

"Just eat it. You've lost blood. You need your strength." He tore off another chunk and bit into it hungrily, then set it on the knapsack as he chewed. "Give me your knife," he said.

"Where's yours?"

"I didn't bring it. I didn't think I would be gone so long. Now we need to bind that wound with something, and all we have that isn't soaked with *meat juice* is our clothing. We're going to use your sleeves. Hurry up, we're losing the light, and we don't dare make a fire."

I handed him my knife, and he used it to cut the laces holding my sleeves to my shirt. In silence, he used the sleeves to make a wound pad and bandage, tied together with the laces. Then we ate without speaking.

From the forest below, a dragon keened mournfully—a long, sustained, desperate moan. It had to be the dragon sire—mourning his baby trapped in what was a literal den of Horrors. I pictured him pacing back and forth in the forest, fearful and uncertain.

I raised my chin and looked Darian in the eye. "I can't abandon them."

"Forget it, Maia."

"Please, Darian."

"No."

"I can't do this alone."

"Face reality, Maia, that qit is doomed. And even if it wasn't, it has a parent still. And even if you *could* get it, which you can't, it's a wild dragon, not a newly hatched qit from an aerie full of humans. It might well chew your arm off."

Tears pooled in my eyes, and I wiped at them angrily. I was sick of crying, even in the dark, unseen. "Weren't you paying attention? Bellua *still* isn't happy. It's personal with him for some reason. The Summer Dragon scared him to his bones. He needs to prove something. Getig is a threat to him somehow, and he won't be content until he has buried the story of Getig forever."

"But why does that mean you have to—"

"Because we need another qit! Your little sire needs a dam. Then the aeries will be back in balance, and Father will have leverage to stop Bellua from taking me to Avigal and who knows what fate. I'm just like every qit we ever sold: slave to the Ministry. Unless I *do* something about it."

"He can't keep you there, or marry you off to—"

"Bellua practically accused me of bringing a curse to the aeries. A curse. Mabir freed *you* from his snare, so that leaves me as the target of his scheming."

Darian was silent for a moment before saying, "Bellua doesn't know you. He's wrong."

"How good that will make me feel when I'm married to some fat old merihem somewhere. Or maybe even Bellua himself."

He fell silent, and for several minutes we listened only to the moaning of the breeze at the corners of the cliff, in the mouths of the crevices.

"And what if they're right?" I said quietly. "I *was* shirking my duties in the forest that day."

"We both were."

I buried my face in my hands. "I keep thinking about Mother's fall."

"This again? What has that got to do with anything?"

"Listen to me. Please. I'm not sure how to say it, so please just listen. Ever since Mother's fall, I've been afraid. It's as if somehow Mother's last words to me were . . ." I couldn't finish.

"What? Her words were what?"

I blinked away tears. "There's something you don't know."

"What don't I know?" Irritated.

I wiped my eyes again, then my nose, and fought back a sob. "Before Mother fell, before she scolded me, before you even got there, *I* saddled Grus."

"So?"

"I don't know if I did it right. I might have left that cinch strap too loose. I should have seen the tear in the strap. It might have been . . ." The sob escaped, and for a few moments I couldn't find my voice. I sucked in a breath. "It might have been my fault. She said, 'A dragon handler with her head in the clouds is cursed.' She used that word— *curse*—and then she *died*. And it might have been *my fault*."

Darian shook his head. "Maia, she checked her own girth before mounting, every time. You *know* that."

"But she was angry and distracted that once, and she used that word. Then she was gone *forever*. And I've never been able to get it out of my head. Ever since that day, it seems that events work against me. I always get blamed. Father's never happy. I'm never good enough.

Bad things happen. When Fren was mauled and Father yelled at me, it was the same thing *again*. It was awful, but it was familiar. As if somehow Mother's last words to me were an accidental curse created by her anger, and her death. And my *guilt*." Tears overcame me.

Darian fell silent, too, finally willing to let me say what I needed to say.

I caught my breath again. "When we saw Getig, I felt such an uplifting, of warmth and hope. As if everything that had ever been wrong might be made right again. I could feel the wholeness of the world. And I wondered if that big miracle might lead to a small miracle for me. A lifting of this accidental curse."

I sniffled. "And then it all went so wrong." I choked on the words. Had Getig really spoken to me in some strange way? Was there something more to be done? Or was he done with me already—my part over—a witness, and nothing more? Or worse, was the message exactly what Bellua said it was?

"I don't know if Getig came to me to lift my curse, or cast it in stone."

Darian frowned deeply, but his anger was gone. "Maia, sometimes accidents happen. You're not cursed."

"But how can I know? With all these signs being thrown back and forth, I don't know what to believe. I don't know who I am. I only know that if Bellua takes me to Avigal, I won't ever be able to return. I just know it. Something is going on, and he can't let our story survive, Darian, and he will do what he must to keep us quiet forever. I can see that much even if you can't. And when he has silenced me, he will come after you. And Father, and Tauman, and Jhem. The curse will spread."

From the forest came another desolate moan, trailing off into a soft chuffing—the cry of a grieving dragon. It punctuated the moment; the last time we had heard that sound was when Grus mourned for my mother.

"The worst thing is, I might deserve it."

Darian said nothing, his head bowed.

I stood abruptly, snatched up my knapsack, and grabbed the larger of the two crossbows. "So I really don't have any choice; I have to figure out a way to save that qit. I can't go back without a baby."

"How does that even make sense? You keep saying that Bellua is going to have his way, no matter what."

I hesitated, unsure how to answer.

"And what if the qit is a little boy? Did you think of that?"

I swallowed. "Yes. But if it's a little girl, I give Father and Mabir leverage. I stave off Bellua. And maybe I show that Getig had something for me, too."

"And you're willing to die for this fantasy?"

I stared out at the deepening gloom for several seconds. "It's all I've got, Darian."

He fell silent again, his face pinched in thought.

I thrust Kaisi's crossbow at him and he took it instinctively. Then I unhooked her quiver from my belt. "You didn't even come prepared." I shrugged into my jacket. "Wait here, Darian."

I left him behind me in the dark tunnel.

––––––

Stars winked in the east as day's colors followed the sun below the western horizon. The light outside was purple and the temperature had dropped. I checked the sky for silhouettes, then hopped over to the wider ledge. It followed the lip of the crevice eastward around a bend and ended at a broken, toothy snag that afforded me some easy steps back up to the plateau. I peeked over the lip, expecting to see Harodhi warriors scouring the tabletop. There was just enough light remaining to tell that all was still, but the Harodhi cave was lit by firelight. Dark shadows moved back and forth in front of it, and I heard voices in pitched tones. I needed to get closer.

Cautiously, I advanced across the plateau, using what little cover was presented—a knob of stone, a thin, scraggly bush, a low spot in the table. Finally I paused behind a low wall of capstone with a crack I could peer through.

Gentle padding behind me. I turned quickly as Darian dropped down beside me. "We don't dare go closer," he whispered.

"Avar—You scared the shit out of me."

"I couldn't let you run out here by yourself." He saw my scowl, then added, "I know—shhh."

I peered through the crack again. "We can't get any closer anyway without putting ourselves upwind of their dragons."

"How did they manage not to be discovered with Father and the others out hunting for an entire day?"

"They have a cave to hide in. And Father wouldn't have taken game from our own valley—he'd have wanted to tire the parents with a long flight, not steal food from our wildings."

He frowned. "What are they doing?"

"I don't know."

There were several guards posted across the cave entrance with crossbows at the ready, probably with the dragon sire in mind. Beyond them, figures milled about at tasks difficult to make out. Behind all, the heads and wings of the two dragons rose above the confusion, the brown dragon of the leader bobbing from time to time, but the Horror not moving at all.

I made out the cage on the cart, the donkeys still hitched to it with their noses in feedbags. The door was open, but the baby cowered against a far corner as one of the Harodhi waved something at it through the opening. Meat? A weapon? I couldn't tell. But when the qit bleated in fear, the man threw whatever it was aside in obvious disgust.

The leader wearing the red sash stepped out of the milling of figures and cuffed the man. Their voices rose in pitch as they gesticulated, pointing at the baby, at something further back in the cave, and out into the night.

"They're arguing," I said quietly.

"About what?"

"About the baby, I think." Realization crawled on my skin. "They're here to steal qits out from under our very noses, and start *bonding* with them. But they have no idea what they're doing. Probably this rider with the red sash is the only one with any knowledge. And he's failing."

"There are so many Harodhi, Maia."

"It almost makes sense. They think they have to bond the qits immediately, so they've brought a bunch of potential riders to take babies from the mountain nests. But they're rushing things and doing them poorly. There are dead babies in the cave. They had their frills cut off and their wing ports done wrong." I looked at the Horror again, with its darkly armored head and neck, lacking a frill at all, unmoving. "Gods, Dare, will they turn them into those things?"

"*Avar . . .*" Darian looked terrified. "What about the riders? They're human, aren't they?"

"Not both of them. Look at the one riding the Horror-dragon." I sought the Horror-rider and found him standing just behind the leader. Covered in black garb but, like his dragon, utterly motionless among the figures scurrying all about. I couldn't see his face except as strange reflections of firelight on a shiny surface. I ducked my head out of sight.

"But they have dragons of their own in Harodh, don't they? Why would they come so far to steal ours?"

"*Avar*, Darian—"

"How would you ever get past them? We would have to plan some sort of distraction."

I could barely see him in the failing moonlight, but I saw him shrug and, despite myself, I hugged him. He pushed me off. "I didn't say it was a good idea or that I would help. I was just saying it would have to be something dramatic to draw them out, like a fire, but timed so that we aren't anywhere near it when they spot it."

"But that would draw Father too, or worse, Bellua and Rov."

"Would that be a bad thing? I'd still rather talk you out of this and trust Father to come up with something. This is crazy." He put a hand on my shoulder. I could tell he was shaking.

Pitched arguing from the cave drew our heads up again. Another flurry of activity flickered against the firelight, and the cart with the corpses was brought to the mouth of the cave. The bodies were unloaded and one of the donkeys unhitched. The leader and another man were engaged in a heated conversation, pointing out into the night, then at the bodies, and then at the plateau.

"They're trying to decide what to do about *us*," I whispered.

Sudden horrific braying made us flinch. The leader's dappled brown dragon opened its mouth and took one of the donkeys by the neck. With a shake of its big head, the cries were ended. The other pair of donkeys tried to back away, screaming into their feedbags, but the cart with the cage on it turned sideways and trapped them. The donkey remaining on the first cart bucked against its harness, screeching in panic. A soldier raised a sword over its neck. I turned away but heard the *chunk* of metal on bone, and the braying ended. Now the baby dragon bleated in fear too. When I found the courage to look back again, one donkey was being butchered. The other was disappearing by chunks into the maw of the leader's mount. The other pair of donkeys watched in wide-eyed alarm.

"That's not how it's done," Darian muttered. "Hunting is one thing, but letting a dragon kill a captive animal will only make it dangerous. They have no idea how to handle—"

And then the black dragon was brought forward. It stopped before the row of dead soldiers, bent down and picked one up by the head.

Darian backed away in a panic. I watched a moment longer, frozen in terror. With calm, methodical movements, it took the corpse apart and swallowed the pieces. My gorge rose, and I swallowed hard to contain it, hand over my mouth.

The baby bleated in fear. Its father answered from the forest behind me with a sad, angry bellow, while the Horror continued to feed. Then I noticed that its rider was crouched down, bent over to gobble something ravenously. I couldn't tell what it was, but the Harodhi soldiers gave him a wide berth.

Darian took me by the belt and dragged me backward, away from the nightmare. The last thing I saw before I retreated was my terrified qit being wheeled deeper into the cave.

S E V E N T E E N

A GLOW ON THE HORIZON heralded the rising of the moon, now two days past full. I thanked the Avar that it hadn't shown its face in time to reveal our panicked retreat.

Its first rays cast a pale column of light into our tunnel as I arrived. Darian huddled deep inside, next to the abandoned dragon's nest. His eyes were huge in the dim light.

"What are we going to do, Maia? What are we going to do?" His words tumbled out in a rush. "They're going to come looking for us again in the morning. They may even come in the night. Who knows what those things can do? We have to hide." He held his hand up, looked in fear at the moon illuminating it, then scrambled noisily up into the dragon's nest and out of its light.

I followed him, though more carefully. "Calm down. We have to think."

"How can I calm down? They feed their dead to that *Horror*. How can you control a dragon that's been fed *people*?"

"I need you to help me."

"This is beyond us, Maia. Beyond us." His face was contorted with fear, his whisper a barely controlled shout. "You'll get us both killed. They're monsters. They are going to kill us. Then they're going to feed us to that *thing*. No, I told you, we sit right here and we wait. End of discussion."

"Darian, please . . ."

"Why are you so determined to *be* a curse?"

I felt the blood drain from my face. Sound and smell and sight and thought were suspended, as if I'd entered a dark limbo. There were no words I could say. For a long minute, there was nothing I could do but observe the constriction of my skin, the welling of my eyes, the opening of a chasm in the center of my chest. All the worst portents of the last several days coalesced into the cold, leaden mass of that word.

Darian had asked if I was willing to risk death for this baby. The real question was whether I could live with a curse for the rest of my days. It didn't matter whether it was real or imagined—inaction would make it real. I was either cursed, or I acquired a qit. It was finally just that simple.

So be it. I wiped my eyes, and set my brave face.

Darian stared silently as I gathered my belongings and climbed out of the nest. As I started toward the tunnel's mouth, he grabbed at my arm. "Gods, Maia, I didn't mean it. I just had the piss scared out of me. Don't go."

I stepped out into the moonlight.

"Maia, come back. I'm sorry."

I wanted to find another approach to the cave; there was no cover on the plateau. I looked down. The entire defile was made up of shelves and the chunks that had fallen away from them. The scree slope rose near enough to our tunnel that I could hop down from here. I sat on the ledge to negotiate the drop and realized it was practically a stair, though some of the steps were taller than others. The moonlight made it easy. I hopped down.

"I'm sorry, Maia!" A hoarse whisper, from deep in the tunnel.

I didn't look back.

———

The valley floor at the base of the cliffs was stony and difficult, and short on cover, but the moon was still low in the sky, and the nearby trees were tall. I allowed my eyes to adjust to the deeper darkness in their shadows. I needed to get close enough to the poacher's cave to assess things and devise a plan. But I knew that once I reached its mouth, there would be guards and precious little cover for me. I was operating on instinct alone—instinct and blind desperation. I struggled to control my racing thoughts. Darian's barb drifted into my mother's last words, then into the arguments of Bellua and Mabir.

Curse. It was distracting, maddening. *Curse.* Over and over again the litany turned, illustrated with images of the ravening Horrors eating the Harodhi dead. Doubt crept into my resolve, but the chorus of damning words always forced me back to the same place: a qit.

I located the trail the Harodhi had used and quickly realized that I'd come upon the scene of their battle with the father dragon. Spatters and puddles of blood showed as ebony in patches of moonlight.

My heart skipped a beat. He was out here still, somewhere. I listened, studied the blackness between the trees, but caught no sight of him. Cautiously I crept into the denser shadows and started up the trail. I stumbled across an abandoned crossbow and examined it. The stock was broken. I set it down again quietly. But here was a perfectly good arrow and another nearby. The arrowheads weren't like the ones we used to hunt deer, with flat triangular blades. They were of military design, square and dart-like, meant to pierce armor. Common to every army that fought against dragons. Even so, dragon-skin is thick and covered with hard plates on the neck, chest, and shoulders—many of their shots had simply glanced off. Would one bow in the hands of a girl be enough to offer a defense? I stuck the arrows in my quiver anyway. They would still kill a man.

Night made the going slow, but I inched my way up the hill, stopping frequently to listen and look all around, in every direction—uphill, downhill, clifftop, forest, sky.

Grunts and moans ahead stopped me in my tracks. Low keening and quiet, sorrowful chuffing indicated a dragon in deep despair. I crouched and shielded my face from the moonlit cliff face and sky, so that my eyes could adapt to the murky shadow. I scanned the forest for a visual cue, finally detecting a bright glimmer ahead and to the right, like moonlight on scales.

Father dragon was in bad shape. He tried to pluck crossbow bolts from his chest with his teeth, but growled in pain and frustration with each failed attempt. His posture was slumped—head down, right wing dragging, left wing held up and back at an odd angle. Several feathered shafts protruded from the alar pectoral, caked with drying blood. It was no wonder he couldn't fly.

He had to be in great pain, yet he'd fought to free his baby from its captors. He'd somehow avoided their snares and traps, and sent a number of Harodhi to their deaths. It reminded me of the tale of one of my ancestors, Malik, who fought off an invading tribe alone, just him and his dragon mount, to rescue his kidnapped daughter. It was nothing less than heroic. My heart went out to him. It would be hard not to think of him now as Malik. But he was also a wounded predator, and I was a girl with a single crossbow, wearing a knapsack full of meat. It was a thin arsenal, a thinner defense. And he was blocking my path.

I knelt behind a rock to watch, and wait. Shortly, he moved up the hill again, slowly and painfully, stepping gingerly on his right forefoot. When he had advanced twenty yards or so, I crept to another hiding place. Little by little I followed him up the slope. He paused often to worry at the arrows in his chest. They didn't look deeply imbedded, but several were oozing black runnels of blood. Walking had to be excruciating.

From up the hill came the bleating of his baby, distant and plaintive. My heart sank at first, but I recognized the call—loneliness and fear, not outright terror. Safe, for the moment.

Malik's head came up and he froze, listening until the cries dwindled. Then he tipped his head back and called twice with a dragon-word, a phrase of his wilding tongue that I could not know. It sounded for all the world like the call of a gigantic hawk.

Baby responded from the cave with another unhappy wail, but it was growing faint, and I realized that the Harodhi were taking it deeper into the cave. When it ended, silence enveloped the forest.

Malik started up the slope again, grunting each time he planted his right forefoot. Suddenly he paused, raised his head, and looked back in my direction.

The hairs on the back of my neck stood up. I was sure I hadn't made a sound, but I glanced around for a defensible position, just in case.

He made a sharp whuffing noise—a warning threat, prelude to attack. My head snapped in his direction, and he charged.

Fear shot through my limbs. I turned and dashed for the trees.

Crashes and heavy footfalls behind me drew nearer. He roared, now fully engaged in the chase.

I screamed, leapt a log, landed badly. I bounced to my feet and darted around a tree. Ahead of me, a dense stand of fir trees surrounded a jumble of boulders. I would have to cross thirty feet of open space to reach it. I glanced back over my shoulder.

Malik rounded some large trees into the open space, closing fast. He roared again, trampled a sapling, then tucked his wings close, ready to pounce.

I sprinted across the gap, leapt between two trees and onto the nearest boulder. A crash resounded at my heels and splinters of wood flew past me. I vaulted a branch, stumbled, felt something swipe at my hair, fell past another trunk into the deep crack between two boulders. I landed on my back, looking up, the wind knocked out of me.

Malik tried to crawl between the trees surrounding the boulders, but the arrows in his side snagged against the trunks. He bellowed angrily and withdrew, stalked around to my left and swiped into my enclosure with a giant forepaw. I scrabbled backward as far as I could, gasping for breath, as he tested the strength of the tree with teeth and claws. It shook but did not give. He growled again in frustration and prowled around behind me, where a single slender tree protected my small redoubt. He pushed against it once, twice, three times. Needles and twigs and cones showered down. Roots groaned and snapped, and the tree fell inward.

I covered my face with my arm, but the boulders and the surrounding trees caught the falling timber by its branches. It settled at an angle like a roof across my crevice, still held by its toes to the earth. Malik bit and scratched at broken roots. He could do no more than shake it, but now he could step onto the boulders that shielded me. A set of talons quested between tree and rock. I scrambled back. He tried the other side, but arrows in his chest and legs snagged on the stout branches. Finally he backed off the rock, to circle and study my defenses.

I fell back, gasping deeply, tears streaming down my face. "Go away," I whispered hoarsely. "Sweet Avar. Avar Avar Avar . . ."

Suddenly he roared in fury and leapt up onto the rocks again. He clawed frantically at the boughs of the fallen tree. Branches cracked and splintered. The trunk groaned as he stood on it and bounced. Shards of wood pattered all around me.

"Go away go away go away . . ."

Again he backed off, then raised his head and roared in utter frustration, shaking the trees and rocks with the thunder of his outrage. I heard his footfalls circling my enclosure, accompanied by low snarling. The undergrowth and trees diffused sound, and I couldn't tell exactly where he was. I pushed myself to a sitting position, brushed hair out of my eyes, removing twigs and leaves with shaking hands. Thankfully, the meat in my knapsack had cushioned my backward fall, but knees, elbows, and palms were scraped and bleeding.

The footsteps moved away and the snarling ceased, but I heard him panting and whuffing aggressively. Twice more he tried to breech the upright trees around my fortress but fell back with painful cries. Long minutes passed in which only his labored breathing disturbed the deep night stillness. Still trembling, I stood up, my head between branches of the fallen tree.

Malik stood in the clearing, head down, panting. He saw me and growled, a deep menacing rumble that I'd never heard in the aeries, not even when Audax was testing Shuja's seniority. This was feral and certain in its intent; he wanted to kill me.

I was trapped there, for as long as I concerned him.

I dropped out of sight again, heart pounding. I needed to convince him that I was not a threat. But how could I do that? He was a wilding—intelligent, but a creature of instinct and emotion nonetheless. He was unfamiliar with any of the commands or dialect that our aerie-born dragons spoke. All I had to work with was my knowledge of dragons, my crossbow, and a backpack full of food.

"*Oh, High Ones,*" I muttered.

I studied my narrow haven quickly. Two large boulders defined it, capped by a third on one end. There was a skinny gap like a short, constricted hallway between that third boulder and the one to my right. A natural entrance. Malik's tail was visible beyond it.

I breathed deeply in hopes of calming myself. I shook so violently that it took several tries to cock my bow and load an arrow. I set it down and removed the knapsack. There were some choice cuts of meat remaining, plus the entire haunch and a few large potatoes.

This was no time for half-measures. I pulled out the haunch and laid the knapsack behind me. Then I picked up the crossbow and crept to the threshold of the crack. Malik was tugging at one of the arrows in his chest with his teeth. He groaned as it drew the flesh around it outward, the barbs on the arrowhead clutching at the plate it had pierced. When it ripped free, he snarled, bit it in three, spat out the remnants as he roared in pain, then licked at the freely bleeding wound.

I took a deep breath and tiptoed slowly out into the clearing. As I was laying the haunch of venison down, Malik spotted me and charged.

But I was prepared. I darted back into the crack between the boulders. He swiped into it with his long arm, but I was out of range, and the arrows still in his chest and legs shortened his reach. He growled furiously, pacing back and forth across the entrance but then stopped to glare in at me balefully.

As much as I wanted—needed—to make a connection with him, Father had warned us many times that a wild dragon will see eye contact as a threat or challenge. I averted my gaze and showed him the crossbow, then laid it down and raised my empty hands. Whether that would mean anything to him or not I didn't know.

He returned to licking his wound until the bleeding had slowed, though he looked up to check on me several times. Many long, excruciating minutes later he sniffed at the air, turned, and found the haunch of venison.

He stepped on it and removed half with a single bite. The remainder disappeared with scarcely more caution, though he worried the bone a little bit before crunching it into shards and swallowing it all.

"*Damn.*" I'd hoped it would last a bit longer. I dug into the knapsack and pulled out two large potatoes. I showed them to him, then lobbed them gently out through the opening.

He sniffed at them, then swallowed them whole.

"High ones . . . you must be starving!" I tried to keep my voice low and calm.

He snarled at me, rumbling low in his chest. But the timbre had changed slightly, and it wasn't all threat now. It made me think of our dragons when they came across something new and foreign. I retreated into the crevice a little further before I caught myself. I'm certain he could smell my terror, but I didn't want to show fear, even though I was trembling and pouring sweat.

"Please leave me alone. I don't want to be your food." Trying to calm him. Trying to calm myself. I recalled Father two days ago tell-ing Darian *it doesn't matter what you say. Tell him a story. Describe the weather. Babble like a lunatic.* Tone was far more important than content. I took a deep breath.

"Avar, but you are terrifying. I mean gorgeous. What a handsome sire you are." He stood panting, studying me. "Normally, a dragon sire is keeping the perimeter, ensuring a food supply for momma and her babies. But here you are, alone, stalking the men who stole your baby. Was that your mate I found? Or is she"—I swallowed—"in the cave?"

He stared at me inscrutably.

Despite myself, I snatched glimpses of his eyes: silver, like the stripes in his markings. He was beautiful, and it pained me to see the arrows in his flesh, the black rivulets of blood beneath them. Despite my fear and sadness and hurt, I found a well of empathy for this no-ble, wilding sire. I purred for him as best I could with dry lips and parched tongue. He tilted his head briefly. Encouraged, I tried to imi-tate the guttural rumble of contentment that our dragons made as they tucked into a meal. He tilted his head again.

"I want to save your baby too. Will you let me help? Look . . ." I fished a piece of meat out of the pack and showed it to him. Then I looked pointedly up the hill and mimicked the mewling bark that qits make when they're hungry, what we called *mowping*. "This is for your baby." Then I put the meat away.

He studied me, not moving.

"Oh, sweet Avar, but you are a mess! I wish I could help you, too." His liquid eyes met mine, and his pupils dilated. Before I could avert my traitorous gaze he growled in rage and leapt atop the fallen tree again.

He ripped it in a frenzy, snapping limbs, pulling upward on the trunk, biting at the smaller boughs. The main beam of the tree groaned and shivered. Bark rained down on me.

I screamed, but then, almost without thought and using all the power in my lungs, tapping all the sadness I felt for this courageous wilding and the full depths of my terror, I did my best to mimic Grus's sad keening. I sustained it at full volume for as long as I could, and finished each wail with a dragon's mournful chuffing.

Malik paused, stared at me, panting heavily. His head tilted sideways.

Baby called back from the Harodhi camp—a long and desolate cry, barely audible.

Malik snarled at me again, then paced back and forth from boulder to boulder above. When he stopped, he threw his head back and called, *keirr! keirr!*

Baby answered again.

He stuck his big head as far as he could between tree trunk and boulder, and roared at the top of his lungs. His warm, stinking breath washed over me, and I cowered in it.

Then he was gone.

———

I waited for what might have been an hour, but Malik didn't return. Once I'd stopped shaking, I stuck my head out between the fallen tree and the boulder. I hurt all over. My hands and knees throbbed. My side ached. I should have been exhausted, but fear still shook me.

I couldn't see Malik. I crept out into the clearing and scanned the forest as far as I could see. The sky was turning turquoise, but the valley was still in dawn's shadow. The air was cool and damp, redolent of moss and dew. A bird warmed up for his morning aria, and busy shade-tails scampered down out of the canopy. The pastoral serenity made the previous night's events feel like a fever dream. But the shattered trees, the ragged turf, and the trails of blood told the truth. My bow was still loaded and cocked. I left it that way and started out after Malik.

His track was easy enough to follow, heading uphill, toward the Harodhi poachers' cave. I spied another potential sanctuary ahead and made certain I was alone before I hurried to it. Then I caught my breath and looked for the next sanctuary. I leap-frogged up the slope this way for half an hour, with the dawn burgeoning in the sky above, before I spotted Malik again. He moved slowly but purposefully, one hundred or more yards ahead, using the trees to the right of the cart trail as cover. I followed his example, though I made a concentrated effort to keep at least one tree in the line of sight between us. He crawled up to the level of the cave and finally curled up behind an outcropping of granite within a screen of cedars. I sensed that he was waiting, considering his situation.

I struggled up the slope, clinging to the trees with my bleeding hands. Soon I was laboring to catch my breath, legs burning, but I managed to close within a few dozen yards of Malik. He had already spotted me and stared with long, hard menace. But he did not move or make a sound. For several minutes we watched each other. Sweat crawled down my back. Whatever happened, for as long as Malik's strength remained, he was going to be a part of this journey. My stomach twisted at the thought of contending with him again. It twisted a bit tighter when I realized that Malik was the closest I had to an ally. An ally who might bite me in two to be rid of me.

There was sudden commotion at the mouth of the cave. The sounds of shouts and tramping feet drifted down on the brisk air. Flashes of sky on metal revealed a mass of Harodhi warriors heading away from me through the pre-dawn gloom and onto the plateau. The Harodhi leader launched his dappled brown dragon into the sky above them, wings cracking. Behind them came the black silhouette of the Horror-beast, with its rough armor and darkly shrouded rider. Something had drawn them out. I peered out between two boles to see what it was, and my heart knotted into a fist.

From out of the crack where our tunnel was concealed, at the top of the rocky stair, a column of thick, gray smoke billowed up to catch the first ruddy light of day. Darian must have set the ancient dragon's nest on fire.

Dare, you idiot. He'd been certain that Father would come, and insisted that waiting was the right ploy. But he'd also been frightened that the Harodhi would hunt us down, possibly even in the dead hours—yet he had gone ahead with his first plan. For me. He'd made the distraction I needed.

I was responsible. He wouldn't be here but for me. I uttered a silent prayer to Getig that Darian was already far away from the source of that smoke.

A patter of stone came from my right; Malik crept along the deer track toward the cave. He saw the advantage in the diversion and was making his move, but I was frozen with indecision. I needed to follow him, though my breath was short and my knees shook. But I needed to know if my brother was safe.

The Harodhi dragons landed near the crevice where our tunnel was hidden, but for reasons unknown waited for the foot soldiers to join them. Then another movement caught my attention in the floor of the valley far below.

It was Darian, dashing for the trees. He disappeared into their shadows, and I gasped with relief. Surely he had heard Malik's roars in the night. For all he knew, I'd become the last meal of a doomed wilding. Yet alone and frightened beyond reason, he'd decided in the black hours of the morning to arrange my distraction anyway. Perhaps it would cover his flight for home, and at the same time send Father a clear signal, even if it meant attracting the poachers and their horrible beast. He had set his blaze, then left before it became visible, to follow my path down the scree stair.

I was flooded with relief and fear. He was safer in the trees, though not out of peril. But he had forced me to immediate action. If Father arrived now, my quest would end in failure.

"*Thank you, Darian,*" I whispered.

Malik crouched low, stalking slowly forward. Soon he would round the last abutment that defined the Harodhi cave opening. I considered all my options, none of them good. I was not prepared for this. I was in completely untraveled skies.

Then a hoarse, feral cry over the valley broke my concentration. The leader on his brown dragon and the black Horror had left the site of Darian's smoke signal and swept to the east, down toward the forest. Had they spotted Darian?

I groaned, horrified. Though there was nothing I could do for Darian, Malik had presented me with an opportunity, however tenuous. It remained my only hope.

From the cave, voices shouted in alarm, crossbows sang, and Malik roared.

Sweet Avar. Darian, High Ones—forgive me.

I vaulted up the last torturous ramparts of the slope to the mouth of the cave and stumbled after Malik, my crossbow readied.

E I G H T E E N

MALIK SLAMMED FURIOUSLY into the Harodhi defenders. Over a dozen bowmen scrambled to avoid his attack or position themselves for a telling strike. One scrambled between the wheels of the cart that bore the stained and blackened kegs, only to be dragged out by his legs and flung the width of the cave. Another tripped in his panic to escape and was crushed into the stone by a heavy forefoot.

Those remaining surrounded Malik. Every time he turned to face one group, others circled to attack from behind. Some of their arrows bounced ineffectually off his natural armor, but others bit deep, and Malik roared in pain. When he charged, the bowmen fell back and circled, keeping him from committing to one target. They stayed in disciplined pairs, and as one loosed, the other reloaded.

My fury mounted with each bolt that struck him. I raised my crossbow, sighted down the length of it, but found the flurry of activity confusing. When a target came into range, the face of my first kill flashed into my mind, and I hesitated. That fly crawling on an unblinking eye would haunt me forever.

Angry, confused, frightened beyond belief, I waited for another opportunity, but when it came I again hesitated too long.

Tears threatened to obscure my vision. *Is this how you act on your commitment?* I chided myself. *What if Darian dies but you fail to save the baby? It would all have been for nothing.*

The combat turned, and another Harodhi paused to sight his weapon. I pulled the trigger. My bolt smacked into his back as Malik turned on him. The man fell with a cry. I gasped in conflicting relief and sympathetic agony. The men next to him fled Malik's talons without any notice of me. As he whirled, Malik planted a rear foot on him, as if to finalize the kill. I knelt down to cock my crossbow. My arms shook so badly I could barely manage to position the next quarrel in the groove. My stomach churned, but there was nothing to throw up. I shouldn't have helped Malik; I might have been spotted. I should have used his gigantic distraction to slip into the cave.

Malik managed to pin two warriors against the far wall, only to take arrows in his haunches and rear legs. He launched himself at the men behind and they scattered.

I saw an opportunity; as the action flowed to the right, I dashed to the left. To reassess my position, I paused behind the upright scaffolding hung with the corpse of a young dragon.

The action still moved away from me. As Malik chased a soldier into the small waterfall, his wings behind him as a shield, all eyes turned their way. Screams and splashing and a horrible crunching noise echoed off the stone. I sidestepped quickly along the cave wall, fighting dry heaves, weeping. My boot snagged in the blood-soaked cloak of one of the newly dead. I pulled it free, stumbled again, continued toward the charnel wagon.

Malik charged again, and the action turned my way once more. I crouched as the swarm of shouting Harodhi wheeled past. One man spotted me and paused, confused. In that instant Malik stepped on him, dug his talons in, and ran after another man with the first still in his grasp. The man's screams ended abruptly, and Malik discarded the crumpled body.

I lurched sideways, hoping beyond hope that I could slip past this conflict and into the cave unseen. I didn't know if I would find my qit, or what I should do if I did. One step at a time. Keep moving.

Another soldier spied me, shouted, and other heads turned. He and a companion broke from the combat and ran my way. I loosed a bolt and hit the lead man in the chest. He fell backward like a sack full of meat. His companion raised his crossbow and aimed at me. I darted to one side and back again, then dashed for a boulder. I heard the snap of his crossbow and a sharp crack behind me, then took a misstep and fell.

The soldier stalked toward me as I scrambled to my feet. He tossed his crossbow aside and pulled a wicked, curved sword from his belt. I stepped into the foot strap of my bow, cocked the lever, fumbled and caused the bow to snap out of my grasp. I tried to back up, but tripped on my bow and fell.

Out of nowhere, Malik appeared, took the Harodhi in his jaws, and shook him like a rag. The man died with a burbling scream. Malik turned as arrows bounced off his haunches or pierced him, and leapt back into the fray.

"*Avar Avar Avar Avar . . .*" I panted as I put a boulder to my back. I found my bow, cocked it successfully this time, and loaded another quarrel. For what seemed an eternity, I sat gasping for breath, retching, listening to cries and crossbows snapping, roars of anger and pain, other noises too horrible to contemplate.

The cave ran back in a maze of crumbling stalactites and stalagmites, spotted with woven piles of branches and bones—the nests of dragons. It narrowed ahead, disappearing into a black crevice. I summoned my courage, gathered my things, and ran.

A roar behind me turned my head. Malik galloped after me. I dodged around a stalagmite, stumbled, scrambled back. Malik accelerated, nose wrinkled, eyes dark with fury. I passed a group of men sitting upright in bedrolls, crossbows leveled, wrapped in bloodied bandages. They looked past me at Malik, their faces contorted with fear. When he charged, they loosed as a group. He paused to rip them from their beds. Then a volley of crossbow bolts stung his rear legs and tail. He whirled about, growling and snarling.

I sprinted deeper into the cave, tripping at least twice on rocks or debris obscured by shadow, before finding the wagon tracks of the poachers. I careened on. The cavern walls closed in on either side, visible only by virtue of bright highlights on a wet surface, reflections of the distant opening behind me. The floor dropped, and I realized that I was running downhill. I collapsed to my knees, bloody palms grating on a rough stone floor.

Behind me: roars, shouts, crossbows, screams. Ahead of me: fathomless darkness.

I crept forward blindly, hand extended, testing each step. The sounds of battle were dwindling. I had to hurry.

The cave was deeper than I imagined and thick with the stench of rotting meat. Something snapped under my foot and flew up, hitting me in the face. I fell, and my hands landed on a jumbled bed of bones, inches deep. There were bones everywhere; this was a lair long used by dragons. I tried to push myself up, and my fingers found something wet and mushy. I recoiled in disgust. There was no way to know what it was.

I stood, and for a minute battled vertigo in the absolute dark. I attempted to find the wheel track, stumbled again, hit my head on a hanging pillar of stone and fell. I struggled to my feet and stood frozen, completely disoriented.

The full weight of my situation drove me to my knees again. I'd come here seeking redemption but found only death and terror. I tried to remember the feelings awakened in me by the appearance of the Summer Dragon, but they wouldn't come. Even Getig had been reduced to an empty uncertainty. I was abandoned and utterly alone. It had all gone horribly, horribly wrong. My mother's curse echoed in my memory.

Behind me, the din of battle ended. The only sound was dripping water.

"Getig, what am I doing here?" I whispered.

From somewhere ahead, a baby dragon keened and chuffed with a tiny voice, then mowped for food. My heart skipped a beat. There followed a harsh shout, the clang of metal on metal, and fearful keening.

I REALIZED THAT MY eyes had adjusted to the lack of light.
The cave opening was well behind me—I'd come farther than I
thought—but enough light leaked in to reveal a forest of strange stone
columns like poured wax, the floor carpeted with bones, and dragons' nests in every open space. A passage had been cleared through
the boneyard, grooved with wheel tracks winding deeper into the cavern. I took a few deep breaths. Somewhere ahead was a trapped and
frightened baby who needed me.

I dried my eyes, checked to see that my bow was still cocked and
loaded, then gathered my quiver, my knapsack, and my resolve. I
picked my way through the bones as quietly as possible and followed
the track down.

Bit by bit, the light source changed. The thin blue light of day fell
away behind me, and the diffuse orange glow of a lantern bloomed
somewhere ahead. Hushed voices echoed in the Harodhi's clipped
tongue. I slipped carefully off the track and peered out from between
the columns.

The way opened up into a natural chamber with fewer columns
and a flat, sandy floor. The lantern sat on a boulder to the rear, throw-
ing everything into bright relief with long, stark shadows. Two dragon
hides were stretched across frames of tentpole pine to dry slowly in
the cool cavern air. Against a low wall to the right, innumerable hides
were folded and piled like blankets. Racks and racks of dried meat
hung near the blackened pit of a cold fire.

Barrels streaked with black stains waited on carts. Dragon bones
had been sorted and stacked by kind against the opposite wall; leg

bones like firewood, wing bones like a delicate nest of kindling, ribs like barrel staves, vertebra like spiny stumps. Skulls.

More than two dozen of them, five or more from adults, but mostly juveniles. There were surprisingly few qitling skulls, however, and I reflected again on the bizarre mutilations of the qits outside.

Here was the center of their horrible enterprise, their stockpiled bounty. But where had all the babies gone? What was in the barrels? Blood? Why?

Anger welled up inside me, and it felt good. It wasn't fear. It wasn't doubt. It was clean and straight and sharp as an arrow. It had purpose and direction. I breathed deeply and quietly, nostrils flared, as if anger was a form of sustenance I could take into my body through my lungs.

Four Harodhi warriors were gathered in quiet argument. I guessed that they debated how to respond to the noises from without. With their heads uncovered, I clearly saw their white hair and translucent skin, ghostly and strange. Behind them was the cart with the cage on it. The two donkeys were still hitched to the cart with their muzzles in feedbags, but their feet were hobbled.

Almost lost in the expanse of the cage was the baby. My heart raced at the sight of it, huddled into a corner, eyes wide, top frill laid back close to the neck in fear, wings instinctively crossed before it in defense. No bigger than a medium-sized dog or bobcat, plus wings. I instantly longed to reach out and caress the soft, dry scales of its neck, to comfort it and give it something to eat. So much like Malik with its tan and silver markings. Beautiful.

One of the ghostlike Harodhi called out, echoes fleeting away. When no answer came, he gave an order. One of the men lit another lantern and pointed it up the slope. I ducked to avoid being seen or blinded. As they slinked upslope toward the opening, their light cast bizarre swinging shadows that confused the vista of the cavern. They passed me by, all four of them, without so much as a backward glance.

I waited until they were well up the trail, then slipped around the pillar and approached the cage. They'd left a lantern behind, and the baby's silver markings twinkled in the light. It was curled into a ball, shivering, keening faintly, its little head tucked under a wing.

I slowed my step. I didn't want to scare it. "Hi, baby." I kept my voice soft and quiet, not quite a whisper. "Shhh shhh shhh." Then I purred as best I could, the way a mother dragon soothes her qits to sleep. It was hard to maintain, as I had to do it with my tongue, whereas a dragon dam rumbled deep in her throat. But the little head appeared out from under the wing. The silver eyes that studied me were wide and trembling.

"Oh, High Ones, but you are cute." I'd said it before I knew the words were coming. "How could anyone do to you what . . ."

The baby keened unhappily, and I fell silent until it stopped.

It looked malnourished, but not desperately so. Some rib showed, but its belly was still round. It seemed that Malik had kept it fed before the Harodhi arrived. Yet the mowping told me it was hungry, that the poachers hadn't been feeding it well, if at all. I looked around to see what they had to offer. There was nothing here but dried dragon meat. Couldn't they have provided anything else? My nose wrinkled in disgust at their amateurism. Of course it was starving—even an infant dragon knew better than to eat of its own kind.

Slowly I pulled my knapsack off and reversed it, so that it was hanging in front of me. Then I pulled out a piece of venison and held it into the cage. Baby's nose twitched, and it unfurled its wings. As I looked for the sheath scales between the rear legs, uncertainty reared up again. If this were a little male, all my efforts would be undone. I needed a dam for Darian's little sire.

But the sheath scales were well behind the pubic bone and facing rearward. "You're a little girl . . ." Relief calmed my breathing. She stood awkwardly and paced back and forth in the cage, eyeing the meat in my hand, but unwilling to take it.

"*Mowp?*" I imitated her request for food. Then I purred some more. She stopped and cocked her head at me. It shouldn't have been comical in these circumstances, but I couldn't help smiling. Her eyes were so reflective—silver like her father's—her ear and top frills perfect the way only a baby's could be. Her broad chest and big feet indicated plenty of growth to come. She was a perfectly formed, perfectly beautiful qitling.

"Come on, baby," I cooed. "I know you're hungry. Come and eat. *Mowp?*"

The door of the cage was closed and latched, but it had no lock. I opened it so I could reach further in. She wailed lightly, so I gently eased the door the rest of the way to prevent it clanging against the bars. I was anxious for her to come to me; soon the Harodhi would return—or worse, Malik. I needed to win enough trust to get her into my knapsack, where the swaddling effect would calm her further, just like a human baby.

At last hunger decided for her. She approached cautiously, then stretched out her neck and gingerly took the meat from my hand. She dropped it to the cage floor and watched me until I withdrew my hand. Then she sniffed at the meat, licked it twice, and wolfed it down.

I purred, said, *"Mowp?"* again, and offered her another piece of venison. She took it more willingly this time, and swallowed it without the taste-test. I purred to encourage her. Qits at this age were ready to bond. I was counting on that. I hopped onto the cart and sat in the doorway of the cage. She retreated into her corner again. "Hungry baby?" I took out another piece of meat and held it forward with my right hand, reaching out with my empty left hand, too.

As she returned for the treat, I allowed my left-hand fingers to brush lightly against her cheek. I purred and cooed. She didn't recoil from my touch, but came closer, sniffing at my pack, clearly starving. I reached in for another piece of meat, and she looked me in the eye.

"Mowp?" Her voice was clear and confident. Despite myself, I stroked her jawline. She recoiled only a little bit, then allowed me to touch her again. The skin was soft and dry and smoothly pebbled— exactly as I always imagined it would feel. I gave her another piece of meat, and she allowed me to stroke the top of her head and around her mouth, my hand imitating the grooming tongue of a mother dragon after a messy meal. "Good baby!" I tried to say, but my voice cracked, and it came out a whisper. A tear spilled onto my cheek. She responded easily to my touch, even in the midst of this horror— starving, and perhaps desperate for some comfort, too. I purred for her as she ate.

Last night I'd asked myself if I was willing to die for this baby. Circumstances had forced the answer then; I had little choice. Now I could finally respond to doubt with certainty: This little life was worth fighting for.

I smiled, and stroked her head. She purred, perhaps an instinctive response to the fulfillment of her basic needs.

Suddenly there were shouts from the direction of the cave's entrance, and a deep, angry bellow resounded through the cave. The donkeys hitched to the cart looked up in fear. Their feedbags went limp. Screams of terror and the clacking of crossbows ended in wet, crunching noises and a gurgling cry. Scuffling, huge feet cracking in the carpet of bones, another scream that ended abruptly. A crossbow snap, crunching, a burble. Then came the sound of a person running, pursued by heavier footfalls, a roar, a shriek of pain, a crack, and silence. The donkeys tested their hobbles nervously.

Heavy steps crunching through bone approached from the darkness along with whuffing and snarling, then a single loud *click* that echoed in the cavern.

I looked around for cover, a place to take the baby and hide. But there was nothing, and I didn't have time to coax her into my knapsack anyway.

One of the donkeys started honking anxiously, and the other joined in. Baby held her head high in an effort to see past the edge of the light, calling plaintively. Movement beyond the pillars, silver flashing on tan. The donkeys erupted into high-pitched braying, kicking against their hobbles and the harness that strapped them to the cart. Baby cried out in fear at the sudden cacophony.

Father dragon rounded the last cluster of pillars. He panted, riddled with yet more arrows, bright blood striping his chest and legs. But he paused only long enough to take in the scene, then he launched himself at me.

I leapt backward into the cage and barely managed to close the door. His head slammed into it, rocking the cage and driving the door inward past its stop. His head entered the cage, but the twisted door was now between him and me. He snapped at me anyway with curved yellow teeth the length of daggers, limned with red along the gum line. Pink spittle struck me as he roared with breath that reeked of fresh blood. I cringed into the corner of the cage, screaming, with baby crowded next to me squealing in fear. Malik snapped and angled his head in hopes of reaching me, failed, pulled out and bit at the cage, shaking it. The donkeys brayed and bucked, their rear hooves cracking against the cart. He ignored them, buffeting the cage with his forefeet. A corner buckled. He reached into the door opening with his left paw, but an arrow snagged on the frame and he withdrew, snarling. He reached in again, his paw questing past the edge of the door. I had my knife in my hand, though I didn't remember drawing it. I didn't want to use it and risk angering him, even though his talons came within inches of me. I retreated as far as I could. Finally the narrowness of the opening and the arrows in his arm forced him to withdraw.

One of the donkeys broke its hobbles and attempted to run, but only pulled its teammate down. The cart lurched, knocking baby and me over. The second donkey struggled to rise, braying in fear.

Malik took the cage in his teeth and yanked. The cage pulled the cart over sideways before crashing to the ground. Baby cried out in fear. I shouted in pain and alarm. My crossbow went off, the arrow careening into the black. The cage landed door-side down, trapping me inside with the qit of a very angry wilding dragon. The cage wouldn't take much more of this abuse.

The second donkey broke its hobbles and scrambled to its feet, and together the animals fled deeper into the cave with the cart scraping and bouncing on its side behind them.

A semblance of quiet returned. Malik circled the cage, studying it, growling low. Baby whimpered in fear. My knees and shins were bruised from falling on the bars of the cage. I caught my breath and rubbed them slowly, concentrating on my predicament. My knife was no longer in my hand. I scanned around until I saw it on the ground several feet away. I couldn't reach it. Baby was in a panic, terrified by her sire's assault. I stroked her chin and nose, purring and whispering, "*Shhh, shhh, shhh . . .*" Malik continued to examine us, no longer growling, but panting heavily.

I offered baby a strip of venison, but she was too frightened to take it. "Mowp?" I said, but she scrabbled at the bars, little forepaw questing out in her father's direction. I tossed the meat out of the cage, at Malik's feet, and said, "MOWP," testily. He looked at it, then at me. Baby cried.

"I don't want to hurt your baby! Can't you see that I'm here to help?" With him mere feet away, it was clear that the arrows in his left alar pectoral were oozing pus. I wanted to cry for him. "I can't treat your wounds; you're too wild. But they're infected. Poor, poor Malik. You're in such bad shape."

He glared at me. I avoided his eyes.

"I don't know if you will survive. But I can care for your baby. I can! See?" Then I made mother noises and offered baby another plank of venison. Baby sniffed at it, but stuck her nose out through the bars again, keening. I petted her head, hoping that her father would see how gentle I was, how unconcerned baby was with my touch. Baby's quivering nose led her back to the strip of venison in my hand. She ate it quickly and nosed into my knapsack for more. Relieved, I pulled out another piece for her, and she gobbled it down.

"See, Malik? See?" I had to fight my urge to look him in the eyes.

He watched me, motionless.

Baby ate another strip of venison. So much food might not be a good idea, but it was the only weapon I possessed.

Malik cocked his head slightly sideways.

He looked down at himself, at the many arrows protruding out of his chest and legs. Then he lowered his head and put his nose to the bars of the cage. Baby stuck her nose through and licked him, forepaws touching his lips. He licked her in return, and growled deep in his throat, a pitch so low that I felt it more than heard it.

He didn't know he was doomed. He had only one thought in his mind: saving his offspring. He had never wrestled with the question of risking his life for his baby. There had never been a question. No question at all. His sacrifice was untainted by selfish desire.

"*Keirr,*" he said, like the call of a hawk. His baby made a strange little honk that sounded almost like *poppa,* then licked his nose.

Realization struck me. "Is that her name?" It had to be. Like an affectionate nickname: his little hawk. "Keirr," I repeated. Malik and baby both looked at me.

Sounds came from beyond the darkness, at the mouth of the cave: shouts and muted conversation, and the call of a dragon. The Harodhi leader had returned with his men. Had Darian escaped? Was he alive?

Malik pulled back from the cage and turned away, growling menacingly again. His little hawk cried, reaching out through the bars, but he started up the path. Treading quietly. Choosing his battleground, away from Keirr. I didn't doubt it.

I had to get out of the cage, but it was lying entry-side down. Malik's assault had pushed the door past its stops and into the cage. I wrenched it out of the way and stepped into the opening, then grabbed the lowest metal straps of the grid in front of me and lifted the cage with all my strength. The straps cut into my fingers. I was barely able to raise it an inch off the floor. Keirr whimpered behind me.

I searched around me, desperate for something to use as a lever. There was nothing to hand. Nearby were some flat chunks of stone, though, fallen from the ceiling—the same material that the plateau was made of. I gathered several of them into the cage with me, and put the flattest one next to the edge of the doorway.

The echoing voices were drawing nearer, curt, angry.

I heaved on the cage again, lifting with my legs. When it was up, I pushed the rock under it with my toe before it could drop again. I put another, thicker rock in position, then lifted again. Baby retreated to the lower portion of the cage, which helped only a little. I managed to raise it another couple of inches, and pushed the next stone under it with my foot.

Malik growled menacingly, now out of sight in the darkness.

I placed another rock, lifted, pushed it into place. I had six inches of space now, but this was taking much too long. I needed a bigger stone. Suddenly baby was next to me, neck stretched out under the gap, testing the fit. I couldn't let her escape. I pulled the blanket out of my knapsack quickly, the remaining meat and potatoes scattering, and threw it over her. She squealed in fear, but I wrapped my arms around her and held her tight. *"Shhh shhh shhh. Oh, little Keirr, don't summon your poppa back here."* She struggled, but once I had her wings pinned to her side, she calmed down. It was a tactic we used in the aeries to move qitlings at need; darkness and the swaddling effect calmed them.

I worked my knapsack up around her body, purring all the while, then drew the strings securely around her neck, leaving her head free. When I pulled the blanket back so she could look around, wide-eyed, she tried to peck at me with her needle-sharp teeth. I brushed the dirt off a strip of venison and offered that to her instead. After a moment, she took it and worked it over. I pulled the blanket back over her head.

Then I heaved on the cage with everything I had. As the floor of the cage began to tip back toward horizontal, it became easier, but the metal straps cut into my fingers until they were slippery with blood. I groaned, pulling with all my strength. It inched up, inched up, the balance of weight nearing a tipping point. I pressed upward until the cage finally rocked back, and fell upright again with a loud clang. Baby cried out, but I purred quietly and reached into the blanket to stroke her head.

The voices grew suddenly louder; the Harodhi had entered the inner chamber. They'd heard me. Growls rumbled in the entrance of the cave.

I slung baby in my knapsack on my back, gathered up as much of the remaining venison as I could stick in my pockets, and stuffed a couple of potatoes into the pack with her.

The voices grew angrier—they had discovered further carnage. I cocked and loaded my crossbow, retrieved my knife, and scanned about for anything else of value. The lantern would be of use—a shuttered type that allowed for a focused beam. Good. I didn't want to illuminate myself, so I shuttered it quickly down to a narrow beam and pointed it backward. Its manufacture was a bit shoddy; I would have to be careful with it. They had to have lantern oil somewhere. A small keg without the grisly black stains looked promising. I sniffed at it, felt oil around the cork. Good. I hefted it under my arm and noticed a quiver of arrows on a makeshift stone bench. I slung that over my shoulder.

I was starving, but I wasn't going to touch the dragon meat. Something else caught my eye: a rolled up bit of parchment next to a leather scroll case, a bottle of ink, and a quill. Despite the urgency of the moment I was compelled to give it a look. I unrolled the scroll.

The sketched cliffs and mountains seemed familiar, but when I recognized them my jaw dropped in terror. It was my home.

The aeries of Riat were drawn in detail, as seen from the air. It was all there: the surrounding mountainscape, the pinnacle that the compound was built upon, connected by a bridge to the homestead on the clifftop, the village and farmlands below, even the river Wilding and the Roaring.

My emotions tried to reject the truth even as my intellect

acknowledged it: the Harodhi were spying on our aeries. They were taking qits, yes, but they were also planning an assault like the one that had taken Cuuloda. There could be no other explanation.

I couldn't stop shaking. This news had to make it out of here if nothing else did. With trembling hands, I rolled the parchment up and stuffed it into its leather quiver, then slung that on my back, too.

The wheel track wound back down into deeper gloom. I didn't know what was back there, but behind me were Horrors and an angry Malik. I would simply have to take my chances with the low road.

Suddenly one of the Harodhi called out, but in Gurvaani, not his own speech, and I froze.

"Dragon rider!" Was he addressing me?

When the echoes died, he spoke again, in lower, more menacing tones. "We have your companion."

T W E N T Y

WAS DARIAN ALIVE?
        I shuttered my lantern completely and peered out between
two pillars of stone. At the far end of the cavern vague shapes moved
back and forth in front of the faint vertical sliver that marked the entrance. Diffused light from the Harodhi's lantern revealed the leader
and his dragon front and center, and others spreading out across the
width of the cavern. Again, boots crunched and cracked in the bed of
bones.

I saw Malik crouched eighty feet or so up the slope toward the
mouth of the cave, but I doubted the Harodhi had seen him yet. Their
eyes were still adjusting to the change in light, and their own lantern
would keep them blind to anything beyond the circle of its glow. All
the better for me.

Then a shadow filled the opening from the outside and the Horror-
dragon squeezed in through the crack. It reflected the lantern light
strangely, the colors shining cold and green instead of orange and
warm. Nothing about this creature was right.

I didn't spot Darian until the leader signaled, and one of his lieutenants pushed a small shape forward next to the boulder where the
lantern sat.

I couldn't see him clearly. He was shoved to his knees almost immediately. Was he hurt? His arms were bound behind his back, and
he shook as if he was sobbing. But he was alive.

"Do you hear me, dragon rider? I know you are there!" The leader's voice had a raspy edge, as if he had been shouting a lot recently.
He didn't need to shout—every footfall, every foreign curse, every

clank of metal sounded sharp and crisp. The last echoes rang in my ears.

"I told you, I came alone." Darian's tremulous voice was as clear as if he was right next to me.

The leader slapped him hard across the face. *"I know you are lying,"* he hissed. "You were with us when this carnage occurred. Your accomplice must have done it."

"It was the father of the dragon baby you stole."

Another sharp slap on the other side of Darian's face silenced him. "A wild dragon does not put an arrow into a man. A wild dragon could not make this assault. You are here with a dragon rider." His accent was thick with Harodhi tone and cadence.

Darian spat, then stifled a sob. "I'm not. By Korruzon I swear I came alo—"

Slap. "Do not speak that name. You are just a boy. Obviously you are here with someone. My men heard you shouting a name last night. Who is Maia?"

Darian spat again. "You should order your men to clean out their ears."

The leader hoisted him up by his shirtfront. "You think you are funny, do you? You think that jokes will help you?" He threw Darian down again and kicked him several times, drawing grunts of pain. I bit my lip to keep from crying out, and aimed my crossbow at the leader. But it was a long shot—even if I hit him, Darian would still be bound and in their grasp. I didn't know what to do.

"Who is Maia?" The Harodhi leader kicked him again.

Darian fought to his knees. "Maia is the greatest warrior in all of Gadia, and he will put your head on a pike to decorate his hall."

A lump rose in my throat at Darian's courage.

The leader pulled a curved dagger out of his belt, blood on it already. The blade flashed crimson, with a rippled cutting edge. Darian shrank back from it as the leader waved it slowly back and forth in front of his nose. "Why are you here?"

Darian stared at the knife.

"Why are you here?" The leader cuffed Darian's ear for emphasis.

Dare, please don't make him mad.

Darian's chin rose. "Because we are looking for you, and now we have found you."

Without warning the Harodhi leader slashed him across the shoulder. Darian cried out in agony.

"No!" I cried, my voice hoarse enough from screaming to be unidentifiable as female.

The Harodhi turned my way again.

"Ahh! So you are there after all. Show yourself, Maia, oh great warrior, or I will kill your companion."

I scolded myself for not seeing through his bluff. He'd never been sure whether I was here or not. Did he still think I was a dragon rider after hearing my voice?

Malik was still and silent, biding his time—patient as only a predator could be.

"Mowp?" said a little voice from behind me.

"Hush, baby. Please," I whispered.

The leader stepped forward, and a lieutenant moved next to Darian with a curved sword held ready in both hands. "Come out, warrior, and show yourself. Perhaps I will let you both live if you cooperate."

I didn't believe him for an instant. I understood now that he feared me still, and hoped to draw me out so he could decide how to deal with me. As long as he didn't know who or what I was, I had an advantage. For the moment at least, Darian was his only defense against the wrath of what he thought to be a mounted warrior.

But he turned and spoke in his brusque foreign tongue, and the Horror-dragon started forward with a deliberate, mechanical stride.

All but the leader himself gave the beast wide berth. As it passed the lantern, I caught a glimpse of the rider's face, and I shrank back in terror.

Like the dragon, its flesh was black. Not beautiful like the ebony people who sometimes traveled through Gadia from the far west, but shiny, pitted, and cracked like the surface of a log in a fire. It was a charred outrage against nature, more like a burnt corpse than something living. And when it left the circle of the lantern light, my terror mounted.

What I'd taken for strange green reflections on the beast's armor were now visible as something else. Green light leaked out between the joints of the black metal on its neck and chest, from beneath the helmet, and through cracks and ragged tears in its skin. The rider's eyes were holes revealing the same green flame within a grisly lantern, the fissured jaw and wasted nose defined by more green light shining up from within the robes.

Baby squirmed in the knapsack.

"Do you see, dragon rider?" The leader's voice rang. "You cannot escape."

In desperation I called back to him, attempting to keep my voice pitched low, and playing up the hoarseness. "I'll destroy your spoils! Pelts, bones, barrels and map. Let the boy go!" I held my breath and aimed my crossbow carefully.

The leader glowered into what, for him, was darkness. He was little more than a silhouette from my vantage.

"You think that I am concerned about these things? I already have what I came for. I don't think I need to concern myself with you any longer. I think, instead, I will kill your boy and send my pet to finish with you. He is hungry. He hasn't eaten since last—"

I loosed my arrow. He cringed at the snap of my bow and the hiss of the arrow in flight, but I hadn't aimed at him.

"Darian! *RUN!*" I shouted, as the arrow smacked into the hip of the soldier standing over him. He lurched to his feet, driving his shoulder into the shocked man and knocking him over. In scrambling up, Darian stomped on the embedded arrow, eliciting a scream of agony, then kicked the man in the head. Shouts rose up all around as Darian kicked the lantern. The leader dodged its trajectory, but it shattered against a dragon's nest and a small plume of flame leapt up. Deep shadows careened and flickered, confusing the terrain.

"This way," I screamed. "*Run!*"

He sprinted into the blackness as best he could with his arms bound behind him. I saw his silhouette stumble and fall, but he got to his feet with a curse and continued. He was running blind. I unshuttered my lantern—only long enough to show him the path—then shrouded it again. More silhouettes followed him down the slope. Then the Horror-dragon and rider turned to intercept him.

But they had turned their backs on an unseen foe. Malik leapt out of hiding onto the monster's haunches with all four sets of talons, driving it to the ground. The beast tried to wheel about, but Malik hung on, raking at wings and back and biting with his teeth, his growls resounding through the cave like an entire pride of wildings. Sickly green light glowed out of the new wounds in the Horror's flesh.

Darian was past them in a shot, but crossbows clacked and snapped from the slope above. The Harodhi arrows splintered on stone all around.

The Horror-rider turned in his saddle, leveled a crossbow at Malik, and loosed. Malik screeched in pain, but clawed up higher on the dragon's back and swatted the crossbow out of his hands. The rider quickly released his harness and leapt from his mount's back an instant before Malik raked the saddle.

Darian's footfalls neared. I opened the lantern again briefly to light his way, but there was a sickening thud, and a crossbow bolt pierced his calf. He cried out and stumbled. I closed the lantern again and, by the tiny bit of light it still cast, found Darian and dragged him into cover with me.

"Darian—you're alive."

"I'm shot, damn it." He flinched when I reached for the slash on his shoulder. "Shot and cut and burned."

"Burned! How? Where?"

"Get these ropes off me."

"Where are you burned?" I sawed at the ropes that bound his arms.

"That thing—it's cold, like ice. Where it grabbed me it *burned*."

The sounds of dragon combat had grown louder, and snarls of pain punctuated the cracking of crossbows. I peeked around the pillar.

The overturned lantern suddenly ignited the ancient, tinder-dry dragon's nest. Light spread as the flames billowed. Malik still clawed at the Horror's back furiously, but the beast rolled over, forcing Malik to leap aside. Other silhouettes picked their way down the slope.

"We have to get out of here." I gathered up the crossbows and the ammunition.

Darian panted heavily, trying to control his pain. "Get out where? They're blocking the only exit."

"No, these wheel tracks go deeper into the cave. I think the Harodhi might have come from this direction. I think we're in the path of *their* exit."

"Sweet Korruzon, Maia! That's what I love about you: The only way you get out of trouble is to get into deeper trouble."

"*Avar*, Darian. What about this?" I touched the arrow in his calf. The slender, dart-like arrowhead protruded from his shin in front.

"No! Don't touch it. Leave it alone. Let's just go."

"Come on, then. This way." I picked up the keg of lantern oil and pulled Darian to his feet. He winced.

"I am going to knock you on your ass when we get home, kidling," he said.

"It's good to see you, too."

I opened the shutters on the lantern just enough to light a sliver of track ahead of us, once we were beyond the fire's light. "Hold this," I said, handing it to Darian, "and put your arm over my shoulder."

"Mowp?" said a little voice from behind me.

"Carefully!" I added.

"What was that?"

There was no time to stop and show him, or even explain.

"By Korruzon's blazing, sulphurous farts! You have a dragon in your pack!"

An angry bellow turned our heads. Malik had backed down the trail, fending off the Horror with his talons and teeth, but the situation had changed for the worse. He gave ground with every exchange, and soldiers were creeping up on him.

Keirr struggled and cried in my pack. *Oh, High Ones*, I thought. *Malik*.

Darian did his best to lurch after me, half walking, half hopping. We turned a corner and lost sight of Malik, but the sound of other footfalls drew near.

"Keep going!" I hunkered down with my crossbow. The silhouette of a man came around the bend and I loosed. He fell with a muffled cry.

"*High Ones*." Darian froze.

"I told you to keep going!" I watched for a moment, as Malik's roars and the scuffling, tearing sounds of dragons in battle continued unabated. I dashed forward, grabbed the downed soldier's crossbow out of his hands, and tried to rip his quiver loose from his belt. It wouldn't let go. The soldier stared at me with pale eyes, gasping for a breath that wasn't going to come. I bent down and with my knife slashed the cords that held the quiver, then retreated with my stomach squirming.

Malik backed around the bend, snarling, forepaws slashing in frenzy at the dark form of the Horror, just out of sight.

"Dare—Malik is in trouble!"

"Who is *Malik*?"

"Malik! Keirr's poppa."

"*Who is Keirr?*"

"Avar, Darian! Don't be so *dense*."

I grabbed his shirt under his arm and lifted, supporting him as best I could. He hopped and skipped after me, cursing.

The cave narrowed as we descended, until at last we came to a slender passage with an ancient, crumbling dragon's nest on either side. Freshly splintered wood blocked the way, and it took me a moment to identify it as the cart that had transported Keirr's cage. The donkeys were nowhere in sight, but they had left the shattered cart behind.

"Go, Dare—through here." I handed him the new crossbow and quiver, then gave him a push. He stumbled over the debris and into the narrow defile without argument. Then I unstoppered the keg of lantern oil and backtracked a little way.

The snarling and scuffle drew near. Malik's roars sounded desperate. The light from the fire uphill was growing brighter, and smoke filled the upper cave.

I hurried to pull wood out of the nests to either side of this skinny doorway, piling it together with the wood of the destroyed cart. It wasn't easy; the dragons were good at building solid nests.

Little Keirr protested with squeaks and squawks at the violent movement. "Hush, baby! Please hang on!"

I poured lantern oil on the wood in front of the narrow opening and soaked the remnants of the rope that had bound Darian.

"What are you doing?" he called.

"Shut up. Just keep moving."

Keirr struggled and squawked in my knapsack. Malik backed into sight again, but two Harodhi warriors leapt past him, with crossbows leveled. I ducked behind a stony column as a bow cracked. The arrow shattered on the wall across from me, and I cried out in alarm. I stuck a bit of the rope into the bung opening of the oil keg, then turned the keg upside down until oil dripped onto the floor. Another arrow cracked on the wall opposite me.

I peeked quickly around the corner. Two Harodhi soldiers were sneaking up on my position, one struggling to cock his crossbow, the other with his weapon leveled.

I opened the shutters of the lantern to light the rope in the keg of oil. Then I jumped around the corner and took in the setting as quickly as I could. The two Harodhi warriors saw me and lifted their bows. I heaved the keg of lantern oil in their direction. It shattered on a stone in front of them, and oil splashed to douse the one in front. They loosed, but both their panicked shots missed me as I ducked back into cover.

The oil didn't ignite immediately, which wasn't a surprise. I crouched down with my crossbow and pulled to cock it. The mechanism was stiff, and one of the Harodhi sprang around the edge of my cover, surprising me. There came a snap from behind me, and an arrow appeared in the man's neck, dropping him. I glanced over my shoulder to see Darian, white-faced, lowering the crossbow I'd just given him. I left my bow and labored instead to ignite the last bit of oil-doused rope. It started to burn, and I tossed it onto the wood in front of me.

"Come on!" Darian hopped away, into the narrow defile. I followed, looking backward.

The oil burst into flames all at once, just as the other soldier stepped into the opening. The oil that had splashed on his robes ignited suddenly. He dropped his bow and threw his arms over his head, screaming. He slapped at himself, spinning about frantically, but the flames only climbed up his clothing to turn him into a blazing torch.

Keirr screamed in fear at my back.

I ran to Darian, wrapped an arm under his ribs, and together we staggered down a long, narrow passageway, shrieks of pain and defiant roars chasing us, and little Keirr screeching in my knapsack.

Suddenly we burst out into a large chamber where the diffused light from behind us dissipated into denser gloom. Darian stumbled and cried out, and his echoes answered from far away. I hauled him to his feet and pressed forward.

"Open the lantern wider," I said.

"How?" He stumbled again, barely managing to set the lantern down without dropping it. I collapsed next to him, grating my wounded palms on the stone floor. His shoulder was bleeding freely, soaking his shirt and mine.

"Maia," Darian gasped. "I hurt. I can't . . ."

"You have to." I flicked the lantern doors wider, burning my fingers in the process. Then I pushed to my feet and helped Darian up. "We have to keep moving. Come on."

We had traveled barely fifty yards when the light coming from behind grew brighter. We crouched behind a rock and looked back.

Malik burst through the opening with the burning corpse of the Harodhi warrior in his jaws. He dropped the lifeless body and licked a flame off his lips. Then he roared with unrestrained fury, upright and wide-stanced with the glowing tunnel behind him like a vision from one of Mabir's most dour sermons.

"Up, Darian! *Up!*"

Keirr cried and whimpered as I hoisted Darian to his feet again. Then I once more shuttered the lantern down to its narrowest opening. The wheel track went down, and down, and down.

T W E N T Y - O N E

I STUMBLED ON, supporting and pulling Darian. He winced and sucked air through his clenched teeth with every step, but kept up with me as best he could. I was grateful for the downhill slope; it would have been impossible otherwise.

Keirr struggled in my knapsack, crying to get out, and in the darkness behind us, Malik followed. I couldn't see him any longer, but I heard his pained grunts and threatening whuffs and snarls.

We struggled on through an alien landscape for what seemed an age. For the first time I was able to really see the strange shapes like melted candles. Stalactites hung from a ceiling out of sight above and stalagmites rose like waxen spires from the cavern floor. Many had joined to form the same sort of distorted, stony columns populating the outer caves. The shapes became truly bizarre as columns swallowed neighboring spears, suggesting deformed monsters or twisted trees. The careening light from our narrow beam gave the pillars an illusion of life, as if they marched off into the deep gloom surrounding us. The cavern was immense, the furthest walls invisible.

Hollow echoes and the drip, drip, drip of water accompanied us at every step. Everything glistened with moisture.

"I have to rest." Darian panted.

My legs burned and the straps of the knapsack cut into my shoulders. A rest sounded wonderful, but we couldn't stop. Malik was keeping pace with us, and I feared what would happen if he caught us. "I know, but we can't."

"Mowp?" said Keirr yet again. It seemed that everyone needed something.

"Keirr, Keirr. Yes. Mowp. But we have to put some distance between us and your poppa."

"Great—you'll stop for a *mowp*, but your bleeding brother has to press on?" He meant it as sarcastic humor, but the truth was obvious: we were hurting.

"Just for a few seconds, then. Let me take the lay of things."

Darian collapsed with a groan onto a rock and set the lantern on the trail at his feet. I carefully shrugged out of the knapsack and set it on the ground too. Keirr had managed to work her head out from beneath the blanket and blinked at me with her beautiful silver eyes.

"Mowp?"

"*Avar,* baby, but you *do* want what you want." I fished into my pockets for a bit of venison. In the wild, she wouldn't have been fed piecemeal like this. She'd have had one huge, satisfying feast off of fresh kill, and then she'd have slept. I held a steak out to Darian. "Feed her this. Please?" He looked up at me, then took the meat and held it for Keirr to gnaw on.

I picked up the lantern and opened its shutters wide, pointing it back the way we came. Perhaps we'd gained some ground on Malik after all—he was nowhere in sight. He must be hurting far worse than we were. But I heard him still.

Then, far up the trail, a pinpoint of light shined back at me. It blinked once, and then disappeared. One reflection.

"*Keirr!*" Malik's distant voice was now hoarse and pained. The echoes rang but then answered themselves from much farther away, repeating, *Keirr! Keirr! Keirr!* His baby looked up and made that peculiar *poppa* honk again. She had a name of her own for her sire that I wanted to be able to say. I tried to imitate it.

"It sounds like you just stepped on a goose." Darian tried to chuckle, but his voice was raspy and his face looked gaunt in the dim light.

"He's getting closer, Darian. We have to keep moving."

"Do you have water?"

"Yes." I passed him my waterskin. "But hurry."

He tipped it up and drank deeply.

"Save some!" He lowered it again and handed it back to me without comment. I weighed it unhappily. It was less than a quarter full. I was thirsty and didn't doubt that Keirr would appreciate a drink too.

I held the lantern in front of me and peered into the darkness. Fifty yards or so ahead the track took a bend to the left and upward, the first upward track we'd come to. The rise would be difficult, but it might buy us some time against Malik.

I handed the waterskin back to Darian, then cupped my hands under Keirr's chin. "Pour some out, Dare. Please." He did, and Keirr lapped it up quickly, with barely a drop spilled. "Mowp?"

"Is there any left?" I asked.

Darian shook the waterskin. "A few drops, maybe."

I frowned. It would be best to sate her needs, so she would remain quiet. Sooner or later, she had to sleep. "Give them to her."

He poured the last of our water into my hands, and Keirr took it all.

"Mowp?"

I pulled the blanket back over her head. "Not now, baby. Not now." I checked the drawstrings on the pack, then shrugged back into it.

Malik's heavy steps and labored panting grew louder. He clicked once, loudly, and was answered with echoes.

"Let's go, Darian. Come on." I knelt, he put his arm around my shoulder, and we resumed our halting progress.

The switchback proved to be an ordeal. How did the Harodhi manage to move carts or wagons over this tortured, stony rise? It was more like stairs than a trail, and Darian had a difficult time with the bumpy ascent. He leaned heavily on me, grunting and cursing with every step.

Suddenly I realized it *was* a stair. The path had been carved out of the strange, molten rock forms, and each step, though now decaying and overlaid with hardened flows of liquid stone, was spaced deliberately for a human stride. It reminded me immediately of Cinvat valley. What other features did I fail to observe before this? What might I see with my lantern opened wide? Finally we came to a flat space, and I opened the lantern shutters again to take a look back. All was still. Under a sheer cliff face, the trail below us where we had paused a few minutes ago was empty. I still heard Malik, but he had fallen behind.

"Breather!" gasped Darian, and I agreed. I was worried that the climb might have aggravated his wounds. He collapsed to the floor, and I set little Keirr down beside him.

"I need to bind your shoulder, Darian," I said. "Your turn to give up a sleeve." He didn't move as I took my knife to the slash in his shirt and finished what the Harodhi leader started. The cut had stopped bleeding freely but still oozed bright red. He was dehydrated, making every drop of blood all the more precious. In the end, I needed both his sleeves in order to bind it securely.

"Now let me look at your leg."

"Careful." His face was deathly pale, his skin waxen. I hid my reaction as I inspected his wound.

The arrow had pierced his leg completely, and the slender arrowhead protruded from his swollen shin, bright red blood oozing out. Bright was bad: rich blood from an artery. The fact that it merely oozed suggested that the artery wasn't severed entirely, though for all I knew his boot was full of blood. I feared to touch it.

"I have to leave it, Dare."

"Okay." No argument.

"I'm afraid what will happen if I try to pull it out."

"Okay." His eyes were closed, as if he were about to fall asleep.

"Get up. We have to keep moving."

He looked up at me, bleary eyed. "You have no idea where we're going, do you," he said, matter-of-factly.

I swallowed. "Yes I do. I am following the Harodhi cart track."

"Great—back to Harodhi-land! Good thinking." He gave a painful chuckle. "We'd better hurry then." He struggled to rise, and I helped him up.

I wanted to have a quick look at the trail we had covered already. "We're about out of oil." I started, as I turned the lantern to the trail behind.

Malik was directly below us. When he saw my light, he leapt up at me with a roar and snarl, scrabbling with his talons on the slippery smooth cliff face.

I screamed in surprise, and Darian shot to his feet, away from the edge. Keirr cried out in panic as I froze in shock at what I saw.

Malik was a nightmare. He was covered with soot and smelled of smoke. The ferocious raking of the Horror had broken off many of the arrows studding his neck, chest, and forelegs. The deep gashes bled horribly, sticky and black. His face was crosshatched with bite-marks, and his left eye was gone, the socket clogged with thick globs of congealing blood.

I cried out in horror, unable to move, caught between fright and devastated sympathy.

He made one more lunge at the lip of the cliff, roaring in anger, but his bloodied and splintered talons fell short, and he slid back down to the trail below. He leapt again, scratching and clawing, but made even less progress. Finally he collapsed on the road beneath us with his head hanging, his wings drooping.

Keirr cried and struggled in my pack.

"Oh poor Malik!" I said, as he chuffed in agony below.

Darian grabbed me. "Poor *Malik*? What is the matter with you?"

"You don't understand."

"I understand that he wants his baby back. How is that difficult for you?"

I pulled away from Darian's grasp and looked down at Malik, panting at the foot of the short cliff below. He barely moved. "You're right," I admitted at last. "He won't stop. We have to keep moving."

"Yes, we do. Gods, Maia, he's a wild animal."

"And you wouldn't be here, alive, but for him!" My echoing words agreed with me.

Darian's lips drew tight and he said nothing more. I put my arm under his again, tears rolling down my cheeks. My baby's laments faded, and I felt her head—once again free of the blanket—resting on my shoulder. I didn't have a hand to spare to give her a reassuring rub.

We pressed ahead, yard by yard, in silence. When I stopped to look around or listen, I saw only distorted candle-wax architecture, heard only the dripping of water and the distant chuffing and snarling of Malik, still in pursuit. The track stayed more or less level for the next hour or so, and we followed it without a break, until the lantern flame started to gutter.

"Oh no, Darian . . ."

He looked at the lamp, then at me, then back the way we had come, and finally forward into the blackness. "Do you have any wood?"

It seemed like a stupid question. The only wood we had with us was our crossbows and quarrels, none of which we dared sacrifice.

But Darian was in bad shape. He had lost a lot of blood; his mind was slipping.

I opened the shutters all the way. "We keep moving until we run out of light." I cast the beam around us, but it didn't go as far as I would have liked. On the trail just ahead I spied something that didn't belong. Only then did the smell connect in my brain.

"Donkey dung!" I said. "There in the road. The donkeys passed this way. How could they find their way in the dark?"

Darian looked at me blankly.

"Don't you get it? If we can catch up to them you can *ride.*"

I pointed the beam forward, but it disappeared into the gloom. I shifted slightly, and it fell upon a shape that struck me as odd. On second look, it became the statue of a man wearing strange, form-fitting clothing, half buried in a column of stone that had grown up around its legs and torso. There was a stump of a statue on the other side as well. I realized then that we stood upon tightly knit pavers, overlaid on either side with the solidified excretions of the mountain, like frozen streams at the feet of the spires. Looking back, I now spied columns and walls of obvious artifice, covered with friezes of ancient deeds and curiously garbed people, who disappeared behind frozen waterfalls of melted stone. I'd walked right past them.

I was reminded again of the city of Cinvat in the valley, but instead of a forest of trees, a forest of stone had consumed and transformed this underground wonder. "Darian, look," I said. But then the lantern flickered and died, and the most profound darkness I'd ever known swallowed us.

Darian squeezed my arm, and I held my breath.

"Maia . . ."

"Shhh."

The silence was vast, and minor sounds like drips or our own guarded breathing were consumed.

"Now what?" Darian whispered.

"Listen."

Malik still followed us, moaning and panting. But something else reached my ears, from even farther away, so distorted by multiple reverberations off cave walls that it took me a minute to realize what it was: Footsteps. Many of them, as of a marching troop of men.

"Darian! The Harodhi are following us now, too."

"What did you expect?"

"I hoped that the entire cave full of old dragons' nests would become an inferno they couldn't pass. That maybe the smoke of it would pour out and show Father which way to come."

"Fires need air. They only had to wait."

I fought panic. We needed to keep moving, but we couldn't see. The risk of stumbling off a cliff face into a bottomless chasm was all too great.

I sat down carefully, to not wake Keirr if she was sleeping, and pulled three arrows out of my quiver.

"What are you doing?" Darian whispered.

"Trying to make light."

I heard him sit beside me. "Good." He said it wearily. He was not himself.

Fumbling in the dark, I sliced a substantial piece of fabric off the hem of my jerkin. I pulled the wick out of the lantern—it was bone dry—and stuffed my fabric into the opening. Then I turned the lantern upside down.

"What are you doing?"

"I'm sopping the last of the oil out of the lantern."

There was just enough oil to dampen the fabric, which I wrapped around the wick. Then I placed the fletched ends of the three arrows around it and guided Darian's hand to the shafts, where he could hold them in place. Some torn strips from my shirt kept the arrow shafts together just above and below his hand.

"Isn't going to work," he said. "You can't light oil without a flame."

"I have flint and steel." I sighed. "In the bottom of my pack, under the baby."

Darian sighed too. "We have to have it. Give me more arrows and your knife. We need kindling."

"How did you start the fire in the tunnel last night?"

"Two sticks and friction. It took me hours, and I rubbed my hands raw."

Malik's panting and chuffing grew louder.

"We have to hurry," I said.

He started whittling slivers of wood from an arrow shaft. "Flint and steel," he said.

I slipped my arms out of the pack straps and gently turned around, slipping one hand under Keirr's chin. She awoke with a chirp. "Sorry, baby!" I petted her nose and chin and scratched behind her ear frills. She purred quietly for a moment, and then said, "Mowp?"

Whittling noises continued as I loosened the drawstring and eased my arm into the pack, feeling down between the blanket and the bag, past her little body toward the bottom. She started to struggle. With my other hand I kept the top of the bag open only enough for her neck and my arm. She raked me inside the sack with her little talons, despite the blanket.

"Ow! *Blazes*, little thing!"

I encountered one of the potatoes, pulled it out, and set it beside me where I could find it again in the dark. Then I reached back in and felt around until I found the flint and steel in its little leather sack.

"Here it is." I held it out until Darian's hand found it and took it from me.

"Mowp?"

"Yes! Yes, I'm getting it . . ." I located the potato again and smashed it against the stone. Then I held pieces up one by one for Keirr to nibble out of my hand.

Malik's growls grew closer, and Keirr honked her *poppa*-word again.

"*Keirr*," said a very large voice, from no more than a hundred yards away. Not a roar, but spoken like a word again, as when he'd touched her nose through the bars of the cage. It was followed by grunts and whuffs that might also have been dragon words.

"Hurry!"

Darian struck steel on flint, and the spark showed wood shavings and short sections of arrow shaft between the fletchings around cloth and wick. He struck again, and I looked back down our trail. He struck a third time, and I saw Malik's good eye reflected back. He growled low. He was too close.

"Hurry!"

He struck again, and a spark stuck in the whittlings. He bent down to blow on it.

"Avar, Darian."

He ignored me, blowing gently. A flame sprang up, and he nursed it with his breath. Suddenly the oil caught, and our makeshift torch sprang to life.

"Let's go!" he said.

I grabbed the pack straps and hoisted Keirr onto my back again, then helped Darian upright. He limped desperately, cursing. Keirr cried plaintively on my back.

Malik's single eye shined back at me from no more than fifty yards away. It bobbed up and down with his stride. He wasn't charging. That was good. But it meant he was pacing himself.

"We have to move *faster*," I said.

"This light isn't going to last long."

"Just move!"

"Mowp?"

"*Baby . . . wait.*"

We labored on, and the chasm began to narrow. Echoes were sharper, more tightly spaced. The path began to climb again, clearly the handiwork of men.

It became a numbing rhythm: climb a step, help Darian up, listen for Malik—whuffing still, grunting in pain. He seemed to be gaining until we reached the top of a stair and found another flat stretch, and then his sounds faded as he struggled up behind us. Darian pulled pieces of arrow shaft out of his pocket from time to time and poked them into the end of the torch to keep it going. The fletchings were long gone, the wick and fabric nearly consumed. Meanwhile, the tramping of feet grew louder.

"There's light ahead," Darian gasped. I looked up. He was right. Beyond the next stair, past a cluster of misshapen columns, a faint blue glow illuminated the misty cavern air.

"Is it daylight?"

"*I hope so.*" His voice was a pained whisper.

The torch began to gutter. I looked ahead to get a lay of the trail as best I could, in case we were suddenly fumbling in darkness. There was a switchback ahead, and another steep stair to climb. I groaned.

Right before the turn, we came upon a large black lump. The donkeys, still strapped to the tongue of the cart, lay broken and dead in the trail. My heart sank. They had tumbled from the stair above, unable to negotiate the incline, bound together as they were. One had fallen and pulled the other with it. *"Damn it."* Tears brimmed in my eyes. I was exhausted, but I'd dared to hope for a little bit of good luck.

"Take some meat," Darian said.

"What?"

"Quickly. Feast that baby so she'll shut up."

He was right. I took my knife to a haunch, flayed the skin back, and carved off a big chunk of thigh, while Darian squatted down on his good leg, wounded leg stretched out in front, his head laid back against the wall. With nothing else to put it in, I wrapped the meat in my jacket. Keirr complained the entire time.

Malik whuffed from the darkness. He was getting very close. The makeshift torch suddenly died. The last lumps of glowing cinder fell out of the embrace of the three blackened arrow shafts and winked out.

"Donkey dung," said Darian.

I laughed briefly through my fear, and helped him up. "Careful— we'll have to feel our way past this bend. But there's light ahead, up this stair."

Our eyes adjusted quickly to the glow from above. It was the equivalent of starlight, not easy to see by, but enough. I understood why Malik hadn't gained on us—his progress had been made in the dark, with only one good eye. He'd kept up with us, fumbling every step of the way, following only his nose. When we reached the light above, would he catch up to us?

"Faster." I helped Darian up another step.

He groaned.

"Mowp?"

"*Shhh,* baby. Hang on a little longer."

We climbed. Shortly I felt movement and heard crunching noises from the knapsack. Keirr had pulled her head back inside the bag and found the other potato. *Oh, good girl . . .*

The top of the stair ended in a platform before one more switchback. By the glow from beyond, I could see that Darian's cheeks were hollow, his eyes sunken. I looked back the way we had come, and though Malik was invisible, I still heard his labors somewhere below.

In the distance behind us bobbed the orange glow of lanterns or torches, and I realized that the tramping of Harodhi feet had become louder. The soldiers appeared between columns for an instant, close enough to make out figures and the flashing of weapons.

"Oh *High Ones*, Darian, they're getting closer."

We took the first step, and he winced, gritting his teeth and panting. He tried to hop to the next step, but stumbled and nearly fell.

"I'm sorry, Maia," he whispered.

"Don't apologize," I gasped. "Concentrate."

I heard water ahead, falling in a steady stream. Not a large stream by the sound of it, but enough to make splashing sounds.

As we took the stairs, Darian paused at each step to get his good leg under him. When we reached the top landing, both of us collapsed in exhaustion.

"A little farther." I summoned what little strength I had left and helped Darian up again, lured on by the promise of a drink. We approached the columns at the top of the stair. Some were manmade, straight and fluted like the ruins in Cinvat; the rest were natural spires that seemed to pour from the roof and spill down the slope like frozen waterfalls.

I hoped to pass through to a view of daylight, but what I found took my breath away. A huge, circular chamber had been hewn out of a natural cavern eighty or a hundred feet across, fifty or more feet tall. It was ringed with eight colossal fluted columns, some still standing clear, some vanishing into ropy waxen pillars. Ornately carved leaf and dragon motifs decorated foot and crown and filled a central flute between. Stone stairs climbed up or down between every pair of pillars, vanishing into black passageways. Four in all. The floor was strewn with bones of animals and dragons, and littered with boulders and shards from the ceiling. The ornately paved floor had been shattered where they fell.

A low wall carved to resemble flower petals contained a pool some forty feet across in the heart of the chamber. A stream of water fell from the ceiling above to splash and dribble on a cluster of giant blue crystals in the pool's center. These were the source of the eerie blue phosphorescence that filled the room. Time had encased them in an ornate, natural latticework of semi-transparent blue and green stone.

It was beautiful, strange, and mesmerizing. But which exit would we choose? How would we decide before Malik or the Harodhi arrived? The many bones suggested that an exit was near. But which passage? The wheel track continued on across the chamber to the right, toward an opening that went down into black oblivion. Was that the right choice? Or would that lead us to *Harodhi-land*, as Darian had put it?

Tears of exasperation stung my eyes. Darian could barely keep up with me as I led him into the vast room. Keirr's weight dragged at my shoulders. I ached from head to toe.

Between the pillars were carvings, depicting things I would never have imagined. Geysers of carved smoke rose above armies in advance. Men in bizarre, jointed armor assaulted towering buildings of peculiar seamless architecture. Strange airborne machinery did battle with dragons of magnificent proportion and breed. The water rippling over the blue crystals caused the light to shimmer, giving the carvings an illusion of movement. In my weariness, I couldn't take it all in. My brain was numb, and I had one thought: Water.

I stumbled to the pool and collapsed at its edge. Keirr complained at being bent over as I dipped my hands into the pool and drank deeply. It tasted of minerals and stone, but it was cold and wet. Darian hopped up next to me and fell with his chest atop the low ornate wall. He drank noisily as I lowered Keirr off my back and dipped water out for her, too.

Over the fall and splash of water, I heard whuffing and snarls. I looked up, but Malik wasn't in sight. Not yet.

"Darian, we can't stay here."

He lay panting next to the pool wall. "I can't."

"We have to go, Darian."

"I can't." He slumped down even more.

I struggled to my feet, grabbed his collar and pulled, but he made no effort to rise. I burst into tears. "*Damn* it, Dare."

He looked up at me with a face drawn and pale, eyes like ghosts. "I'm sorry, Maia."

I dropped next to him, my arms around him, weeping.

He gripped my hands weakly.

Keirr cried in my knapsack. "Mowp?"

It was endearing, but so single-minded that I didn't know whether to laugh or cry. So I laughed through my tears. I released Darian, then dragged my jacket closer and opened it. The donkey meat had soaked the leather with blood. I opened the drawstring on the knapsack and let Keirr scramble out. She went straight to the meat and started licking it. I sliced pieces off with my knife to feed to her. She devoured them hungrily. At the same time, I pulled a strip of venison out of a pocket and took a bite, then found another and held it out to Darian. Our last. "Dare. Take this. You need it."

He didn't take it.

"Darian?"

I looked over at him in panic, thinking that he had passed out or had even died. But he was staring at something with wide eyes. I followed his gaze to the wall above the passage where we had entered. There was a single carving.

"It's *Getig*," rasped Darian, in awe.

My breath caught in my throat. There was no mistaking him—the twisted horns like gnarled trees, the tall, elegant neck frill, the proud posture, even his immense scale next to the carved human supplicants at his feet—all were accurate. Carved by the people of Cinvat, long, long ago.

The memory of Getig's molten gaze flooded me with sudden warmth. Once again I felt an overwhelming sense of the enormity of creation and my tiny place in it, the essence of the Summer Dragon that had eluded my recall. It seemed so easy now that I wept tears of shame for having ever lost that memory.

I looked around the room again. Above each of the four passages was another magnificent dragon of noble aspect. Clearly High Dragons, by their regal bearing and massive scale. Each was different; the one to the right had great stag-like antlers instead of horns, its frills and wings with edges scalloped like oak leaves. The one to the left was slender and lithe, with a graceful bearing and smooth features. The one opposite Getig was the largest, yet it had been carved in such a way that it appeared almost insubstantial. Background elements showed through it, the wings trailed away into clouds. Of the four, it was the only one that looked out of the carving directly at the viewer.

"Waeges, Menog, and Oestara." I named them from right to left. "Autumn, Winter, and Spring."

"What does it mean?" he whispered.

"I don't know." I could barely speak.

Keirr nuzzled my hands, looking for another pre-cut piece of meat, drawing me back to the moment. I sliced a bit off and fed it to her. I finished my plank of venison and continued to portion out the donkey meat to my wilding baby until, at last, she seemed satisfied. All but a few bites were gone. She came to me and put her nose in my face. She licked my lips.

I was so weary and overwhelmed that at first I didn't realize what she wanted. But it soon came to me. It was simple. When wilding dragons finish a kill, they groom each other. She was licking my face to clean it of blood. If I were Keirr's mother, I would do the same in return. And so, with tears in my eyes, I took her little head in my hands and kissed her nose as if I was a dragon dam and she was my qit. I kissed her mouth. I kissed her chin and tasted the blood that had dribbled there. I wept, and she licked the salty tears from my cheeks. I dipped some water from the pool and washed her face with my hands. She started to purr, and almost without thought I purred in response. Then I folded her into my arms and hugged her, stroking her cheeks and scratching behind her ear frills. I continued to kiss her lips and chin and nose, cherishing every second of connection, because I now knew what I had to do.

Darian was losing blood and could be dying. I could not rescue him, carry this baby out of here, and contend with Malik too. I was responsible for Darian's injuries. Whatever else happened, I needed to get Darian out of here, and I couldn't manage all three of them. I had to give Keirr back to her father and save my brother's life.

It meant going to Avigal with Bellua, agreeing that I was cursed and that Getig had spurned me. But there was no other option left. Things had changed. I couldn't save Keirr and Darian both. I was out of strength, and Darian was running out of time.

I held her close and sobbed. She licked my ear, since my face was pressed into her smoothly pebbled neck. She made no sound as my shoulders shook with anguish.

"Maia," said Darian.

His hand slapped my shoulder weakly. "Maia!" With urgency.

I opened my eyes. Malik stood twenty feet away.

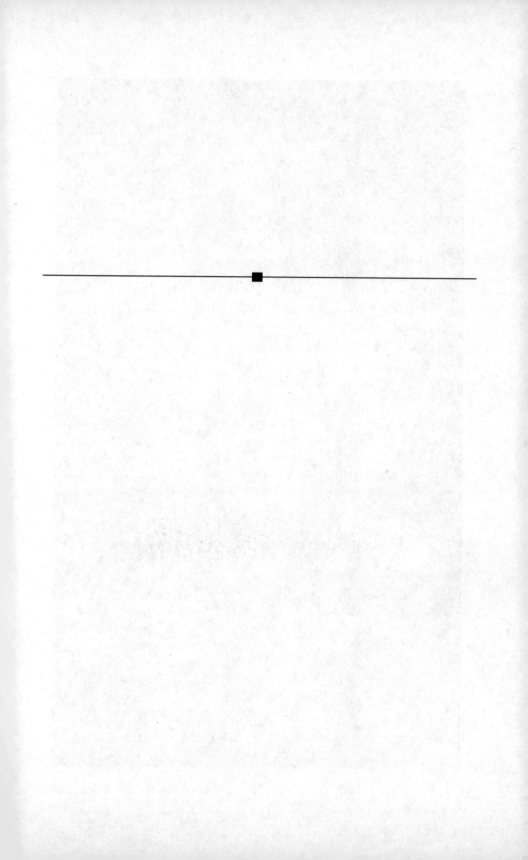

A N I N S T I N C T B U R I E D in exhaustion told me to run, but I
held my breath instead, frozen in numb anticipation. How long
had he been watching me?

Keirr cocked her head at me quizzically.

"Maia!" Darian scrabbled backward weakly. "You have to run."

If there was reason to run, it was already too late. I would never
get Darian up in time.

"Leave *me* and go!" he said, as if reading my mind.

I shook my head slowly.

Keirr turned and, spotting her poppa, bounced joyfully over to
him. Her chirps and playful barks were more than I could ever hope
to learn and repeat, the sounds of a happy, sated qit with energy to
burn. He lowered his head to greet her, accepting her playful swats
and swipes in silence. She stood on her back legs to reach his muzzle
and licked his nose happily. Though his lips were burned, he returned
her affectionate kisses and allowed her rambunctious greeting to
blunder against the wounds in his legs. He kept his head lowered, and
licked at her face and ear frills whenever she came near his mouth.
She was clearly delighted to have her poppa back, and she wanted to
be entertained. But the chuffing noise that rattled deep in his chest
indicated that he was in anguish, even during this joyous reunion. He
closed his good eye, and did not move either to rebuff or encourage
her play.

Keirr bounced back to me, crawled into my lap, licked at the donkey meat lying on my jacket, and *mowped* happily. Then she snagged
the last remaining chunk of meat and trotted over to Malik with it in

her mouth. She dropped it in front of him and danced around it excitedly. Her playful enthusiasm brought a lump to my throat.

"Keirr," he said, quietly. She pounced on his right paw, chased her tail for a turn, then pounced on his other paw in an effort to draw a response.

"Keirr," he said again. Then, "Mfff [purrrr]."

She skipped over to his lowered head and raised her nose to his. He rubbed his chin against her cheek, and she licked his bloody lips. "Mfff [purrrrrr] [rumble]," he said. She sat and looked up at him, and I allowed myself to breathe.

Malik looked at his wounds, and at his little Keirr, and at Darian. Then he fixed me with his remaining eye, breathing shallowly and painfully. I met his silver gaze at last, without fear. He studied me long and hard, unblinking. His ruined face was impossible to read, but he no longer snarled or whuffed with menace. He seemed to be waiting for me to do or say something.

My brain was a weary tumult of frustration and sadness, embroiled with thoughts of Mother and Father and family, Mabir and Bellua, foreign poachers and Horrors. All the events of the last few days spiraled into this moment, in this strange blue-lit room with High Dragons looking down from the walls. I was exhausted, ready to accept whatever fate had been ordained for me.

"She belongs to you," I said finally, my voice cracking. "I'm sorry." I could barely whisper. "I'm sorry for your loss and pain. I wish I could help you."

The tramping of Harodhi soldiers echoed up from the cavern beyond, and orange light tinted the air. Malik turned his head in that direction, then back to me. He closed his eye and hung his head low. Keirr rubbed her cheek against his chin. He keened sadly, quietly, as our dams had done the night of Brood Day. Then he rumbled softly to his qit, and she looked at me. He rumbled again and her ear frills and wings drooped. He licked her face and rumbled one more time.

She came to me, slowly, her silver eyes wide, and crawled into my lap. She looked back at her poppa and keened almost inaudibly.

Malik picked up the piece of donkey meat at his feet and walked over to us, his tattered face mere inches from mine. He dropped it on my jacket and licked his qitling's face one last time.

I could barely believe what was happening. Malik knew how badly he was hurt, could feel his strength ebbing. He knew that he would be unable to care for his qit. He had reached a decision much like mine.

Tears streamed down my cheeks, and I struggled to find my voice. "I promise . . ." My words caught as I swallowed the lump in my throat. "I promise I will take good care of your little Keirr." I looked him in the eye.

His mangled head dipped slightly, as if in acknowledgment, and then he turned away. His baby cried after him, but he limped painfully across the chamber toward the far exit, leaving a trail of bloody footprints as the sounds of pursuit grew louder. Then he stopped and looked over his shoulder at us. "Mfff."

"Maia." Darian propped himself up on his hands. There were tears in his eyes, too. "We have to go."

I wrapped my arms around Keirr to gently pin her wings to her sides again, then worked my knapsack up around her. I put the meat in with her, pulled the drawstring, and stood. I left the blanket and my jacket on the floor, and held out an arm to Darian. He gripped my wrist, and I pulled him to his feet.

Malik waited until we were but a few feet behind him, and then he led us into the far passage, beneath Menog, the Winter Dragon.

I paused once to look back at the carving over the opposite door, the door by which we had entered. In the rippling blue light, the Summer Dragon seemed poised to take wing.

———

Malik took the lead, and we followed him up a dark stair, the glow from the chamber of High Dragons fading behind us. We passed branching tunnels that led up or down into abysmal darkness, but Malik seemed certain in his path. Finally it struck me that he knew his way. He had been here before.

Darian struggled, his eyes closed, his mouth set in grim determination. He could barely put weight on his left leg, and hopped along painfully. As the darkness grew more complete, I was only able to manage because the steps were man-made, regular, and shallow, and because I could follow Malik's labored breathing ahead. My legs burned, my back ached. Several times Darian stumbled, and in catching him I bumped the arrow in his leg. I worried each time that I'd aggravated the injury, or that his gasps of pain would alert the Harodhi following us. Though she didn't struggle or try to claw her way out, Keirr's movements in my knapsack frequently threatened to pull me off balance.

I became delirious with pain and exhaustion, but I forced myself to keep moving. Darian and Malik had it far worse, and both were depending on me. I tried to distract myself by figuring out where we might be. I guessed that we had turned westward in the great cavern before we'd come to the chamber of the High Dragons. If we found an exit, we might well be viewing a sunset from the opposite side of the ridge that separated Riat from the far valley. We would be very far from home in a dangerous wilderness full of predators.

I dropped that line of thought—it only led to more hopelessness. Instead, I focused on the next step, and the next step, and the step after that.

The echoing rattle of armor and tramping feet was louder, and I realized that I could see by thin orange light. I turned to look back down the long, straight stair. Torches bobbed in the distance.

"Darian, hang on," I rasped. He said nothing, but squeezed my arm weakly.

I climbed with renewed purpose, terrified, and hoped that they couldn't hear us over their own din, or see us past their flickering lights. Darian concentrated on maintaining his balance, so I supported him as best I could.

But they were gaining. Malik grunted and wheezed ahead of us, and we followed, laboring in a nightmare of fear and pain. A stone turned my foot. I collapsed with a grunt, cracking my shins on the stair, and Darian cried out, clutching his leg. Keirr screeched once— only once. But it was enough to alert our pursuers. Shouts echoed up to us, and their tramping became a raucous clatter. Fear propelled me to my feet and gave me the strength to haul Darian up again. I threw his arm over my shoulders, reached around to grab him by the belt, and lifted him off the ground. I carried him that way up ten or twenty steps, until suddenly, mercifully, the floor leveled off and continued on a straight and level course. I shuffled forward, on the verge of collapsing, until I realized that I could no longer hear Malik.

I halted, setting Darian down so that he could lean against me as I gasped for breath. Keirr keened at my back. The landing now obscured my sight of the Harodhi on the stairs below, but their clamor grew louder and the aura from their lights bobbed closer and closer. I pulled a crossbow off my shoulder and stuck my toes in the foot strap to cock it. My arms were so weary that I barely managed to pull it taut. Torches and then heads appeared over the top step, coming quickly, as I fumbled to position a quarrel in the groove.

"*Damn it,*" I hissed. By their light I could now see a passage intersecting this one on either side, at the top of the landing. I'd passed right by the openings. Did Malik take one of those paths?

Eight or ten soldiers poured over the lip of the stair. One pointed at the floor, where Malik's blood trail shined in their light, leading this way. Was he so far ahead of me that I'd lost him? Another pointed at me and shouted, and there was an exultant cry. I loosed, and was rewarded with a scream, but now they kneeled to cock their own weapons.

"Oh, sweet Avar, *Darian . . . I'm sorry.*"

Malik suddenly burst from the passage on the left and charged through their ranks, clawing and biting. They screamed and scattered. Two fled shrieking down the stairs, but the rest scrambled to escape talons or teeth. He swatted them like insects, grabbed them in his jaws and hurled them into the wall, or flung them headlong down the stair. At last only two remained. As one attempted to finish cocking his crossbow, Malik raked downward with a big paw and drove him into the floor. The other crawled, wounded, toward the passage on the right. Malik simply stepped on him, bent down, and crushed the man's spine in his jaws. The wily old predator had doubled back in the dark to ambush them, using us as bait.

Shaking, I slung my bow again. "I'll be right back, Dare. I'm going to grab one of those torches."

Malik still waited at the top of the stair, watching down the way we had come. As I picked up one of the Harodhi torches, I peeked over the lip. There were more lights approaching from below.

I hurried back to Darian and helped him up. "Hold this," I said.

He took the torch without comment, and we staggered forward. Malik followed behind, looking often over his shoulder with his good eye.

We made better time with the way lit before us, but the sounds of pursuit were growing louder, and much too quickly.

"Light," said Darian. He pointed with the torch. "Light! There!"

Fifty yards ahead were ascending steps, illuminated with the cool blue light of day filtering down from somewhere above. The litter of bones on the floor grew thicker, indicating that an exit was near. Now alerted to it, I could smell pines and feel fresh air in my lungs.

Relief flooded me, giving me strength. Darian felt it too and dared to test his bad leg again in order to help.

"Blessed Avar! We're going to make it, Dare! Hang on!" He set his jaw and wrenched his tired body into action beside me. We lurched to the stairs. Malik joined us, and we climbed slowly, too slowly, toward the light.

Shouts sounded behind us, and bows cracked. I ducked, looking back, but Malik had spread his wings as a shield. A pair of bolts pierced his wing membranes to chatter off the stairs. Others struck him with sickening thuds, and he roared in pain.

"*Come on, Darian!*" I dragged him backward up the steps, panting. Malik turned, shielding us with his body and backing up, growling.

We reached the top step and saw daylight. The hall to the outside had collapsed in several places, and giant boulders sheltering dozens of abandoned dragons' nests cluttered the way, but the path was open. Glorious, blinding sunlight streamed in. We picked up our pace, negotiating bones and rubble in a stumbling dash for freedom.

In the dark behind us crossbows sang, Malik roared, and men screamed.

Suddenly, one of the boulders at the mouth of the cave moved. A head snaked up, emanating a sickly green light, and two tattered wings unfurled. As the Horror stood up, the dragon of the Harodhi leader stretched its wings and rose behind it. They'd been waiting for us.

THE BLOOD DRAINED from my face as I staggered to a halt. Darian sagged against me. *"Korruzon, pissing blood . . ."*

The Harodhi leader barked an order, and the Horror started forward. Malik had ripped huge chunks of flesh from the Horror's legs and neck, wounds that now glowed with sickly green light like vents in some outlandish, walking furnace.

I nearly pulled Darian over in my effort to retreat. He stumbled with a cry, and I tripped on him, caught myself, but then lurched backward off-balance into a giant, crumbling dragon's nest. Keirr grunted at the impact.

It was hopeless. We could never outrun this monster, and there were soldiers closing behind us. We were trapped.

I staggered between Darian and the Horror and stepped into my crossbow to draw it, shaking. Keirr bleated in terror, ending with her poppa-honk at volume in my ear.

Bracing myself, I loaded a quarrel into my bow, aimed, and loosed. It careened harmlessly off the eyeless helmet of the Horror-dragon. The rider raised his crossbow and leveled it in my direction. His non-eyes glowed balefully from the holes in his burned face, sighting down the shaft of the arrow. I stopped breathing.

Darian's bow snapped, and his bolt struck the rider in the chest just as the rider loosed; the Horror's quarrel went wide, lodging in the nest beside us.

Keirr squawked. I gasped in amazed relief at Darian's shot.

The monster looked down at the arrow in his chest. It was a strike that would have felled an ordinary man, but the Horror simply looked up, cocked his bow, and drew another arrow from the quiver at his belt.

I dropped to my knees, stunned.

The Horrors advanced. Keirr scrabbled at the drawstrings of my knapsack, screeching in fear. Darian wrestled with his bow in front of me, as the Horror-rider put me in his sights again.

Suddenly Malik's giant form flew over our heads to land with a bellow in front of us. He charged with full fury into the Horror and rider, slashing and biting and roaring.

Keirr squawked and tore at the knapsack. One forelimb emerged below the drawstring to rake at my shoulder.

"Baby, NO!" I shouted, but the words meant nothing to her. I backed against the nest, effectively pinning her, and cocked my bow again. Shouts from behind reminded me that we were surrounded. I loaded another arrow and peeked around the nest. At least half a dozen Harodhi warriors twenty yards away spotted me and raised their crossbows. I recoiled as arrows cracked and splintered on the boulders around me. I took a deep breath and looked around the nest again, this time down the length of an arrow. At the first target, I loosed, but missed, then retreated again. No answering shots came— they must have all been reloading, indicating a breakdown in the discipline they had used on Malik before.

"Maia!" When I turned my head, Darian thrust his bow at me, loaded and ready to shoot. I passed my spent bow to him.

I glanced around the nest again to see that the Harodhi had all taken cover.

Malik and the Horror battled in frenzied fury. Talons slashed through the air. Where the Horror struck, Malik's blood sprayed. Where Malik connected, chunks of black flesh crumbled like coal, leaving glowing holes. The savagery of his initial assault had driven the Horror back, but now Malik gave ground, backing toward us, stumbling and clawing to maintain position. I marveled at the ferocity of his attack, given the extent of his damage, but I realized that his strategy had changed: he didn't expect to survive. He held nothing in reserve. This was his last stand.

"Look out!" Darian's cry turned my head. A Harodhi soldier mounted the boulder to my left, raising a sword to strike. Darian's arrow caught him under the chin and spun him over backward. Then Darian hopped backward to another boulder that might offer him better cover. I retreated to join him.

"This is it, Darian. We have to get out of here soon."

"How?" He gritted his teeth in pain. "That thing is blocking the way." His face was frighteningly pale. A trail of blood had followed him across the sandy floor. But he cocked his bow and reloaded it.

He was right. We had nowhere to go, and even if we could get past one of our attackers, in one direction or the other, we would still be far from home, alone, exhausted, and wounded.

Darian no longer had the torch. I spotted it in the gravel just a few feet away, snatched it up, and thrust it into the nest that had been our cover. The wood was ancient and tinder dry. Smaller twigs and grasses caught fire almost immediately.

"What are you doing?" asked Darian, horrified.

"Covering our rears and *making smoke*." I pulled the torch out again and gripped it together with my crossbow.

Two Harodhi scrambled behind boulders to our left, flanking us. I grabbed Darian by the shirt and pulled him behind another rock. A crossbow bolt whistled past my head.

Darian's bow hung in his hands, and he grimaced in pain. "Are you hit?" I asked in a panic. He shook his head no, pointing at his leg. I took the bow from him and slung the strap over my shoulder.

"This way!" Soot from the torch stung my eyes. Darian hopped and cursed and scrabbled after me, onto a slab of collapsed ceiling that inclined upward, like a broad ledge against the cave wall. It would provide cover from every direction but directly behind us. But as I edged around an ancient nest, Darian slipped and tumbled over the slab's edge, out of my grasp. I grabbed for him, but an arrow smacked next to my arm, sending a shower of dust and pebbles into my eyes. As I recoiled, I heard him land with a grunt out of sight, almost directly beneath Malik's shuffling feet. I screamed his name, but he didn't answer.

Two Harodhi dodged to closer cover, stalking me. I couldn't go after Darian without exposing myself to their bolts. I scrambled backward with one crossbow leveled, the other slapping on my side. Keirr had freed her other foreleg and now hung on my shoulders with her talons, keening into my ear. I was gaining elevation, effectively trapped on a high, canted ledge.

Malik's snarls weakened, his roars taking on a desperate tone. I could neither hear nor see my brother. The leader and his dragon skulked into the cave, seeking a path around his hideous thrall to join battle.

Suddenly I saw Darian hopping and limping in a desperate dash for the outside. The Horror's battle with Malik and the movement of the Harodhi leader had opened a gap. He found a boulder to fall behind, then scrambled out of my sight.

Gods, Darian! Run!

The burning nest erupted into a raging fireball, igniting other nests nearby. Smoke billowed up to the roof of the cave. Desperately, I looked outside, in vain hope of seeing Father and Shuja in the sky. It wasn't enough. I lit another nest as I sidled past it up the incline.

A Harodhi warrior stepped out from cover, his crossbow leveled, looking for me. I loosed and hit him mid-torso, then ducked behind a huge nest on the edge of the rock shelf. It was the last cover remaining to me on this upward climbing ledge. As tall as it was wide, the branches and bones that made up its most ancient base were rotted and crumbling. Dragons had reinforced its decaying structure so many times that it overhung the cave floor below.

I jammed my torch into the base of it close to the lip of the slab, hoping to make more smoke without exposing myself to an inferno.

Malik roared and thudded into the side of the ledge below and to my left. Though he had the Horror's neck in his maw, he couldn't crush the armor. The beast continued to rake Malik's legs and neck. And now the Harodhi leader on his dragon had made his way through the rubble to emerge from the smoke behind Malik.

I spanned my bow and pulled an arrow out of my quiver—my last. Now I had one shot, and then I was helpless. I discarded my empty bow.

Three Harodhi stepped out of cover and crept up the incline toward me. Another appeared further back. They had their wicked curved swords in hand. They were out of arrows too. But then the smaller nest down the slope burst into flame. I lost sight of the soldiers in the plume of fire and sparks. Their shouts told me they had retreated from the searing heat.

The Harodhi leader drove his dappled brown into the fray. It pounced on Malik's right haunch, raking and biting. As Malik roared in fury and pain, the nest erupted into towering flame. A pall of dirty smoke stung my eyes and lungs as the base of the nest settled.

The Harodhi leader was directly beneath it.

I saw a chance. With my arm, I shielded my face from the heat and sat down as near to the nest as I dared. I kicked at the base with my heel, Keirr screaming on my back. Hot cinders shot out of the gaps and sizzled on my skin. The Harodhi leader shouted, looking up at me as I knocked a flaming timber loose from the pile. The nest settled once more with a growl, then collapsed all at once. I scrambled back as the blazing woodpile spilled over the ledge and buried the Harodhi leader in flaming cinders. The Horror pulled back from Malik as the leader's dragon screamed in terror.

Three soldiers charged up the incline of my ledge, through the smoke and flame of the other burning nest. I raised my bow and backed up to the furthest end of the ledge.

There was nothing beyond. The cave opened onto a steep slope that fell away into a stony canyon. I saw Darian outside, lying on a ledge below the porch of the cave floor.

I couldn't jump—the fall would kill me. But Malik was next to the ledge, almost directly below me. With barely a thought, I leapt, mimicking Keirr's *POPPA* honk at the top of my lungs. Little Keirr squealed in fright.

Malik started at the impact when we landed with a grunt on his back. But his good eye fixed on me as I stretched out along his spine.

The dragon Horror lunged at me, its breath stinking of burnt flesh. I fired my last bolt into its glowing maw. It recoiled with a hoarse, gravelly shriek. I dropped the crossbow and threw my arms around Malik's neck. Little Keirr gripped my shoulders with desperate fear. *"Go!"* I shouted, but Malik was already under way.

He sprinted to the lip of the opening and launched into the air with a cry of pain. Vertigo threatened to drag me from my perch as the ground fell away from us all at once. The Horror screeched and leapt after us. I heard the dry crack of its leathery wings. Malik flapped weakly against the arrows in his alar pectorals, keening in pain with each stroke. The world careened madly as he slid sideways, unable to get power from his left wing. I squeezed his neck to keep from sliding forward off his back, and hazarded a look to the rear.

The Horrors were barely a dragon's length beyond the end of Malik's tail, and gaining. The beast gauged Malik's trajectory, climbing to drop on us from above.

"Malik! Fly!"

The Horror sculled above us, rear talons reaching for me as Malik slipped sideways suddenly, screeching in agony. The monster missed and flapped upward, positioning for another strike.

Malik's maneuver had gained us a few seconds, but he lurched and cried out again, unable to flap any longer. The best he could manage was a downward glide.

The earth rushed up at us crazily. Malik spread his wings for a landing but hit the ground hard. I lost my grip, slid down his right wing and off. I stumbled several feet before momentum threw me face-first onto moss and stones. Malik slid forward, tumbled once, and finished on his side, unmoving.

I pushed to my knees in a spinning universe, tried to stand, but collapsed. I was on the side of a mountain, across a valley from the cavern, which spewed a column of dirty brown smoke into the sky.

Good Avar, let Father be nearby, I whispered.

Keirr struggled in the pack behind me—she at least was alive. I started to crawl toward Malik, but the Horror sculled to a landing between us. It too hit the ground hard, its wings in tatters from the fight with Malik. As it straightened and turned toward me, chunks of black flesh crumbled from its legs and neck where Malik had mauled it. Blackened bone and ligaments showed in the holes, green embers fading in the margins. It limped badly, one foot mangled. The rider on its back unlimbered his crossbow and fixed his sickly gaze on me. One arm hung limp at his side, shredded by Malik into a string of bone and dimly glowing ligament. His right leg was in tatters. Darian's bolt still protruded from his chest.

I stood unsurely, trying to find my balance. Keirr squawked and thrashed, threatening to pull me over. I stumbled backward as the

Horror raised his bow and loosed. Nothing happened. He looked at his weapon with the slow deliberation of an imbecile. The bolt had evidently been lost at some point in the battle. Without another arm to aid in loading the crossbow, it had become a useless weapon. He tossed it aside. The impossible beast that was his mount advanced, and I staggered back, fumbling beneath my knapsack for the knife in my belt.

The beast lurched forward, but then stumbled. Its right foreleg came apart all at once. Chunks of burnt meat fell away from charred bones, and the elbow joint separated. The monster crashed onto its chest and squirmed in the bracken and grass, struggling to regain its feet. It screeched, and I caught sight of my arrow, still imbedded in the back of its throat, before a spray of ash erupted from its maw. Green sparks spewed from the numerous rents in its neck. The foliage beneath it curled and blackened, and then the beast collapsed. It stopped moving. The dim green glow in its many open wounds began to fade.

The thing was dead. Finally dead. I didn't realize I'd been holding my breath until I gasped in desperate relief, but then the rider reached down and unbuckled his harness, slid off of his dead mount, fumbled the black sword from his back with his one good arm. He limped toward me, his mangled right leg dropping cinders.

I panted as he stalked toward me steadily, but I stole looks at his mount. They were not invulnerable after all.

I shrugged out of my knapsack, lowering it carefully to the ground. Released the drawstrings so Keirr could scramble out. She staggered at first but then hid behind my legs, keening. I pulled my knife, gripped it in my teeth. A rock the size of my head sat at my feet. I lifted it and pressed it to shoulder height.

The Horror approached with stubborn, mechanical will. I advanced on him, gaining speed. He limped forward with cinders falling out of his torn robes. As he raised his sword, I lifted the stone over my head, darted inside the radius of his swing, and crushed his helmet. Glowing dust splashed out from under it. He glared at me with one non-eye from beneath the ruined helmet and opened his mouth in a rasping hiss.

With a wail of fear, I grabbed at the arrow still protruding from his chest with one hand and wrenched it sideways. With the other hand I took the knife from my teeth and slashed at him. I was now too close for him to use his sword. He dropped it and clutched my arm. His grip burned with unnatural cold. I screamed, but stabbed and slashed frantically. More glowing dust fell from his throat, from his arm, from his cheek.

His robes had fallen away to show leather and steel armor, rent where Malik had ripped him but with no sign of blood. I couldn't tell where armor ended and flesh began. His helmet was riveted to the skull. Serrated cheek guards merged with the flesh. Deep, ragged holes riddled his charred skin. Instead of lips he had only scars, revealing brown and crooked teeth filed to points. He tried to draw me close to them, but I stabbed at his face and neck.

"Why won't you die?" I screamed, stabbing in desperation. Keirr screeched somewhere behind me.

Finally the monster fell to the ground. I fell with him, but I didn't—couldn't—stop stabbing and slashing. Not until arms wrapped around me from behind.

T W E N T Y - F O U R

"**M**AIA! MAIA! STOP! It's all right. Stop!" Father's voice.
I pulled free and tried to stand, but my legs gave way, and
Father caught me. A shadow enveloped me, and I twisted to see Shuja's silhouette limned by the sun. Father wrapped me in his arms again
and knelt beside me. I looked to the sky. I didn't see the Harodhi
leader on his dappled brown dragon, but other dragons circled down
toward us: Rov on his massive Cheien, Jhem on Audax. Bellua, too. I
didn't even know his dragon's name.

Father held me tightly, rocking, his fingers in my hair. His cheek
was moist.

"Darian," I said. My throat was raw from shouting, from inhal-
ing smoke and ash.

"Where is he?"

"Where is Darian?" I echoed, dumbly.

"Maia—where is he?"

"He's outside of the cave. He's hurt." I put a hand to my head,
where a painful throbbing threatened to burst out through my eyes.
Now that fear had left me, all strength seemed to have fallen out of
my body, all sense out of my mind, though a tiny voice, keening, sliced
into my awareness like a blade.

"Keirr . . ." I looked around for her. She was across the field with
her poppa, beyond the dead dragon Horror, licking his face, crying.

Father held me tighter, but he shouted to someone I couldn't see.
"Check outside the cave for Darian!"

"Tauman has him," said Jhem. "I've got her, Magha. Go to your
sons."

My ears were filled with shouts and snapping dragons' wings, then a big shadow wafted down to join us. Father kissed my forehead, then was gone, and Jhem cradled me in her lap. She brushed hair out of my face and looked me over carefully. "That will be a nasty bruise. Avar, girl, but you are a mess."

"Bellua!" yelled Tauman.

"Maia, what have you done?" Jhem's tone was filled with amazement.

"Darian! Darian! Wake up, son!" Father's voice, panicked.

"He's alive," said Tauman. "But he needs help."

"I found my baby," I said to Jhem, matter-of-factly.

"What?" She turned toward Malik, took in the rest of the scene, and her jaw dropped. *"By all the High Ones . . ."* A whisper.

"Maia," Darian moaned. "Where's Maia?"

"She's safe," said Father.

"Blessed Avar," said Darian, a soft exhalation.

"Don't let him lose consciousness." Father's voice again. Concerned, I turned my head to see Father next to Tauman, who cradled Darian in his arms.

"What happened there, Darian?" asked Tauman. "Darian! Stay with me! What happened in the cave?"

Darian winced against the light. "That was Maia."

Father and Tauman looked at each other in surprise.

"Maia?" said Father.

"And the dragon sire."

They looked at me, puzzled.

Darian put an arm across his eyes. "How did you find us?"

"We followed your signal fire," said Tauman.

Father nodded. "That was good work, son."

"That was Maia too," said Darian.

They looked at me again, and Father muttered, "Dear, sweet Avar . . ."

But then Bellua's voice interrupted. "I'm here. Put the boy down." Father and Tauman laid Darian down on soft turf.

"How bad is it?" Father looked scared.

Bellua studied Darian's eyes, felt his neck for the pulse, and probed his body gently. "Bad. He's lost a lot of blood. His boot is full of it. He's lucky to be alive."

"They both are."

"Water," said Darian.

I groaned and pushed up to my knees again, but my head swam. Jhem pulled me closer. She poured some water onto a kerchief and tried to swab my forehead. I pushed her hand away.

"Keirr." I couldn't stand, so I crawled toward Keirr and Malik. They were beyond the dead dragon Horror, which seemed to be crumbling slowly, like a sand sculpture in rain.

Jhem grabbed my arm and pulled me back. "What are you doing?" She sounded terrified.

Malik struggled with long, shallow, rattling breaths, while his baby keened. He was still alive. Was I the only one who could hear them?

Another rush of air announced the arrival of Rov's huge white Cheien. The Dragonry officer dismounted easily. "There's a dead dragon in the cave. One of the Harodhi forest breed, by the look of it. And I think the rider is still in the harness, under a burning pyre."

"You need to see *that*." Father pointed at the Harodhi Horrors on the ground beyond me. But he remained with Darian, folding his jacket under his son's head as Bellua examined the arrow in his leg.

Rov came over to Jhem and me. The dead man-thing lay a few feet away, the dragon Horror a few yards beyond that. Rov stumbled to a halt when he saw the thing at his feet but made no comment.

The sickly green fires had gone out, leaving the blackened husk of what once had been a man. As we watched, it settled, the charred flesh inside the armor crumbling little by little.

When Tauman saw it, he reeled in revulsion. "What in the name of all Holiness is that?" He left Darian's side for a closer look.

"That," said Rov, "is a Horror. Perhaps *now* you understand my urgency."

Father shook his head. "When I was in the Dragonry, we fought men and animals, not these abominations."

"How is such a creature possible?" Tauman said with disgust.

"The forces that conspire against all of creation never rest." Bellua bent over Darian, applying a tourniquet to his leg just below the knee. "I share Captain Rov's sense of urgency, all the more now that the meaning of recent signs has been made so clear."

When the merihem spoke, my skin prickled and shrank. I tried to block his words from my mind. The grisly corpse and the conversation surrounding it had distracted everyone, so I pushed to my feet slowly, testing my legs. I felt better. My head still hurt, but my balance had returned. I started toward Malik and his qit.

"See how death and disaster follow this girl," Bellua said. "Everything she touches is cursed." I didn't have time for him.

"Enough," said Father.

"Every omen said . . ."

"Enough!"

Keirr ran to me, keening, then led me past the dragon Horror, back to her poppa. Life still trembled in his great body.

He lay very still, laboring to breathe. His left wing was crumpled horribly beneath his body. His chin rested on bloodied earth. Crimson trickled from his nose. His good eye hung half open, already glazed over. His body shivered with every inhalation.

Bellua kept talking as he tightened the tourniquet. "I tried to warn you, Broodmaster, but you chose to dismiss my words. Now calamity has visited your aerie."

Keirr keened plaintively. When I knelt next to Malik's head, she climbed into my lap, put her front feet on my shoulders, and looked at me.

"Oh, my poor baby," I whispered.

Bellua's voice was an irritating noise that wouldn't stop. ". . . calamity in the form of this stubborn and disobedient . . ."

Malik's eye opened, the vertical slit of iris struggling to focus. I reached for him.

"Maia!" Father rushed toward me, pulling his bow off his shoulder and nocking an arrow. "What in the name of the Highest are you doing? Get away from there!"

Keirr scooted behind me as I jumped up between Father and Malik with my palms raised. "No!"

Father looked back and forth between Malik and me. "No." I kneeled down again beside Malik.

"Wait, Magha." Jhem placed a hand on Father's arm.

"That's a dangerous, wounded wilding." Father was almost pleading.

"No, he's not." My voice cracked. I reached out again and touched Malik's cheek with my fingers. He didn't flinch or make a sound. Keirr began to lick his nose again. He keened very quietly, deep in his throat. It was long and mournful, and ended with a rattling chuff.

When Father saw Keirr, his face turned white, and he lowered his bow.

"He saved us," I said.

Rov and Tauman joined Father and Jhem, as I stroked Malik's jaw and ear frill. "It's okay, poppa," I whispered. "I will take care of your little Keirr. I promise."

As if in answer, Keirr curled up in my lap, keening, and reached out with a paw to touch her poppa's lip.

Everyone—even Bellua—fell silent, watching.

Malik's eye closed. The solemn hush of the hillside was broken only by the rustling of leaves in a light wind, the creak of leather and scuff of paws on turf, Keirr's quiet distress, and Malik's rattling chuffs. Every breath seemed more difficult than the one before it. His last exhalation was a long, slow keen that ended as a whisper, and then his body relaxed at last, settling with a few quiet, leathery creaks and rustles. I pressed my cheek to his and wept.

No one said a word. Keirr stuck her nose up from under my arm and licked my face. It was a qit's way of asking for comfort, so I drew her close, my head still resting on Malik's, and kissed her nose tearfully.

Footsteps approached, and then Jhem's arm slipped around my shoulder.

"What happened here?" Father's tone was hushed.

"I'll tell you what has happened." Bellua wiped Darian's blood from his fingers with a kerchief. "You have reaped what you've sown. Your stubbornness echoes in your unmanageable daughter. See how death and omens of death follow this girl everywhere she goes."

I could take no more of Bellua's voice eating at my head. I eased Keirr out of my lap and pushed to my feet. "You have to be the first to pass judgment with your poison tongue." I advanced on him, fists clenched at my sides. "But I will tell you what happened. *Getig* led me here, Darian followed, and then this *wilding* saved our lives."

I grabbed the leather scroll case off of my back and fumbled it open. "This. Look at this. I found it in the cave. They were watching us. While you were busy planting your ugly little words in everyone's ears, these monsters were making plans." I ripped the drawing of the aeries out and threw it at Bellua's feet. He didn't even look at it, but Rov picked it up and unfurled it.

I took a step toward Bellua. "You came to our aeries certain that you understood everything, but the Summer Dragon upset your . . . your idea of things, and it scared you. So you twisted everything into . . . into . . . a shape you could control. You spun curses and omens out of thin air to manipulate us. And everybody let you get away with it! No one else, least of all *you*, gave any concern for anything but their own needs and wants." I swiped tears off my cheeks angrily.

"This wild animal showed more bravery and . . . and selflessness than anyone here. And now you're trying to do it again. Something happened that you couldn't control, so you try to tie it up with your words. *Well, you can't.*"

Keirr bumped up against my leg and keened apprehensively. I knelt down and drew her close. "Whether you like it or not, I have a qit now, too."

All eyes dropped down to my baby.

Bellua's mouth opened and closed twice before he found words. "What you have done, clearly, is obtain the last qitling that Captain Rov needs to fill his requisition. Praise to Korruzon! I suggest that you turn the qit over to him now and save yourself worse punishment. Then set your mind to the journey you are about to take with me, to Avigal—"

"I won't go!" I looked around the circle of faces for support. "I have a qit now. The aeries are whole. And Rov has the qits you gave him. This qit is *mine*."

"Captain Rov?" Bellua held out a hand in my direction.

"Father . . ." I said.

Father stared at Keirr with wide eyes, his mouth down-turned and uncertain. When Rov handed the drawings to him, his eyes grew wider still and his hands trembled.

"Are you all blind?" said a weak voice.

Bellua started toward me. I put my arms around Keirr protectively.

"Listen to me!" said the voice again, a bit stronger. It barely sounded like Darian.

With ashen face, Father studied the drawing of the Harodhi spies.

"Can none of you see what is really going on here?"

Finally, everyone paused and looked at my brother. He had propped himself up on one elbow. His face was pale, his cheeks hollow, but his eyes sparked defiantly. "Maia took a qit from a wild dragon, with his blessing, and then rode him to safety. How can any of you fail to see the wonder in that?" He looked from face to face. "She showed courage when I was cowardly. She was resourceful when I was in complete panic. She applied every bit of knowledge about dragons that Father ever taught us in order to communicate with a wilding sire and his baby. She not only saved my life, but she acquired a qit for herself and alerted us all to a Harodhi threat."

"She put your life in peril," Bellua snapped.

"If Maia had obeyed you, that monster lying at our feet would still be in these caves plotting against us, and we would *all* be in peril." Darian winced as he leaned forward. "As far as I can see, the Summer Dragon was here for Maia. Not for me, though I wanted to think so. And not for you. But for *Maia*."

Bellua glowered. "Praise be to Korruzon that he can turn this child's wicked disobedience into a blessing—"

"You *don't get it*. Korruzon didn't use Maia to show us a threat. Getig used the threat *to show you my sister*."

Everyone looked at me suddenly, and a lump grew in my throat as I looked back at my brother. He lay back abruptly with a sigh of pain.

Bellua stared at me longest, his eyes wide with conflicting emotions. Anger, certainly, but also fear and confusion. Finally he started toward me again. "I won't have theological matters explained to me by a—"

Father stepped in front of him. "No, Bellua."

The merihem pulled up with a look of surprise on his face.

"You have been wrong from the beginning," said Father. He pressed the Harodhi drawing into Bellua's hands, then Father looked back at me, and his chin went up. "We've all been wrong. I've certainly had something shown to me, something I should have seen a long time ago. They've already begun to bond. By your own logic, the Most High ordained this moment, but, as Darian says, for Maia."

Jhem's hands gripped my shoulders from behind. I looked back at her. She held her quivering chin high. Tauman came up and put his arms around us. Jhem pulled me closer and leaned into him.

"Maia has a dragon to raise now," said Father. "She won't be going to Avigal with you after all."

Bellua's face was a thunderstorm. "Captain Rov. Your qit." He pointed at Keirr again.

Rov studied me for a long minute, then shook his head slowly. "No. The offspring of such a dragon as this one should breed more like him and not be spent on a battlefield. The aeries need such blood." Then he nodded at me. "And this young woman has more than proved her worth. My requisition can fall short one dragon."

Bellua trembled with barely restrained emotion, but he looked more than a little bit lost as well. He dropped the chart on the ground. "This isn't how it ends, Magha. There must be an investigation to determine how this fits with doctrine. We will go to the source— Korruzon—for the answer." He strode back to his dragon—directly past Darian—and climbed into the saddle. "Bring the boy to the Temple," he said. We watched as his dragon lifted into the sky and wheeled toward Riat.

Father returned to Darian's side. "Jhem, take Darian to Mabir. We'll meet you there." He and Tauman started to lift Darian as Jhem mounted Audax.

"Wait." Darian signaled to me to join them. I went to his side and knelt down close. Little Keirr stuck her head up under my arm.

"I told you that you weren't cursed," he whispered, and he grinned at me, his chin bunched up in pride.

Unable to speak, I mouthed the words, *thank you.*

Father looked at me curiously, but then he and Tauman eased Darian into the saddle in front of Jhem. My brother's smile was replaced with a grimace of pain when they launched. I wasn't done worrying about him.

Rov clapped Father on the shoulder. "The acquisition train will have to finish its journey without me. The Harodhi had designs on your aeries. Expect them to try again. We'll need to investigate these caves and make sure they aren't a liability, and seal them off if they are, then consider how best to defend Riat. I also want to hear the full story from this remarkable young lady. Then I will fly directly to Avigal to get reinforcements for Riat. In the meantime, we should muster up a militia to watch these caves. The Harodhi aren't done here, I guarantee that. They'll be back, and probably soon." He spat on the Horror sprawled in the dirt. "I'll be burning that before I do anything else."

Father nodded, but his face was creased with worry.

Rov looked at me. "Broodmaster, this is no small thing. Harodh was close to a second devastating blow. I believe your daughter may have saved you—all of us—from disaster." He clapped Father on the shoulder again, then picked up the chart and started toward Cheien.

Father came to me, and a smile touched the corners of his mouth. Finally he shook his head slowly and pulled me close for a bear hug.

I wrapped my arms around him and squeezed. Despite myself I wept again, but they were tears of release and of happiness.

When he pulled away, he placed his hands on my shoulders. His face wore a new appraisal. "I want to hear that story too, before Mabir or Bellua or anyone else has a chance to pick it apart. It appears that I owe you more than an apology—in fact, I'm in your debt." He kissed me on the forehead. To my great surprise, a single tear rolled down his cheek. "I've been distracted. I'm ashamed that I didn't realize how much like your mother you really are."

He knelt down to look Keirr in the eye. My baby looked back at him without blinking, and he smiled. "And you, my little friend. Aren't you a wonder? What an unexpected turmoil you caused. What an amazing outcome. And so much for me to think about." He stood and put his arm around my shoulders. "Darian is waiting." Worry lines creased his face once more. "Come on, Maia. Let's get your qitling home."

PART II
The WILDING

GRAEDEN SHOVED THROUGH the crowd surrounding the Dragonry paddock, craning his neck for a better view. Words like *slaughter, massacre,* and *lost cause* fell in whispers around him. He pushed to the railing to see the Dragonry teams as they landed. Three, four, five of them. "Where are the rest?" he asked, alarmed.

A tall man in farrier's clothes turned to him. He paused and spared Grae a stern look. "Don't be stupid, boy. Can't you see that's all that's left?"

Grae felt his throat close with grief. Out of three dozen teams that left this morning to retake the aeries of Cuuloda only these few returned. They'd been weeks gathering their numbers and planning their assault. Graeden's drawings of the layout of his home informed their strategy. He'd sat in on every session, accompanied the scouts on reconnaissance. This failure seemed impossible.

The dragons were slashed on chests and heads. Their wings were in tatters. One bore an extra rider—it could only mean that he'd lost his mount. A half-dozen merihem dashed out to meet them, followed by attendants with stretchers and satchels of gear.

Grae vaulted over the railing and ran to join them. He grabbed a rider by the shoulders and spun him around. "What happened?"

The man's face was slashed across one eye, blood caked on his cheek and in his shirt. "What do you think happened? Get off me." He pushed Grae's hands away.

Men jostled Grae as they passed. A rider collapsed onto a litter, one arm held tight against his chest where the armor had been torn away and only his bloody shirt remained. A dragon crumpled to the ground and his rider leapt down to help a merihem staunch the flow of a gaping wound on its shoulder.

"We have to go back," said Grae, to no one in particular.

"You're in the way, son," said a merihem, shoving Grae aside with hands already covered in blood. Another soldier rushing in from the barracks bumped him, said something angrily that Grae didn't hear. Wheels creaked, and he turned to see a traction rig being rolled out. With nets and manacles, it would immobilize an injured dragon so it could be treated safely.

An arm around his shoulder guided him back toward the rail. He looked to see a big soldier in leather lancer's gear. "I want to help," Grae said.

"You can't help by standing in the way," said the man.

He shrugged the soldier's arm off. "You don't understand. That was my home. That's my aerie. My family. I have to do something."

The man's expression softened, and he sighed. "You're the brood-master's son?"

He nodded. "They wouldn't let me go with them." His chin fell to his chest.

"You'd have died too, son. I'll tell you what you do now. You take your dragon and you enlist in the Dragonry. Get some training. Join a talon. Then kill as many of the Harodhi that created those monsters as you can." The soldier gave him one last shove toward the crowd of onlookers.

Graeden staggered back, his head swimming, eyes blurred with unshed tears. He swung his legs over the rail. Fought his way back out through the mass of people; refugees, many of them. Rejoined his mount, Kiven, waiting obediently outside the Dragonry barracks.

He absently stroked Kiven's neck when the dragon lowered his head. He stared up at the mountains in the direction of the pass through which the defeated teams had returned. The peak blocked his view of the Cuuloda aeries further up the long valley, but the sun was bright on those most distant spires.

His heart pounded and he closed his eyes. His fists clenched at his sides. Yes, that's what he needed to do—murder Harodhi. Make them pay. As many as it took to bring this war to an end.

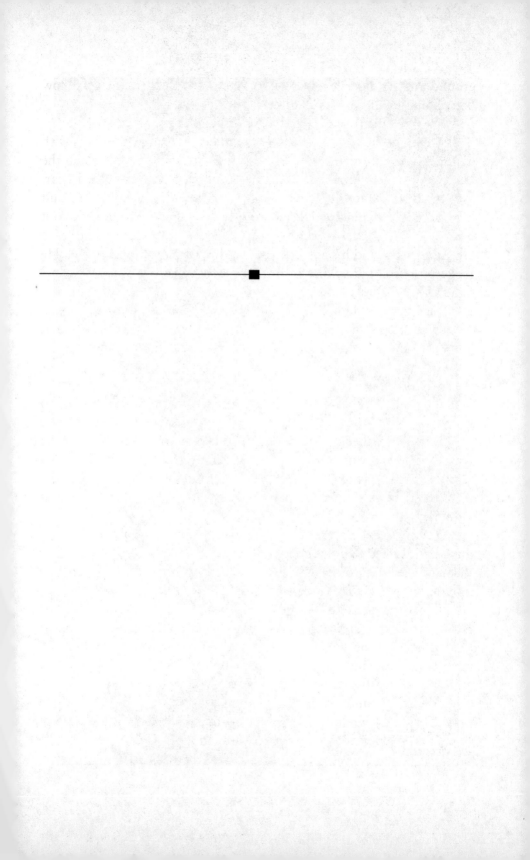

"RELAX, MAIA. Focus on Keirr. Let the pain flow off you."
Mabir sat in a chair behind me in the winter stable, his graving tools arrayed on a table to our right, the broodmothers gathered round. His needle jabbed into the base of my skull like a wasp's sting, but I embraced the pain. I'd been waiting for this day all my life. The bond mark was a rite of passage for every dragon rider. I knew what to expect, yet I couldn't push the pain aside. "I'm sorry. It's not the needle. It's Darian. I can't stop worrying about him."

Mabir touched a cool, damp cloth to my neck. "I understand. We're all worried. But Bellua and I will pull Darian back. It's simply a matter of time. Let's concentrate on your bond mark. Relax. Don't think about Darian or Bellua or anything else. We're nearly done."

When I closed my eyes all I could see was Darian lying still and pale in the Temple, unconscious into his fourth day. His fever ran hot, and Mabir said he mumbled constantly in a strange delirium. I took a deep breath. "Darian followed *me*. He would be all right if I hadn't—"

"Maia, Maia, Maia." Mabir swabbed my neck with something that stung. "The Wisdom of Haom says, *There is no future in the past.* You acted with initiative and courage. Good has come of it, with the exception of this strange wound in Darian's leg that doesn't want to heal."

Good *had* come of it. I looked down at Keirr, curled up at my feet, tiny snout under leathery wing. After four days in the aeries, the skin of her cream-colored belly was stretched drum-tight and her ribs no longer showed. I reached down to lightly brush the matching bond mark at the base of her skull, and she whuffed a deep, contented sigh. The scabs were already falling off. Baby dragons heal so quickly!

When we started work on Keirr's bond mark the day after her arrival in the aeries, I held her tight and hummed a tune Mabir taught me. The old dhalla's gentle touch and his voice harmonizing with mine had calmed her. I started humming it now, in hopes that it would calm *me*.

"Good, Maia. That's right." Mabir harmonized and adjusted his tempo ever so slightly to gather my voice into the ritual.

I concentrated on the calming tune, and little Keirr responded in her sleep with a sustained, harmonizing tone. Dragons love music, and this music resonated in her bond mark. Grus joined in quietly, then Athys and Coluver. A soothing energy washed over me.

Mabir hummed quietly, the tap-tap-tapping of his tools in my neck point and counterpoint to the beating of my heart. Occasionally he dropped into a chant as the rhythm of his tapping changed, or spoke in a monotone as he switched tools. It wasn't idle noise, but part of the ritual somehow. I listened to his voice, ancient and pleasant, and willed myself to sink into the strange concert of music, rhythmic pain, and bone-deep ecstasy that seemed to ebb and flow with the cadence of his work. Keirr's blood and mine were mixed into the ink he used. This was Temple Science, the ritual graving art of the Rasaal that bound dragon and rider together. When I concentrated, I could feel the tempos merge in a curiously soothing way, as if each tap knitted our bond a little tighter. My heart tied to hers, and hers to mine.

I would wear the mark proudly, of course, but it almost seemed unnecessary. Keirr and I started to bond from the moment I met her. Our experience in the caverns together was a more powerful link than any the dhalla could draw in our skin. I still woke every night from dreams of burnt monsters chasing us, to find Keirr crying in her sleep beside me.

There were moments when memory overwhelmed me, especially if I was alone. I would try to concentrate on good memories, of mother laughing at something I said, or flying with Father through cloudless skies with the wind in my hair. But soon anxiety would creep beneath the joy, like spiders under a worn but beautiful tapestry, and then images of dead things would erupt and tear the fabric: walking carrion, pale men with arrows—my arrows—thudding into their bodies, a human torch, dragon babies crawling with flies, barrels blackened with dried dragon blood, flames and darkness and—

"Maia! Relax."

I shivered and let go my breath.

Darian's qit, Aru, lay next to me, a deep coppery color, almost black, with lighter copper markings on his shoulders. I could talk about this, at least, without choking up. "Aru is really unhappy. He whimpers through the nights, and he doesn't eat enough. He shadowed Keirr and me all day yesterday, but he isn't his usual playful self. He needs Darian. He needs the last ring in his bond mark."

Mabir touched the cooling cloth to my neck. "Yes, it leaves him with a deep wanting. He senses your bond mark in the making and is drawn to it. But we have to wait until Darian is ready. Bellua has graved deep healing into his wound, but it remains angry and red. I fear that he may lose that leg before we save his life."

"Father told me." Mabir returned to his needles, and the stinging resumed. He took up the melody once more. Aru whimpered, pushing his head into my hand. "But what about Darian? Won't his half-finished mark leave him with a wanting too?"

Mabir pressed something cold and pungent to my neck. I winced and turned. His face was somber, but when his eyes met mine, he smiled. "We're done. Your mark is finished." I touched cool dampness at the back of my neck, where Mabir had applied a thin poultice.

He took my hand in his and met my eyes, looking back and forth between them. But he didn't answer. *What aren't you telling me?* Finally he squeezed my hand, then let it go. "Let me worry about Darian. You have an important task to perform now. I know it will be very hard for you, but you must love this baby with all your heart, and show her that she is the light of your life." He smiled at his little joke, and I couldn't help but smile back. I felt a moment of joy. It was done. Keirr and I were bonded.

"If you still have any doubt that the Summer Dragon's appearance marked a turning point in your life, banish it now. With this mark, your life *has* changed. I know that you feel the weight of rules and expectations—all young adults do. But this bond will define you for years and years to come. It will shape your understanding of freedom, and commitment, and friendship. It may take you to places you never imagined you would go and reveal your inner self to you in unexpected ways."

He smiled again. "This strikes you as a lot of ceremonial gibberish, I can see. But in ordinary times we would make much of this occasion—Tauman received his final marks in the Temple, and we celebrated for two days afterward. When your brother is well, we'll have a proper celebration, I promise. The important thing is that you understand the solemnity of the bond, and raise your baby with love and trust."

He squeezed my shoulder gently. "But of course you will do that." His eyes twinkled out of the creases made by his smile. Mabir seemed younger in that moment, as if the weight of his long years had been lifted.

He stood and rubbed his hands briskly together. "I need to get back to the Temple to see how your brother is doing. Fren's bandages need changing, as well. He's still delirious with pain, but his fever has begun to drop."

That *was* good news. But to be completely free of the weight of Bellua's bad omens, I needed for everyone to emerge whole, Fren included. And most importantly Darian.

"Dhalla, what happens if Darian's bond mark isn't finished in time? Can it fail?"

He turned and began to wipe his needles down with alcohol one at a time, ordering them in a folding leather case on the table beside him.

"Dhalla, will Darian's bond mark fail if we wait too long to finish?" I pressed.

He practically stabbed the last needle into the case. "It might. Yes."

"And what will happen to Aru if it does?"

We both knew the answer to that question. "We will lose him. He will have to be destroyed."

My blood pounded in my ears, and for a moment I felt faint. My hand involuntarily clenched on Aru's back and he squirmed under my fingers. I looked down at him, throat tight, and caressed his head in apology. His eyes were open, but he stared vacantly at nothing, ear frills drooping. Darian's injury and Aru's plight twisted in my gut. "You have to finish Darian's mark." My voice cracked on the words.

"No point in getting angry, Maia. They have to be together for the bond to knit, but Bellua has forbid moving *or* graving on Darian while his own marks are doing their work in the boy's leg."

I knew it. I knew that Bellua would be in the middle of this crisis, keeping Darian and Aru apart. Without Aru, my little Keirr would have no future mate, and Bellua might still get his way. What kind of holy man was that? "I blame Bellua. This is his fault."

"Shhh. He brought me here, don't forget. He's waiting for—"

I lowered my voice, but spit the words out defiantly. "I blame Bellua."

"Maia, you can't judge—"

"I blame him! None of this would have happened if he hadn't tried so hard to turn the sighting of the Summer Dragon into something—"

"He comes from a rigid school of thought. He only acted on his beliefs."

"From the moment he knew we saw the Summer Dragon he worked to bury the story and—"

"Maia—"

"And silence me! Why do you defend him?"

"He is a holy man. He is bound by his oaths."

"His *oaths*? What kind of holy man would—"

"Maia, please. You don't understand. He made a choice to be what he is—he gave up a personal life. Loyalty to Temple and nothing else. His teachings and his vows are everything he has. When confronted with events he couldn't explain, he retreated into his doctrine. It's not that he's opposed to you, but that he knows no other way."

"You disagreed with him at first, but then you . . ." I silenced myself, unwilling to accuse Mabir openly.

His sagging face told me he understood. He had sacrificed me, deferring to the religious authority of the Rasaal and swallowing his own misgivings in order to appease his conscience and his own vows. He ended up satisfying neither. It wasn't Bellua's oaths that troubled him, but his own—sworn to a system he had come to doubt.

Mabir shook his head slowly, his shrewd old eyes bright with unshed tears. "But you proved him wrong, didn't you." He sighed and dabbed at his eyes with the end of his beard. "And in doing so, you shamed this old man. My faith was tested, and I failed."

His simple admission surprised me. I didn't know what to say.

His beard trembled. "Faith . . . I have long struggled with the question: Is it something we aspire to discover and nurture within us, or something we lose as we grow old? It comes so easily to the young. But you showed me what I'd lost, and rekindled it in this old heart. I am grateful, and humbled. I hope you can forgive my weakness."

I put a hand on his arm. "Of course, Dhalla! If you hadn't, I wouldn't have a qit of my own!" I tried to smile reassuringly for him. He smiled back and grasped my hand readily. I squeezed his in return.

I had another question to ask. I wasn't a dhalla and had no experience with the Temple Science, but I'd been thinking about it for days. I took a deep breath and leaned toward him. "What would happen if you finished Aru's bond mark partway with *my* blood in the ink? Would it save Aru if Darian's healing takes too long or if he dies?"

His head snapped up, and his dark eyes grew wide. "A *shared* bond mark?"

My new graving throbbed. "Would it be bad?"

His beard shook with the quivering of his open mouth. "I could never, would never think . . . No, it's not possible," he finally sputtered. He took a deep breath then let it out. His eyes were focused far away. "It's never been done, to my knowledge. We would have to augment your mark as well. It would violate the rituals of the Science. I'm not even sure I would know how to integrate it."

His eyes focused on me now and the look he gave me was troubled. "Bellua could have me defrocked or worse if he found out."

"Could he find out?"

"Sweet Avar, girl! The very thought."

I shrank back, but he reached out a shaking hand to touch my shoulder, and studied me with an odd mixture of fear and fascination. "No, no! It's that this is very dangerous ground we tread. But I understand your fear—I don't trust Bellua either. I fear for Riat if he is allowed to manipulate events to fit his chosen narrative."

"Would it save Aru?"

Mabir couldn't speak. Keirr squirmed awake and reached out a paw to bat playfully at Aru's nose. He didn't respond except to blink.

Mabir looked from Aru, to me, to Keirr, then shook his head as if to dislodge an irritating thought. "No, no. I can't. It's too risky."

"Dhalla—"

"No! I cannot!" He clutched the leather case of instruments close to his chest. "You don't understand. I couldn't possibly explain without teaching you so much . . ." His words trailed away to leave an unhappy twist on his lips.

I kneeled down to hug Keirr and Aru both closer to me. "Would it save his life?"

"It might, but if Darian should die yet Aru survive, or if he even *saw* the bondmarks, Bellua would know we had done something—that we . . . that *I* had violated ritual. Broken with the Temple."

"Interrupted his foul magic, you mean."

He stared at me for a long moment, brow furrowed. "Those are harsh words, girl."

"His manipulations are foul."

"We cannot discuss this any longer," he said, then collected the rest of his things and fled the stables. I jumped up to follow him, thinking I would press my case before he got away. But as I passed through the stable door I saw Bellua, pacing slowly away toward the bridge to the paddock, black coat wafting on a breeze, his hands clasped behind his back. Mabir paused beside him. "I'm ready to go," the old dhalla said, then hurried across the bridge.

Bellua looked over his shoulder at me, his face expressionless, eyes shadowed. He'd been shuttling Mabir here on his dragon, Zell, so the elder dhalla could render our bond marks. He should have waited in the paddock with his mount. My whole body went cold. *Had he been listening?*

"I'll be with you in a moment, dhalla!" he called. Mabir stopped on the bridge with slumped shoulders, though Bellua didn't see it. He'd already turned to saunter my way. I ducked back into the stable, my chest pounding, and gathered my little dragons close.

"MAIA. CONGRATULATIONS on your bond mark. I know this is a momentous occasion for you." Bellua stood in the stable doorway, a silhouette dark as the mouth of a cave.

I hugged Keirr and Aru close to me. "Thank you."

"May I come in?"

I shrugged, and he entered slowly, his hands behind his back. His face drew long, brows knit, the corners of his mouth tightly bent.

He spoke to the floor. "Originally I intended to stay behind only to write my report, but now I remain until Darian is well again."

Waiting for Darian or Aru to die, you mean.

"More than that, I need to study this new situation. I promise to be patient, to see what comes of the portent and your place in it. I fear that I may have been hasty. I have chided myself for it—I know you deserve greater recognition than I gave. I must wait until your brother comes out of his fever before I judge, though I've watched you with your new baby, and I think you have a natural gift. I have nothing but admiration for your resolve, and for the way you tamed that wilding sire. Surely Korruzon was present in that hour."

He paused, as if waiting for me to acknowledge his words. He sat on a bench, brushed a fleck off of his coat. I waited for him to continue, certain that anything he said would be a lie. He'd spent an entire day seeking leverage he could use to bury my story before it rose to challenge the teachings of the Rasaal. But since I came home with Keirr he'd been silent, only shuttling Mabir from the Temple to the aerie and back. I feared at one point that he would insist on applying my bond mark himself, but he didn't interfere. I'd barely seen him at all.

He cleared his throat. "I'm sorry for actions and words that seemed to dismiss your value. I hope you will forgive me for my harshness. I concede that my judgment may have been premature."

Again he paused, staring at me expectantly. I had nothing to say. I certainly wasn't going to thank him after all he'd put me through.

He shook his head. The corners of his mouth drew down even further, and he fidgeted uncharacteristically. "Words are not serving me now. I should learn to trust my first impressions. The first time I saw you, I saw something special. Remember? I called you a wild-flower. More appropriate than I knew at the time." A near smile revealed a dimple in one cheek, and his expression lightened, but it quickly vanished as his face resumed its somber lines. He looked down at his hands. "I let my teachings cloud my instincts, and I am sorry. You have schooled me, Maia."

I couldn't read his eyes, though I swear he meant to look sad. His words eerily echoed what Mabir said just minutes ago—the second apology in less than half an hour. Was it genuine? Or another manipulation? I didn't know him well enough to tell. But I'd seen him at his most emotional, on the hillside where Malik died, when everyone stood against him at last. I didn't trust him.

He held out a hand, palm up, like a peace offering.

I took only his fingers for the briefest possible handshake. He continued to search my face, but I couldn't think of anything to say that wouldn't be a lie or half-truth. Something shadowed his expression, some intense emotion that stirred beneath the surface. Keirr squirmed against me, groaning with an echo of my discomfort. I looked down at her, relieved at the interruption. Finally Bellua stood, bowed crisply, then turned and left.

I waited until Zell's wingbeats receded into the distance before I exhaled. At last I stood up, pushed the rolling stable doors open wider, and peered out with a shiver.

The compound was quiet. Tauman and Jhem hunted with their broodfathers again—the sires' reward for good behavior following the theft of their broods. After hunting all week, the ice vaults were filling up with meat. Meanwhile, Father and Rov shuttled back and forth between the village and the cavern, mustering up a small militia of locals to keep watch until Rov could return with real Dragonry regulars.

Lazy cloudlings dotted the sky, but I saw no dragons. I sighed in relief and stepped out.

Keirr trotted after me, head held high, her nostrils quivering as she studied scents my nose would never know. She'd been subdued when we first brought her home, clearly missing her poppa, looking lost amongst the press of unfamiliar adult dragons and strange human beings. She stayed close to me at all times, but over the last few days her confidence had grown. Already she caroused like a normal, playful qit—splashed in the watering trough, growled and pounced on her food, attacked and defeated piles of straw bedding.

My only job was to teach her proper dragon manners, but her boundless energy was exhausting. Fortunately Athys and Coluver adopted her readily, and I was grateful for their help in keeping her corralled.

Aru plodded out after us, head low and tail dragging. I stopped to wait for him, and Keirr took my cue as an excuse to attack. He reared up to fend her off with his paws, but she snagged his tail in her teeth and soon they spun around each other in a tumble. Finally he flipped her on her back with an oversized paw and sat on her. She growled with mock anger, wriggling joyfully. I laughed despite myself. She never took "go away" for an answer. It was good to see them bond since they would be mates one day. Soon each would get a final circle of runes added to their bond marks to tighten the emotional cords they created with their play.

Aru pinned Keirr with almost no effort—he outweighed her by half—and sat with limp wings, ignoring her struggles. When her happy barks turned to pained yelps, he growled at her.

The big shadow of his mother, Grus, fell across them. "*Qit*. Aph, qit," followed by a scolding click of her tongue. Aru rolled aside, and Keirr scampered to my side for sympathy. I rubbed her ear frills. "You asked for that you know, scoundrel." She cocked her head at me, silvery eyes blinking.

Aru began to walk drag-tail toward his mother, but stopped, looked at me, started my way, paused again, then hung his head and sat. Poor little Aru, lost and confused. Grus and I touched eyes for a moment, and then she bent down to lick at his ears. I knelt beside him too and scratched under his chin. He didn't move, even when Keirr licked his nose.

"Qit, boi," said Grus, and keened sadly, then tilted her head from side to side, indicating a word she didn't have or couldn't pronounce. After watching Keirr and her sire recently in the caverns, I knew Grus probably had a dragon's word for what she meant, that we ignorant humans didn't know and couldn't say.

But her understanding impressed me. *The qit and the boy.* It was the same thing I'd worried about all day. "Aru needs Darian, and I bet Darian needs Aru."

"Qit nneedsss boi," she said, and nodded. Wise momma dragon.

Their bond marks needed finishing. Something had to be done, but once again the adult humans played their appointed roles, did what was expected of them. Even Mabir, despite admitting that he distrusted Bellua's motives, still cowered from the merihem's shadow. "*The Wisdom of Haom said, There is no future in the past.*" That's what he told me. *So then why are we listening to Ancient Haom? Isn't he from the past? Isn't your inability to confront Bellua mired in the past?* The contradiction was absurd.

The more I thought about Bellua's short congratulatory speech the less I liked it. *I must wait until your brother comes out of his fever before I judge.*

If Darian dies, you mean, you will blame me again. He couldn't even position himself in a lie without leaving a back door open.

I shook my head in anger, then stood and patted Grus on the nose. She looked up. Athys and Coluver joined us, surrounding little Aru in a protective wall of dragon dams.

"We're going to *fix* this, momma dragon. I don't know how yet, but I'll figure it out."

She did not blink, but tilted her head to one side briefly. "Fik-ssss," she said, then rumbled and clicked another phrase deep in her throat, tilting her head again, to the other side. Were those dragon noises a word, like those that Keirr's poppa spoke to her in the caves? I tried to imitate the phrase, though my rumbling would never rattle anyone's bones, and I had to click with my tongue, but Grus nodded and repeated the phrase.

———

The broodmothers watched Aru and Keirr while I descended the stair from the storehouse to the ice vault to gather their dinners. I didn't want to leave them alone—or to be alone—any longer than was necessary.

In days long beyond counting, my ancestors built an aerie between the crags atop this spire of stone. Over centuries, the compound expanded to cover the pinnacle, including the broodhouse, the tack house, and all the other buildings. Eventually a new paddock floor built of stone enclosed it all, like a roof over the original aeries. A section of the ancient paddock was walled off as an ice vault to store food for dragons and humans alike. All the buildings on the aerie had trapdoors that led to the ice vaults.

Six ancient dragon-sized doors on the north face of the pinnacle, three on the outside and three within, contained the original broodhouse platform between them. Relic of a time long gone. The space was filled with straw to deaden the air and hold in the cool temperatures. I don't think we had ever opened those doors. Father talked about walling them up.

Thin light filtering down the stair from the storehouse glistened on ice and damp stone. Echoes were sharp, but died quickly; the air seemed dank and lifeless. I hurried to my task.

Similar to the gantry platform, we used a basket-hoist powered by the aqueduct to move goods up or down between the ice vault and the storehouse above. I loaded chickens and melons onto it quickly.

When we were small, Darian and I would take turns riding the hoist when we thought we could get away with it, while one of us stayed behind to operate the water valve. If you did it right, the basket would shoot up and hit the stops above, and the rider would fly into the air. It made a racket, and we would laugh until our sides hurt—well worth the scolding we'd get when Father caught us. I couldn't help but smile at the memories. Then my throat tightened. *Please, Darian, get well.*

By midsummer, the ice in the vault became glassy and thin and wet, but the air still turned my breath to steam. Hopefully Fren would be well enough come winter to replenish the stores. I saw him in my mind's eye, smiling a greeting, winter sun bright on his cartload of ice, sawn from the frozen high mountain lakes. He would ask me, *How is your shadow doing?*

My heart began to pound, and I shook my head, but the nightmare images flooded in, churning like a whirlpool: Fren slumped in a pool of his own blood, clutching at a gash he could not hold closed. Darian crying out in pain, an arrow in his leg. Poppa dragon's last shuddering breath. Bottomless fatigue, cries and screams and pain and fear, and behind it all a cold inferno of green flame contained in the corpse of a dragon, with a dead rider glaring balefully at me from its back, stalking me despite wounds that would have killed a normal man.

At times it seemed like nothing that happened before our journey through the caves was real, that I'd been born into that howling darkness with a full set of false memories. I'd bolt upright in my bed, streaming sweat, unsure where I was, and realize that it was merely a nightmare. Then I would touch Keirr, picture the Summer Dragon in my head, and come out the other side. For a time.

Mabir said it was a kind of madness that follows a harrowing experience. Father agreed. They said it would lessen with time, that I should concentrate on my qit.

But right now I stood alone in the ice vaults, the ancient catacomb where dead flesh lay preserved, where sound and smell and time were suspended, and the shadows seemed to whisper my fears.

Why was Bellua so threatened by me?

I imagined him looming over Darian's sick bed, his needles in his hand, tap-tap-tapping into my brother's leg with his Temple Science. What was he doing, really?

"Maia? Are you okay?" Jhem stood at the mid-point of the stair, the carcass of a white-faced deer across her shoulders.

I didn't remember picking up the burlap-wrapped packet of meat in my hands. I hadn't heard Audax's wings or the scrape of his talons on the stone ceiling, though I heard it now. Several dragons.

"You look like you've seen a ghost, Maia. Are you okay?" She laid the deer on a shelf.

I took a deep breath. "I'm okay," relieved that my voice sounded strong. She came forward as if to embrace me, but I held the packet of meat up between us. She clasped my shoulders instead.

"Jhem, I have to talk to you about something."

"Talking is good. It will help—"

"No, no. I mean Darian. We have to get Darian and Aru together and make Mabir—"

"Where's the basket? Hello?" Tauman tramped down the stair. "We've got meat up here that needs to be on ice." He spotted Jhem and me, took the packet out of my hands, and set it on the basket hoist. Then he yanked the lever to open the valve and set the small waterwheel spinning. The basket started to rise. "Let's go! Work to do! Your baby and her mate are up there waiting." He started toward the stair again but stopped and took a second look at Jhem and me. He frowned. "What?"

I inhaled and set my jaw. "I have a plan."

THE VILLAGE OF RIAT nestled in slumber below the cliffs as we glided silently down to the Temple. I rode with Jhem on Coluver, Keirr swaddled in the knapsack in my lap. Tauman had Aru strapped into the saddle pack on Athys, with only the little dragon's head sticking out. We took the broodmothers because they were calmer than the sires, less likely to tussle with each other or make awkward noises. We needed to get in and quickly out again with as little fuss as possible.

The Temple filled the top of a low shelf, outthrust from the cliff north of the Roaring. Though commanding a position of authority above the roofs of the village, it was accessible by an easy, winding path. Its ornate columns and curved roof were all but invisible in the half-light of dusk, but through stained glass windows, lights within sparkled out like will-o'-the-wisps in the darkness. The attached aerie hadn't housed dragons since the death of Mabir's mount, but would know dragons once again when Mabir's acolyte, Tulo, was old enough to bond with one. The two wings of the building embraced a large courtyard where we landed with little more than a rush of air and the gentle scrape of talons on stone.

"Quickly now," I said, sliding down from the saddle with Keirr in her pack in front of me. I landed with a grunt—she had gained a lot of weight since our ordeal in the caves less than a week ago.

Tauman handed Aru down to Jhem and me, then hopped down to join us. I'd been worried that he would disapprove of my plan or think it childish. But he'd only nodded as I explained the situation and recounted my conversation with Mabir. Darian and Aru needed to have their bond marks finished, I argued, and Darian was his brother, too. He wanted him whole and healthy and both qits successfully integrated into the aeries.

At first, he insisted that Father be made aware of our plan, but Jhem and I disagreed with him. "Father will want to be direct about it, and then Rov will get involved and Bellua will find some way to make me the villain," I said. "Then we'll be locked in another long debate about signs and portents."

"We need someone to keep Bellua and Rov occupied while we get Darian," said Tauman. "But you're right. Forgiveness will be easier to get than permission. So instead, we wait until the next time Father takes them to the caves. They've been going almost every day. That should give us two hours or more."

The opportunity came that very evening. And so we found ourselves smuggling the aerie's two new qits into the Temple, with a two-hour window. I hoped it would be enough time.

The double doors of the Temple resounded with the drawing of the latch, then the left-hand door swung open. The scent of incense spilled out, and the acolyte Tulo emerged with a lantern, his dark hair in disarray, as if he'd been roused from his bed. Mabir appeared behind him, eyes wide.

"I *thought* I heard wings. Dear sweet girl! What are you doing here—And Jhem, and Tauman!" When Aru moaned unhappily in Tauman's grasp and the old dhalla saw Keirr too, his face changed, hardened. "I see. I understand."

"You have to finish Darian's bond marks," I said.

"Of course," he nodded. "I half expected you might try something like this, young scoundrel. Come in then. Come in. Tulo—see to their mounts. Water and feed them but don't unsaddle them. Stay with them until we are done inside."

Tulo headed into the darkness with his lantern, and Mabir turned to enter the Temple. Tauman passed Aru to Jhem. "Can you handle this?"

"Of course I can." Jhem seemed hurt by his question, though I didn't get why.

Tauman considered for a moment, then nodded. "I'll stay here and keep an eye out."

"Thank you." Jhem kissed him quickly, then she and I followed Mabir inside as fast as our squirming burdens would allow.

The dhalla led us by the light of ensconced candles through the great, circular nave of the Temple, large enough to accommodate his *tinnen*—his congregation—plus several adult dragons. We followed him past the raised dais in the center from which he delivered his sermons. Past wooden columns carved in the semblance of dragons, framing the now dark stained glass windows. To the arched doors of the inner chambers—Mabir's offices and sleeping quarters, and the rooms that served as a hospital for the sick and injured. Taking a candle down from its niche beside the doors, he waved us inside.

"Sweet, meddling Avar," he said quietly as I passed, but his eyes didn't scold. He looked uncertain but not scared as he had the last time I'd seen him. "You are a catalyst after all, aren't you, girl? You vanquish any doubts I had that the Summer Dragon came for you. *Change* follows you." He sighed. "But this feels right to me. I've cowered from Bellua too long and made too many compromises. And besides, *you* are my brood, and Riat, not Bellua or the distant Temple in Avigal or the seminary of the Maktaa." He cupped my cheek with one dry, comforting hand as I passed.

The air changed in the inmost chamber. I'd never been in this room before. It felt colder, smelled of sickness and sour decay, dried blood and ointments. Soft moaning came from the far wall, and I struggled in the dimness to see the source. Blocking the candlelight with my hand, I saw beds lining the outer walls, separated occasionally by wooden panels carved with dragon motifs. Mabir hobbled toward the source of the sound and waved me to follow. "Bring the qits. Hurry!"

Now I made out shapes like tables and chairs. We came to a bed where a figure lay unmoving. It was Fren, I realized. "He sleeps now," Mabir said quietly as we passed, "but he has been awake off and on. We spoke two days ago. He had a good day, though he struggles still."

We passed several empty beds before we came to Darian. He moaned hoarsely as we approached.

Mabir pulled up a chair and table, and unrolled his graving tools from their leather pouch. "Bring Keirr, Maia." I carried my qit into to the circle of candlelight and exposed her neck. Mabir nodded. "This will be the simplest mark to finish, so we'll do it first—the final ring of script tying Keirr to Aru and he to her." I held her and hummed the calming tune as the old dhalla gently but steadily tapped the words of bonding into her skin. She never squirmed once, even when the runes were applied directly over bone. Finally Mabir wiped her neck with an astringent cloth and said, "Done. Good job. Be proud of your little lady." He smiled briefly, then signaled for Jhem to bring Aru.

Jhem pulled up another chair and sat with Aru in her lap. Darian stirred and blinked against the candlelight, his hair matted and pressed to the side of his head.

"Aru!" he said weakly but happily. Aru honked a greeting. Darian held out a hand and Aru licked it, his tail lashing back and forth. A lump rose in my throat. It was the first time he'd been conscious since our ordeal, but somehow Aru's presence stirred him awake. Now I knew we were doing the right thing.

"Roll over on your side, boy," said Mabir, arranging his inks and needles on the bedside table. "We're going to finish your bond mark now." Darian did as he was told but seemed only vaguely aware, his movements cumbersome and awkward as he collapsed into his bed like a sleepwalker.

Mabir warned us back with a glance. "Give us room. You may sing with us, but don't crowd. Aru will be fine right here. He wants this mark finished, he'll be no trouble." Jhem set Aru down and backed away to sit on another bed. Little Aru laid his forepaws on Darian's bed, as close as he could get without crawling in beside him, and laid his head on the mattress. Soon the tap-tap-tapping of Mabir's tools began. Aru's anxious whimpers settled into gentle keening that harmonized with Mabir's chant.

I found a chair and sat down, relieved to have Keirr's weight off my shoulders and in my lap instead. The rhythmic tapping and singing had a calming effect on me. I could almost feel tension releasing from the room. The gloom receded somehow, as if the flames in the candles had gained confidence. Keirr sat very still, watching Mabir with intent curiosity. Little Aru's head lay on the bed beside his bond-mate, eyes closed in bliss.

Before I realized that any time had passed at all, Mabir called to me, "Your turn." My eyes must have been closed because the candle-light dazzled them.

"What?"

"This was your idea," he said. "I haven't stopped thinking about it. I know how to do it now. On Aru, I've hidden the runes atop other runes, angling in to deep, clean flesh. Eventually the marks will emerge, but for now they'll be hidden in plain sight. It is insurance against disaster, and Bellua be damned. But now is when we must do it, while the blood runs free."

Jhem came to me with shock in her eyes. "What are you up to now?"

I passed Keirr to her, still swaddled in the knapsack. "It's some-thing Mabir and I talked about before. I didn't think he would to do it. I didn't expect it, I just wanted Darian and Aru's marks finished."

"Enough talking. Come," Mabir said.

Trembling, I dragged my chair to Darian's bedside and sat. He had slipped into unconsciousness again, a bubble of spit on his lips. Aru still rested one paw on the blanket next to Darian's head, the lit-tle dragon's every breath punctuated with a sigh.

Mabir looked at me, then at Jhem. "We will tie Maia to Aru, a shared bond mark. It will lend Aru strength while Darian recovers, and possibly save him from death if Darian should fail. This must be our secret."

Jhem and I traded glances, and she nodded apprehensively. "Of course," she said.

"And you, Maia, maintain the poultice on your neck as long as you can. When it falls off, wear your hair loose to cover your neck. Don't let Bellua see it. I can't use the same trick with your marks as I did with Aru. Human skin isn't thick enough."

I nodded.

"And don't say anything to Darian. He needs to grow into these marks. They can't be clouded with negative emotion. I know your brother, and he won't like sharing his charge. He'll adapt better if he's given time to focus only on *his* bond with Aru. Eventually I will break the news to him myself."

With one more glance between us, Mabir began. I sat with my back to him as I had done only this afternoon. His tapping and singsong filled the silence. *This was your idea,* I told myself. *You cannot wince or cry out.* Where earlier I allowed memories to intrude on my courage, I found it strangely easy to evict all sensation. It felt more important, bigger than Keirr and me alone. The stakes were higher, and so I steeled myself more deeply. Now I held in my resolve the life of my brother's bondling and perhaps of my brother, too. It *did* feel right. Mabir's melody entered my soul. I heard Jhem in harmony. I summoned my voice and joined, and soon Keirr and then Aru entered the chorus. The calming tune aided me.

It felt the same, at first, as it had this afternoon, but before long differences became clear. I knew that Aru was troubled even before he squirmed and keened in confusion. More surprisingly, I sensed Darian's moan before it escaped his lips. These new marks drew on something broad and unfamiliar compared to the runes of my own bond mark, and when Aru groaned in harmony with me in a moment of pain, I understood. This was the new language that Mabir had contemplated and applied, the additional circle of runes that bridged Aru's ties beyond his bondmate, Darian, to me. These were the runes that Bellua might observe and know were foreign to the teachings of the Rasaal, the gravings that might damn Mabir, written into *my flesh.* Only then did I finally truly feel the dhalla's fear. I was a conspirator now. Mabir and I were joined in defiance of the Rasaal. This might save Aru and his bond with Darian, but it might condemn us all, and Father, the aeries, and all of Riat with us.

Mabir's voice released me. "Done. Relax, young lady. Find a seat away from us, and I'll finish with the last ring of marks on Aru and Darian."

I couldn't speak. I only nodded in agreement as I rose from my chair. Sweat poured off my body and I shook uncontrollably. I wandered a distance away and slumped into a seat. I tried to understand what had happened, to fit it into a single context that made sense, but I couldn't. I felt divided, elsewhere. The room spun. My own bond mark hadn't affected me so. Aru and Darian both sighed with relief as Mabir's tapping continued. Groaning, I began to raise a hand to my head . . .

But a vise-like grip caught my arm and held it short. I jumped with surprise, turned, unaware that I'd sat next to Fren's sickbed. His skin was pallid. Gray fingernails dug into my skin. But his eyes shone wide and bright in the flickering light. Not manic, but full. Full of fear, or hope, or revelation. I froze.

His voice came in a papery rasp. *"The dhalla told me of your adventure, Maia, and I knew. I knew that you were a sign to me."* I tried to pull my arm free, but his grasp held like iron, completely wrong for a man who had suffered wounds such as his. *"A sign that Asha has not been displaced, that the world is still true. I will wear my scars with pride, for they helped to send you on your journey."*

Asha? What did he mean? The man was delirious, certainly. As I tried to wrench my arm free, Fren went into a spasm, back arched, and his eyes rolled back into his head. He whispered as if into a void, *"One will lead, one will follow."* Agony pinched his words and a tear escaped his clenched eyelids. *"One will rise and one will fall."* A shallow semblance of awareness returned to his face, but he still spoke into the shadows. *"There is darkness coming. Getig shows you grace, but it's elusive. Your scars can hold you back unless your light is strong."*

Then his eyes turned full on me, bloodshot and harrowed. *"Hold to the light, Maia. Hold to the light of Getig, of Asha."*

A thread of saliva ran from the corner of his mouth as he collapsed again on the bed, his eyes closed halfway in the sleep of delirium. His fingers relaxed, and I withdrew my hand.

Trembling, I rubbed the marks Fren's nails left in my wrist and looked to Jhem and Mabir. If they had heard any of it, they made no sign.

What had just happened here? Who or what was *Asha?*

Mabir put the last of his tools back into his pouch and looked at me with a mixture of relief and anxiety. He said something, but I didn't hear it. I nodded anyway.

Jhem walked over and pulled me to my feet. I shook my head and returned to the gloom of the Temple infirmary. Aru bounced happily next to Darian's bed, licking the hand that dangled there.

"Look at them," said Jhem. "We can't separate them now. They belong together."

"You're right." Mabir's eyes twinkled at me. "More than that, they both need to be near Maia, so that Aru can draw strength from their new runes, and Darian from Aru. I'll explain to Bellua that I chose to finish their bond marks without his approval. He'll be angry, but that is my burden to bear. Let me wrap Darian's leg and immobilize it, so he's safe to travel."

I squeezed my baby tight as Mabir came to me, put his wiry arms around us, and hugged us warmly. "Thank you, little catalyst, Getig's little Maia."

Getig's Maia. I didn't know how to respond to that, but when he tried to release me, I gripped his arm.

"What is *Asha*?" I said.

Mabir's face paled. "Where did you hear that name?"

"From Fren, moments ago."

The dhalla looked to Fren, then to me, and his color faded. He trembled beneath my touch. "Sweet Avar. Not now, Maia. This is not the time. Holy Avar, but these are strange times indeed. Speak that name to no one. No one! I will explain when I can."

He pulled away from me and hobbled to Darian's bedside. "Jhem! Maia! Gather your babies and send Tauman in. It's time to get you all home."

TWENTY-EIGHT

DARIAN SLEPT the next two days in the winter stable, with Aru and Keirr and me close by. Father scolded us mildly for our escapade, in Bellua's presence. But he smiled slyly and winked at me once as Bellua spewed angrily about this affront to his authority. The merihem insisted on studying Darian's finished bond mark long and hard, but he made no judgment about Mabir's work, and never looked at my neck. I tried not to think about him, saying nothing when he came in from time to time to examine Darian, though I wore my hair loose and never turned my back to him. He didn't once resort to graving in Darian's wound, even though he always brought his tools and my brother remained gray and still. Did it mean that he saw improvement? Or would he dare to withhold aid and let my brother die?

I stayed by Darian's bedside except to feed our qits or relieve myself. Jhem brought my meals, and Father and Tauman stopped in regularly. We tried to wake Darian frequently to pour some broth down his throat, but Father worried that it was too little nourishment after such a long fast.

Aru improved, however. Where before he'd been confused and unhappy, now he seemed content to lie between Darian's cot and mine, and even tussled with Keirr like a qit ought to do. That at least was a relief. I realized that I could *feel* him the way I felt Keirr. Before, I'd been unaware of that bond with my own qit. I'd thought it was merely my deepening love for her. Now, because of Aru, I understood that the bond mark truly did unite us in a way difficult to describe. If I yawned, they might both curl up in their beds. If my stomach growled, they would *mowp* for a meal. If one of them stopped to scratch behind an ear frill, I might feel a tickle behind my ear. If I thought too hard about it, my insides got quivery. I noted a difference, though—the link to Aru seemed weaker, less commanding, as if Aru truly was shared and not mine alone. Would that be a problem in the future? Would his loyalties be divided? Weakened? Or broadened? Not even Mabir could answer that question.

On the third day, I realized that a flush of color had returned to Darian's cheeks and the wound in his leg appeared less swollen. The rotten, gangrenous smell was gone, the gravings successful at last. As Bellua looked on in silence, Mabir pronounced Darian officially on the mend, and Bellua stayed out of the aeries the rest of that day.

Darian's laughter woke me the fourth morning. He sat in his bed, with Aru bounding around him in circles. Though he'd lost weight, his cheeks were pink. I jumped out of my blankets and took him by the shoulders, cautious to avoid the giant hug that I really wanted to deliver.

Keirr stretched and crawled out of her box to curl at my side. Darian scratched behind her ear frill as she purred a greeting to Aru.

"Maia, I'm home! When did that happen?"

"Four nights ago. We rescued you from the Temple hospital—"

"Rescued? From the Temple? The last thing I remember is falling. The Horror in the cave. I ran past it."

"You don't remember the mountainside, after we escaped from the Horrors? You stood up for me."

He shook his head slowly but then nodded as a light dawned in his eyes. "Yes, I do remember that now. I think I remember the Temple, too." He touched the back of his neck. "How long have I been asleep?" He looked around the aeries as if seeing them for the first time, a smile forming on his lips.

"Over a week. I have so much to tell you, but you have to swear silence. Things have gotten strange around here." I couldn't stop looking at him. His cheeks were hollow, but when he smiled he looked so much like his former self that I had to smile, too.

"Not so strange that we don't have *food*, I hope, because I'm starving."

I laughed. "We still have food. You stay right here—I'm going to get Father."

As I started to run for the doors, Darian grabbed my sleeve. "Maia, thank you." His voice cracked.

"For what?"

He shook his head, a look of perplexed amusement adding humor to his hollow cheeks. Then he laughed out loud. "I don't know! I've been asleep or something. But thank you anyway. I'm pretty sure you've taken care of me."

I smiled and kissed his cheek. "You have no idea."

———

Mabir visited more often once Darian awoke, and even spent two nights in the winter stable with us. He didn't talk to me about Fren's cryptic words though, and I was afraid to bring them up because Mabir and I were never alone, and I worried that Bellua might be listening at the door. I caught Mabir studying me oddly a time or two, but he acted as if he were doing something else. Once, I found a chance to quietly ask him, "When? When can we talk?"

"Soon," he said. "But not here. Not now."

Darian was too weak to walk, but he ate like a qit, and his face filled in again. His improved condition freed me to begin working with Keirr. One of the first tasks, now that the bond marks were applied and healed, was to create the ports in her wings that would allow us to strap a saddle harness around her body. Father summoned me into the courtyard, and Mabir joined us with his graving tools readied, a burlap sack at his feet.

Father stood beside the "porting horse," a sawhorse contraption with a block of wood in the center sculpted to fit the underside of a qit's wings between the wing muscles and her hips. The thought of cutting my baby made my stomach turn, and Keirr responded by shrinking and struggling. Naturally, I held her close to calm her, but Father clicked his tongue like a dragon dam. "You can't treat her like a pet, cuddling her and kissing her all the time. She's going to grow very quickly. She's going to be smart, and she's a natural predator. It's time to start treating her like the adult animal she will become very, very soon."

I nodded. "I know. It's just that . . ." I looked up at him sadly.

He smiled back. "Don't think I don't understand how you feel,

Maia. The bond mark has increased your empathy for her—not that you didn't have plenty of that already. But we must do what we must do, so let's do it well, right? We'll get her in position, then you hold her, and *be firm*."

Together we moved Keirr next to the porting horse and stretched her wing out with the block nestled against her side. Mabir put a hand on my shoulder and smiled encouragement. Then he opened the burlap sack and produced a block of ice from the vaults. He laid it on Keirr's wing where it joined her torso, and together we calmed her struggles.

Father took his skinning knife with its short, curved blade, freshly sharpened and washed in alcohol, and pointed with it. "Take note of the veins here, behind the wing and here, in front of the leg. They feed the membrane of the wing, and they're important in a young animal whose wings have more growing to do than any other part of her body. Always leave at least two fingers' width between them and the incision. Keirr's are well placed, so this won't be a problem. When her wings are grown these veins won't be nearly so critical." He raised the blade, and I winced. "Don't worry, she has less feeling there than you imagine, and ice numbs the skin. It will be over quickly."

Without thinking, I began Mabir's calming tune. He joined me, as did Father, humming in low harmony. Mabir removed the block of ice, and then Father sliced with deliberate care through Keirr's wing membrane into the block of the porting horse, directly next to her body. He reversed direction and returned, removing a thin, lozenge-shaped bit of skin. She barely struggled until Mabir bathed the wound with an alcohol-soaked swab. But with continued singing and gentle force we kept her restrained long enough for him to grave sigils around the opening. The runes arced around the margin, then stretched out several inches into the wing membrane like arrowheads. "This will promote scar tissue with elasticity and strength," he explained.

"I feel it! In my own side, like a tingling."

Father nodded. "That's the power of your bond mark at work."

We repeated the process on the other wing. Last of all, we wrapped a clean bandage around her torso and through the wing ports, to prevent them from healing closed, and applied a poultice to the incisions to numb them and stop any bleeding. It had taken less than twenty minutes, but now my Keirr was prepared for a life in the skies with me—*me*—on her back. My joy at the thought seemed to calm her, because she turned and licked my face, her silver eyes squinting with trust and acceptance.

Father patted my shoulder. "Good job. Take a few moments while we do Aru's wing ports." He and Mabir took the porting horse into the winter stable.

I took Keirr's head in my hands, kissing her on the nose.

"Don't you worry, little one. No matter how big you get, you'll always be my baby."

She blinked back at me.

"Mowp?" she asked.

I floated on a cloud for the next several days, lifted by Darian's recovery and Aru's rebounding spirit. My bond with Keirr was a new uncharted landscape that only grew broader and deeper. Mabir showed up once in a while, mostly to check on Darian or confer with Father, and he still refused to discuss Fren's words. I filled Darian in on most of what he'd missed, but I didn't tell him about *Asha* or the shared bond mark, fearing, in part, that he might be upset by it but figuring, too, that what he didn't know he couldn't accidentally tell to someone who would make ill use of it.

We rarely saw Bellua and Captain Rov, who spent most of every day at the caverns or otherwise kept to the manor house. Bellua hadn't left, as he'd said he would if Darian recovered. But we saw less of him, thank the Avar. I didn't think about either of them much but avoided Bellua when he lurked about the aeries.

I had plenty to keep me occupied.

Young dragons are hard work. Besides feeding and bathing, they need training of all kinds. It begins with language lessons—simple commands, mostly, certain words and phrases that will be important throughout their lives: stay, come, go, halt. Their favorite would be the word for *up*, "Hai!" But those days still awaited us.

First: names. Dragons understand the concept. They use names willingly and even invent their own—Keirr's own sire named her.

Shuja called my Father "Magha," an easy name for a dragon to pronounce, whereas the "T" in "Tauman" was more difficult, and so my brother's Rannu called him "Dauman." "Jhem" came out of Audax's mouth with a soft "G" as "Ghem," and so on. Shuja called Tauman "Boi," to his embarrassment, and Jhem "Ghirw," or *Girl*, as best we could decipher. Social status was not lost on dragons.

"Mai-ah," I said, patting my chest as Keirr nosed about for another piece of salmon. "Mai-ah."

"Mowp," she insisted.

"Who am I, Keirr? You are . . . *Keirr*." I patted her chest. Then I patted my own again. *"Mai-ah."*

"Mowp." She'd been fed already, so she wasn't hungry, but salmon was easily her favorite treat so far.

I held the lump of fish at arm's length, out of her reach. Patted my chest again. "Maia."

She sat and looked at me with her head cocked sideways, a pose becoming very characteristic of *study*, of deep thought. "Maia," she said, perfectly. Then "MOWP." Assertively.

I laughed and gave her the treat, scratching behind her ear frill. I sensed the part that our bond mark played in the transaction. It somehow helped her to know what I expected from her. Impressive science, the Temple's art of graving. That, or a very smart qit. Or both. I often wondered how my ancestors had managed dragons at all without the graving science, or had the art come first—and for what purpose? As far as anyone knew, the science was older than history.

The whole process intrigued me, though. I listened close to the adult dragons when they clicked and rumbled to each other, thinking always about my mother's comments so long ago, and the way that Keirr's poppa told her to come to my side, to stay with me, with only a very few rumbled sounds. They weren't just random noises, I knew that much, though they were hard to differentiate from each other. I continued to listen and mimic them when I thought I detected something. More often than not the adult dragons looked at me as if I were deranged. Perhaps I was.

One day I watched in fascination as Keirr played with a chicken carcass I set out for her lunch. She backed off from it several paces, hunkered down as if she prepared to spring, and closed her eyes. She clicked and opened her eyes wide, head bouncing high, then looked at her meal with her head cocked.

"What are you up to, little girl?"

She crouched down again, closed her eyes, and wiggled closer to her target. She clicked again, then her eyes popped open and her head went up, tilted to the other side. I laughed aloud, but she ignored me and repeated the process one more time: crouch, eyes closed, creep closer, click, then look up with something akin to astonishment.

And then it was over. She pounced on her quarry and dismembered it thoroughly. Something had happened that escaped me. I wished I could be in her head while she performed this ritual, whatever it was. I saw it once more the next day, this time with Aru as the unwitting victim, with a full-on mock battle afterward. I never saw it again.

Keirr astounded me with how quickly she learned words, and Aru with how quickly he followed suit. They were eager to communicate. Aru learned to say Keirr's name quickly, but she struggled with Aru for some reason. It always came out "Owoo," or entirely as the rolling dragon "R." We worked on it.

"Bukaw" was chicken. "Mmuu!" for beef. "Spsh" or "hwssh" or any combination that evoked splashing noises was "fish," though we were far from naming species—all words that I adopted because they were easy for her to speak.

Darian disliked barnyard sounds entirely, though. He worked hard with Aru to get him close to actual words in our language, but the best his qit could do with *chicken* was "k-kkn." *Cow* gave him much less trouble, to my brother's relief. One day Darian sat rubbing the scar on his leg, frowning as if it hurt, and snapped, "Your dragon sounds ridiculous clucking like a chicken and mooing like a cow. I wish you wouldn't teach Aru that they're acceptable words. I don't like it."

The filigree of graving around his scars didn't make them any prettier. I could see that his leg probably still throbbed, but I was in no mood for attitude. "When you're feeding him yourself you can teach him whatever words you please. I've got my hands doubly full."

When he started to object, I turned my back on him and marched straight to the storehouse, with Aru and Keirr trailing behind. They waited with anticipation as I went below to the ice vault and gathered food for their mid-morning meal, primarily chicken, Aru's favorite. When the basket hoist reached the top, they circled hungrily.

I showed them the basket full of chicken carcasses. Keirr asked for one politely by clucking quietly like a hen. "Buk buk," she said, and I tossed her a prize. She snatched it out of the air, tenderized it just a little, and then swallowed it one piece at a time. Aru watched, eyeing the remaining birds.

"You have to ask, politely," I told him. "Watch Keirr. Hey, baby, want another?"

"Buk buk buk," she said, and I rewarded her with another bird.

"Get it?" I said to Aru. He looked at me, tilted his head to one side quizzically, straightened it again. Nosed in for a bird, but I pushed him away. "Buk buk," I insisted.

"Buh," he said.

"Not bad. Try again: Buk buk bukaaaw."

Keirr responded, perfectly: "Buk buk bukaaaw," and I gave her a chicken. She tore off a leg and rolled it around in her mouth with great relish, looking at Aru. Teasing! I smiled.

Aru tilted his head first at Keirr, then at the diminishing bounty of chickens in my basket, and said, "BUK BUK BUKAAAAW!"

After a moment of stunned silence, I broke out laughing. Keirr did too, the wheezing laughter of a dragon. "Oh, well done!" I tossed Aru a chicken and he made short work of it.

"BUK BUK BUKAAAAW!" he demanded, and I tossed him another. He lashed his tail excitedly and wheezed a bit himself. My sides were starting to hurt.

"BUK BUK BUKAAAAW!"

Darian was going to kill me.

Aru began to cluck like a hen whenever he spied me. Whether I'd intended it or not, it worked to get Darian out of his bed. He started testing his leg with short walks around the stable, using a cane at first. Aru scampered happily at his side. Within a few days, he'd finally regained enough strength to join me in the paddock, though he limped badly and probably would for a while yet. He held his tongue, but worked hard to eliminate chicken noises from Aru's vocabulary.

It was too late, though. I encouraged Aru with additional gifts of poultry when no one was watching. Keirr found *Buk Buk* much easier to say than *Aru*, and adopted that as her name for him. Jhem started using it as a nickname too. Tauman wasn't above teasing Darian about the size of his pet chicken. Father reprimanded us only mildly.

Darian almost turned himself inside out with anger. "You've turned my dragon into a chicken!" he fumed. But he'd asked for it and he knew it. And besides, it was funny.

Throughout those days, Father drilled me on other things. While I played *chase* with Keirr and Buk Buk in the paddock to develop their leg strength, he might pass by and quiz me, "What is the dragon-skin sky?"

"Fair but cold. Higher than dragons can fly."

"That's right. And what is the ragged sky?"

"Continuous rain in a dragon's range of flight, but dead air."

"What's the anvil top?"

"Severe weather and dangerous turbulence, mixed air below."

"And what do you see today?"

"Short towers, at the middle or top of a dragon's range, rising air below them, bad air inside, but fair weather. They might become anvil tops as they move east."

And so on. Most of this we already knew, but Father was determined to drill it deeply into our heads, so we would know how to avoid dangerous air and oncoming weather. I enjoyed the lessons—they made me think about the day when Keirr and I would fly together for the first time. By midwinter, Menog's Day, she would be big enough. Right now, while she still romped and played like a kitten, it seemed impossible that she could get so big that fast. But dragons are predators who depend on size as much as anything for their success. They double in size six times in their first year.

When their wing ports were healed, Father produced training harnesses for them. They strapped on like miniature saddles with a cinch around the waist and through the ports, straps across the chest and shoulders, and a weight where one day a rider would sit above the forelimbs just in front of the wings. Darian and I took turns tying a long lunge line to a ring on the chest of the harness, and then ran our qits in big circles in the paddock. At first they didn't like the contraption on their backs, but with rewards of *bukaw* and *hwshh* they soon galloped with their little wings spread, chortling with dragon glee. They couldn't possibly fly yet, but they already discovered nuances of control by angling their wings forward and back, to feel lift or decline.

Darian made a point of taking care of the feeding as much as he was able, and not just because he didn't want Aru doing livestock impressions. Once I caught him wincing as he limped up from the ice vault, and when I started to unload the basket hoist for him, he pulled my hands away. "I need to get my leg back in shape and loosen up these scars. You should play with Keirr. You've earned it." He looked down at the trough he dug in the dirt with his toe. "Maia, I owe you. I owe you a lot, actually." He looked up at me again with red in his cheeks. "I *am* sorry. The truth is, I really am proud of you, kidling, and I shouldn't have been such a butt."

A lump rose in my throat, but I swallowed it. "You're sappy." I kissed his cheek. "But thanks."

The summer felt settled, embracing me in a way I hadn't felt since before Mother died, except perhaps for that amazing day I watched Getig from the ruins and followed him into the forest. I realized that the bond growing with Keirr resonated with that feeling somehow. My empathy expanded out to Aru and Darian. We cooperated better, laughed more. We went to bed every night exhausted beyond words, but it felt wonderful.

If only Bellua had returned home like he said he would. Instead, too many times I felt my skin prickle and turned my head in time to see him look the other way. His former belligerent attitude was gone, and he seemed almost lost. But he remained in Riat, watching, as if waiting for something.

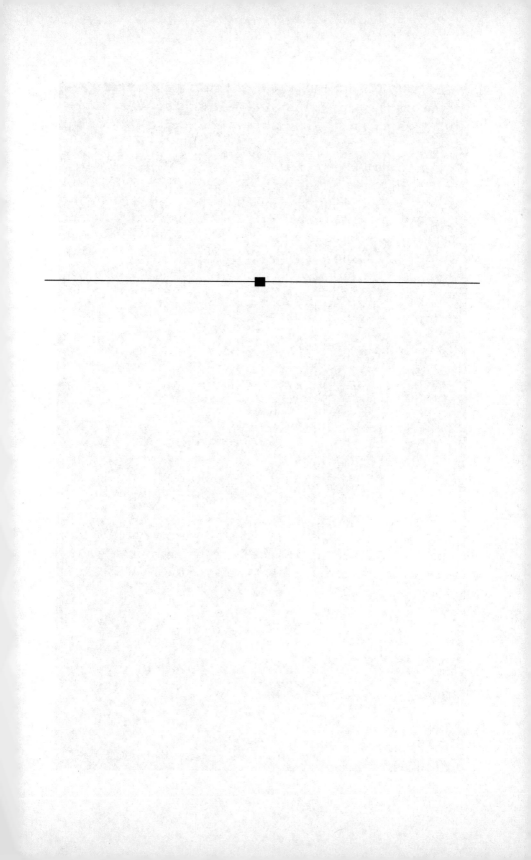

I WHEELED A FINAL barrow-load of bukaw, muu, and hwshh, supplemented with melons and seasonal vegetables, into the stable. When the qits were ears-deep in food, Darian and I slipped back out to the courtyard, only to find Mabir and his acolyte Tulo, Father, and Rov waiting for us. The look on their faces told me that this was more than a casual visit. Tulo had a quiver across his shoulders. Father and Rov carried their longbows.

Mabir placed a hand on my shoulder. "Maia, it is time to tie up some loose ends." Father and Rov looked on with stern faces; apparently they'd already agreed to let Mabir do the talking. Darian seemed oddly apprehensive. Only then did Bellua emerge from the shadow of a tree in his dark garb.

Mabir patted my shoulder. "Captain Rov has determined that parts of the caves must be sealed for the sake of security. I've convinced him to let me visit before they are lost to us. I'd like to see the areas you described in your report to Captain Rov."

Bellua shifted uneasily at the corner of my vision. Areas he would rather Mabir didn't see?

"I want you to accompany us," Mabir continued. "I want you to show me the rooms you encountered and talk to me about them. It would be nice to chat. Can you do that?" He turned his head so that only I could see his face, and winked.

I nodded, though goose bumps rose at the memory of the caves.

"Good," he said.

"You'll ride with me," Father said.

"Darian will stay behind to watch the qits," added Mabir. "It's fair enough. You've watched his bondling for days."

"We're going *now*?" My stomach lurched. I felt completely unprepared.

Father gripped my other shoulder in one of his huge hands. "Captain Rov leaves soon to gather reinforcements for the aeries and the caves. We've waited long enough. Now's the time."

Father and Rov whistled to their mounts. Shuja and Cheien stepped out of the stable, stretching their wings, then followed us across the bridge to the paddock where Bellua's Zell waited. Father helped Mabir onto Zell's back, in front of Bellua. Tulo joined Rov on Cheien. I climbed onto Shuja with Father, and we buckled in.

It felt strange not to have Keirr with me. I'd barely spent more than a minute without her for days. It seemed like a betrayal to sneak off while she was eating. "We'll be back soon, right?"

"Don't worry about Keirr," Father said. "Jhem and Tauman are here. She'll be fine for a couple of hours." Then he whistled and shouted, "*HAI!*" Shuja leapt into the sky and his great wings pushed against gravity. Soon the aeries and Riat fell away behind us. The forest and ruins flashed beneath, then the valley of Cinvat was spread below us.

Shuja reached the cave in less than half an hour, where it had taken me a night and much of the following day to make that journey on foot.

Smoke came from the cave mouth, where I saw figures gathered—townsfolk, conscripted by Rov into a temporary militia. I'd assumed that's where we would go, but we flew on past the cave, the plateau, and over the next valley beyond, around the shoulder of the mountain to the far entrance where Darian and I fought the Harodhi leader and his Horrors. My stomach squirmed. I pressed back against Father. He hugged me to him.

Rov and Cheien landed first, scattering a black knot of scavenging crows. We circled until he waved us in, then Shuja beat back momentum with strokes of his wings and lit on the porch of the cave.

"Smaws bad," he said with his rumbling dragon's voice: *smells bad.*

Father patted the shoulder of his wing. "That it does, my friend."

Just beyond Cheien lay a pile of charred timbers and bones, the remnants of the nest I'd dumped on the Harodhi leader. The blistered corpse of his dragon stuck out in an array of ribs hung with blackened flesh. What hadn't burned was rotting faster than the crows could squirm through the debris to eat it. Lined up against the far wall were other skeletons—human skeletons—picked clean already. The carnage and the smells wiped the past week of joyous distraction out of my head. Nightmare images crawled beneath my thoughts.

"There's no need to tremble, Maia. We have militia here too. It's safe now. Take a deep breath."

I nodded and slid down from the saddle. The leathery crack of Zell's wings turned my head. Father and I dismounted as Mabir unbuckled, then Father and Bellua helped him down. Everyone dismounted.

"How did we miss seeing this entrance all these years?" asked Mabir.

"The opening is concealed by this overhang." Father pointed to the ceiling. "We'd have never seen it but for Maia's fire. There's some evidence that a bridge of stone once connected to the far slope. It's a wonder to me how much of our own history we lost in the wars with Gurvaan."

"Sadly true." Mabir picked his way carefully into the cave. When he spotted the corpse, his nose wrinkled in disgust, his eyes grew wide. "Is this the Horror?"

I shook my head as Father answered. "No, this is the Harodhi leader. The Horror is across the valley."

Mabir came to me and put an arm around my shoulder. "My dear sweet girl, only now do I begin to understand what you endured." He frowned and hugged me tighter. "You showed great bravery. Wear that with pride as armor against the nightmares." I linked my arm with his to steady him. He patted my arm and we started forward.

Bellua and Father followed, with Shuja and Zell behind. We caught up to Rov and Cheien. Tulo stood close to them, wide-eyed, clutching his quiver of drawing tools to his thin chest. The boy had some talent as an artist and came to draw pictures of the carvings for Mabir. A small group of nine or ten townsmen emerged out of the gloom of the hall. They were armed with crossbows and spears, though three also wore sheathed swords at their sides. They seemed relieved to see Captain Rov and his giant mount. I realized then that Rov had brought them provisions in a duffel bag. He passed it to the men as their leader gave his report, then he signaled us to follow.

The townsfolk gave the dragons plenty of room, but they all stared at me as I passed. "Greetings, young ma'am," said one of them, and smiled. "Ma'am," said another, touching his breast briefly, a greeting or sign of courtesy unfamiliar to me. Then he gave a sidelong glance to Bellua, and I paused. This unusual attention left me unsure what to say, so I nodded a silent greeting.

When my eyes adjusted to the light of torches set in sconces along the walls, I could better see things I'd missed before. Though badly eroded from countless centuries of moisture, friezes decorated every surface from knee-height to ceiling—of men and women in odd costumes, in scenes of daily routine, martial regimen, or bizarre conflict. Mabir touched them reverently, his eyes glistening. "Remarkable! I'm tempted to linger, but Tulo has already made drawings of this hallway for me. I truly want to see the chamber you described with the waterfall and the four doorways."

"That's further along," said Rov. "There's a long stair, but the steps are not steep. I think you can manage it with our help."

"You plan to close this entrance?" Mabir's smile faded.

"We must. It's a risk, and offers the easiest way out of the caverns for the Harodhi. We've barely begun to explore the other passages. The wise thing to do is seal every entrance we find, and then post guards."

Mabir looked disappointed. "Let's not dally then."

"I wish Fren could be here," said Father. "The best archer in all of Riat. Perhaps in all of Gadia." He took Mabir's other arm. Tulo followed our descent.

The way was as long as I remembered. The sharp smell of dry stone and ancient dust triggered a flood of memories, but I turned them aside with less trouble than I'd feared. Perhaps I was healing from the madness. Or perhaps the presence of Shuja and Cheien, a pair of trained Dragonry mounts, drove the darkest shadows away.

More than that, Mabir would finally explain *Asha* to me, if we could get away from Bellua and the others.

We emerged into the chamber with the fountain and the four doorways, each surmounted by a massive carving of a High Dragon. The supernatural awe I'd felt before filled me again, the grandeur not at all diminished by the presence of so many torches. The trickle of water from the overhead source echoed eerily, the blue luminance still cast rippling life upon the carvings. I wasn't fleeing for my life this time. I could look deeper. Here, next to the fountain, was a stain from Darian's wound. Here were Malik's bloody footprints, dried on the stone floor. And all around us, scribed into the walls, was a story.

Bellua followed Rov and Cheien around the perimeter with his hands clasped behind his back, into the furthest passage on our left, beneath the carving of Waeges, the Autumn Dragon in her leafy splendor. Tulo and the three militiamen followed him, and then Zell. Father and Shuja lingered behind.

But Mabir clung to my elbow, trembling. Tears shimmered in his eyes. "Show me," he said, his voice cracking. "Describe again your experience here."

I pointed to the eastern entrance, beneath the carving of Getig. "We entered there," I said.

"*Of course you did.*" A whisper.

"What is this place?" I answered. "You've made me wait long enough. Tell me what this is, and tell me about Asha."

Mabir's eyes glittered in the light of the scattered torches. "Yes, I have, and I apologize. This is difficult for me, because it awakens knowledge I'd buried for years, decades. Forbidden knowledge. Heresy. You cannot know this, and yet I am compelled to tell you."

My heart pounded in my chest. For several minutes Mabir let the sound of falling water alone fill the silence.

"This room," I said. "It's the Cycles, isn't it."

"Yes. More than mere history. These images may be older even than Cinvat." He sat on the wall containing the pool and faced the image of Getig.

I sat beside him. "Dhalla, what is *Asha*? Is it one of the Avar?"

He looked at me sidelong, and a smile touched one corner of his mouth. "It is an old name, my dear. An old name indeed. It predates Korruzon and the ruins in our forest." He scanned about the chamber: Bellua and Rov were out of sight down the hallway beneath Waeges, but Father approached us with a casual restraint that made me think that he knew our conversation wasn't meant for others to hear. When Mabir saw him, he smiled at me and then waved Father over.

"Come, Magha. You might as well hear this too. Your family history is in the telling."

Father's face lit with curiosity and he dropped down beside Mabir. Shuja sat a few strides away and clicked once or twice, looking up at the carvings as if they made sense to him.

———

"In ages past, before Korruzon, there was *Asha*. This was a temple that revered Asha. It's a name once given to the original Source, but not the tale the Rasaal tells, of Korruzon as world-creator, who pushed mountains and seas into their present shapes with the writhing of His preordinal body. It is simpler, but harder to explain, too.

"Asha is a name, but not for a deity. It means *Truth*, no more, but no less—the Eternal Law, whether one understands it or not." He presented the entire room with his extended arms. "This is Asha as they understood it. Look at the carvings. Above each door, marking each transition to a next phase, you see a spirit embodying a season. Getig as the Avar of material abundance and fullness—see the sun high in the sky, above fields of crops. Now move counterclockwise around the room, the way the planet spins if you view it from the pole."

I wasn't sure what he meant by that, but I didn't interrupt.

"Observe images of fields being harvested but also of conflict. What are those machines? I have never seen the like. Sweet Avar, the detail is astounding!" His lips were quivering. "Then comes Waeges in the north, the Autumn Dragon with her leafy mien."

Mabir shivered. "If Getig symbolizes a tipping point, then Waeges signifies a world at the midpoint of mad descent, when Order gives way to Chaos." His face fell all at once, and his voice caught in his throat. "And then, after Waeges, we see full-scale war."

A tear slid down his cheek, and I looked to where his gaze directed me. An image I'd barely studied before: dragons carved into a smoke-filled sky, battling strange beasts with rigid wings and odd ovoid shapes, like whales festooned with sails and other artifice. Not natural creatures, but constructs. And in the terrain below, more strange machinery, like horseless wagons with bizarre ballistae or other weapons unknown built into their frames. Buildings burned, people turned anguished faces to the sky.

"Menog in the west marks the low point," he continued, "the setting of the sun. Perhaps the most intangible of the Avar. See how the sculptor rendered His wings as transparent. Even in stone, the background shows through. Brilliant. Menog symbolizes the spiritual center that remains when all else has fallen into ruin—the true heart of us. And He is the promise of Renewal; note the seeds at his feet. Between Menog and Oestara, the conflict ends in ruin, but in the midst of the decay, at the edge of the season, people return, buildings are erected, fields are sown. Peace settles again. The Avar of Spring, Oestara, rises with the sun on the southern wall, and the cycle begins anew."

The creases of his face were damp with tears.

"You see here a telling not just of seasons but more importantly of the Cycles, the greater turnings of a cosmic wheel. The seasons turn. A life is born, gives birth to another life, then passes. Entire civilizations rise and fall again. There is always another turn waiting. That's what the Cycles are—the perpetual reawakening of Asha. The Avar, whatever they are, are all *of* Asha, whatever Asha *is*. For many ages, the followers of Asha, the Ashaani, embraced an abstract philosophy that sought only *Truth*. They never dared to confine Asha to a description, for words limit, confine. The Ashaani made communion with Asha through spiritual practices, not rote ceremony; with questions, not infallible answers; a philosophy of careful doubt coupled with exploration, humility seeking knowledge."

I shook my head. "I don't understand."

Mabir leaned toward me. "You can only know what you know. Belief is not the same as knowledge. Belief is an assumption of knowledge despite a lack of evidence. Or so the old faith explained. The Ashaani wanted proof, and made ways to test every thought. Many of our sciences are but shadows left from their time. The new Temple—the Rasaal—took what was *Asha* and renamed it *Korruzon*, which shifted the narrative of the universe. The Cycles still remain in our philosophy, but in the High Dragon Korruzon we were given an ultimate, undying champion, a living manifestation of the true God—not merely an explanation of rebirth and renewal. Korruzon displaces Asha's inevitable turnings with purpose, replacing Asha's simple acknowledgment of life and death with authority that will encompass all things at the ultimate end of time. The Rasaal speaks of mysteries that the Ashaani wouldn't give voice to, because they chose not to believe in anything they couldn't weigh or touch or see. Or so the *new* faith says." He sat straight again. "Of course the names of the Avar are known throughout Gurvaan. Every loving home has an altar to Armath. Metalworkers honor Kreela, and farmers revere Amrah. And so forth. But the Rasaal gave them a new explanation, as the many guises of Korruzon."

He fell silent. Father and I locked gazes for several seconds, and I sensed that he deferred to me. Why? Because I had seen Getig?

I touched Mabir's hand. "You say that all Avar are *of* Asha. The Rasaal says they are all guises or reflections of Korruzon. What's the difference? Why does that make Asha so scary to Bellua?"

"Because the Rasaal disavows the greater Cycle. It teaches that all of creation will proceed to an ultimate end, with Korruzon as its Redeemer. But the Ashaani, who revere Asha, believe that Korruzon—even though he has been physically present for hundreds of years—*will pass*. That undermines Bellua's entire faith. It makes Korruzon *of* Asha, too.

"When Gurvaan conquered us, the Ashaani were declared heretics and put to the sword, hunted and sacrificed on the altar of the new truth. Convert or die. Few survive, and their church is hidden. Magha, your father's father begged my silence when I was but the youngest acolyte of the new religion. He didn't want you or your father to hear the stories or learn the ancient scripture because he feared it would put the aeries at risk. He converted for your sake. I've held this close all these years. Please forgive me."

Father wore an expression I hadn't seen on his face before: Wonder. Ghosts haunted this ancient place, it seemed. The ghosts of an old philosophy or a buried truth. I looked for Bellua and Rov again—these truths would trouble Bellua—but they were nowhere to be seen.

"I admit I didn't know what to believe," Mabir continued. "The old ways were simple and humble. They valued Truth, *whatever* it might be. They sought to move closer to Truth by discovering what was clearly *not* true. And yet the new faith compelled me. I grew eager to know everything the Rasaal knew that the Ashaani did not. Nonetheless, I sought to temper my acceptance of the new order with an admiration for the old. Alas, the Temple of the Rasaal would allow only its own teachings."

I finally understood the difficulty he faced in defending me, even if I still felt that he'd betrayed me before. He had struggled with this conflict all his life, finding a comfortable middle ground, only to see it challenged by my encounter with Getig.

Peace transformed his expression as he studied the wonders of this temple to Asha. Neither Father nor I would interrupt his reverie. Finally, he turned to me again. "Maia, Fren spoke the name *Asha* to you. Did he say anything else?"

I looked between Father and Mabir. I swallowed. "He said, '*I knew that you were a sign to me, that Asha has not been displaced, that the world is still true. I will wear my scars with pride, for they helped to send you on your journey.*' Then he said something strange, '*One will lead and one will follow. One will rise and one will fall.*' Then he said that there is darkness coming. That I should hold to Getig, and to Asha."

Mabir didn't speak for several long seconds, with the splash of water and its eerie echoes the only sounds.

"What did he mean, dhalla?"

"As you might guess, Fren is an elder in Asha's hidden church. His simple forest life masks a well of knowledge in the old ways. But he spoke from delirium. It may have been no more than an expression of his faith."

I shook my head. The religion of our lives in the aeries was the *work* that we did, with very little time for thoughts about the finer points of history. "Dhalla, what do *you* believe?"

He dabbed at his eyes with his beard, studied me for what seemed like an age, then bent to pick up a long stick. He turned to the fountain. "One of the lessons I recall from my childhood came from the Ashaani—that of the Eddy in the River." With the stick he pointed toward a rivulet coursing a path through the matrix of stone and crystal. "Do you see that spot where the stream swirls into an eddy behind a loose stone?"

I nodded.

"What is an eddy? Is it a thing that you can hold? Could you remove that eddy, take it to another place and still have an eddy? Of course not. And yet there it is. Water moves through it, for a time becomes its substance. Then the water moves out. All things are like that eddy, dependent on a very precise set of circumstances to exist—persisting for a time, occasionally for a very long time. But it's all in motion. You are made of the food you eat, the air you breathe. Much of you has moved on. Your skin sloughs off, your hair falls out. Trees grow from the forest mulch, then topple and decay, or they're hewn into lumber and made into houses. The houses fall, the wood rots. Mountains are torn down to reveal the bones of sea creatures imbedded in the cliffs. Languages change and become new languages. Beliefs are altered by other beliefs. All things have the appearance of solidity, but it's an illusion, a trick of perception drawn from our eternal entrapment in the present. Only memory reveals the truth, yet even memory is but an eddy in your mind.

"Religion may be the most ephemeral eddy of them all. It persists with a name and a building where the faithful congregate over generations. The faith the first generation embraced might be unrecognizable to the last, even though the building and the name have remained unchanged." He reached out with the stick and poked a pebble into the eddy. The swirl of water changed shape.

"We are all eddies in a great stream of perpetual change. The universal engine never slows, never fails. It is the Evertide. A simple truth that threatens the authority of the Rasaal."

I didn't know what to think at first, but when I recalled my experience in the valley of Cinvat where a forest grew up through the bones of a lost civilization, it made sense.

He took a long breath before continuing. "Fren may have been delirious, but he would not be alone in wondering if Getig's appearance kicked a stone from beneath the foundation of the Rasaal." Mabir's chin jutted out, his mouth firm with resolve. Tears glistened in the corners of his eyes. Then he looked at me. "I have spent my entire life doubting the faith I championed." He turned back to the fountain and pushed the stone out of the path of the rivulet, and the eddy disappeared.

"Before your experience, Maia, I was still torn. But now I know. When answers are so difficult, an assumption of certainty is a hindrance. The path of acceptance, of not-knowing, is closer to the ways of the Ashaani than of Korruzon. By leaving you open to the voice of the universe—or of Asha, if you will—doubt can lead you where certainty never will." He smiled, a look of joy tinged with regret.

"That's what I believe."

———

Shuja stood and whirled, looking toward the northern portal, beneath Waeges. He clicked once, loudly. Echoes returned.

"What is it?" Father stood, too.

"Fee-t. Come fass-t."

I heard them too, and then Tulo burst into the chamber at full speed. Father and Shuja were already at the door as Bellua and then Zell charged through. "Get out!" Bellua shouted, pointing at us. "Get Mabir out of here!"

Two of the militiamen rushed through the door next, one of them dragging the third, hanging limp in his arms. Then Cheien backed out with Rov beside him, loosing arrows through the door into the darkness beyond. Something had chased them out of the deeper cave.

I grabbed Mabir's elbow—fear had charged him with unexpected energy. I steadied him as he made for the exit below Menog's image. Bellua met us there with Zell beside him and took Mabir's other elbow.

Shouts turned my head. Cheien and Shuja, side by side, their wings folded back tight, lashed out with talons at figures running through the portal. The two militiamen laid their wounded comrade down and drew their bows. Father loosed arrows now, too, at the shrouded mass pouring through the door.

Harodhi.

THIRTY

THEIR ARROWS FILLED the air, but the Harodhi died quickly with a slash of talons or snap of jaw. More streamed out to replace them. Father and Rov were forced to retreat, their dragons following in their defense. But something was off. The Harodhi seemed panicked, as if they fled something.

One of the militiamen took a crossbow bolt in the chest. He fell backward, his crossbow clattering to the floor. Bellua had hold of Mabir, so I dashed to the townsman's side. He looked up at me and gasped, "Ma'am, you must leave."

I took up his crossbow and slung it over my shoulder, then sat him up with my arms beneath his and pulled him backward. He groaned in pain but did his best to help me with his feet, then scrambled upright.

Rov returned volleys with his longbow at a rapid pace. Another militiaman fell with an arrow in his neck. Father loosed directly into the face of a fighter who had slipped past Shuja, then nocked another arrow. I pulled the crossbow off my shoulder.

From the Waeges portal came a rumble, and then screams of terror. Several more Harodhi soldiers tumbled out in full panic. The air suddenly turned icy cold, and a shadow emerged.

Gigantic. Intangible. Like a winged shadow cast upon the walls. The air around it rippled like heat-shimmer off hot stone. Two Harodhi soldiers, too slow to escape its touch, dropped, clutching their heads.

I heard Mabir cry out behind me. He and Bellua stood motionless. "*Go!*" shouted Father, looking back at us. He and Rov and their mounts backed toward us quickly now, maintaining a wall that no Harodhi passed.

But the thing did not follow us. Its presence was insubstantial, confusing. It strode or swarmed into a position between the portraits of Getig and Waeges, and crouched with cat-like menace.

The Harodhi now had room to spread out, threatening to surround Father and Rov, Shuja and Cheien. I eased the militiaman down and then spanned his crossbow. He watched, handing me a bolt from his quiver. I loaded it, listening as Father's shouts and Rov's commands took on a tinge of panic.

Suddenly every nightmare image from my first trip through the caves exploded in my head. Not trickling in and then spilling out, as they'd done over the past weeks, but all at once—an eruption—as if they'd been forced into my mind from without. I froze, stunned. Pain burst behind my eyes. I heard screams all around and knew they were fearful. Vaguely, I saw the flurry of attacks by Shuja and Cheien. My vision tunneled past them to the thing hovering like ichor in an eddy of shadow. I knew it was looking at me. It had no eyes, but it saw me. Through me. Into me. I was reminded of Getig's meaningful gaze, but where the eyes of the Summer Dragon lent warmth and purpose, this abomination offered only fear: Darian's festering wound, fire, pain, exhaustion. A heroic dragon's dying breath. Blackened carcasses, with cold green flames lighting wounds that should have killed them. A fly crawling on an eyeball. My own fears, turned back on me like weapons.

But I've already faced these specters and won.

Aru, his strength ebbing, Darian unwaking.

Darian lives!

My mother, seated on Grus, scorn in her voice, disappointment on her face. Guilt pierced me, and I faltered, cried out in shock.

A dragon rider with her head in the clouds is cursed.

Did it speak to me? Or evoke my own voice, testing me? It didn't matter, it couldn't show me a fear I hadn't fought already. I'd faced these demons, put them behind me, and won my Keirr.

Arms trembling, I loosed my bolt. The arrow passed through the shadow and struck the far wall. The militiaman cried out in pain but pressed another arrow into my hand. I spanned and reloaded, gasp-

ing. Steadied my aim, loosed again, and dropped a fighter coming up
on Father's right. Something whistled past my head. I spanned the
bow, felt another arrow in my hand, chose another Harodhi warrior,
missed wide to the right. After each shot I met the eyeless gaze of the
thing, fought a blindness of pain behind my eyes. Loosed again. Then
there were only three Harodhi warriors standing, then two, then
none.

We all stood panting, waiting. I realized that Father had lifted the
soldier beside me and pulled him back. Shuja backed up next to me on
my right, Cheien on my left.

The thing stretched, hovered, diminished a bit perhaps, but threw
my fear at me still. I forced myself to think of Keirr, and new images
flooded into me, of my own broken bones and of Keirr crumpled like
a discarded chicken carcass.

I'm not afraid of you. I tried to mean it.

"Gods, my lady! Get out!" The weak voice of the townsman.

Shuja roared defiance, then Cheien. Bellua and Mabir were out of
immediate danger, well up the stair behind us. Only myself, a
wounded militiaman, Father and Rov, and our dragons remained. All
of us had faced fear before and overcome it. We wouldn't fail this test.

The creature threw this morning's nightmare at me, blended with
the one from the night before, images of carrion and blood and fire
and screaming faces, a litany of my worst dreams jumbled together.

But every day I wake.

The shadow reared. Wings like smoke spread out to either side,
spanning the distance between Getig and Waeges.

"I'm not afraid of you!" I shouted.

It showed me an image of myself, small and frightened, and then
crushed into bloody paste where I stood by an intangible force. I cried
out but loosed my last arrow into the place where it swam like a black
fog. The thing swirled, coiled, and charged.

Shuja and Cheien leapt to meet it, roaring defiance, and slashing
with talons and teeth. Where they ripped, it swirled like smoke and
dissipated. When it struck back, our dragons roared with pain and
confusion, though it left no marks. Cheien gave ground and it followed, but Shuja swiped at what might have been wings. When it
turned to Shuja, Cheien delivered a flurry of blows. It seemed scat-

tered now, like a fog of rain evaporating over a fire. Then it retreated, but our war dragons followed unrelenting.

It faded, and then disappeared entirely. We waited several minutes, but save for our labored breathing and the ever-present trickle of water, only silence followed. Every face was streaked with sweat. Cheien plucked an arrow out of his foreleg with his teeth. Shuja shook several arrows out of his left wing and roared, but his tone was different than I'd ever heard. Anger with an edge of fear.

"Sweet Avar, what in the name of holiness was that?" asked Father.

"Cold," said Shuja. "Cold fire."

"Like the Horrors," I said.

No one answered, but realization struck me with the force of a dragon's tail swipe that the thing had been in my head, reading my memories, taunting me with them. I felt a tickle in my right nostril, on my lip, and touched it—blood stained my fingers.

I wiped it off on my pants and turned to see Father supporting the militiaman's head in his lap. The man's eyes were fixed on me, and he reached out with a shaking hand. "Young ma'am, you are unhurt?"

I nodded yes, shocked at his pale face. He smiled weakly. "You were brave," he said, then coughed. A spout of blood splashed on his jerkin and ran down his chin and neck. With a shudder, he crumpled in Father's embrace. Father placed a hand over the man's eyes and looked at me. I fought back a sob. I didn't even know his name.

Rov knelt next to me, where one of the Harodhi lay. "This one here still lives." A crossbow quarrel thrust up from the man's chest. Blood pumped out around it.

Bellua joined us and bent close to the pale face, made even more ghostly by blood loss. "What was that apparition?" he demanded.

Rov repeated the question in the strange cadence of the Harodhi tongue, and the foreigner replied haltingly, eyes darting back and forth between Rov and Bellua, blood trickling from his mouth.

"He says it forces them somehow."

Bellua frowned. "That makes no sense. They had battle rage."

Rov spoke again in the harsh tongue and shook the man when he seemed about to pass out. The answer was a mumble. "It drives them, he says. Like dogs. Fills them with something . . . a word I don't recognize. Something to do with, not hunger, but *eating*. He says it's not one of them, and he begs for mercy."

The man muttered something else.

"What?" said Bellua.

Rov looked disappointed. "He wants to go home."

The man stopped breathing. The blood oozing from his wound trickled to a stop. Silence surrounded us, but my heart pounded in my ears.

"How did it get into our heads?" I said.

Bellua turned to me slowly. He was deathly pale, clearly shaken by all he'd witnessed. "What do you mean?"

"How did it . . . ? Didn't it . . . ? It was in my head, using my fear like—it didn't do the same to you?" Panic rose in me as I realized that the thing had attacked only my mind. No one else's. And I'd said so aloud, to Bellua. Given him a new weapon that he wouldn't fail to use.

But he said nothing. He only stared at me with shock. Or fear. Or horror.

"That decides it," said Captain Rov. "The caves will be sealed as soon as possible. Magha, I won't be leaving immediately after all. I can't leave now. I'm sorry, but I'll have to draft Tauman as a courier to Avigal with requisition orders." He went to the other downed militiaman, hefted his limp body over one broad shoulder with one arm. Rov winced, and I saw a Harodhi arrow in the other. "Let's get these men outside."

Father only nodded, then gathered the dead townsman in his arms. Bellua struggled but finally lifted the third. I took Mabir's arm. We left through the Menog portal, Cheien and Shuja bringing up the rear. No one spoke again until we'd emerged into the full light of day.

WE LEFT THE BODIES of the militiamen on the porch of the cave, in the care of their fellow townsmen, with a promise from Rov that he would return before nightfall. On the flight home, I said nothing, and Father asked no questions. He only crushed me in the protective circle of his arms and cursed once or twice under his breath.

I hurried to the winter stable as soon as we landed, leaving Jhem to help Father with Shuja's saddle. I rushed past Cheien as he landed with Rov and Tulo. Darian wasn't around, and I didn't look for him. I only wanted to see Keirr, to wrap my arms around her and sob into her neck.

I thought I'd improved, that the worst of my trauma lay behind me, but my wounds were opened anew. Keirr licked the tears from my face and wriggled happily. Her cheerful purring soon calmed my shakes. When she mowped eagerly for her dinner, I was finally able to dry my eyes.

She cocked her head at me. "Mowp, Maia. Hwssh."

"A sentence! You funny girl!" I caressed her cheek. "Well, that deserves a reward. Fish it is."

We crossed the bridge toward the paddock, but as we approached the corner of the storehouse, I heard Bellua's voice. I pulled up short and restrained Keirr with a silencing hand wrapped around her muzzle.

Mabir spoke. "Don't make a false correlation. You don't know that it has anything more than coincidence to do with Maia."

"Then why was it in her head and not yours or mine? What is it about her that puts her at the center of . . ."

"Of what?" Jhem's voice.

Bellua snapped, "I don't know! Whatever this is. First a manifestation of Korruzon in Summer's garb, then the business with Horrors, and now . . ." His words trailed off again.

I kicked myself for saying anything at all about the creature's presence in my mind, in my mind and no other, sifting through my fears the way a dog paws through garbage. Had it *spoken* to me, too, using my own inner voice? Or did it simply evoke my fears with language I supplied myself? The memories were muddled, elusive. Was I losing my mind? I felt that word nibbling at the edge of thought again—*curse*. Its best attack had been an image of my mother. I pushed the thought aside angrily.

Father's voice. "You imply that her presence summoned it. That's unfair."

"That's not what I said, only that once more she is present at a moment of crisis and has contact with things that none of the rest of us have contact with."

I'd heard enough. I marched around the corner. "Was *that* a shadow of Korruzon too? Was it one of the Avar?" My voice cracking.

Bellua paused for a moment, then spoke with measured cadence. "That was most certainly *not* a shadow of Korruzon."

"Then what was it? It attacked me, in my mind, like someone else telling me what to think, or feel. It used my own fears to try to frighten me, blind me. It didn't do the same to you?"

Bellua shook his head.

"It didn't try to get inside your thoughts?"

"No."

Father's hands braced my shoulders from behind me. "I saw it drop at least two of the Harodhi just by engulfing them. But I didn't see whether they got up again."

If it had touched me like it did those men, would it have won full access to my mind? Is that why they fell screaming? Shuja and Cheien sounded confused when they met it in combat. The thing had entered my mind with precision and purpose, even if that purpose was a mystery. What was it? I didn't want to call it "the thing" forever. I needed to know what it was.

"When the last of them fell, it seemed to lose strength," said Father. "And it faltered when Maia shouted defiance at it. Then our dragons took it apart quickly. The last Harodhi to die claimed no bond with it before he died. He said it drove them."

Bellua spoke to Father. "It raises another question—or a familiar question: What was it that Darian and Maia really saw on—"

"We've covered this ground," said Mabir. "Your warnings are as shapeless now as they were then."

"What shape would you like? The shape of that aberration in the cave was ominous enough, don't you think? *'For the powers of deceit are ancient, and prosper in the shadow of ignorance.'* " He looked at me as he said it, his voice rising. "So says the Rasaal. I should contact the Rasaal for guidance. I should take Maia back to Avigal."

Mabir spoke patiently. "Other scriptures offer an explanation for what it might have been: one of the *Edimmu* or *Utukku*, the dark manifestations of the Avar."

"That was not of the Avar."

" *'As day precedes night, so Light recedes, that Darkness may surely follow.'* "

Keirr's head pressed under my hand. I cupped my fingers under her jaw to keep her silent while I waited to hear Bellua's answer.

"Heretical scripture," he said. "I wondered if your visit to the caverns would awaken the past in your ancient heart. Be wary what you wish for. You do not want such a thing to manifest as real. And be wary what you reveal about your true yearning, old man."

My stomach tightened with concern for Mabir, but again he answered calmly. "If answers are needed, then should we not look everywhere? Or should we cling to assumptions and bring about our own demise?"

"Do not question the teachings of the Rasaal."

Mabir nodded slowly. "I question only *your* assumptions."

"And I act only to prevent another calamity in the wake of this girl's actions—"

"Why don't you trust me?" The words were out of my mouth before I'd considered them. "You know I didn't ask for this. All I ever wanted was what I have right here." I laid a hand on Keirr's head.

He stared at me for several seconds, anger threatening his careful facade. "It's not you I distrust, Maia. Ultimately, it's the darkness I fear. It seduces, and it lies. I am familiar with the old religions, and they are too accommodating. Evil pries at their cracks, slithers in through the flaws in their doctrines. For whatever reason, forces have gathered around your innocence, but it's impossible for me to know what they are. I would hate for you to be exploited."

"How can you be so sure that you're right?"

"It's not a question of right or wrong, Maia, but one of awareness and obedience. I have given my life to the Rasaal, and to Korruzon—who's kept the Empire safe for hundreds of years. The Temple's strength is in its structure, a bulwark against the darkness. We are stronger united, Maia."

"Then why do you fight us?"

"I don't fight—"

"You do too. You've been horrible to me since the day you arrived. You don't fool me. You interpret everything so that it fits your doctrine, and you leave no room for discussion."

"Because there *is* no room for discussion. I speak from knowledge. The Rasaal is the absolute true source of—"

"What if it isn't? What if you're wrong?"

His face hardened. "You're a child. You don't have experience enough to challenge—"

"But Mabir does, and you don't like it!"

"I—"

"We need to know what that thing in the cave was, and you are no help. What was it? What did it do to me? Why haven't we seen it before? Why are you so much more concerned for the Rasaal than you are for the aeries, or Riat? Or me?"

"I don't fear for the Rasaal, but for your home province of Gadia and the empire that nurtures it. *And* for you."

"Then tell me what it was!"

He stared down at me with eyes like granite, nostrils flared. "I don't know what it was."

"How can you not know?" I could hear my voice rising and hated it, but I couldn't stop. "What good is your rank and all your learning if you can't explain what in Korruzon's name that thing is?"

He took a deep breath. "History is not an open book. Only some truths are clear to see."

"The truth scares you."

His face twitched, and I knew I'd touched a nerve. So I pressed it harder. "You only ever see what you've been told to see. You're so afraid it was something that shouldn't exist, something you shouldn't believe in, you pretend it was something else."

"I don't speculate. There is danger in assumptions—"

"Mabir had a name for it, but you didn't like it. *Itimuu* or *Edukku* or something."

He took a deep breath and let it out slowly through his nose. "History shows us this much: that the religions of the past were but stepping-stones to the present, many of them deeply flawed. That's why they were branded as heresies, so that the cancer of their distortions could be cut out of the Temple body. Mabir risks much by entertaining them." His eyes sparked. "And so will you, if you listen to him."

Father stepped between Bellua and me, putting his nose within an inch of Bellua's. "You might want to reconsider before you think to threaten my children."

Bellua held his gaze until footsteps and the padding of a dragon turned our heads. Tauman and Darian approached us on the bridge, with Rannu and Aru right behind.

"Gentlemen. Lady." Bellua looked only at Jhem when he said it. Then he turned and sped across the bridge to the manor, where his rooms were. I didn't watch him go.

Father's eyes followed him only for a second or two, then he patted my shoulder.

Jhem touched my chin. "That was well said, Maia."

"Agreed," said Father.

Mabir nodded solemn agreement.

Before I could respond, Tauman joined us. "What's going on? Rov told me to gear up for a trip. Where are we going?"

Father set his jaw grimly. "Just you. You're going to Avigal."

Tauman's eyes widened with surprise. "What? Why?"

"Something new has come up, and Rov has drafted you as a courier to the capital to deliver requisitions."

"I thought *he* was going to—"

"I'll explain while we saddle Rannu. Jhem, have Kaisi put together provisions for a long journey: jerky, hulled oats, dried fruit. She knows what to do. We'll need coin from the reserves, too. One hundred pieces of silver, ten of gold."

"Of course," said Jhem and shared a look of concern with her husband. She would be responsible for three dragons while Tauman was away on Rannu, and weeks or months separated from her mate and her bonded human might leave Athys nervous or despondent.

"Be sure to watch Audax," he said. "Don't let him get the upper hand. You have to be strong with him."

Jhem's chin dropped, and she winced at the remark. I knew the incident that wounded Fren still weighed on her.

"I'll help," said Father, fixing Tauman with a stern eye.

"Athys and Grus have practically adopted Keirr," I said. "I'll engage Athys as much as I can."

She smiled at me. "Thank you." She started to walk toward the manor but turned and threw her arms around Tauman, burying her face in his shoulder. "This is so sudden." When she pulled away again to look at him, her eyes brimmed with tears.

He kissed her forehead and stroked her hair. "I'll be fine. You'll see. We can say our farewells later."

"Do you trust me?" Her eyes were unsure and questing.

"What choice do I have?" he said.

Jhem's face fell, and she broke into a run before she'd crossed the bridge, passing the Dragonry Captain at mid-span.

Father leaned close to Tauman. "Tame your tongue, boy. You choose this moment to be her taskmaster? Learn some patience."

"Because you're such a great example of patience?"

Father squinted. "Your timing leaves—"

"Gentlemen," said Mabir, pointing.

Father glanced over Tauman's shoulder and sighed. "Save it. Here comes Rov." Then he got in the last word, pointing at Tauman's nose. "Make it right with her, boy."

Tauman's eyes held Father's, but he nodded. When he and Father turned to Rov their faces were composed, the clouds rolled back.

Rov handed Tauman a scroll case sealed with black wax. "Take this to the Ministry of the Dragonry. I've requisitioned Dragonry regulars, plus masons and engineers to seal the caves." Then he handed over another scroll, tied with black string, affixed to one end of the parchment with his seal. "This note authorizes you to pay for expenses along the way with Dragonry script. Get invoices for travel expenses, and they'll be paid."

Father clapped a hand on Tauman's shoulder. "I'd save that for a last resort. Use the metal first and keep a ledger. Keep a low profile while you travel; press gangs will look greedily on a lone dragon and rider. That's bad enough. But men would kill for a letter such as that. Wear your sword and bow, so they know you're not to be trifled with."

"I can do that." Tauman looked grim.

"He can't be gone beyond Menog's Day," said Father. "That's rutting season, so obviously I need Rannu here."

"He won't be delayed. Following what happened in Cuuloda, this will be a priority."

Father looked Tauman in the eye, at the same time pulling his ring—his broodmaster's signet—off his finger. He pressed it into Tauman's hand. "Wear this. You'll have a broodmaster's signet and Rov's seal as defense."

"And mine." Bellua had returned, also bearing a scroll case but sealed with red string and red wax. He looked at me as he passed, but his expression was unreadable. He placed his scroll case into Tauman's hands. "I prepared this for the next courier. I didn't expect it would be you. I'm sorry about that. But take it to the Rasaal. Give it directly to Poritor, in the Ministry of Acquisitions. His name is inscribed on the outside."

"What is it?" asked Father.

"A report, and a request for instructions from the Rasaal, and—depending on their orders—a request that some personal effects might accompany Rov's requisitions. Nothing more."

Mabir nodded slowly. "You could go with Tauman. Why stay?"

Bellua looked at Father and Tauman, then at Rov. But his gaze stopped on me.

"How can I leave?" he said. "Someone must represent Korruzon in Riat."

I STOOD AT THE PARAPET and watched Jhem escort Tauman out, my arms wrapped around myself even though the air was warm. Soon they disappeared into the dusty late afternoon sky.

Darian and I fed our qits, then led them back to the winter stable to bed down for the night. I stroked Keirr's ear frills while I filled Darian in on what happened in the caves. He listened without comment, lying next to Aru, though his brows were drawn tight and his lips pursed in thought. I realized that at some point he'd fallen asleep. He was still mending, and an ordinary day of work wore him out. Aru and Keirr breathed slowly and deeply.

I'd been talking to the twilight.

Father's whisper startled me. "Grus needs some time in the air tonight. Would you care to join us?"

I nodded yes.

Father led Grus from the winter stable across the bridge to the tack house, where he had her saddle readied. Rannu's saddle berth stood empty, which put a sinking feeling in my stomach. We saddled Grus in silence. Father climbed aboard, then offered me a hand up. We strapped in—me in front, his arms around me.

Grus leaped eagerly into the deepening sky. The air was cool and sinking, so Grus had to row hard with her wings to gain altitude. Eventually we climbed into the last of the fleeting sunlight and circled.

Father had taken me on flights like this since I was small. I loved the freedom of the sky, the crispness of the rushing wind, the feel of powerful muscles working beneath me. But melancholy rode with us tonight, not least because Grus keened softly, still mourning her latest stolen brood. She was the most sensitive of our broodmothers and almost surely felt the tension between the humans in her world as well.

Only the winking of lights in windows indicated where Riat lay, all but invisible in the shadow of the mountains on the plains below. The aeries capped a pinnacle of stone which thrust like a ghostly finger above that darkness. Far to the east, banks of thunderheads flickered aggressively, as on the night following Getig's appearance. Tauman would be flying through that.

"We've been raising dragons in Riat for twenty generations," Father said, breaking the stillness. "Since before the Empire took our province and established its rule. There is dragonlore passed down from the beginning that you have yet to learn." He paused while Grus banked into a shaft of light. "Dragons are sensitive to the rhythms of the cycles, their nature attuned to a coming necessity. When hard times approach, dragons lay larger clutches. They make more little dragons, so that there's a greater chance some will survive. They don't think about it, they just do it, like when a cat or a horse puts on a thicker coat before a hard winter. A wild dragon lays two, maybe three eggs. In an aerie, the normal clutch is five, sometimes six eggs. This year our dams laid seven, eight, and nine eggs. So I've had a sign of my own in the nature of the cycles, and it mirrors your sighting of Getig. Change is coming, whatever Bellua may want us to believe."

He pulled me closer, wrapped his arms tighter. I sank into his embrace, willing the events of the day to recede. But they wouldn't. I frowned. "What are the Avar, really?"

Father hesitated before he answered, and then he spoke haltingly, as if searching for the right words. "Once, long ago, during my time in the Dragonry, I befriended a mercenary man from the far reaches of Telamon. He insisted that the Avar only manifest as dragons—or we only see them as dragons—because dragons are so important in our culture. In his land, he said there are no dragons, because it's a hostile desert that can't support such large predators. Instead, the Most High take on the appearance of great horses. He suggested that they might not be gods, but creatures of nature, or as he put it 'reflections of the greater tide.' The important fact is not *what* they are, but *that* they are. That seems a lot like the Ashaani idea, doesn't it? The merihem would call that blasphemy, but the merihem would also agree that the High Dragons are mystical beings of spirit and something *more* than the stuff of our world. Sometimes they linger and offer guidance, as in the case of Korruzon. Sometimes they just appear and vanish again, and who can say what it means."

I shivered. "I remember when the fishermen said they'd seen Khordad moving in the tides, and everyone thought they lied. A few days later they hauled in an astounding number of fish. But then the blacksmith—I can't remember his name—said he saw a vision of Vashita in his fire, and a week later he died when his shop burned down."

"Grogen. His name was Grogen."

I considered a universe that turned like a grindstone with us as the grist, and my brow pinched into a frown. "So we are merely the playthings of mystical dragons and horses."

"Heh. It seems that way sometimes."

"And no one really knows what they are."

For a few moments, Father let silence express whatever it was that troubled him. "I saw Korruzon that one time," he said at last. "He was amazing. A gigantic presence, dark and inspiring and terrible and uplifting all at once. But if I hadn't, I might believe that all talk of High Dragons was foolishness meant to keep the weak-minded in shackles. The dhalla and merihem see only the words in their scriptures. They make words their slaves, and use them to enslave others. The Temple is as much a construct of words as it is stone and mortar." His voice grew heated. "Even the painted-glass windows, rather than looking out into the real world, give us illusions of fantasies they want us to see instead. The real world is never so easy to define as their—"

His words ended with a growl, and he kissed the back of my head. "I'm sorry. I'm the wrong person to answer your question. There was little discussion of belief in our household, and now I know why. It seems my whole family embraced a lie in order to keep our aeries but in support of our conquerors. I don't know how I feel about that either, except that we do well by our village and farms. We've preserved something that might have been taken from us. But I shouldn't poison you with my lack of faith. Not after what you've been through. I'm confused too. I don't know what that monster was, or what it did to you."

He sighed. "I wish I knew what I believed."

I'd always admired the stained glass windows with their depictions of historic events—Korruzon as a towering, noble presence above his many subservient aspects—the Avar that populated our stories. Was Getig among them? I couldn't even remember. And now those windows had been cast into shadow, not only by Mabir's revelations but by my own father's words. His simple confession of uncertainty moved and troubled me.

I breathed deeply. "Mabir said doubt can lead where certainty never will."

"Perhaps," said Father. "But it's a more difficult path."

"Maybe we're not supposed to know. Maybe we're really only supposed to ask."

"That would be the Ashaani idea again, wouldn't it?"

Grus found a rising current, and we spiraled upward in silence for several minutes. I leaned back against Father, glad to have his arms around me.

After a few minutes, however, the silence became uncomfortable. "I'm sad that Rov is sealing the caves," I said. "I want to know more, but we won't see them again as long as we're at war. Except in Tulo's drawings. What if the answers to our questions are there, and we've lost them?"

"Rov does what he must as a military man. I understand that. But it's Bellua you need to watch out for. He's angry and frustrated. Count on him to turn this against you."

I suddenly felt like such a burden. Again. Tears stung my eyes.

"I fear for you, Maia," said Father. "It scares me to think that you've been targeted by . . . I don't even know how to say it. If the world was right, we could enlist Bellua's aid in figuring out what we faced today."

"We can still ask Mabir."

"And we should, though we'll need to be discreet."

He laid his cheek against the side of my head. "Asha. I honestly never heard that name before today. But I like the idea of simple, unadorned Truth that need not dress up in garments and declare itself, truth that simply *is*. I'm surprised and pleased at this change in Mabir, too. That came from you, you know. You opened his eyes just by being you. Maia, you saw the Summer Dragon! Treasure that. Let it balance against what happened today. Don't ever forget it. Someday, I hope the meaning will become clear to you."

"That's what Jhem said."

"Really?"

"Well, she said that things happen for reasons that don't make sense until later. If ever. Sort of the same."

"She's right. And that's a lot like the Ashaani idea too, isn't it? Perhaps one day the meaning will become clear to all of us."

I huddled tight against the wind, and Father responded by pulling me deeper into the circle of his arms. I turned my head to look at him in the failing light, hair blowing across my eyes, his features blurred through my tears. And I thought I'd never seen him so clearly before.

———

Jhem returned well after dark. I didn't even see her; she only opened the stable door to let Audax in. He curled up in his nest with Coluver and they made cooing noises before rumbling to sleep. Jhem made herself invisible for the next few days. Had Tauman offered one of his unimpressive apologies? Scolded her with silence? Or maybe made amends? I looked for her when I could, but she didn't want to be found.

Father and Rov took turns standing watch in the paddock each night, eyes scanning the sky. I lay in bed waiting for exhaustion to bring sleep, my thoughts circling endlessly from curses to Horrors to apparitions. I hoped Father could take me to visit Mabir without Bellua looming, to ask the questions that kept me awake, but Father was gone with Rov at the caves during the day. He reported that the thing—we still didn't have a proper name for it—stayed gone, for whatever reason. That was small comfort.

At nights I tried simple prayers to Getig, for understanding. I trusted that whether he was an aspect of Korruzon or of Asha, I was talking to the right Avar. I had no idea if I was doing it right. How is a prayer answered? It wasn't like having a courier drop into the paddock with a message.

By day I tried not to think about it, but Darian obsessed over it. "Father just stood and loosed arrows into the Harodhi?"

"Yes. I told you that already."

We were exercising our qits in the yard, running them in circles on a lunge line. At the moment, Aru was having his turn. "I know," Darian said, "but I'm trying to picture it in my mind. He didn't dodge, or shift around?"

"I don't know. I suppose, but—"

"And Shuja shielded him with his wings?"

"I think so. It happened so fast—"

"Just like the wilding sire did for you and me. Like he knew that's how the Dragonry mounts do it. Do you suppose they do it out of instinct?"

"Maybe. Honestly, how would I know?"

He looked at me askance. "And the thing in the air, was it—"

The Thing. "Darian, please—you've asked me every question at least three times. Take up your slack—Buk Buk is tripping on the lead."

"*Don't call him that.*" Darian turned back to Aru, shortening the length of the lunge line. Aru grabbed the rest of the slack in his teeth and shook the rope like a terrier, then pulled backward on the line until Darian stumbled to his knees. Beside me, Keirr wheezed with the dragon equivalent of laughter, her tail lashing.

Our qits had grown over the last month, doubling in length, quadrupling in weight. Keirr's shoulders came above my knees, Aru's to mid-thigh. They were strong too, and their wings now spanned nearly as great a reach as Darian's arms plus mine. It made me proud but also a little sad to see my baby turning into a dragon so fast. No more lap-cuddles, though she still mowped like a nestling and sulked when I scolded her.

Because of his size, Aru ran faster, leapt higher. But Keirr learned more quickly, and Aru often followed her lead. Darian took that as a challenge. The competition pushed all of us to improve faster.

Which thrilled Father, of course. "What excellent qits they'll produce one day!" he said. Often.

That didn't help Darian in the present moment, though. Aru tugged again and Darian toppled to his elbows with an angry cry of pain. I ran to Aru's side, yanked the lunge line in his mouth down hard, and grabbed a fistful of ear-frill. "Aru! Shame on you, bad boy!" Then I clucked like a scolding dragon dam, which caused his head to droop and his tail to sag. He would learn the words and tone of voice eventually. But for now it was enough that he knew I was displeased.

Keirr skipped past him, said, "Buk Buk" and clucked her own tongue mockingly.

"Keirr! Hush now. Shhh! No more of that." She dipped her head sheepishly, but looked at Aru and delivered a last tiny cluck. I suppressed the urge to giggle by frowning pointedly.

Darian sat in the dust and rubbed his scarred left leg. The wound still gave him trouble. Though his limp improved, his strength hadn't returned yet. "He obeys you better than he obeys me," he said.

The embarrassment in his eyes made me bite off the jest I had readied. I wanted to tell him what Mabir and I had done, but Mabir's instructions were clear. *Don't tell Darian.* I led Aru to his side, and he popped his qit on the nose with a reprimanding cluck of his own. Aru sat with his head hanging.

"Are you all right?"

"I'm fine."

I sat next to him and put an arm around his shoulder. He shrugged it off. "I told you, I'm fine." He pushed to his feet and put Aru back to work.

———

I took my anger out on the chicken carcasses I prepared for Keirr's dinner.

For most of our lives, Darian had been my big brother, my muse and commander. He expected me to follow him in the natural order of things. The appearance of Getig gave him a brief time as the center of attention, with the assumption that the Summer Dragon appeared for *him.* Even though he stood up for me after our trial in the caves, I knew he probably felt smaller than me for the first time in his life.

I chopped the last chicken in two with the cleaver, left the blade imbedded in the block, stared at bone and meat and blood. "He has bad dreams, too." The words came out even as the realization hit me. "The things that happened to us haunt him, but he's too proud to admit it."

Keirr looked at me curiously.

"Of course that's it. I should have thought of it before. He covers it up well. Or maybe not so well."

Keirr blinked.

"Can you say, 'Darian?'"

"No."

"Of course you can. Say, 'Darian.'"

"Boi."

"You're awful." I suppressed a giggle. "Say, 'Darian.'"

She rotated her head. "Drrrrrrym." The "R's" rolled melodically. Only dragons were capable of that pleasing sound.

"Good! And you are a rapscallion, Keirr. Can you say 'rapscallion'?"

She considered for a moment. "Yhes," she said.

Keirr's new favorite word. Everything good was "yhes." *Hwssh, Maia—Yhes. Bukaw—Yhes.* Scratches behind the ears—*Yheeess.* She would often nod her head for emphasis. Keirr completely understood *yes.*

I laughed despite my mood, impressed by the fact that, regardless of what she could or couldn't say, she knew the meaning of *"Can you say?"* Language was part of her, part of what dragons are. As I fed and watered them, I listened to their alien conversation, a completely strange collection of clicks, rumbles, purrs, and whistles. I recalled Keirr sneaking up on a chicken carcass with her eyes closed and her ear frills fully deployed, clicking, and her odd response when she opened her eyes again. Something related to sound had happened, and it happened in their speech, too. I thought of Shuja in the cavern, clicking once loudly before announcing, "Fee-t. Come fas-t." Keirr's poppa, Malik, had made the same clicking sound as he followed us through the caverns. Our dragons only made the singular click when they were away from the aeries. At home, a click was usually followed by several more in diminishing volume, either quickly or slowly, then a rumble or purr. I knew that was important, but I didn't get how. Not yet. I wondered how much Mother had figured out, and what she could have told me about dragon speech.

And I thought about the two mothers who lived in my head—the one who talked to dragons, and the one who cursed me before she died.

Word came that Mabir and Bellua had declared Fren recovered and healthy, and allowed him to return home. I expressed disappointment that he wasn't in the aeries, working for us as Father promised. "He needs to see his family and settle his personal affairs," said Father. "But he'll be back before long. I still owe him a debt." We'd been stabling Fren's horse in the tack house, and his son, Domu, had long since collected her without my even noticing. I wanted to see Mabir again too, but I wondered if Bellua had put himself between us.

One day Fren walked out of the forest into our manor yard, on the exact path he'd taken to deliver a load of wood chips almost two seasons ago. I dropped my shovel and pail.

"Fren!" I ran to him, with Keirr trotting behind me. I wanted to throw my arms around him and hug him hard, but I worried about aggravating his wound. I stopped and held out a hand.

"Young ma'am! It's good to see you!" He pulled me into a warm embrace. "I'll take a hug, please, m' lady." I gave it gladly.

I drew back to look at him, overcome with happiness. He'd shaved the beard grown during his unconscious weeks, leaving only his goatee. I remembered him with more girth. His loss of weight wasn't obvious in the Temple hospital, but it was now. His shirt and vest were new—Father had paid for those.

I felt redeemed at last. The aeries were finally whole. "How's your shadow, Fren?" I asked cheerfully.

He smiled and wiped a tear off my cheek with a thumb. "My shadow is well."

"Mine too. You don't know how relieved I am to see you." The slate of Bellua's omens was finally wiped clean.

"I'm here to start work—" he began, but then his eyes grew wide at something behind me. I turned to see Keirr, sitting politely, her head tilted to the right. "This pretty silver creature is the wilding?" he said. "Look how big!"

I clicked for her to join me. "This is Keirr. And Keirr, this is Fren. Please say *hello* to Fren."

Keirr took a step forward, then sat again. Such a little lady. "Herrro, Phrrrem," she said with the beautiful, rolling dragon "R"s.

Fren shook his head in amazement. "If my horse ever said such a thing I would fall right off her!"

I scratched her chin. "Keirr, if it weren't for Fren, you wouldn't even be here. His injury brought us together." She looked at me sideways.

Fren smiled at me with eyes crinkled.

"Oh, Gods, Fren. Can you ever forgive—"

"There's nothing to forgive. I survived to meet this silver wilding and to see you again."

I leaned closer to him. "Do you remember speaking to me in the Temple?"

His smile faded and his brows pinched, revealing something between concern and puzzlement. "I wish I could remember, lady ma'am. But Mabir told me about it. It's true, what I said: I'll wear these scars with pride. The rest of it—I don't know what it means, but don't you fret over it. I'm here to get my strength back and loosen up these tethers across my body."

"I wish I could talk with you about that. But . . ."

"But what?"

"I don't want to get you in trouble."

Fren looked concerned. "What sort of trouble could you possibly—"

"Bellua," I said, lowering my voice, even though I knew he was nowhere around. "He doesn't like Asha or the old tales. He watches every move, records every word. If he learns that you are an elder in a forbidden church, I don't know what—"

"So Mabir filled in some gaps for you," he said, with a tight-lipped smile that failed to mask his concern. "That is just as well." The bend in his brow deepened. "I've long kept my faith to myself, with Mabir's indulgence. If Bellua is the sort of man you fear he is, I don't want to alert him to my beliefs. I know too many others."

"I haven't even told Darian." Not the only thing I hadn't told him.

"It saddens me to say it, but perhaps that is for the best. At least for now."

"Nobody knows but Mabir, Father, and you and me. We should keep it that way. We shouldn't give Bellua any reason to watch you."

"Assuming I didn't already babble something unfortunate while I slept. Something he overheard." He looked at his boots for several seconds.

"I want to know about Asha."

Fren looked up. "There are ears about, here in the paddock. We have no real reason to spend time together. I know nothing about raising or training dragons, and you have no need of saws or axes. We'd have to be discreet. But nothing could honor me more than the chance to offer you guidance, Maia—you who have demonstrated the spirit of Getig so well."

I shook my head. "It would put you at risk."

Fren's face constricted. "I want to stay close, keep an eye out."

"You'll be close enough to find easily. At least there's that. When the time seems right, I'll find you?"

He nodded again.

"You shouldn't have to hide your beliefs," I said.

He crushed me in another hug. "Come," he said, releasing me at last. "Walk me in to find your Father."

———

Routine settled on the aeries. Summer bled into fall, Getig yielded to Waeges. Leaves on the fringe of the forest turned brilliant red and gold against the dark backdrop of pines. The air grew cooler, the wind more likely to bring the ragged sky of low, rain-swollen clouds. Father and Rov continued to watch the skies at night.

Aru and Keirr doubled in size again. Father introduced them to bigger training harnesses suited to their new girth, with substantial weight where the saddle would be. "In the wild they'd be testing those wings already," he explained. "They might well take a long glide down from the aeries. We can't have that. Ambitious wildings injure themselves all the time. Instead, this will discourage them *and* make their legs and wings all the stronger."

I had no contact with Fren. I would see him from time to time through the trees, but I dared not even wave. It made me angry; there was a time when Fren would have swung me up on his horse for a ride. Now we acted like strangers, because of Bellua.

For his part, the merihem laid low and stayed out of our way, tending his Zell with surprising affection. Which made sense—she was the only friend he had here. But the depth of his apparent love for her surprised me. Emotion he never showed to his fellow human beings. I wondered if I should question my opinion of him, but shut the thought down.

Waeges' Day arrived, when the village lit bonfires and feasted the most needy in honor of the changing season, in the spirit of Balance. Father, Jhem, Darian, and I held a feast for Kaisi and her family and for others who had no kin of their own but supplied us with goods or labor over the course of a year. Darian and I took turns watching the qits with the dragon dams, but otherwise spent all morning and afternoon in the kitchens. None of us were great cooks, but we followed recipes that my grandparents handed down: venison stew with root vegetables and wild herbs. Pilaf with rice, berries, garlic, and onions. Yams and baked apples drizzled with honey. Rov took a portion of the feast to the militiamen on duty in the caves. Bellua and Mabir and Tulo cooked in the Temple for those less fortunate. In the end, it didn't matter if the food wasn't terrific. The spirit of giving was the important thing.

Routine settled again when the holiday was over. Then, three weeks after the Feast of Waeges, the sky filled with dragons.

THE THUNDER OF MANY WINGS drew us all to the paddock. Tauman on Rannu landed first. Behind him came a dozen
dragon-rider teams.

"Korruzon's blazing farts!" shouted Darian, his face beaming.
"Look at them, Maia! Did you ever imagine such a thing? How many
different aeries are represented here, do you suppose?"

"I have no idea." Many were gathered here, in full Dragonry regalia. Every dragon had sigils painted on the surface of their wings in
big, bold strokes. Harnesses shone with polish, the saddles were be-
decked with quivers and pouches and metalwork of various func-
tional sorts. Many of the mounts wore armored plates on their
shoulders and necks. Spears were strapped along their spines, atop the
folded "kite" that was a rider's last resort should his mount be killed
in the air. More than half the riders were armored—one of them a
woman, to my surprise. They wore swords on their backs and crossbows at their sides. Long spikes poked out from the plates on their
shoulders, and several more thrust out from their backs. I knew from
Father's stories that they were meant to deter the claws or teeth of an
attacking dragon. I pictured these warriors assaulted by Horrors, and
a chill moved through my ribcage.

Darian grinned back at me. "I see at least four aeries that I can
tell, and a couple of them look like Riat dragons, don't you think?"
His enthusiasm didn't feel right; I found the spectacle ominous, not
exciting. Despite my unease, it thrilled me to see some of our babies
home and safe. I wondered if they would recognize their parents, or if
the parents would know their qits.

I pointed. "That one for sure looks like Grus, but with Shuja's coloring."

Darian whistled low. "Wow. This is great! Look at all the top bows! I've always wanted to see one." Several of the saddles bore huge, elaborate crossbows mounted in front, with a hand crank on the side, a boxlike structure on top full of arrows, and complicated machinery everywhere between, including cables in channels in the dragon's harness. "So the dragon can cock the bow with its elbows," Dare explained. "All these years we've been listening to Father's stories and selling qits to the Ministry, but this is the first time we've had the Dragonry here, in *our paddock*."

I felt Keirr's head press against my side, and I reached around her neck to scratch under her chin. Her eyes were wide as she wrapped a wing over my shoulder. "Hoo?" she said.

"They're Dragonry, Keirr. Military."

She looked up at me in confusion. I think she expected names, but this was impossible to explain within the confines of her vocabulary. "Many names," I said. "Many names." She pressed closer. This was something huge and new, completely outside her experience. She clicked, and clicked again.

Tauman and Rannu trotted in our direction. "Make way!" he shouted. "We'll need every bit of the paddock to get them all in."

Darian and I retreated to the bridge and tried to name the aerie each dragon came from as it landed.

"Adaz aerie, in Evir," said Darian. "It looks like Zell—lean and dun, with speckles."

"And those three could almost be littermates—from Sando in the north of Treven."

Darian's voice fell. "Several there from Cuuloda."

"Yep." The sight of them put a lump in my throat. Dark and muscular, like Shuja. He'd come from the aeries in Cuuloda. A stark reminder.

We watched in silence for several minutes, until Darian pointed. "What's the aerie in Kaul?"

"I don't remember, but that one's a long way from home."

"They're Dragonry, Maia—they're *all* a long way from home."

"Not those two. I swear that one belongs to Grus, and that one to

Athys. Look at how they hold their heads high and look all around. They know they're *home*. I swear they do."

Then Jhem ran past us as Tauman slid down from his saddle. She leapt on him, wrapping her legs around his hips. He engulfed her in his arms, spinning her around with his face buried in her neck. She laughed.

I laughed. *Darian* laughed.

"Are you well?" Tauman asked her.

"Yes! And Coluver is well, and Audax has behaved himself, and Athys will be overjoyed to see you."

"Where's Father?"

Jhem held his face in her hands and kissed him before she answered. "At the caves, with Rov."

"I need to go tell him that we're here, then."

"No! Don't go. Not yet." She enfolded him in her arms again and laid her head on his shoulder. Weeks apart had softened the hurt feelings, it seemed. I grinned, and caught Darian beaming, too.

"I'll go," said Bellua, suddenly beside me.

Tauman looked up. "You would do that?"

"Of course. Your dragons are weary. You all need a rest, and food and water."

"It's not only us." Tauman's smile vanished, and he relaxed his hold on Jhem. She released the grip of her legs to stand beside him. "There are refugees approaching on the north road, from Cuuloda."

Bellua stepped to the rail of the bridge. "I don't see them."

"You will. They'll be along soon enough."

"You left them unguarded?"

"Oh, they're not alone."

A squat brown dragon with bowed legs came toward us, with armor plating on his shoulders and chest. A thin ribbon of white fabric wafted on a slender whip, mounted to the saddleback; its rider was a "ribbon officer," the leader of this talon. He dismounted and approached us.

His skin was not nearly so pale as the milky-white skin of the Harodhi, but not so brown as ours. He was tan with freckles on his cheeks and hands. I knew of these people—they lived far north and east, in the mountains of Idwal. He made me think of Jhem in his coloring, though he was tan and yellow, not red. He wore no gravings other than the bond mark and a double talon of rank on his right arm. Hardened leather armor covered his chest, shoulders, and thighs. He plucked a dragon-leather helmet with attached goggles off his head and tucked it under his arm. His short-cropped hair was so light as to appear almost like straw. I'd never seen the like. He held a hand out to Bellua.

"I'm Sergeant Cairek ad Seijas, good merihem, an' this is my mount, Taben ad Gath." His dragon nodded. "Pleased t' be here at last." He had an oddly pleasing accent.

Bellua took his hand and bowed. "Bellua ad Reitleh. Welcome! Welcome. Do you have a communication for me?"

"Nay," said the Dragonry sergeant. "Were you expecting something?"

Bellua looked concerned. "Yes, I was."

"I'm sure it'll be along shortly, then," said Cairek. "Where is Captain Rov?"

His apparent lack of concern tightened Bellua's frown. "He's in the caves with the broodmaster. I assume Tauman filled you in?"

"Aye, he did." He turned to Jhem and held out a hand, bowing ever so slightly. "You surely are Jhem? Your husband told me many good things about you, ma'am."

Jhem took his hand and bowed in return. "He probably told you about all my awful qualities too, then." Tauman's mouth drew tight. He was awful to Jhem about half the time, critical and unrelenting. But she probably shouldn't have been so glib.

Cairek let the jibe go without comment, turning next to Darian. "An' this would be young master Darian, with his new charge . . . ?"

"Aru," said Darian, scratching his qit behind the ear before he remembered to bow and take the sergeant's hand.

"He's a handsome character, i'nt he?" Cairek's smile was easy and pleasant.

Then he turned to me, bowing deeply. "I take it you are Maia. Getig's Maia, hey?"

My face burned with sudden embarrassment. I glanced at Darian, and his face reddened with an emotion that also pinched his brow and puckered his lips. Then I glimpsed Bellua, who stared down at me with his mouth pressed into a straight line. I didn't know how to respond. At last I took Cairek's offered hand. "Yes. Pleased to meet you."

He bent to Keirr's eye level with a look of wonder transforming his face. "An' this would be the wilding then, hey?"

Tauman harrumphed. "Some might say that Maia is the wilding." I wrinkled my nose at him.

"Keirr," said Keirr.

I scratched her neck. "That's her name, and she wants you to know it."

Cairek grinned, but didn't look away from her. "We've heard your story as far away as Ebrolin, m'lady." His tone was soothing, his delivery so relaxed that his voice had a calming effect. I liked him immediately.

"Really?"

"Aye. I'm most pleased to make your acquaintance." He stood. "We have refugees from Cuuloda close behind. They want to meet you as well, I think."

I glanced at Bellua again. He stood stiff and ruddy-faced, his eyes drawn as narrow as taut wire.

"I'll start the food," said Darian with a sidelong look at me, then he darted toward the storehouse.

"This will put a strain on resources," said Tauman. "We've gone from six adult dragons to eighteen, with brood season approaching."

"It's harder than that," said Cairek. "We're going to need a place to pitch tents for dragons an' riders alike. An' given the lay of things, we'll need to clear forest to make room. I'm sorry for the hardship, Mr. Tauman, but it can't be helped."

Tauman nodded. "There's another talon of Dragonry on its way as well, accompanying the masons and the engineers Rov requested for the work on the caves. They're ground huggers with all their big machinery, so they'll be several more weeks, arriving just before Menog's Day, when resources are most guarded. And then they'll need food and a place to pitch their tents, too."

Before I could ingest this conversation, two more Dragonry riders approached, and Cairek turned to them. I expected them to salute, but they stood casually, poking gloves into belts and loosening the straps on their armor. "All in and ready for orders, sir," said one of them.

Cairek held one hand toward them, the other toward us. "These are my talon leaders, Ajhe ad *missed that*, and Marad ad *that one too*. Their mounts, Deka ad *somewhere* and *somebody* av Cuuloda are at the watering trough." Names flying everywhere. I would be lucky if I remembered Cairek, Ajhe, and Marad. The only aerie name I'd recognized was the last, Cuuloda. I liked the way they introduced their mounts, though—complete with lineage names from the aeries that gave them birth. That appealed to me immediately. A bonded dragon and rider depended on each other for survival. It only made sense to introduce them as honored *persons*. The men bowed and smiled as Cairek named us in turn for them.

I thought to myself, *Keirr av Riat. No, Keirr av Malik*: Keirr, daughter of Malik.

When Cairek introduced Keirr and me, the two men bowed deeply. "Honored, young miss," said Ajhe, and "Most pleased, m'lady," said Marad. The same odd deference I'd received from the townsmen in the caves. I bristled inside—I didn't want to be notorious. I only wanted to raise my qit. But I bowed courteously. "The pleasure is mine."

"I'll go find Rov and the broodmaster," said Bellua. He spun and marched across the bridge to the stable.

––––––

It took an hour for Jhem and Darian to haul enough food up the lift from the icehouse to feed every dragon, while Tauman and I manned the saddle jib. We used a cart to roll the saddles to various parts of the compound. The paddock was soon arrayed with them, each with a soldier's kite propped open above it and their bedrolls laid flat beneath. By the time Father and Rov returned with Bellua, the riders relaxed under their makeshift tents, their mounts lined up at the watering trough or eating from piles of vegetables and meat.

With Shuja and Cheien unsaddled and fed, we gathered at the north end of the paddock next to the gantry and looked out over the parapet to the northern plains.

Cairek spoke with Rov. "I need your orders, sir."

Rov crossed his arms and considered. "For now just post a standard watch schedule."

"Aye, sir. And Broodmaster, sir—"

"Call me Magha."

"Aye. Magha, sir, we'll need t' knock down more of your timber to make enough room for roosts."

Father growled low in his throat. "Yes, that already occurred to me. No more than you have to. I treasure my forest."

"Aye," said Cairek. "We'll need t' make a couple of saddle jibs for ourselves, with a little help."

"I can put Fren on that. He'll give you good work."

"You understand, Magha sir"—Cairek looked uncomfortable—"that eventually we're going to need barracks."

Father looked across the canyon between pinnacle and clifftop, at our forest, and nodded.

"I see the refugees," I said, pointing.

Through the mist from the Roaring, at the edge of the stretching shadow of the mountains, a string of carts and people wound between the low foothills, riding animals and driving other animals before them.

"That's a long journey from Cuuloda," said Jhem.

"They've had an escort," said Bellua. "Look up."

In the sky above them nine dragons circled.

"They're not part of my wing," said Cairek. "We only spotted them this morning as we neared Riat. Look twice, good Bellua. They're Juza. I imagine they have the communication you seek."

Juza! The Juza were Temple warriors, like the Dragonry but trained within the walls of the Maktaa, the religious school of the Rasaal. They were elite fighters, like warrior-priests. Fabled. The best of the best. *The Keepers of the Flame*, some called them. I'd never seen one before.

"Why are the Juza here?" said Father.

"It's not unheard of for them to escort refugees," said Cairek.

"But not the norm. Am I right, Bellua?"

Bellua turned to Father, unable to hide his surprise. "I didn't know they would send Juza."

Father placed both hands on the parapet. "I want to speak with their commanding officer, whoever he is. And the refugees' leader as well." He scowled. "So the Temple is involved in earnest now."

"When weren't they?" I said, before I could stop myself.

Bellua's lips twitched with unspoken words.

Father nodded, then looked over his shoulder at me with volumes of questions and concerns in his eyes. But he said nothing.

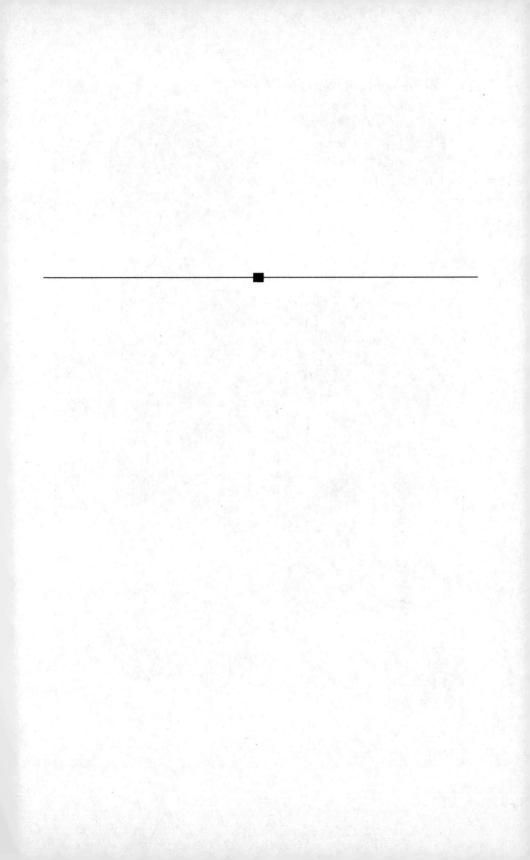

THE LEADER OF THE JUZA settled on the bridge, and his dragon sauntered toward us in the half-light. Its face was crimson, as were the wings it stretched and folded. Yellow bands twisted through the rust on forelegs, chest, and shoulders, and rippled like flames as it walked. Old stories told of dragons that breathed fire; if those tales were true, they should have looked like this magnificent animal.

The Juza kept a breed of dragon to themselves, the Torchbearers. All the Juza rode Torchbearers. By some accounts they were the offspring of Korruzon Himself. Could this be one of those? Did they breathe fire? If so, it would explain the other name for the Juza—the Keepers of the Flame.

The Juza rider unbuckled from his harness and climbed down. His armor and the clothing beneath it, his sword belt and scabbard, his bow and the quiver at his hip—all were black as smoke. Only the white sash around his waist and the bright red fletching of his arrows broke the theme. He was stocky and square, closely shorn with a razor-sharp hairline. Gravings much like Rov's covered his face and neck.

"I'm prelate Addai," he said, with a crisp bow. "Where is Bellua? I bring orders for him from the Temple." His accent was strangely sharp, his mannerisms more so—the strut of a rooster in the body of a bulldog.

"The inner courtyard," Father said. "Captain Rov is with him, and the leader of the Cuuloda refugees—"

"This is the boy, Darian?"

Darian looked apprehensive. "Yes, that's me."

"And that would make you the daughter," said Addai, turning to me.

"I'm Maia, yes."

He looked me up and down, inspected Keirr. His eyes were sharp and small, like punctuation marks within the pattern of gravings. The hairs on my arms rose.

He turned to Jhem. "And you are . . . ?"

"Jhem, sir. I'm Tauman's wife."

"Of course. The stunning red hair. My pleasure, ladies, gentlemen." He turned to Father. "Who will see to my animal?"

His *animal*?

"I will," said Jhem.

Addai gestured and clicked to his mount. "The others are this way?"

Father nodded and gestured him in. He marched past us into the courtyard.

Jhem's jaw dropped as she watched him go. She held up a hand for Addai's unnamed mount to sniff. "He didn't even introduce us."

Darian shrugged. Father threw me a glance loaded with meaning, including *I don't care for this guy,* but especially *be on your best behavior.*

I touched Jhem's arm in passing and gave her a quick kiss on the cheek. She nodded thanks with an angry eyebrow cocked. "Let me know what happens."

We followed Addai in and waited to take our places at the table. There was another man already seated.

The refugee leader had a belly that sagged over his belt, jowls that hung like flaps on either side of his drooping mustache. His clothes appeared shabby at first but on second look showed gold threads and lustrous fabric; a man who'd known wealth and easy excess, starved by circumstances into a shadow of his once substantial self. He sat across from Father at the courtyard table and paused in wolfing down the food before him, perhaps remembering that table manners were among the garments worn by civilized folk.

Cairek looked away, as if the man's hunger made him uncomfortable. Rov and Tauman watched the newcomer in silence. Darian took in everything with eager interest.

Addai stood at Bellua's side, handing him a scroll sealed with red wax. "Merihem, here are your orders."

"Thank you." Bellua frowned and broke the seal.

I sat beside Mabir. It was the first time I'd seen him in weeks. "Mabir! Why don't you come by more often? I've missed you."

He gave me a cautionary glance. "I am old, child, and I travel at the mercy of others." I could barely resist leaning in to whisper questions, but if my lips so much as twitched, he shook his head *no* almost imperceptibly.

Bellua unfurled the scroll and looked up at Addai. "What about my things?"

Addai caught me watching them. "Read first," he said, meeting my eyes. "Then I'll explain." I matched his gaze, studying him, trying to catch any quirks of behavior that might reveal his mind. His gravings, I now saw, weren't like Rov's at all. More intricate, more square and choppy, embellished with flames around the perimeter.

Bellua's expression became opaque as he began to read.

Father held an arm out toward our hungry guest. "Everyone, meet Borgomos, head of the Merchant's Guild in Cuuloda." Only now did I note his Staff of Office, leaning against the arm of his chair. Fancier than our local Headsman's staff, it was fashioned of ebony, grooves and empty holes indicating where precious inlays had once adorned it. The symbol of office that should have topped it was missing. Only two holes remained where it was once attached. Why would his Staff of Office be stripped of its jewels?

"Addai ad Rasaal," the Juza leader introduced himself with a bow. "We met briefly, this morning, in fact."

The Guildmaster dabbed his lips before he spoke, as if to confirm his former affluence. "And I thank you for your escort." He started to rise.

The Juza leader waved him back down. "Don't get up. You're famished. Eat."

"It embarrasses me to eat alone."

"Think nothing of it," said Father. "It's the least we could do for you after your long journey." He and Addai remained standing.

"I thank you, sir. And, Broodmaster—"

"Call me Magha."

"Thank you, Magha, for your kind hospitality and your care for my folk. I'm eager to know what we can do for you in return."

"It's almost winter," said Tauman. "The only new food coming in will be whatever harvest the fisherman catch."

Father nodded grimly. "You're right. But I'll not turn folk away. We'll tighten our belts. Cairek? Your men can hunt?"

"If you mean do they know how, aye, of course they do. But we're not here to feed refugees. We're here to defend the aeries an' guard the cavern until it's sealed."

"You'll have to help feed yourselves." Father fixed Cairek with a stern eye. "I raise dragons for the Dragonry, and that requires resources. I'm a charitable man, but Riat is not a charity, and I'm not a quartermaster. Our supplies are going to be stretched to the limit when brood season hits."

Cairek dipped his tawny head once in deference. "Understood, Broodmaster. We've foraged before."

"There's more news that may affect the way we handle this," said Tauman, leaning elbows on the table. "Korruzon and Emperor Ahriman have instituted a new policy."

Father's eyebrows pinched together. "What's Ahriman up to now?"

"Charters."

Father slapped the table in disgust. "This again? I thought we'd rallied and defeated this notion."

"We did, but it took every aerie last time, remember, and Cuuloda was the strongest. Ahriman wants the outlying aeries to apply for charters. Take on investors and expand."

"And how is that going to help us now?"

"With investors, we can buy food from farther afield, bring it in. Cover the shortfall and still expand."

"With debt that must be repaid."

"We've already added a breeding pair."

"They won't be breeding for another year."

"I know, Father, but hear me out. If we take advantage of this opportunity, we can emerge stronger than ever."

Father scowled at him. "These aeries have been in the family from before counting. I won't give ownership to a bunch of wealthy strangers. Ahriman demands too much control."

"It may be our only way. Like it or not, we depend on Ahriman's gold."

"And Ahriman depends on our expertise in retur—"

"And it may be the only way you can afford to help the Cuuloda refugees."

Father glanced uneasily at Rov. "So much for your promise that I'd be repaid for expenses."

The Captain was impassive. "The Ministry communicates that the next wave of reinforcements will bring grain and forage to supplement the winter stores." He turned to the Guildmaster. "However, *your* sudden appearance effectively negates the boon."

Borgomos looked shocked, and froze with his napkin just shy of his lips. "I don't wish to be a burden, obviously."

"There's danger for you here," said Rov. "The caves are still infested with Harodhi warriors and other things. Until we get them sealed, there's a chance of Cuuloda's fate repeating here in Riat. I recommend that you continue on to Taskis. We can't protect you."

Father spoke. "And where would they go? Taskis is the nearest city that could handle them, but it's as far from here as Cuuloda was, and with two great rivers to cross. They've seen hard times already, and they're our brethren. It will be a sad day when the Dragonry leaves the people to defend themselves."

Rov shook his head. "I don't disagree. But we have to be practical, and as you say that means putting the aeries first. I'm sorry, Guildmaster. I have tough decisions to make."

Borgomos leaned forward, both hands on the table. "Your indulgence, Captain. We've been through this once before already. When the Dragonry arrived downstream from Cuuloda, in Chaaladan, we became the burden. The Dragonry had priority. That's why we're here. I've already spent all but a few coins of my life savings on the road from Cuuloda, feeding my people. We lost only a few very old and very young survivors."

I pondered the use of the word *survivors* to describe persons who died along the road and noted again the missing inlays in his Staff of Office. Now I understood. He had truly given everything.

Before anyone could interrupt he continued, louder, making it clear that he intended to be heard. "My people fled from hell. Many lost family, some of them torn and eaten before their very eyes by monsters too horrible to describe." His face grew pale. "I was in the village below the aeries and saw very little at first—silhouettes in the sky, too many dragons to have all been from the aerie. But I assumed it was Dragonry until they descended on the village. Horrors. Attacking anything that moved. Women, children, animals. It didn't matter." His chin began to tremble, and he looked down at his hands.

"Those of us who escaped did so only by luck. I fell into the river and let it take me. Eventually I crawled out on a bank, under a forest canopy, and lay unmoving for fear of being discovered. I admit that I showed no courage at all. Not after seeing—" He sucked in his breath to compose himself. "More than anything else, they eat. Insatiable. It's the only thing that slows them down, the opportunity to eat something. Anything. Many fought back, or—like our broodmaster— killed their own to prevent worse." He fell silent.

No one spoke. My heart pounded as I recalled the monsters Darian and I battled in the caves.

Mabir reached across the table to touch his arm. "Two of our own have had encounter with the Horrors, in our own mountains. We understand."

Borgomos looked up, directly at me, and then to Darian. His eyes returned to me, and he nodded slowly. Took a deep breath. "We heard. We heard the news in Chaaladan, and it gave us hope. First, to learn that one of the Avar of old had appeared, but then to learn that a broodmaster's daughter had defeated one of the monsters in such a way. To claim a dragon for herself. We took heart, and we knew where we had to go first, even if you turned us away."

His face contorted with suppressed emotion as he looked into my eyes. "Many among us wanted to see this miracle child and her qit for ourselves."

I felt my face flush and knew that Bellua was probably furious. I didn't look at him, but I couldn't look at Borgomos either, or at Darian or anyone else. Addai especially. I didn't know if his views aligned with Bellua's, but already I distrusted him.

"Certainly Korruzon watched over her in that trial," Bellua said. There was something different about his tone. Not as strident as I expected. But I turned my face away from him, sure it reflected the fact that I wanted to crawl over the table and throttle him.

"I didn't do it alone," I said, keeping my voice calm. "Darian helped. And we had a dragon with us."

"A wilding dragon, by the reports we heard," said the Guildmaster, "who you rode like a princess of Gadia from the old tales. And Darian, though wounded, fought like a prince."

"Not so much," said Darian, frowning. "Maia saved my life, not the other way 'round."

"The wilding only acted to save his qit, not me," I said.

Borgomos's eyes were red, but a smile now creased his cheeks. "I'm sure the story grew before it came to us."

"I have no doubt," Bellua said, his tone now stripped of emotion.

"It doesn't matter," said Borgomos. "The important thing is that it gave us hope, and strength to make the journey. For that I am grateful."

Now I did hazard a look at Bellua and was surprised. He didn't look angry so much as tired. Something had changed in him since reading his orders from the Rasaal, something that shifted his outlook on the whole affair in a way I didn't understand.

Addai stood over him, with a look of concentration as he spoke to the Guildsman. "A sort of pilgrimage, was it?" His eyes flicked to me.

"We knew that the first flight of bondlings comes shortly after Menog's Day," Borgomos said. "We've come far to witness Maia's first flight with her wilding. It would mean a lot to us."

"Would it now?" Addai said, his face cast in stone, etched with the jagged runes of his gravings.

Borgomos's chin twitched for a moment. "Please understand, sir, it may seem a backward thing to one of such learning as yourself, but we took hope where we could find it."

"Is there not a dhalla among you?"

"No, sir. Just simple folk. Our dhalla and all his acolytes were lost."

Addai said nothing, but I understood his questions with their careful tone: he sought some level of heresy, evidence that my story had turned into something unacceptable. Bellua's report to the Rasaal no doubt colored his expectations. Addai coupled religious certainty to a warrior's pragmatism, like all of Bellua and Rov's worst qualities rolled into one person. Where Bellua made me suspicious and angry, Addai terrified me.

He folded his arms. "I'm concerned with the situation I see in Riat, overrun and overburdened. I concur with the Captain that we find as many skilled laborers as remain amongst the Cuuloda refugees, then send the rest on their way to Taskis. We can't be burdened."

Father looked stunned at this blunt appraisal. "Spring would be a kinder season to run them out," he said, with no attempt to soften the sarcasm in his words.

"We are weary," Borgomos pleaded.

Addai showed no flicker of emotion. "There are bigger concerns. As has been pointed out, our mission here is to protect the aeries, first and foremost." He addressed Father. "Give them enough food to see them off. Don't let them settle in. I want them gone."

"They just got here. And so did you for that matter. You know nothing about our ability to help—"

"I am not without sympathy, Broodmaster, but I'm here to accomplish a task, which is to protect—"

"A heartless task, it seems."

"Your ability to produce dragon qits is the very first concern. I happen to be an expert in the finances of aeries—"

"*I* happen to be an expert in the finances of *this* aerie," Father said.

Cairek cleared his throat. He'd been sitting and watching quietly, his brow drawn in concentration. "Protecting the aeries. That's the reason we're here, innit? So what threat do we face in the caverns?" His eyes moved from speaker to speaker. "Can you tell me that now? I would think it an important part of the decision."

Addai stood with arms akimbo. "I wish to hear this as well."

Father looked at Mabir, but Rov answered first. "There's a Harodhi contingent in the caves—human foot soldiers armed with crossbows and swords. We've faced them on three occasions, but they're weakening. As to the other, we don't know what it was. There is disagreement."

Borgomos's eyes grew wide.

"Something accompanied the Harodhi on their last venture out of the deep caves," said Bellua. "Something unidentified in Temple scripture. It attacked in ways we can't understand or properly explain."

"Can you try, please?" Addai said.

"It appeared as a shadow vaguely the size and shape of a dragon," said Rov. "And followed a team of Harodhi skirmishers into the chamber, a place where many paths converge. It mostly hung back and didn't finally engage us until the last of the enemy was down."

"Except that it attacked the girl from the beginning, using some sort of power of the mind," said Bellua. "Or so is the story." His tone struck me strangely again; I wondered if he chose words designed to feel out this newcomer, Addai.

"And no one else suffered the same," Addai said. "Yes, I read your report."

"I would love to know your thoughts, prelate," said Bellua.

"When I've had a chance to settle in and digest what I learn, of course."

I realized that I didn't know who had authority over the other—Bellua or the Juza leader. Mabir was strangely silent. Borgomos sat with his hands in his lap.

Addai pinned me with his tiny eyes. "In fact, I want to hear things from Maia's point of view."

Bellua straightened. "When *Maia* has experience enough to explain—"

"Experience?" Cairek interrupted. "It sounds to me like she's had the only experiences that matter."

That shut Bellua up cold. In my mind, I thanked Cairek for stating something so obvious it shouldn't have to be repeated.

Addai clasped his hands behind his back, his beady eyes unreadable behind the gravings. "Go ahead, child."

I swallowed and glanced around the room. All eyes turned my way. "It never had form. It was shadowy and weak in a way, but powerful at the same time. I loosed arrows at it, though they passed right through. But I got the sense that it was"—I struggled for the right words—"studying me."

Addai leaned in. "Explain."

"It was in my head, digging around. It showed me things that it thought would crush my spirit."

"Showed you things?"

I nodded. "In my head, like when you read a book and you see the pictures in your imagination, only stronger. Clearer. Pictures from a horrible book. In the end, I think it simply wanted me to be terrified."

"Were you?"

I swallowed. "Yes."

"How do we know the supposed attack wasn't all in your mind?" His face was unreadable.

I stared at him. "It was so deeply in my mind that it gave me a nosebleed."

Bellua frowned. Addai studied me without a word. Borgomos stared at me with glistening eyes. I couldn't look at him. I thought of all the prayers I'd offered to Getig, hoping for some insight into the monster. All the unanswered prayers.

"She stood fast against it," Father said. "Shouted defiance at it."

"But when it attacked," Rov added, "our dragons took it apart as if it was made of paper. It dissipated and vanished, and we haven't seen it since."

"I've been thinking about that," I said. "It was strong while the Harodhi attacked us. But when it had to defend itself alone, it seemed diminished. Like it drew strength from them somehow."

Cairek nodded in appreciation. "It was no Horror, then, but something else completely."

"And that's where, so far, answers fail us," said Bellua.

Mabir's robes rustled as he sat up straighter. "I can offer an explanation, though only as a word from the ancients, not as my opinion necessarily—"

"Careful, old man," said Bellua.

Addai turned his intense gaze on Mabir, who continued regardless. "I've studied the old traditions. They explain that when the world falls out of balance the *dark* Avar gain strength and presence—manifestations of balancing forces—the other side of Asha, who the ancients revered."

Bellua scowled. "All Avar are reflections of Korruzon, and so it could not have been Avar."

Mabir shrugged. "So you keep saying—"

"*Asha* is a dead mythology of the past," said Addai, his face twitching beneath the sharp gravings.

"But they offer us an explanation."

"It was a demon," said Bellua. "One of the *rahza*. Avar are reflections of Korruzon, and *rahza* are not."

With a freckled fist, Cairek thumped the table once for attention. "My dhalla always told me that the *rahza* were made of flame or filth, an' were shaped like men. Sounds more like Horrors to me." He cocked a blond eyebrow, having stunned Bellua to silence a second time. "Let's hear the dhalla out, hey? Perhaps the old traditions can teach us something, even if their terms or doctrine were wrong."

Mabir watched Bellua and Addai for several moments, as if awaiting an argument. It didn't come, so he glanced at Rov. The Captain shrugged.

Mabir bowed his head to draw a deep breath and gather his words. "In Ashaani scripture, the *Edimmu* and *Utukku* were balancing forces that heralded the end of a cycle. They manifest to tear down the old world in preparation for the new, like termites in the rotting body of a tree. The Edimmu came of Shadow, manifesting emotion: fear, despair, anger. In every story, the Edimmu precede the Utukku, the Blight. The Utukku always follow. When society breaks down and war blankets the land, they too appear, bringing physical hardship—decay, disease. Starvation. Desolation. Death."

"Bedtime stories, to frighten small children," said Addai.

"Perhaps. But this 'other' in the caves caused fear in the Harodhi and attacked Maia's thoughts with emotion. That sounds unnervingly like Edimmu. But there's more to consider. The Ashaani would say that *potentials* have been unleashed. This could be the first appearance of something that will only grow in power. No one living has experience of any of it—unless Maia now does, somehow." His eyes flicked to me. He looked scared. "I don't like the way our paths cross their beliefs. The appearances of the Summer Dragon and now of this Shadow creature together are a warning. If it was Shadow or Blight, then, barring some miracle, what follows is inevitable."

"And that is?" Borgomos's face was white.

"The congregation of the Edimmu is the fearful, the desperate, the angry. It feeds on fear and grows on desperation, but it delivers anger. Upheaval and destruction. The end of a cycle."

I thought of the carvings of war and death in the cavern. My pulse pounded in my chest, in my fingertips on the table, in my ears.

"Our own local lore remembers one such, but it was both Shadow *and* Blight. A statue stands timeless in the ruins, where Maia and Darian saw the Summer Dragon. It is a remnant of a previous cycle. The black dragon was known as the Dahak. It began as Shadow, but it grew powerful over time. And it turned the world to ruin."

My pulse throbbed in my neck.

Finally Cairek spoke, a strand of his straw-colored hair hanging in his face. "We plan for the worst. Seal the caverns and pray that Maia bought us enough time with her courage."

Borgomos pushed his plate away and looked around the table from face to face. "What about us?"

Cold, dense silence choked the room as Addai and Rov exchanged looks. Father's face grew darker. I could tell that Jhem grabbed Tauman's hand below the table.

A breeze rattled the bamboo canes above.

When no one else could find words to break the trance, Darian muttered, "You could hear a pixie fart in here."

Addai's eyes snapped to Darian, but he took a deep breath and spoke to Father. "Be mindful of what happened to Cuuloda, Broodmaster. We'll have our hands full enough protecting the aeries. We dare not absorb Cuuloda's burdens."

"We fight this war *for them*, don't you think?" Father turned to Rov, the lightning glint in his eyes. "What is our purpose—what are we doing here if we don't protect each other?"

Rov's eyes didn't so much as flicker. "There are engineers and war machines and another talon of Dragonry on their way. We have too many mouths already."

"It's for the greater good," said Addai.

Borgomos was ashen.

"*Burdens?*" I said, before I knew the words were coming. "You're all a bunch of cowards."

"Lady, don't take risks on my behalf," said Borgomos.

"We should take these people in, until they're strong enough to move on or find their place."

Addai's chin went up. "These matters are beyond your understanding, young—"

"What's hard to understand about compassion?"

"Child, it's a more complicated issue than you can possibly—"

Father leaned across the table at him. "You couldn't choose a crueler season to turn them out. Menog's Day is just around the corner. Let them celebrate in a village, amongst countrymen."

Borgomos stood abruptly and turned to face Rov and Addai. His clothes were tattered and dirty, but he squared his shoulders and straightened his back. He was clearly done groveling. "You should listen to your dhalla when he names your shadow beast in the cave. Call it Edimmu if you want. Or call it by its other names; we have seen them all. They're real. Fear, Despair, Anger. They stalked us all the way from Cuuloda. Along the way we also met Disease, Starvation, and Death."

He let the last word ring off the walls around the courtyard, then turned and took up his Staff of Office, stripped of all precious material that he could sell or barter. "We can face them again here or face them on the road. The difference hardly matters. As to cowardice, that's not for me to judge. I'll leave that to you."

Rov studied the room long before he uncrossed his arms. He looked last at me. "Very well. You can stay until the engineers and equipment arrive. You'll have that long to prove your worth. Those who cannot will have to continue on to Taskis."

Father looked daggers at Rov and Addai, placed a hand on Borgomos's shoulder. "This isn't over, Guildmaster. You have time. I'll find places for as many of your people as I can."

Borgomos looked Father in the eye as he shook the offered hand. "Thank you again, Broodmaster."

"Find Jhem. She'll let you down in the basket."

Borgomos bowed, then turned to me and offered a hand. When I took it, he placed his other atop mine and squeezed gently. "Lady," he said.

As Keirr and I emerged onto the patio of the ruins, the sun peeked through a hole in the dark sky, lighting the scene as if by a soft lantern. It looked so different now. No water flowed in the stream. The undergrowth was brown. Flowers were replaced by prickly seed-heads on brittle stalks. Fallen leaves chased each other in the breeze like qits at play, skittering around the statue and collecting in drifts against the broken wall. Empty trees scratched at the ragged sky. I almost expected to see Waeges glide in over their bare tips the way Getig had a season ago.

Keirr stepped high, touching trees and rocks with her nose and footpads, licking everything and clicking constantly. I wondered again at the significance of the habit. I listened and watched for clues, but it still wouldn't come to me. As always, it brought my mother to mind.

Together we approached the statue of Menog and the Dahak. Dried moss on the upper surfaces crumbled under my touch, so I brushed off as much of it as I could reach to reveal more of the sculpture. White Menog curled above the black Dahak, one forefoot gripping the monster's neck. But the Dahak didn't look the least bit defeated; its jaws were opened wide, talons raking. Even the thumbclaws in the wings ripped at Menog's hide. Both Edimmu and Utukku—Shadow and Blight—Mabir had said; a monster that heralded the end of an age, long before even Korruzon. What a battle that must have been—two Avar in a titanic fight to the death, with the fate of the world in the balance.

The wind swirled and I pulled my jacket closer. Change *had* engulfed us. There could be no doubt.

Cairek's men had felled a huge patch of trees north of the manor, right to the edge of the cliff so those on duty could see the paddock and the village below. Father wasn't happy about that; he had a favorite path between the manor and the Roaring that was now laid bare. They left only a few of the biggest trees for their shade. They built nests from the severed limbs, reminding me of the wildings' nests woven of branch and bone. The trunks were set aside until they could be turned into building material—more work for Fren that would keep us apart. Leftover twigs and branches were gathered for cook fires. Father grumbled, "There's another entire wing on its way. I'll have no trees left at this pace."

At least the Juza had taken up residence in the Temple stable and yard and not on the clifftop, though Addai was here most of the time, conferring with Bellua or simply strutting about with his hands on his hips, watching. Or circling overhead on his magnificent Torchbearer. The Juza were always fully armored and fully armed with sword, bow, and quivers of red arrows.

Rov and Cairek planned future structures with Father, barns and barracks and tents that would come with the next wave. It was clear this was no temporary arrangement. The Dragonry was here to stay.

Their conversations always left Father miserable. *Sad angrr* Grus would have said.

With as few as three dragon-rider teams camped in the paddock, there wasn't room enough to run the lunge line, so Father gave us permission to take Aru and Keirr for walks outside the compound with their weighted harnesses on—within bounds. For Darian, that meant constant visits to the Dragonry on the clifftop. He was obsessed with them, asking questions of the riders, inspecting the gear. It's all he talked about. I preferred the silence of the forest.

Keirr sat on the patio, turning her head from side to side and clicking calmly, eyes closed against the light.

"It all began here, when we saw the Summer Dragon," I told her. She opened her ear frills toward me and clicked again, though without opening her eyes.

"Now it's all become so strange. You and I get to come of age together in an armed camp." I rubbed her ear frills, and she cocked her head at me. "But this is your world, isn't it? Dragonry, Juza, Rasaal.

Shadow and Blight. You were born into a world with *Horrors*. This is all you know."

This had once been a sacred place. I suppose I always knew that, but I understood it now, even if the faith of those long distant people eluded my understanding. Keirr's history was tied to this spot, which only deepened the feeling of sanctity for me. I kissed her nose and scratched her chin.

I'd given up on prayers—they seemed no more useful than wishes. Perhaps I prayed to the wrong Avar. But the ruins soothed me. They always had, even before Getig showed himself to me here. They *felt* like Truth, even if I didn't know what that meant.

I needed to talk to Mabir. Or Fren, but I'd barely seen either in weeks.

"Come on, qitling," I said. "Let's go home." Keirr trotted happily after me, but the forest seemed all too quiet.

Suddenly I heard the solid thwack of an arrow hitting a tree. I knew that sound well enough, though I couldn't place the direction until I heard it again. I pinched Keirr's snout gently and held a finger to my lips, then edged closer to the source.

Fren stood in a clearing, head turned hard left, bow arm extended and an arrow knocked. Shirtless, lean and chiseled from a working life. His scars stood out. Vivid stripes surrounded with the healing script, some of it scribbled up the sides of his neck and down his left arm, but it was most concentrated in the center of his chest.

He released his arrow and it smacked into the tree again. I craned my neck for a look. He turned at the snap of my footstep. "M' lady! I apologize. I didn't know there was anyone about." He set his bow down, grabbed up his shirt and crawled into it. "Just trying to loosen up these scars whenever I can and get my bow strength back."

"I'm so sorry, Fren. Do they still hurt?"

He smiled. "M'lady, our scars give us strength. They toughen us. There's no shame in scars."

I didn't know what more to say. I stepped out of the undergrowth to see his shots.

The target, carved into the side of a dead tree, sported a perfect cluster of three arrows in the center. "Wow. You're a really good shot. Father always said so."

He looked at his cluster of arrows, then at me, then back at his grouping of arrows. "Well, a man gets a reputation." Then he looked at me with his brow puzzled into a frown. "Is there something I can do for you, young ma'am?"

———

Father opened the man-door to the brood platform and gestured us in. When I was small and angry and needed a swat on my behind, his eyes looked just like this.

Keirr was still just small enough to enter that way if she crouched with her wings folded tight and ducked her head. She clicked and nosed everything. Fren looked about as if he occupied hallowed ground.

Father squared off in front of me, hands on hips. "What is this about, then?"

"I've made a point of staying away from Fren."

Father nodded encouragingly, as if to coax the rest of the thought out of me.

"I didn't want to risk drawing Bellua's eyes—"

"Good. I don't need Bellua or Addai focusing any attention on either of you. It's bad enough already with Borgomos and his folk practically venerating my two wilding daughters." He absently patted Keirr's cheek as he said it.

"But I need to ask you something I should have asked the day Fren returned."

Father looked very dubious. "Which is?"

"Fren is the best archer in all of Gadia. You've said so yourself."

"Yes. So?"

"So, you should hire him to teach me archery."

Father only stared.

"Hire him to teach me how to use a proper bow. Darian too, for that matter. Who would argue with you, after what we went through and the dangers we faced? And *may yet* face."

Fren grinned and looked Father square in the eye. "It would be my honor, Broodmaster."

"Seriously?" said Father to me. "You *fly* in four weeks—"

"I know."

314

"Are you ready to take on more work?"

"Yes!"

He shook his head, staring at me. Then a chuckle parted his lips.

"Why is that funny?" I asked.

He smiled. "Because you're right. Also because you have no idea what you're in for but—like your Mother—you go there anyway."

———

"**W**hat did you get me into *this* time?" Darian asked one afternoon, after Fren added more sand to the bags we hefted.

"This is how my father taught me," said Fren. "And it's exactly how it's done in the Dragonry. Ten more pulls on each arm for complaining."

Darian groaned, but after that moment he applied himself. He even became competitive.

Father had ordered new bows for Darian and me from the bowyer in Riat, but they would be weeks in the making. Meanwhile, when we could arrange to be together, Fren put us to work. We performed endless calisthenics designed to improve our upper-body strength: push-ups, pull-ups on a bar hung in a stable doorway, endless repetitions hefting bags of sand upward while bent over, standing, kneeling, lying down. Braced across a bench holding a board-like position on front, back, sides, to build our torso strength. I understood that these were the muscles we'd use to draw a bow. But this was *work*.

Despite my ulterior motives, Fren and I never had time alone together to talk. I got the feeling he'd developed doubts about such pointed conversation. I'd ask a simple question, like "What are we doing here?" And he'd answer, "Feed the dragon. Clean the pan." What was that? A riddle?

In between, we still had duties to perform with our qits. Though she was long and lanky, Keirr's shoulders now came nearly to mine, Aru's skinny frame topped Darian's ears. Father introduced new saddles, our first with actual straps and buckles, not just tied together out of rope. They were old, Darian's in brown like Tauman's, mine a dark gray with copper stitching, like the one that fit Grus. Mother's colors. That alone pleased me beyond words. But it got even better.

They had seats. We would ride at last. Darian and I looked at each other with so much obvious excitement that we broke into laughter at each other's expressions.

Father grinned large. "That's the saddle Tauman used to break Rannu in. And Maia, yours is the one your Mother rode when Grus was young. These young ones want to test their wings. But we won't let them. Not until they're strong enough to fly with a person in the saddle."

We led them to the saddle jib, practically skipping with excitement. Keirr and Aru sensed our mood and fidgeted as the new saddles were cinched into place.

I gave my baby a hug around the neck and patted her cheek, uncertain how she would react. She looked back at me, silver eye flashing, and said, "Up, Maia?"

I laughed. "You smart, funny thing!" I climbed the step rungs on the forward harness strap, and she shifted to accommodate the change in her center of gravity. I swung my leg over and found both stirrups; she shifted back again. As I transferred my weight in response to her movement, she became excited, jumping and bucking, swaying from side to side. I heard Darian laughing, but I couldn't take my eyes off Keirr. She looked back at me with one eye, then the other, nodding and wheezing with dragon laughter. She had seen people on the backs of dragons all along, so this wasn't strange to her. And clearly, better than a saddle weighted with sand.

We rode them around the paddock in circles until feeding time, then again until the sun went down. The day was over before I knew it.

I'd never been so sore. I hurt in places I didn't know I had, which surprised me, having ridden on dragons since before I could remember. But this was different. Keirr was a rambunctious youngster, and I'd never spent an entire day on a dragon's back before—certainly never alone, and not on the ground galloping like on a horse. It was the most wonderful pain of my life.

———

The next day, Father greeted us with bridles for their heads, too—something no dragon I'd ever seen was required to wear. Their eyes would be covered up, making them essentially blind.

"It's going to be tough on them at first, but this is an important part of their training," said Father. "I'm going to set up an obstacle course in the paddock, now that we've got all the intruders settled elsewhere. They'll have to trust your commands. When they don't, they'll run into things, trip, bump their heads and wings. I won't lie— you'll get banged up too. But this is how qits in the Dragonry are taught to trust their riders. These bridles will help them learn. The faster they absorb the commands, the sooner they'll be rid of the headgear. Trust me, they'll learn fast."

And they did. Keirr was especially trusting, and so she learned quickly, but Aru wasn't far behind because pain is an excellent teacher. The commands were few and simple, words they already knew. "HAI!" for example—leap *up* or hit a barricade. Posts in the direct line of travel taught the commands for left and right. *In* and *out* told them when it was safe to spread their wings. Inflection indicated speed or intensity, so *whoa* was slow, WHOA! a full stop. Every command was accompanied by a slap or tap on the neck, as well. "Our words and signals become part of their environment, like another sense they have to learn," Father explained.

Keirr and Aru both clicked throughout their workouts, their ear frills opened wide. By the end of the second week they navigated ever-changing obstacle courses simply by listening for our commands or responding to the touches on their necks.

"Feel your bond mark," Darian said one day, at the end of a long session. I reached behind and touched the back of my neck. It was hot, like sunburn. I reached down to Keirr's bond mark. It was the same way.

"It helps us," Darian said, with a quizzical grin. "That's how we feel them, and they feel us."

In between, we trained with Fren. I tried to frame questions that would get me the answers I sought about Asha and Truth, but without alerting Darian to my agenda.

"Fren, how do you know what's true?"

"Feel the contraction of your muscles and pay attention to your pain."

"That's not an answer!"

"Do you understand your question?" He winked at me and turned his back.

It started to annoy me.

It was good work, though. It kept us distracted from the difficulties of an aerie overburdened with dragons and people. We barely had time to think about Horrors or *Edimmu*. If I spied Addai or Bellua lurking about, I'd do exactly as Fren demanded: I'd concentrate on my muscles and try to direct the pain, or I'd pay close attention to the movement of Keirr's body beneath me. She tested her wings constantly. She wanted to fly, I could tell. Always, we were conscious that Menog's Day approached fast. Our first flight loomed.

Every evening we collapsed into exhausted, blessed sleep. After another week, Father delivered a surprise. "Now you're going to learn to trust your dragons. This time *you* will be blindfolded. They have to learn something they're only beginning to comprehend: where you are in their space, and how important it is to protect you. And *you* will learn that you're not in charge. Your relationship to your mount is as equals. You learn together. You fly together. You are a single unit, a *team*. You must learn to accept their input as a part of your environment, like a new sense you've been given. If you thought the last two weeks were hard, ready yourselves. We'll go hard, and the only break you'll get is your exercise sessions with Fren."

The next few days were brutal. Father and Shuja ran our mounts on a tether lead through a new obstacle course, shouting commands, whistling and laughing. Even though Keirr and Aru used their new words enthusiastically, the communications were more physical than anything else. We learned fast to anticipate our mounts' next movements by subtle cues in shift or balance. Soon after, Keirr and Aru were able to judge when the communications were necessary, and when we just *knew*.

Off came the blinders and blindfolds. We spent the last days of autumn simplifying our commands down to a minimal patter of words and touches, the very personal language that made bridles unnecessary. Keirr was very happy to be done with the bridle. Oh *yhes*.

Aru was soon ready for the final training course, being strong enough to leap from the paddock and flap to the roof of the aerie with Darian on his back. His exuberance pushed him forward, with Father cheering and letting the lunge line out for higher and higher leaps.

"He's advanced for his age, boy!" Father said, and Darian glowed with pride. "He made it with two downbeats of his wings. When he can do it with one downbeat, he'll be ready for the sky."

Keirr worked hard to keep up and reached the rooftop two days later, though it took her three flaps. "That's fine," Father said. "She's small, but she's strong. That was really very good." We followed up with days of practice flights to the aerie roof and landings in the paddock. It gave our young dragons a new appreciation of the command HAI—not just up, but *flying*. Then one day, Aru made it from paddock to roof with a single flap of his wings. The next day, with me hunkered close to her neck, exhaling forcefully into the back of her neck, my face pressed to her bond mark, so did Keirr.

Meanwhile: "Fren—what is the meaning of life?" I knew my questions were getting ridiculous, and I guessed he was likely to give me another non-answer.

"Lift the sandbag. Count. Lift again."

Damn.

Darian enjoyed the structure of this new daily work, though. He surpassed me in weight and repetition for each exercise, but I pushed him hard. My competitive spirit demanded no less. I wasn't about to let him forget who had saved whose life in the caverns. We weren't soft people by any stretch—raising dragons is hard work. Riding an animal that weighed eight or ten times what I did was work too. But soon I saw changes in my physique; I developed round biceps, broader shoulders, and the veins in my forearms stood proud. The growing muscles in my chest made my small breasts seem embarrassingly large. But if I felt at all masculine, I needed only to look at Darian. While I became lean and hard, his arms and chest swelled with new muscle. His limp vanished, and he began to imitate the casual, easy swagger of the Dragonry riders.

I suppose I did, too.

THREE DAYS BEFORE Menog's day, Father gave Darian and me harnesses to wear on our first ride. They were old too, the very ones Tauman and Mother used on their first flights with Rannu and Grus. But they were in good condition. Darian's was brown, to match his saddle. Mine, likewise, was deep gray with copper stitching. We spent that evening in the tack house cleaning and inspecting the saddles and adjusting the harnesses while our dragons slept.

We could hardly call them qits anymore—Keirr's shoulders now came to my nose, Aru's to Darian's forehead. With the rest of the year's growth to come, they weren't their full size yet and wouldn't fill out for several more years beyond that, but they weren't babies in any sense either. I scarcely had time to mourn the end of that too-brief period, though. Keirr and Aru shared our excitement and surged through their paces with enthusiasm we could barely contain. We knew their instinctual behavior could overwhelm us if we didn't work them hard. They wanted to fly. I was never so grateful to have Father telling me what to do.

Two days before the celebration he handed each of us a burlap bundle tied with string. "Since we didn't have a proper celebration for your bonding, I give you these instead. I'm very proud of both of you."

Each bundle contained a new shortcoat of leather with buckles for our harnesses, and winter chaps for our legs. Folded inside were lined gloves and a set of the laced leggings that dragon riders wear as safeguard against blacking out at the bottom of a steep plummet. The laces are drawn tight, and then when the legs are bent sharply they constrict, preventing blood from pooling in the legs and numbing the brain. The very thought shivered my body with a mix of fear and excitement.

Finally we discovered new goggles made of soft leather with polished glass lenses, smooth and distortion-free, unlike ordinary window glass.

I stood speechless, overwhelmed with emotion. I felt like an empress, and Darian beamed with pride. We were almost there.

Mother visited my dreams that night—but smiling, not angry. Speaking the tongue of dragons.

———

Menog's Day marked the changing of the season, when autumn surrendered the last of her color to the hard gray of winter. The people of Riat celebrated with lit candles in every window. Families visited the graves or memorials of their ancestors to lay chrysanthemums— autumn's final blush—in their memory. In the evening, villagers along the central canal launched paper boats dressed with candles and dried flowers. Soon after the sun's last glimmer, the river Wilding became a serpent of twinkling lights, seen in glimpses between the buildings. The villagers watched the progression of lights, singing or making silent prayer from shore, while children skipped and raced to follow their skiffs. Some boats ended in a blaze as paper or flowers caught fire, but that was part of the spectacle, and part of the story.

Tonight we gathered on the brood platform with our guests. Bellua and Addai stood next to Rov. They conferred in low tones, but I couldn't hear them and chose not to try. Mabir tended to services in the Temple. Father had invited Borgomos, but he declined to join us, saying only that he'd planned something with his people. Fren had disappeared, no doubt to a ceremony of his own.

Cairek stood politely apart from all as we waited for the lights to appear, though he stole looks at me from time to time. His men lined the parapet of the paddock or watched from the clifftop. Many of them had already lit candles of their own. The Juza patrolled the night sky.

My hand found Jhem's as we waited. Keirr stuck her head under my arm as if to say, "No, you are mine." I hugged her neck, but didn't let go of Jhem's hand.

The sun went down, the shadow of the mountains streaking across the plains quickly on this shortest day of the year. Singing floated up from below before we saw the first of the lights in the river, bobbing and winking as the paper boats that carried them were jostled on the stream. It was beautiful. When I'd seen this ceremony before, it was mere spectacle, the meaning lost on my young mind. Now I understood the simple beauty, an image of every man or woman who ever lived caught in the currents of their lives, a story of life and its fragility. I smiled. How was it that Mabir described Menog? *He is the spiritual center that remains when all else has fallen into ruin— the true heart of us.*

"Look," said Darian, pointing to lights in the sky north and east.

"What is that?" said Jhem. They rose beyond the far porches of Riat; first a few, then more, until a soft glowing cloud undulated like a dragon's wings against the rise of night.

Father's hand found my shoulder and gripped it. "It's Borgomos's people. They've hung candles from kites, and fly them in the evening breeze. Kites shaped like dragons, to honor their history. It is the way of Cuuloda." After a pause he amended that. "Was."

We looked on for several minutes in silent appreciation. It was creative and beautiful, more appropriate to the aeries than candles in a river. "They're honoring those they lost," I said.

Father's hand squeezed my shoulder. He didn't release it for several long moments. "That's right," he said, and then stopped speaking. I turned to see his face, directed at the lights in the distant sky. His eyes glittered and his chin was taut.

Then, one kite rose above the others, higher and higher, until there was no mistaking the meaning. "I think that one's for you," said Darian.

Despite myself, I glanced at Addai and Bellua in time to see them look away. A shiver ran down my legs. I didn't ask for this. We watched until the horizon was black and the last candle—my candle— winked out against the backdrop of stars.

Afterward, Father, Tauman and Jhem, Darian and I took lanterns and walked with all our dragons through the army camp, to a point on the clifftop overlooking the fall of the Roaring. One year or another, if the weather didn't permit flying, we held our ceremony here.

Rov and Addai didn't want us in the air at night, so instead, each of us by turns carried a bouquet of dried chrysanthemums to the precipice and said a few words, aloud or to ourselves, in honor of those gone before us.

Father went first, and stood in silence for a space. Then he said simply, "I miss you, Father and Mother. And I love you still, Reiss." It always struck a lonesome chord in me when he spoke her name. He didn't do it very often. He threw his flowers into the tumult of the Roaring and they vanished.

Tauman lowered his head, lips moving quietly in private thought. Jhem leaned against him, also speaking to herself. They threw their bundles over together. Darian followed with similar quiet reverence.

I didn't know what to say. I could see Mother in memory's eye, riding her Grus, smiling in sunshine, laughing in winter, singing the qits to sleep, scolding me with her last words. As I stood there washed in spray amidst the deafening thunder of the Roaring, all the days I had lived felt like water swirling through the eddy of my time on earth. Like beads on a string—countable, finite. How many beads since Mother's fall? Pride and excitement blended strangely with my nostalgia, bringing tears to my eyes. *Menog's tears are good tears*, Mother would have said.

I pulled the flowers to my chest. I couldn't toss them in without a word, but I didn't know what to say. Perhaps tomorrow when I flew with my Keirr for the first time, perhaps then. I tucked the bundle of flowers into my jacket.

Her remembrance belonged in the sky anyway.

THIRTY - SEVEN

THE SKY WAS ON FIRE.

A towering wall of cloud loomed, a vertical wave of moving air with a curled and tattered crest, blazing red in the pre-dawn light.

"A Morningtide boiling up, on the first day of the New Year," said Father, "And on the day of your first flight."

"Is that a good sign?" asked Darian, from somewhere behind him.

"This could be a once in a lifetime event. Wait until Bellua sees it. Wait until we tell him a Morningtide also rose on the day Maia was born. HA!"

The Morningtide was a fabled cloud formation. Every so often, dense, moist air rolled off the ocean to the west. Warm dry air from the east rose against it, stood it on edge, and piled it high against the uplift of our mountains, a wave waiting to break on our tall shore. It offered an opportunity to soar to heights seldom achieved, sliding across a cliff face of cloud as it mounted into the sky. When a Morningtide arose, supplications were made, ashes were scattered, the Avar were praised.

"It's beautiful!" said Jhem, the breadth of it reflected in her eyes.

"Hurry!" said Father, but we didn't need encouragement.

Kaisi thrust hot meat rolled in flatbread into our hands as we started toward the bridge. I wasn't the least bit hungry. I ate half and gave the rest to Keirr.

She and Aru received their favorites for breakfast, followed by a mop bath. Then we rubbed them down with oil, in part to polish their hides for show but mostly to warm up their muscles. And ours. And perhaps to calm us down too. My hands shook so much that I stopped working to stare at them. Darian spotted me, but held up his own hand, trembling like a spider's web. I smiled, and he gave me a wild-eyed grin.

Finally, we led our bouncing dragons to the paddock and under the saddle jib. Shuja, Athys, and Coluver already wore their best gear, and pranced eagerly nearby. It reminded me of the Brood Day flight—Jhem in her white, with hair knotted high, Tauman polished and ready, Father in his service black. But this was different. I was part of it. The day I had dreamed of. Fought for. Risked my life for. The hairs on my neck shivered.

Rov, Bellua, and Addai stood together by the bridge. Nice of them to stay out of our business today, I thought. Cairek and Addai had agreed to ground all their fliers while we took our first flight. "They'll be a distraction to the qits," Father had explained to Rov.

But they weren't going to miss the show. Every last one of them had an identical moment in their past. They knew what Darian and I were about to experience. They lined the clifftop. The roof of our storehouse too.

Father inspected our harnesses, tightened our laces, buckled our coats at the neck. "Listen up. The Morningtide isn't like other cloud formations. It will push you high, fast. It's a powerful thrill for even a seasoned flier, but I can't deprive you of the experience. You'll be safe as long as you follow my instructions."

He finished adjusting our gear, then put one hand on each of our shoulders. "Here's the most important thing: you know the tooth on Mt. Zurvaan we call the Crag is a peril in a Morningtide. The currents will push you up, and if you get too close to the Crag at too great an altitude, you won't be able to escape before the swirling winds suck you down into it. The key is to exit before you reach that height, then glide back for another run. We'll stay well away from Zurvaan. Just follow me. Got it?"

We nodded.

"Darian will go first. Aru is stronger, and he'll be easier to stabilize. Then, Maia, you'll come at my signal."

"Count of two," I said.

"Remember your drills, and you'll be fine. Believe it or not, we've done this before. We know what we're doing." He winked at us.

Tauman shouted from the parapet, "Father, I think you should see this." We joined him at the wall and looked over the edge.

Every street and square in town was filled with people. The banks of the river Wilding were packed shoulder to shoulder. Balconies and windows. Even rooftops.

"Look!" said Darian, pointing back across the village below. "Like last night."

On the far side of town, where the refugees were encamped, two kites like dragons' wings with long streamers rose above the distant rooftops. A cloud of smaller kites bobbed up beneath them.

"I'm not sure whether that's touching or dangerous," I said.

"Why?" said Jhem with a puzzled frown. "They're only cheering you and Darian on."

"Because Bellua will see it as a sign that they hold Darian and me in some sort of reverence. I have no clue how Addai will react."

"They honor themselves, under the circumstances," said Father. "Holding to tradition in the face of catastrophe, despite Rov and Addai trying to run them out, judging their every word. Cuuloda was proud, and we should be proud of their tribute." He clapped his hands. "Now, they're here for a show. Let's give it to them."

Darian and I leapt into our saddles and buckled in, checked every buckle twice. Father inspected each three times at least, repeating his instructions. I barely heard. I already knew them all by heart anyway. Keirr pranced with anticipation.

"Let's go!" shouted Father, and he ran to Shuja. Tauman and Jhem were already harnessed in; Athys and Coluver launched into the air. Shuja turned around and looked at our young dragons and said something in the click-rumble speech of dragons. Then he leapt straight over the broodhouse before ever opening his wings.

"Showoff," said Darian. I shared a look with him, and he grinned like a maniac, then slapped Aru on the neck and shouted HAI! He compressed himself close as Aru leapt, filled his wings with air, and pushed to the roof.

I leaned close to Keirr's ear, pulling tight the lower grips on the forward sweep of the saddle on either side of her neck, and felt the chrysanthemums tucked in my coat rustle. "Are you ready?"

She turned her head enough to fix me with an eye that twinkled silver. "Yes," she said, dipping her chin. Her diction had become so good.

I rubbed her bond mark, bent my legs tight against the laces, and took a deep breath. "Okay, girl. HAI!"

Keirr launched, pressed down against the air once with her wings, and lit easily on the roof next to Aru. "*Hey, Buk Buk*," she said. Aru joined me in laughter, lashing his tail and nodding. Darian grimaced at the chicken noises, but in the end he shook his head and smiled with us.

The rush of wind on wings grew behind us, and suddenly Father shouted, "ONE!" as he led Tauman and Jhem in a pass over our heads. They swept across the valley and then up again.

Darian nudged Aru up to the edge of the roof, with nothing but valley and village below, as Father and the rest came about for their second pass. "This is it!" Darian said aloud, pressed close to Aru's ear.

Shuja's black form streaked close overhead.

"*TWO!*"

Darian shouted HAI, and Aru leapt into the air like an arrow from a bow. I felt a moment of panic when he dropped out of sight, but soon he glided out over the valley on a flat line, with Athys and Coluver to either side and slightly ahead, aiding him with the draft off their wings. Darian let out a war whoop that echoed from every cliff.

I watched closely, observing how Athys and Coluver shepherded Aru higher into the sky. Coluver separated slightly to the right. Aru instinctively moved left to stay in Athys's wing draft, and together they drifted toward the cliff to the north, past the Roaring. If Athys got too far ahead of Aru, Coluver was poised to descend into her place. Occasionally they allowed Aru to flap on his own. Over it all I heard Darian's cheers and Aru's happy barks.

They guided him into an updraft and nudged him into the spiral. He rose high above, where Tauman circled with him at the top of the column.

I looked for the others. Jhem dived toward the aerie, but I couldn't see Father and Shuja.

"*ONE!*" he shouted as they streaked past over my head, startling me.

"Holy crap balls!"

Father's laughter followed him up and around.

"Get ready, Keirr," I said. My pulse quickened.

Keirr stepped to the lip of the roof, then nestled into a crouch like a cat poised to spring. Wings up and bent, ready to catch a volume of air. Head tucked down and back. I laid forward on the saddle, pulling tight on the grips. She was ready. More ready than I was, I thought, when I looked over the drop and saw the landscape far below. My stomach tightened. The aeries plunged straight down for hundreds of feet. Compost pits graced the bottom of the pinnacle.

I swallowed the lump in my throat. Then I adjusted my goggles and grinned. Ha! I wasn't about to die in a hill of dragon shit.

I looked back for Father. He streaked toward me. I took a deep breath, timing his arrival.

"*TWO!*" he yelled as he flashed by.

"*HAI!*" I shouted, bending tight against my laces.

Keirr lunged across the point of no return with a powerful leap and pressed into the void. She fell at first. I rose weightless against the harness straps. Vertigo wrapped me for a brief, frightening instant as she opened her wings and the landscape rushed up at us. Keirr was half the size of Shuja, less stable, more vulnerable to wind, and completely inexperienced. But she filled her wings and flapped once, then again. We rose abruptly. My stomach dropped, then Keirr found a smooth, descending glide line. A shout escaped me that was not fear, but the release of fear transformed. My laughter greeted Shuja and Coluver when they pulled in ahead of us.

"*HAI yes!* Maia, *yes!*" said Keirr.

Our trajectory took us over the village. Children chased us in the streets far below, cheering and clapping. Then Jhem peeled off and Keirr followed Shuja to the left, toward the cliff face warming in the sun. She struggled only once, but Coluver ascended beneath us with a perfectly timed nudge that pushed us back into Shuja's draft. We rose quickly.

"*Yeeeeees!*" shouted Keirr. Shuja answered with a happy roar.

Keirr answered in kind—the first time I'd ever heard her roar. I cheered and laughed, and heard my echo's joy.

We reached the cliff in no time, where the sun's warmth created a swift updraft. Spiraling, we rose higher, Coluver guiding Keirr away from the rock with gentle buffets of air from her wings. If Keirr seemed to falter, Shuja would roll over and give her a boost from beneath with a wingblast. Between them, they kept Keirr's flight path smooth and steadily upward, past the clifftop and higher still. This was a dragon's own knowledge, I realized. Something they simply knew how to do. How many people got to witness such a thing, let alone be a part of it?

The compound receded. The village became a collection of gray boxes, a patchwork of farms and fields blanketed the plains to a horizon lost in mist. I remembered the dried flowers tucked in my coat, but this wasn't the time or place. Not yet.

To the west, the vertical face of the Morningtide rose higher still. Father whistled to get our attention as we banked in circles at the top of the rising column of air. "Listen everyone! We're going to rest here for a minute, then we're going to ride the wall! Follow behind us until we get there, then Darian, you follow me. Maia, you follow Tauman, and Jhem will come behind. Go where we go. Remember to stay away from the Crag. This is it! The ride of your life!"

I'd have been content to stay on top of this spiral, circling endlessly, but soon the adult dragons tucked in three abreast before us. Darian and I fell naturally between them and behind, where their drafts would assist us. Together we turned toward the Morningtide, traveling south along its face. It obscured anything beyond our own ridge, from the distant south along the escarpment, all the way north where it was pierced and torn by Mt. Zurvaan's ragged teeth. Cloud filled the valley of Cinvat, pouring upward; the winds from our side of the ridge met it and were drawn skyward. When I looked up at that amazing wall of churning air, I worried that Father had lost his mind.

He whistled and separated with Aru right behind. They banked together toward the wall. Tauman whistled next, and I followed with the sharp wind braising my cheeks. The rising tide filled Keirr's wings and we floated with it effortlessly, higher and higher. Shuja and Aru soared far above, wings outspread, riding the mounting wave. Currents pushed us slowly northward as we vaulted higher. The roiled face of the Morningtide, only a hundred yards away, shined brighter in the growing light.

The wind became strangely silent. It didn't rush past us but rose with us. We were part of it. Calm filled me. For the first time in my life, I could see beyond the mountains that framed our valleys to high mountain lakes, towering scarps, and deep hollows. My heart soared at the thought of exploring them with Keirr. I had never been so high on a dragon before. Never. I looked down at clouds. The plains were almost invisible in the morning haze. The feeling the Summer Dragon had inspired in me awoke again in my heart, the sense of place and connection, of time and purpose.

But no, it wasn't the same. Bigger still. The world from this vantage had no horizons.

I pulled the dried flowers from my coat. They were wrapped in paper and not too terribly damaged. What better way to honor Mother's memory? I was flying. The words found themselves.

"I think I know you now, Mother. You were like me."

I smiled and let my bundle of chrysanthemums go. The blooms and stems separated in the current and swirled around us as we mounted higher, laughing, into the tallest canyon of the sky.

WHEN THE MORNINGTIDE finally crashed, its wave poured down as rain for days. We couldn't fly in such weather so we gathered in the winter stable to relive our first flight, talking and laughing about it 'til late into the night. Jhem and Father and Tauman joined us. Rov, Bellua, and Addai left us mercifully alone.

At one point, Darian recreated his first war whoop, laughing.

And Keirr said, "WHOOOHOOO hooHOOoo hooHOOoo hooHOOoo . . ." Imitating Darian but adding the echoes off the cliffs as well. After a moment of stunned silence, we broke into laughter. Even Keirr and Aru lashed their tails and nodded. Her impression was so good that I almost felt the presence of bluffs on either side of me.

Something about the way Keirr looked at me afterward made the memory persist. She looked engaged.

———

Late in the second day of rain, I came across Cairek sitting with his legs dangling over the edge of the brood platform, unconcerned with the drop in front of him, a breeze ruffling his blond hair. I had a pail in one hand, a mop in the other, and a broom pinned beneath one arm. I was disheveled and exhausted, and I really didn't want to be seen. But he turned at my footstep and smiled. "Hello, Maia," he said.

I was trapped. I dropped the pail, sloshing cold water on my leg. Cairek suppressed a laugh. "You look like you could use a break. Care to sit for a minute?" He patted the stone beside him. "You've got a wondrous view of the valley from here."

I set the mop and broom down and sat next to him. I ached all over.

"I sneak in here sometimes just to find some quiet," he said. "I hope you don't mind."

"I do it myself sometimes." I smiled to let him know it was okay.

"So, I watched your first flight. That very first drop is unnerving. I remember it well—a life-changing moment. But my first time on Taben was my first time ever. You've flown before. You're a natural, even considering you were born to it. And of course no one doubted your bravery. You rode that tall sky well, my lady."

I shivered with the memory, and felt a glow at his casual praise. "It was scary, but fun."

He chuckled. "Aye. Most impressive, that cloud. I can't tell you how badly we all wanted to ride that. I'm glad your da' turned you home when he did. Some of my men would never have forgiven him." He winked at me. Once again, his easy manner put my apprehensions at ease. He fell silent, and I had nothing to say, so we let the stillness envelop us. He labored at something with his hands. Whittling on a piece of wood. He saw my interest and held up his work for me to see.

He'd carved a stylized dragon, wings folded together above the torso, head pulled back against them, tail curled along the feet on one side. A rider was indicated between wings and neck, with her hands on the dragon's frill. "Hey, that's good," I said. "You're an artist."

"Me? Nah. But my father's family have been carpenters for generations. My da' makes furniture, an' he always had a good eye, liked to embellish his pieces. I guess I picked up some of his talent." He began scratching in lines to indicate scales.

I watched for a minute, fascinated to discover this hidden side of the Dragonry sergeant. His freckled hands moved confidently and easily over the wood. "I could carve you a stick figure," I said, "if I started with a man-shaped stick."

He laughed, a warm and hearty chuckle that bled tension out of the air like magic.

"Where are you from?" I asked.

"Born an' bred in Tenny. That's a village in the far end of Idwal. The conscription teams came an' swore me in six years ago. My older brother stayed to carry on the trade, but I was born to be a dragon rider. They said I 'had an aptitude.' " He looked at me with a dimple and a twinkling eye.

"What's it like, your home?"

"Well, not so different from Riat. Colder in the winter, hotter in the summer. Definitely drier. Pretty. Stone buildings though, mostly. Friendly people. Lots of craftsmen, like here, only they don't breed dragons. Woodworkers like my da'. They build weapons there too, an' produce arrows and quarrels." He worked quietly for a spell. "Last time I was back there, it had fallen on difficult times. The forest was just about lumbered out, not that there was much of a forest to begin with. But it made things hard for the craftsmen. You know that lumber is one of the things Gurvaan covets in Harodh? They have some of the biggest trees you ever saw."

"Is it hard? Being so far from home?" I asked.

"Oh, sometimes I suppose it is. But I've made the Dragonry my home. Taben has become my most constant friend."

"Will you go back when the war is over?"

His expression grew ever so slightly less cheerful then, and he paused in his whittling. "Over? This war is more than twenty years old. I doubt it will be over any time soon. An' when it ends, there will be another."

"Are you career, then?"

He looked sideways at me, perhaps realizing that Father might have taught me that term. "Nay. I've only a short time left, but first I have to live that long."

I didn't know how to respond to that. It was cold and pragmatic.

"The crispies will have something to say about that, of course."

"The what?"

The flicker of a grin tempered his frown. "The crispies. A name we have for the Horrors, because they look burnt. But of course you know that already."

The snick of blade on wood filled the following minutes.

"I don't suppose it's really funny, is it," he said, eventually.

"Actually, it sort of is." I smiled.

"Interesting. Darian always wants to know about the tactics, the equipment, the war. But you asked me about my home. I like that about you, Maia." He looked up. "You know, I could come to love a place like this, assuming Taben an' I get to retire, that is. Wunt his fault he became a warrior. He deserves to live out his life this way—stud to future generations." He chuckled again. "You might say the same thing about me." He looked at me, his eyes lingering a moment. Then he looked quickly away, as if he'd embarrassed himself. It made me grin. "How is it that a pretty little thing like you doesn't have suitors falling all over themselves for your hand, hey?"

In answer, I indicated the bucket and mop, then pointed at the wet spot on my leg.

Cairek laughed out loud. "No, I'm serious."

I shrugged, my turn to be embarrassed. "They'd have to get through Father first. And to be honest, I'm not that interested. There's nothing around here but farmers and shopkeepers, and they're really more interested in marrying into the family than anything else."

"Not one of them has caught your fancy? I find that hard to believe." Again his eyes lingered on mine.

"Well, maybe." I felt myself blush. "But I'm busy most of the time, especially since you came—the lot of you, I mean. And what I really want to do is raise dragons."

Cairek smiled. "That I understand. So what do you think of my Taben? Good stock?"

I considered the question. "Not bad. He's strong, and he's agile. A little bowlegged."

"Ha! He is that, aye. Always thought so myself. Luckily, he's a dragon an' not a horse."

I giggled.

"Pretty little valley, this. Reminds me of home, when I was young an' there were still trees aplenty. You're a lucky young woman."

More silence followed as I watched Cairek put the final touches on his little wooden dragon. I knew he was right. The last few days I'd felt inordinately lucky. Sinfully lucky. I allowed his fantasy to mingle with mine—perhaps one day he would return and make a proposal to Father for my hand. I drew up my knees, rested my chin on them, feeling at once foolish and strangely at ease.

"Here you go then, Maia," he said, and handed his dragon to me. "Something to remember me by."

During the third day of rain the caravan of miners and engineers arrived, despite roads clogged with mud or riven by streams. Another talon of dragon-rider teams landed in the paddock, wet and hungry, with orders to report to Rov as their commander. Rov seemed to know many of them already, embracing them as old comrades. A passenger climbed down from one of the dragons, a tall, straight soldier with white hair and goatee. He wasn't Dragonry. I could tell from his awkward dismount he was more accustomed to a horse. I sidled closer as he approached Father, so I could listen in.

"*Staelan*," he named himself. "I will be in command of the Barrage."

"*What* barrage?" said Father.

"*My* Barrage. Ballistae. Boltcasters. Barricades." I didn't know what any of those things were. "As soon as the weather clears we'll be mounting them on these paddock roofs. You need some palisades too, I'm afraid, but I see you have plenty of timber. Here are my orders." Father glared with taut mouth at the papers Staelan thrust into his hands.

On the fourth day, the rain dwindled to a slow drizzle, and the crack of wings drew me out of the stable. Cheien and one of the Torchbearers stretched above the storehouse roof. I crossed the bridge to the paddock but halted at the corner of the building when I heard Rov's voice: "We've found everyone with health and skills. It's time for the rest to go, as agreed."

"*As agreed?*" said Father. "The people of Cuuloda never *agreed* to leave. They only submitted to an order they couldn't possibly defy."

"Broodmaster, there's a reason civilians leave battle zones. They're vulnerable, and protecting them occupies assets better assigned to other duties. They consume resources better spent—"

I charged around the corner. "I can't believe what I'm hearing. Sending refugees out into the wilderness in the heart of winter."

Rov looked at me in surprise. Beside him Addai stood with his hands clasped together. Though he raised his eyebrows, his face was unreadable beneath the intricate gravings. Were all the men with writing covering their bodies as arrogant as these two?

"They're all that's left of Cuuloda," I said. "This isn't a battle zone. Not yet, anyway. Give them a chance."

"I found places for less than a third of them," said Father.

Addai turned to Father, his tiny eyes unblinking. "Borgomos himself is of no use to us. He is overweight, with skills only in the exchanging of coins. A service we hardly need."

"Bookkeeping is a valuable service. I offered him such work, but he wouldn't take it unless he knew his people could stay."

"Bookkeeping is what determines his fate, I fear," said Addai. "The harsh but simple arithmetic of mouths and resources."

"He has other qualities. Leadership—"

"We have leaders enough, Broodmaster."

"He's a man of rare courage and strength. He could have run far with his riches, but he didn't."

Addai's mouth stretched into a thin, taut line.

"I thought the Juza were part of the Temple," I said. "I expected that to mean they were taught compassion, maybe. Or charity."

Addai's eyes snapped to mine, and his face twitched once before he spoke. "It's not an easy decision we make, young woman. But the Empire must keep its aeries safe." He looked at Father again. "You can't lose sight of that, Broodmaster. We're here to protect *your* dragons, *your* aeries, at all costs. That's our duty now. At all costs, do you understand? You should be more grateful."

———

On the fifth day we harnessed in for our second flight, which stood in stark contrast to the first in almost every way. Keirr and Aru struggled with dead air below torn clouds. Only their eagerness fueled them against the cold. The village streets were empty. And our mission was somber; Father insisted on escorting Borgomos and his ragtag survivors as far as we could.

Addai insisted on providing a winged guard. He and three of his Juza shadowed us all day.

On the way to find Borgomos, east of Riat, we flew over the war machines that the newcomer, Staelan, referred to as his "Barrage." Everything was covered with tarps, surrounded by tents and cookfires where soldiers waited for the weather to break. They'd be all over the paddock soon, unavoidably close all the time. More depressing than the massive intrusion was the cold necessity of all this war machinery. Borgomos's sad retreat was evidence enough of that.

We found him by following the singing of his people, accompanied by the basso rumble of their wagon wheels, a chorus that lifted sadly above the monotone of slow rain. Thirty or so carts and wagons threaded along the Wilding river road, intermingled with goats and the occasional pig, or bedraggled dogs and men on foot. People from the outlying farms met them as they passed, with baskets of food or parcels of goods like candles or firewood. Borgomos walked at the head with the aid of his stripped Staff of Office. He turned and waved at us when he heard our wings.

I raised my hand in response, but couldn't match his enthusiasm. I felt awful for them—so many able-bodied people who might contribute in Riat somehow but were obligated to leave with their sick and disabled and elderly. Which meant their children came too, huddled against the cold and wet. The small towns along the way to Taskis wouldn't be able to absorb so many lost souls; they had little choice but to make the entire long journey. My blood pounded in my ears. It made me so angry. We weren't in control of our own aeries, and it seemed that things would only get worse.

We followed them until the day grew thin. Father landed briefly to speak with Borgomos but didn't want to risk Aru or Keirr being unable to climb back into such a dead sky, against sinking air. So he ordered us to stay aloft until he returned.

When he rejoined us, I saw that they'd given him something. At first glance he seemed to tuck a shield under his arm, but I quickly realized it was two or more kites lashed together.

We parted with Cuuloda's last survivors below the first and shortest set of falls beyond the farms. When at last we returned to the aeries, snow swirled in the air.

———

Rutting fever takes adult dragons in the heart of winter. We shut the broodparents in the broodhouse for a week or more of privacy. They wouldn't eat or drink until they were finished, so there was little to do but check in on them from time to time. They lay intertwined in their nests, barely moving, nuzzling and rumbling softly. In the wild, dragons found a quiet cave and hibernated for as long as a month, engaged only in this surprisingly tender act.

But for Darian, Aru, Keirr, and I, the sun returned. We took to the skies as often as we could. Rov couldn't stop us; this was our *job* now. Imagine.

When Father, Tauman, or Jhem accompanied us, we went further afield to stretch our dragons' range, and Father gave us lessons at every opportunity. The first few days we practiced barrel rolls, pulling tight to our mounts' necks to minimize our gravity. "Tuck your head next to her neck or risk blacking out." Within the third week we practiced the deep, dizzying dives that made our leggings necessary. In between lessons, we ran up mountain ridges with wings as thrusters, leapt into updrafts for spinning rides to dizzying heights. We saw timber felled for the new barracks, visited high cols and frozen mountain lakes. Fren cut ice for the ice vaults and waved when we shouted hellos. Our dragons grew stronger and so did we, and it was all play. It felt like freedom—at first.

We watched from the air as Staelan's barrage was hauled up on the winch platform and assembled on the roofs of broodhouse and storehouse. Darian always circled in for a closer look at the war machines, whizzing barely over the heads of Staelan's men within earshot of his angry shouts. I wanted no part of the ugly things. Like giant crossbows on gimbals, some designed to loose as many as twelve enormous arrows at once, others like catapults that hurled no missile, but rather snapped upward and stabbed simultaneously with many sharp spears. The perimeter of the paddock sprouted log cages pinned to the stone paving, with spikes pointing outward—Staelan's "palisades." Men could move in and out of them easily but dragons could not.

It all represented the end of life as I knew it. My home had become a military installation.

Work began in the Cinvat valley too. The engineers cleared huge swaths of forest off the ridge, right up to the edge of the ruins, and began work on a road along the path to the caves. A road hadn't occurred to me. Of course they would need a road. But did it need to be so wide, if all they planned to do was seal the caves? It angered me

that the statue of Menog and Dahak stood exposed, its forest enclosure shorn away to make room for an ugly dirt road.

When Father or the others couldn't accompany us, Cairek appointed two of his teams to tail us and two others to fly patrol beyond
them. The Juza took turns as well. Their mission, it seemed, was to
hem us in, keep us close. We understood that it was necessary, but we
knew also that young wildings yearn to test the greatest heights early.
Keirr wanted it, I knew. It was clear in the direction of her gaze, the
language of her shrugs and nudges. I wanted it, too.

Our games with Darian and Aru turned quickly from sparring
with each other to losing our escorts. We dodged through trees and
narrow canyons. They always found ways to drop into our paths and
warn us back. The exercise made Keirr and Aru nimble. Their strength
and confidence grew. Keirr and I learned each other's inaudible language. If I leaned forward, she knew I wanted more speed. If I tightened into my laces we would dive. The hitch of her shoulder indicated
a turn to come, a change in the set of her wings meant a change of
speed. We learned the currents and channels of our mountain very
well in the bargain.

One morning Darian cocked an eyebrow at me. "You've got an
eye on him, haven't you?"

"Who?"

"Cairek."

"What? He's nice, I suppose, but no, I don't." I felt the heat of a
blush on my cheeks and hoped Darian couldn't see it. Cairek spoke to
me often, complimenting my progress or making small talk.

"You've got that little dragon he carved for you on your nightstand."

"That doesn't mean anything."

"He talks about you all the time."

"No, he doesn't."

"Yes. He does."

My stomach knotted. I'd let his fantasy mingle with mine once, but
it was just a fantasy. Wasn't it? This brought it a little too close to the
brink of reality. I liked him. He made me feel comfortable. I liked his
tawny hair, his freckles, his blond stubble. But I really didn't want attention, much less romance. Not with everything else going on. Please.

Cairek and three of his teams accompanied us the day we finally ditched our escorts for the first and only time. Glimpses of blue and sunlight pierced the ragged winter sky. Addai and his Juza had been gone on some patrol since the day before, so we felt unhindered. The spring-like mix of sun and showers alone might have tempted us, but when Bellua decided to join the escort as well, I'm not sure Darian or I were rational. We wanted nothing more than to lose him and find some solitude.

A low-hanging cloud allowed us to slip through to a higher outcrop, where we knew of a hidden ledge. After several minutes of silence, Darian said, "Ha! We lost them."

The ledge looked over a dark and untamed valley north of Mt. Zurvaan, swimming in and out of view as low clouds scudded between the peaks below. We dismounted to stretch our legs. I held my gloved hands over my cheeks to warm them up.

Out of Zurvaan's arm above us and left thrust the Crag, a jagged spire taller from base to tip than the pinnacle the aeries were built on. Beyond it, the peak of Mt. Zurvaan rose above swirling mist, close enough to see clouds pulled from its stony point like spider silk.

"Look at that updraft, Maia. Imagine how high that could take you. Higher even than the Morningtide."

"You'd pass out from air starvation."

He smiled. "Eventually. But what a view you'd get first. And from that height, you could glide a long, long way without effort, to places we've never seen. And probably never will."

I studied him in the silence that followed. He looked unsettled, lost. We had grown closer in recent weeks but somehow further apart at the same time. We were together almost every day, but we rarely talked. When we were flying, we didn't have to think about nightmares or expectations, but on the ground, Darian was stuck in my shadow, still. And every time it seemed like he might break through and be his own familiar self, someone like Borgomos would show up with praise for me—"Getig's Maia." Or Addai would build his schedule around my flights.

"Imagine it, Maia," he continued. "True freedom, alone, with four horizons to choose from. No one dogging you. That's what launching off the top of Zurvaan would feel like. Don't you ever wish that nothing had been decided for you, that all you had to do was imagine what you wanted and it could be yours?" He clenched his jaw and looked at me. "What am I saying? You've already done that. You plucked Keirr out of the wilderness with nothing but your determination, when everyone told you *no*."

Unsure where he was going or how to respond, I only listened. Wind moaned around the corners of our ledge. Darian looked out at the tortured cloudscape. "Can I make a true confession, Maia? I'm envious of the way you went after Keirr." His gaze shifted to the blade-like spire of Zurvaan, disappearing then reappearing through the whorl of clouds. "I know you were driven to it, but still, it must be liberating to decide what you want and just go after it, as if nothing else mattered." He looked at me. "How did it feel? Was it exhilarating?"

I shook my head. "No. Not at all. It was terrifying."

"But isn't it good, looking back, to know that you had to make a choice, and so you simply"—he shook his head—"*made* it?"

"Darian, you have no idea what I went through. There was no choice to make. I explained it to you in the caves; how can you still not get it? Bellua threatened to take me to Avigal, to be interrogated by Korruzon Himself—assuming that wasn't a plate of shit. I had. No. Choice. It was either acquire a qit, die trying, or be a slave to Bellua's ambitions. Probably raped, possibly killed to quiet some assumed heresy. It was the only way I had of getting out from under Bellua's boot heel. I was desperate."

"But you did it. You took the spread of the sky and made the only choice you could make, right?"

"What else could I have done?"

He stared at his knees for a long time, nodding. "Freedom is a lie, isn't it," he said at last. "Desire is a trap, unless you do something insane."

"What are you talking about?" I bit my lip, not sure what to say next.

He studied the northern horizon for a minute, and I followed his gaze. Jhem once told me that on a clear day you could see all the way to Cuuloda from the limbs of Zurvaan. What did Darian see? What was he looking for?

"After the caves, did you have bad dreams?" he asked.

I looked up at him, surprised. His face was drawn and dark.

"Yes."

"Do you still?"

I nodded.

He met my gaze. "Yeah. Me too."

"But we're still here, aren't we. We're tougher now."

He smiled, but shook his head. "Maia, when that Horror grabbed me, I thought my life was over. I thought it was going to eat me. The only thing that stopped it was you. They used me to draw you out. But instead, you rescued me. Then I got shot, but you led me to safety. You tamed the wilding father."

"But you rescued me too, Dare. You lit the fire, or I'd have never made it into the cave. I'll never forget the way you stood up to the Harodhi shaman. You made it possible for me to bring home *Keirr*. And you fought hard, even though you were badly injured. Like Borgomos said—like a prince of Gadia."

"But don't you see, Maia? I'll always be the other character in your story." He looked at me. "The one that got in the way and had to be rescued." He turned his face away again, and my heart ached for him. He would never be Broodmaster, but at least he'd been the next oldest, until my notoriety eclipsed even that.

"We're not a story, Dare."

"You don't think so?" He looked at me with his chin elevated, a half smile on his lips, and I knew he was right. We were a story at least as far away as Cuuloda.

"Then they're telling the story all wrong. I couldn't have done it without you."

Darian shrugged. "I'd like to think that Getig held something for me too. Something more than just . . . more than . . ." He held his arms out to the world. "Something. I just feel disconnected. Even Aru—it seems like he goes to you as often as he comes to me." I felt a tingle at the back of my neck and tried not to look horrified. I reached out and put a hand on his arm.

"Don't take this wrong, Maia," he said quietly. "I'm really, really proud of you. It's only that . . ." His face became pinched as he surveyed the tattered heavens.

"What?" I asked him.

He looked at me again. "It's that I'm ashamed. Of myself."

"Why ashamed? Darian . . ." I stumbled on my words as I considered what our shared bondmark might be doing to him, what unintended damage it might have caused. I'd only suggested the idea to Mabir out of fear for his life, and that of Aru. Mabir had asked me to remain silent, and I'd agreed not only because he'd asked me but also for fear that Darian might let it slip at the wrong time. To the wrong person.

In the span of that pause hung the balance of Darian's bravery. He stood up abruptly.

"Don't try to make me feel better. I'm not that upset. I don't know why I brought it up anyway." He clapped his hands, startling Aru and Keirr. "Up!" he shouted, sounding an awful lot like Father. "Weather is clearing on that peak." He indicated the narrow blade of Zurvaan over his shoulder.

"We should head back, Dare. We don't want to get Cairek in trouble."

"I'm going to give it a try."

He leapt onto Aru's back and started buckling in before I could stand up. "Darian! What are you thinking?"

"I'm not thinking." He grinned. "I'm doing." He spun Aru about.

"No!" I shouted, and Aru turned back to me.

"Confound it, Aru!" Darian slapped the left side of his neck to turn him back again.

"Darian," I shouted. "There's no air up there." I checked my girth quickly and scrambled into my saddle as Darian and Aru stepped off the ledge into an updraft.

I buckled in, then turned Keirr around. "*Ghee*, baby. HAI!" We launched into the slipstream too.

I'd forgotten to pull my goggles on, and the wind blinded me with tears. "Higher, Keirr, HAI!" I said, wiping my eyes, getting my goggles arranged. I recovered in time to see Aru peel out of the curtain of rising air and wheel toward the jagged crest of Zurvaan.

"Buk Buk, HAI!" said Keirr.

By the time I rose to the same height and followed them, Darian and Aru clung to the icy windward face of Zurvaan, well below the

peak, tiny as flies. I could tell the currents were fierce. Aru couldn't
hold his wings' shape against the torrent. He attempted to climb, but
finally leapt from a broken shank of stone into the gentler gale on the
lee side of the peak. I gasped in relief and turned Keirr to follow
them.

They glided downward in tight spirals, the cliffs resounding with
Darian's joy.

Zurvaan loomed above with snow swirling around its ancient
shoulders, wielding the Crag like a stony scepter.

––––––

We dived steeply through Buk Buk's trail, caught his spiral and hovered in right above him. Then Keirr pushed off Aru's rump with her
back feet and propelled us up again. Darian yelped. Aru tumbled for
an instant with an angry *"Keirr!"* but then thrust off into a flat dive
down the slope of the mountain. We streaked after.

We caught up to them, suspended in an updraft off a sharp ridge-
back, and nestled in alongside. Darian still laughed. "Oh, my. Oh,
Maia, you have to try that. It's like Aru and I were *one*, thinking and
reacting together. We simply . . ." His face contorted in his effort to
find words. "Connected. Like a belt into a buckle, or the two halves
of an apple you just sliced in two."

"That was crazy dangerous, Dare—"

He grinned at me, catching his breath. "Yeah. I think the fear is
part of it. I do. Not only that, but I know how to take that peak now.
Not on the windward side, but up the eastern face, in the lee. There's
a calmer updraft in the center. I felt it." His smile shrank. "Uh oh,
well. Playtime is over." He pointed down to the east. "There's our
escort."

Below us several dragon shapes glided slowly toward some objec-
tive further down the face of the mountain. But they weren't Cairek's
men looking for us. More than their ungainly mannerisms and burnt
skin, their tattered wings gave them away.

Darian's face fell but his eyes grew intense. "Horrors, Maia. Korruzon's flaming ass. More Horrors."

Where could they have come from? Yet another uncharted doorway into the mountain? There were five more dragons further down

the hill. Darian and I recognized those as Cairek, Bellua, and our Dragonry escorts.

"They don't see the threat," said Darian. "Why aren't they looking up if they're looking for us? *Idiots.*"

"Darian, you have to fly home fast and get help."

"Why do *I* have—"

"Because Aru is faster than Keirr!"

His eyes froze on mine for a second, then he nodded grimly. "What are you going to do?"

I looked down the face of the mountain and shrugged. "Warn them."

"Gods. Be careful." He tapped Aru on the right side of his neck. "*Home*, Aru. GO!" Aru angled off the lip of the updraft and sped for the aeries.

I nudged Keirr out of the stream, and we began to fall slowly on her outstretched wings, studying the situation. Three Horror dragons had position on Cairek's men, and wafted down quietly for a surprise attack like eagles on rabbits or dragons on deer.

"LO, Keirr!" *A steep dive, now.*

She turned an eye back toward me—a wide eye. Then she drew in all but the fingertips of her wings and stretched her neck out straight. Profiled like the fletching on an arrow, we slid forward off the updraft, then accelerated straight for the band of Horrors. I bent my legs hard against the laces, pulled flat to her neck, and took a deep breath.

A canyon opened beneath them. I tapped Keirr's neck in simple communication. She clicked an acknowledgment, pulled forward just a little bit, tucked her wings in completely, and plummeted. The beasts rushed up at us, their silhouettes fractured and wrong, but not in a way I could identify before we hurtled through their formation and down. I thought suddenly of the shadow creature, the Edimmu. Where was it?

The Horrors roared. Leathery wings cracked to life behind us.

THIRTY-NINE

WE SHOT TOWARD Cairek's men circling with Bellua below, Keirr steering us with only her wingtips and tail to keep her profile narrow and fast. I had no intention of stopping.

"*Below!*" I screamed, and their heads snapped up. Then I burst through their formation like an arrow. Shouts and commands erupted behind.

"*Heeey,*" I said and Keirr flattened out. Tapped her on the right side, and she circled wide toward the mountain, to seek another updraft. I looked back.

Two of the Horrors, their surprise ruined, sculled into a hovering position above Bellua, Cairek, and his teams. The third twisted round them all and came after me.

"*LO! Keirr!*" I screamed in panic, and she drew wings and tail tight. We plummeted again, but not fast enough. It gained on us, pushing with its wings as it fell. Already I could see the sickening green glow deep in the cataracts of its flesh.

"Gods, Keirr! It's too fast. We have to be nimble, like 'chase' with Aru. *Chase*, Keirr!"

Keirr was terrified, but engaged. I turned her loose to use her instincts. I would only be dead weight anyway. She torqued rightward abruptly, did a half barrel roll to press us toward a rocky tower, righted herself again to swing behind its broken margin. I pulled hard on the saddle grips to keep myself close but cracked my head against the side of her neck. She ran up the backside of the tower with assist from her wings. The Horror shot around the prominence well below us and started rowing upward. Good, we'd added distance. The

Horror was fast, but it was huge too, and needed more room to change directions. We reached the top of the tower and Keirr dove into a rising stream of air, rode it higher. I looked down to see Cairek's men engaged in a circling, tumbling battle with the other monsters. Only three teams, battling to keep Bellua safe from the Horrors. Bellua's dragon, Zell, wasn't made for this. She was an older nurse dragon, not a youngster or trained military.

One of our escorts was missing. Cairek, but I didn't have time to look for him. The Horror following me stepped from the tower into the updraft, where its adult wingspan gave it an advantage. It rose after us, shoveling huge wingfuls of air behind itself. How could wings so riddled with holes even function?

"Ghee, LO!"

Keirr turned left and plummeted toward the opposite margin of the tower, then behind it, through a crack between two pillars. Out into a turbulent expanse of air. Lost her equilibrium and tumbled. I lost hold of the saddle as she spun, blood rushing to my head. She stuck out a wing and fanned her tail, swung upright again, but at cost of momentum. She bottomed out of the dive—the blood flow to my head reversed abruptly. I swooned and blacked out. Awoke a second or three later, to find Keirr looking back and screeching in fear. The Horror was upon us, sculling to arrest its own speed so it could bring its weapons to bear.

Instead of foreclaws it wielded two long, downward curving blades, like scythes bolted below the dragon's elbow, enwrapping in metal whatever stump remained of the leg beneath. It raised them like the two blades of a giant scissor. Keirr twisted again and propelled us sideways at the last instant. One of the ugly blades whistled in the air above my head. The Horror's momentum carried it past us. We put distance between us again.

The beast wouldn't stop. It turned and flapped after us. Keirr bounced down a ridge of stone, pushing off each protruding rock with legs and wings to change direction and add speed. Twisted through a series of crevasses, forcing the Horror to take longer routes. Found favorite air currents that added distance between us. But the beast had strength and experience to draw on that we didn't. What space we gained with agility and maneuverability, the monster took back with dogged persistence. It stayed close, no matter what we did.

I felt Keirr's desperate energy. After playing on the mountain all day, she was close to exhaustion. I tapped the side of her neck and turned her toward open sky where I could get my bearings. The Horror followed. We found a rising column of air and rode to the top. The beast entered the current and lifted after us.

Above the next ridge, two other Horrors chased Bellua. Even though the Dragonry aided him, his dragon struggled to elude the monsters. Where was Cairek?

The Horror drifted nearer. The rider raised a crossbow, cocking it. From this high vantage I saw the abomination clearly, and my stomach knotted. His legs were splayed open like a frayed end of rope. Muscle, tendon, and bone were woven into the construction of the saddle, which knitted into the ribcage of the beast with brackish light seeping out through the fissures. Charred hide and black armor blended grotesquely, one burnt corpse woven to another. "Crispies," Cairek had called them.

Keirr tipped sideways—too soon. The Horror followed and gained more air. Keirr was beginning to panic, but I didn't know where to direct her. The aeries were in the opposite direction, over another ridge. Turbulent winds swirled above its sawtooth spine, but help would come from that direction or not at all.

"Home, baby, take us *home*."

She thrust straight down, then folded her wings close. I squeezed my legs and clung to her neck as she fell, both of us gasping for breath. I didn't have a weapon on me, not even a knife. What were Dare and I thinking, evading our armed military escort?

Keirr bottomed out of her dive and inertia gave me weight. I squeezed my legs and pulled close to her neck to keep from blacking out again and to minimize my profile to the wind. She sped a long way on momentum alone, head pulled back against her neck, ear frills covering my head and shoulders. I glanced back to see the Horror streaking out of its dive close behind us. The rider raised its bow. I tapped Keirr and shifted my weight to steer her left, then twice to the right. He loosed, but missed us by a wide margin.

The Horror suddenly thrust backward and up, sculling to a hover as one of the Dragonry teams dropped between us, top bow cracking. It was Cairek! Two of his teams sped our way with the other two Horrors in pursuit. I didn't see Bellua.

Cairek had bought me time to flee for home, but I couldn't abandon him or his men. I guided Keirr into a long, wide turn around the fight, circling up and behind—not followed, as near as I could tell. A new current pushed us higher.

We were exhausted beyond words, running on desperation alone. No energy left to draw on but each other's. In that pause I realized how tightly we were bound. Connected through trust and language and endless practice together, yes, but also through our bond marks. Was it more even than that? Sweet Avar! Is this what Darian meant? Throughout the chase I seemed to read her intention, anticipate her movements. She responded almost as quick as thought to my directions. Minds almost blending. At some instants we'd been Maia/Keirr, and at others Keirr/Maia.

I closed my eyes briefly to will myself into her body, to seek out that point of connection and tap it again. I listened. In that instant I heard Cairek's men shouting communications to each other. Top bows chattering. Wind in fabric, wind on leather of jacket or wing. Even around the edges of my goggles. Keirr clicking. The single click. Not the conversational click, but the—

With the first faint echo, the answer struck me like a bolt of fire.

Playing with her chicken carcass, stalking Aru. Imitating Darian's war-whoop—echoes and all—so well that I could *feel* the cliffs. And the conversational home-click with its repetitions, like echoes. Unlike the single click away from home.

Those echoes she listened for.

With the certainty of wind in high places I understood this now. She'd explained it to me herself with her imitation of Darian. Keirr and her kind listened for the echoes of their vocalizations to feel their world, the breadth and depth and volume of it. Then later, they told those pictures to each other with their language. Their three-dimensional language. They spoke in echoes.

I realized that my judgment of these high spaces—their heights and hollows and fathoms—paled next to Keirr's. I would never, ever see them as well as she did.

And now, I needed to see them well. An unwinnable stalemate swirled below me. I marveled at the Dragonry's skill—I could no more navigate such a battle than I could tie snakes into knots. Cairek's battle was a slow retreat. He understood the same thing I did—that help would come from Riat. That we must move this fight in that direction. Bellua and Zell still lived, struggling to avoid the Horrors without getting in the way of the Dragonry. Cairek's men rained arrows down with their topbows, but it had little effect on these burned monsters. They never tired. Melee was not an option—the very touch of the things did damage. Soon the Dragonry would run out of ammo and face the same desperate exhaustion that had nearly overcome Keirr. However ungainly the Horrors were in flight, they were unrelenting, and they wanted the merihem. The thought of letting the crispies have him entered my mind.

I couldn't do that. I stretched out and touched Keirr's bond mark. Warm. She looked back at me with a beautiful silver eye. With a minute's rest and the chance to assess the situation, I knew what to do.

This was our mountain. We knew the chutes of air, the dead spots and live spots. We knew where to scull, drift, rise, sideslip. With shouts and touches, I guided Keirr into a steep dive that took us straight toward the nearest Horror. It had gained position on Bellua and banked for a strike. "Tag it!" I said close to her ear.

As we neared the beast at full speed I shouted, "Heeey! *Heeey!*" Keirr reached down with her rear claws as we flashed past above it and pushed off the monster's head. I watched behind. Bellua twisted clear, and the thing turned to follow us. I pressed myself to Keirr's neck and shouted, *"GO!"*

We shot like an arrow toward the ridge. The beast followed immediately.

Good. But he gained on us, faster than the one with the blades for arms. Fear poured through me. If we misjudged this timing, we were doomed. Keirr grasped where my commands directed her and why. I sensed it immediately, like an electric jolt to her purpose. We aimed low at the cliff face and the Horror angled in high, meaning to trap us.

At the last moment we bent our line sharply upward, caught the fountain of air gathered at the base of the cliff. The monster failed to adjust to our sudden momentum and hit the airstream at a hard angle.

As we shot past an arch of stone, the wind drove the Horrors full into it. Green glowing chunks shattered away. The raging air of the channel hurled us skyward. We whirled and spun in turbulence. I pulled close to Keirr's neck, striving to see more than glimpses of sky or earth. Cairek and his teams followed me. Casualties? I couldn't count that fast. At least one Horror still followed. We tumbled until Keirr found her equilibrium, flipping us over and up.

A shadow enveloped us. The beast with blades for arms dropped down from above. I screamed—there would be no retreating from their horrible reach. But with all her strength, Keirr pushed *toward* the monster, inside their range. Folded her wings tight as the blades whipped past behind us on either side. Then she kicked hard against its throat, bouncing away before the blades could be raised again or the jaws could snap. With another push of her tired wings she gained height on the falling beast.

With a snap of dried leather and a rush of air, the monster closed the gap.

Jaws opened behind us, throat gaping like the flue of a hellish furnace. The rider pulled its crossbow taut.

Keirr turned sharply again, over the top of the thing's head where its bite would be least effective. The jaws snapped, brushing against her side. She yelped in pain, and I felt the snag in her flesh, a touch of cold in my side. But the tooth failed to find purchase, and we plummeted past the beast even as the rider fired his crossbow. I heard the bolt puncture a wing membrane.

Keirr tucked her right wing in tight, shielding a painful wound in her body, using her left to keep us in a tight spiral as we fell. It only slowed us a little. It was lethal speed, and the mountain rose quickly. I pulled as close as I could to help her find a center of balance. At the last instant she opened both wings and flattened out toward a broken ridge.

It rushed at us too quickly. Keirr dropped her hips and hit hard, all four legs compressing like springs. I didn't adjust in time. As she bounded off again my legs were relaxed against the laces. The blood rushed out of my head and I blacked out a second time. I awoke dizzy, sound and sight muffled in fog, the taste of bile strong in my throat.

Keirr screeched in fear. Darkness. No, shadow. The beast was upon us again, and Keirr spiraled desperately against my dead weight. I pulled close. A vision of Keirr and me crashing into the side of the mountain. My eyes opened wide to see that, no, we glided on a flat, downward incline at top speed, away from the mountain, the beast trying to match Keirr's last sharp turn. But the image persisted, now ripping me from my harness and dashing me on the rocks, the same way that my mother died.

I understood. *Edimmu. I know you for what you are.*

Keirr splayed open on a tripod, like the youngling I'd seen in the cave so many months ago. I felt her pain in my sides and gasped for breath. The physical sensations were new—the thing was stronger.

Where are you hiding?

Tumbling down a cliff face, blood splashing with every impact. I felt my bones break, and I cried out.

I'm whole, on my bondmate's back. Keirr's movements and reactions made me sure that she wasn't subject to the evil. Or was she fighting it, just like me?

A shadowed canyon rose up opposite us as we fell. I saw a dragon-like silhouette perched on a ledge, ragged wings flattened together above its back.

I see you, Edimmu.

The shadow backed into deeper shadow. In the same instant the Horror with the bladed arms fell upon us again. Image of blades scissoring across Keirr and me. I felt the frozen pain of sharp steel.

But Keirr has turned again.

Sensation of crushing cold as teeth closed around my body. I screamed in agony.

But we are clear of it, in sunlight.

The Horror thrust wingfuls of air behind, closing fast, but its attentions turned suddenly as a silhouette descended from my left. I twisted against my harness to see more clearly.

Shuja!

Father loosed arrows into the Horror's maw. Shuja dropped down on the back of the interwoven nightmare and tore the rider off with a terrier-like whip of his head. Pieces of burnt Horror spun off to either side. The dragon Horror snapped at him, but Shuja grabbed its wing in his foreclaws, kicked with his rear legs and wings, and shattered the monster's alar shoulder. He pushed off with a roar, and the beast tumbled away behind us, struggling as it fell, with one wing flapping and the other twisted like a broken kite. It cracked across a ridge of rock, then slumped unmoving into a narrow defile.

I gasped in relief as more Dragonry teams streaked past above us to swarm the one remaining Horror. Soon it plunged with broken wings down a rough escarpment and into a deep canyon. My head hurt. The horizon insisted on tilting, but I patted Keirr on the bond mark, panting. We caught a draft up to inspect the ledge where the shadow thing had perched when it assaulted me. The ledge was empty, snaking back into a dark cleft. I listened for the Edimmu, tried to open my consciousness enough to hear.

Nothing. Cold trickled on my upper lip. Jhem called my name, and I spotted her rising below me on Audax. Tauman was behind her on Rannu. Where were Darian and Aru? I didn't see any of the Juza, either.

Bellua and several dragon teams wafted down beside a dark shape, stark against the snow of a mountain crevasse. We circled closer. Not a Horror. One of our own. My eyes chased the sky until I found Cairek and his Taben and knew they were safe.

I closed my eyes in anguish. One of us, our own, broken on the rocks. My stomach heaved. Oh, Gods. I pulled tight to Keirr's neck. *"Home*, baby. *Go home."*

———

Keirr plummeted once, too exhausted to hold the frame of her wings against a sudden swirl of air. I lost awareness when she caught herself at the bottom of the fall. Awoke and pulled tight again. Strange disassociation between there and not there. The sky was up, yes, that was correct. Father had warned us that the whiplash of gravity in our heads could cause injury. I'd blacked out twice today. Three times.

The aeries careened into view. *"Home."* Not my voice—Keirr's.

Rush of wind as she caught our momentum in her wings. Rough landing, Keirr exhausted. She collapsed in the paddock, me draped on her neck. Footsteps. I released my harness straps and tumbled out of the saddle. Keirr tried to catch my fall, but I hit the ground hard. Looked up. Was I lying down or leaning against a wall? A ballista man grabbed my elbow to help me up, two other Dragonry soldiers behind him.

"Ma'am? Are you hurt?"

I shook his hand off my arm and stood beside my Keirr, images from our ordeal repeating in my head, stacked one atop another, dizzying. Vertigo, fear, the illusions of pain thrust at me by the Edimmu. I kept expecting the monster to violate my head again. *Avar. Getig. Asha. What is happening to me?* I could feel shakes coming on. Tears pooled in my eyes, but I refused to cry in front of these men.

I urged Keirr to her feet. When she stretched her wings, the soldiers backed off and parted before us as we turned toward the bridge. Their commander, Staelan, shouted them back to their posts. "Keep your eyes on the skies!" Only then did I notice that the ballistae on the rooftops were all drawn and loaded with missiles the size of tentpoles, aimed to the north.

We started across the bridge to the Manor Yard. I wanted only to put Keirr in her bed and see to her wound.

Movement. Fren lowered his bow as he came toward us, his step quickening.

The sight of him made me pause, and Keirr stopped beside me.

For weeks I'd waited for some sort of insight from him. Or from Mabir, or Getig. Some answer to the questions that burned in my head, the prayers I sent against my fears. All I got were riddles. Or silence. Or monsters. Yet somehow, amidst all this chaos—or perhaps because of it—Keirr and I connected in a way more powerful than I could possibly have imagined. I put my arm around her neck and trembled at the memory, so emblazoned in my mind that I could see the mountain in the sinking afternoon light, smell the thin, crisp air, feel the shudder of her wings as the icy wind burned my ears. I still heard the echoes of her call. I would never stop hearing them.

Today, a dragon-rider team lay broken on the mountain. Even if the rider survived, the team was sundered. Would Bellua blame me? What would that rooster Addai think? Cairek? A year ago, without Edimmu or Horrors or Avar touching down in our forest, my world had been a simple place. Today the heights of its spirals and the depths of its darkest chasms were immeasurably far apart.

Our mountain, a hollow thing full of nightmares—there was a

riddle for you. Harodhi and crispies—and the Edimmu tunneling into my head like a snake in a wall.

"Miss Maia, are you hurt?"

He was out of focus. "Fren, you have to answer me. What are the Avar?" I heard the tremor in my own voice.

He gaped like a fish and blinked. "Miss Maia. You're injured."

"What is Asha?"

He ignored me, staring into my eyes—which only made me angry. "*What is Asha?* What are the Avar?"

"Miss Maia, we need to sit you down—"

"*Please* don't say 'Miss Maia' again." I saw concern in his eyes, but I didn't care. Fear and fury, and signs and monsters, and religious parrying all jumbled in my head, cut with images of eyes and blood and fire and falling.

I grabbed his shirt for support. "There are Horrors in our mountain and some damned shadow thing in my head, and I need to know why. *What is Asha?*"

He closed his eyes for a moment, then answered my question in the same infuriating manner as he'd answered every other: with a riddle. "Asha is neither 'Who' nor 'What.'"

I heard the thunder of wings behind me. I didn't have much time. I twisted his vest in anger. "I've been patient while you and Mabir and Bellua play 'keep-away' with the truth. I've prayed for understanding, but what is prayer? Breath on the wind."

He made sure I'd met his gaze before he answered. "Prayer is work. Prayer is action—"

"Damn it, Fren! No more riddles. *What is happening to me?*"

He looked above and behind me, where sound grew full of shouts and whistles and leather snapping. He took my shoulders to fix me with his eyes. "Anything I can name is merely a facet of Asha. But Asha is all facets, and now already I've said too much, because I've given you an image in your head of something that cannot be seen."

I groaned in frustration. "I want to hit you, Fren . . ."

"Prayer is also silence. Often, the things you seek come to you in a moment of silence."

I swung at him, and he grabbed my wrists, saying, "Shhh, now," the same way I might have soothed a troubled qit. Sharp smell of cut cedar.

I twisted free of his hands and shoved away from him. "The things I sought came to me through trial, and in moments of terror."

He hesitated before he reached for me, but when Keirr hissed he withdrew his hand. I grabbed her ear frill and turned her around. We faced the returning flights of dragons.

———

Even as I turned away from Fren, Darian arrived with Mabir clinging to one elbow.

"Father told me to get Mabir, but Aru couldn't carry us both," said Darian. "I've just gotten him off the hoist." He eyed Fren curiously as he asked me, "Are there any wounded?"

"Yes. Oh, gods, Mabir . . ."

"Are you hurt?" Darian asked me.

Stop asking me that. I shook my head *no*. Winced, nodded carefully. "I blacked out. Twice." No, three times. But I didn't say it.

"Sit her down," said Mabir.

"Keirr is injured. I need to—" My vision swam, like looking out through water. Darian eased me to the ground, and Mabir knelt in front of me. He peered deeply into one of my eyes, then the other, as dragons and riders surrounded us. "You've injured your head, probably slammed it against Keirr's neck when you were unconscious." He wiped my upper lip with his sleeve. It came away with a red stain. "You need to rest, immediately. Let Darian look after Keirr."

"I met the Edimmu again. Oh, Mabir." Now the tears flowed freely.

His face sagged even as his eyes grew wide. "*Sweet mercy,*" he whispered.

Cairek's voice called Mabir urgently from the maelstrom, and the old dhalla stood. "Sweet girl, I'll be back. Darian, don't let her fall asleep." Then he was gone.

Somewhere in the confusion I heard Bellua shout, "Give him room! Back away!"

Darian kneeled beside me, leaned in close and whispered, "What happened, Maia? What'd I miss?" He seemed almost desperate to know.

Before I could begin to form an answer, Father rushed up to join us with Rov close behind.

When Rov spotted me, he charged forward. "There is a dragon dead on the mountain, and his rider may not survive the night."

Father turned and stepped between us. Rov tried to push past. "We lost a man and a dragon today, a good team, while playing nursemaid to these pampered—"

"That was *my* team, Captain." Cairek joined us, pulling off his gloves. "An' I'm here to tell you, she saved at least one life today. She's not to blame."

Rov pushed Father away but stood fast, pointing first at Darian and then at me. "Don't think I'm impressed by your celebrity. I'm not. I'm growing weary of it. While you play at games of chase, my teams and Cairek's teams go hungry. Your dragons are afforded the luxury of food that no other here enjoys."

"Is that true?" I asked, horrified. "Then feed Keirr and me what everyone else gets. I didn't ask for special treatment."

"I'll feed my aeries as I see fit, Rov," said Father. "You don't know what *I've* done without."

"She risked her life an' that of her dragonkin to draw them off," said Cairek. "She killed one of them on her own, just with her knowledge of the terrain. Please, sir. Stand down."

Rov still glared at me, but his lips were no longer twisted with anger.

Darian's expression was guarded and dark.

Another rush of wings and scuffle of feet accompanied the arrival of Addai and his Juza, at last. Keepers of the Flame. Voices and shouting traced his path through the gathered crowd. When he pushed through, he squared his shoulders toward me. "Bellua was right," he said. "Something connects you and every intrusion of darkness into this world of light."

Cairek stepped in front of him, his freckled nose wrinkled. "She saved our lives today."

"But I wonder on the coincidence of her presence each time—"

"Don't bother. The coincidence was entirely that of a clear day, when the Horrors could most easily study the terrain they covet. Maia spotted them before we did. End of coincidence." Cairek leaned toward Addai. "Or perhaps you meant the other coincidence, in which *you weren't there*."

Addai's chin rose another fraction of an inch and his nostrils flared.

"She's a distraction," said Rov.

"If she hadn't warned us, we'd all be dead," said Cairek.

"Aye," said one of his men, behind him, and the crowd began to murmur again.

"There's a point you're all missing," I said, as loud as I could without shouting. I stood up, one hand braced on Keirr's neck. Grimaced against the pain in my head. When the crowd failed to go silent, Father whistled loudly then turned to me with a questioning cock of the head.

I spoke again, as loud as I could without invoking mind-numbing pain. "What you haven't considered is this: We already watch both entrances to the caves. Both entrances that we know of. So unless these Horrors flew all the way from Cuuloda, there must be another way out of the caverns."

Rov's mouth snapped shut, and Addai's tiny eyes narrowed, limned with tattoos of flames.

I squeezed the hair at the back of my head, hoping to numb the pain beneath my scalp. "And how many more like it? How do we seal them all?"

Cairek broke the silence first. "We need to do reconnaissance."

"We should seek every window into the mountain, at least. Agreed," said Rov. "Hopefully they are few."

"We ought to go in, root them out before their numbers build." Cairek met Rov's eyes, but the Captain shook his head *no*.

"We don't have the manpower for that. We don't know what their numbers *are*; we'd have to leave defenders here at all times. It would only divide our forces."

Cairek nodded with a grim set to his mouth.

Then Rov turned to Darian and me. "*You* will stay out of the mountains from here forward. I won't spare men any longer so you can chase each other's tails. Stay east of the cliffs, in the city and farms. No farther."

I thought of the Edimmu again, lurking on a shelf in the shadows, piercing me with daggers made of my own fears. I'd felt it break my bones and slice me in two. "I might know where that opening is." My head throbbed, and I felt another trickle on my upper lip. "I saw the Edimmu again."

Rov stared at me with confusion working behind his stern mask, until Cairek touched his shoulder to get his attention—Bellua and Mabir had entered the circle. The gathered soldiers fell silent.

Bellua shook his head. "The wounds were too grievous, and moving him made them worse. He is gone."

I felt the paving strike my knees, and knew I had fallen. Darian's arms under mine eased me to a sitting position. Keirr's tongue on my face. Mabir starting toward me, his face wrung with concern.

Rov looked up at the machinery on the aerie roofs, at the log palisades caging the perimeter of the paddock. "We have lost our first." He took a deep breath and blew it out slowly. "Six of us"—he looked at me—"counting Maia, weren't enough to take down three Horrors." A cold acknowledgment, and as close as Rov would ever get to apologizing. "How many are we now? Two dozen Dragonry, myself included. Nine Juza. I can't count you, Broodmaster, because Shuja is one of the broodsires, he can't be risked in battle. Thirty-three of us in the air. Even with Staelan's Barrage and all his foot soldiers, I fear we may have brought too little force, and too late."

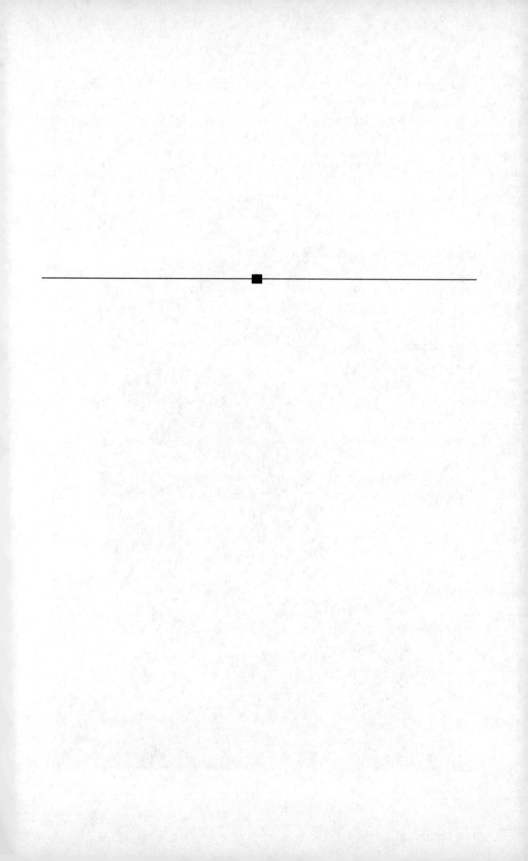

F O R T Y

I WOKE IN MY BED in the manor, crawling out of a long dream. Charnel things made of corpses and steel haunted me, a shadow spun lies to test me. Worse than lies—twisted truths.

Why wasn't I on my cot in the winter stable? Where was Keirr? I froze halfway to sitting up, my skull thudding as if a boulder rattled within it. I swung my legs over the side of the bed with a groan.

"There you are," said Father, from a chair in the corner. He put down a book.

Suddenly I remembered why I was here, and my pain sharpened. "Was there a memorial?"

"Yes. His wingmates wanted to inter him together with his mount on the side of Zurvaan, where they fell, but Rov wouldn't allow it. 'Too many man hours,' he said. So he was buried in a place of honor on the Temple grounds. They left his dragon on the mountain, though. A sad waste, that." Father's eyes were red and weary, the corners of his mouth crooked. "His name was Daarm, and his dragon was Timsah."

"Where's Keirr?"

In answer, her head poked through the open window. "*Hey, Maia. Up.*"

"She wouldn't let us close the window. Or the blinds, or the shutters." Father's grin made his eyes less harrowed.

"No wonder it's so cold in here," I said with a smile. I swung my feet to the floor carefully, then stood to cup Keirr's chin and let her nuzzle my face. "Hey, baby." Her tongue was too wet and too hot, but I didn't have the energy to push her away. "Oh Gods, I hurt."

"You're grounded, you know."

I turned too fast and winced. "You're not going to let Rov keep us off the mountain, are you?"

"As a matter of fact, I am. I bear responsibility for what happened, too. I should have been there. I should have taken you to those high crags myself, though I didn't know you were ready. I should have known you were ready. I should have considered that we don't have the caves secured yet, and we don't know what we face."

"I—"

"But that's not why you're grounded. Bellua grounded you because you injured your head in one of your blackouts, and he grounded Keirr because of the gash in her side. He treated that without need of graving, by the way, and closed the hole in her wing."

Keirr nudged my head affectionately. "I knew that monster snagged her. Poor baby. I suppose I owe Bellua thanks."

"The way I heard it, he owes *you* thanks. As soon as you're fit again, I'm going to do a better job of teaching you how to control your bloodflow. If it's any comfort, I'm grounded too, while Shuja recovers from his wounds."

"What wounds?"

"Burns on his paws and in his mouth, like what you described before, how the Horrors burn with cold. He tore the thing apart, but he paid a price."

I sat on the bed again, holding one hand up where Keirr could reach it with her tongue. "I remember you putting ice on my head, trying to keep me awake. How long did I sleep?"

"Two nights and the day between. You'll rest today, but tomorrow you go back to training."

"I thought I was grounded."

"You are, but I've had your bow and Darian's for a couple of weeks now. I should have given them to you sooner." He gestured toward the corner where a brand-new bow and quiver leaned against the wall. "Another in a long list of things I should have done. Darian's already returned to training—with Fren. I should also tell you that I've had every fletcher within a day's flight making arrows for me. There's a cache in the manor, the winter stable, and the ice vault. I'll show you once you're up and about."

I felt no elation at the gift. I was grateful, yes. Relieved more than that. But not elated. It was a beautiful compound bow with cams and pulleys that increased its range and power—a proper adult weapon like Father's or Tauman's. But I knew why he gave it to me with such grim practicality. Before yesterday, he'd allowed Darian and me time to grow with our mounts, but now he felt guilt over the delay and wondered if Darian's bow or mine could have saved a pair of lives.

———

We trained with a desperate sort of resolve. What remained of the forest behind the manor yard served as the backdrop for our hay bale targets. We shot from the bridge, in full sight of Bellua and Addai and all the gathered soldiers. Except for Fren's commands, our workouts were hushed. We didn't speak of Asha or religion, dragons, or lumber, or even the weather. The silence between Fren and me hurt, but I didn't want any more riddles or sparring over how little he had to say. I only wanted to learn *this*, and well.

"Don't aim," Fren would say. "Feel the arrow. Feel the target. Feel the truth of their connection. Allow the arrow to inform you of its intent."

It sounded crazy, but I considered my connection to Keirr, which wasn't something I thought my way into. It came from the center of me, or even from outside of me. Father sometimes called Shuja his "other self." I understood that now. It wasn't the same, but it was similar. An arrow wasn't a conscious thing, but it had intent, nonetheless, and habit and range and deadly purpose.

"That's good, Maia," Fren told me. "You have the right mind. You are relaxed but strong. You learn quickly." Darian kept up as best he could, but I was simply better at this. It bugged him, but I didn't care. It had nothing to do with him. I would never be caught without a weapon again.

One day, my eye seemed flawless. My first arrow hit the center of the target. Then the second. Then the third. Then the fourth and fifth in a tight cluster. I knew each arrow and saw its path as if it were a silver cord. The sixth and seventh and eighth. The ninth. From somewhere on the barricades behind me came a low whistle of appreciation. Fren observed and said, very quietly, where only I could hear it, "You're touching Asha now, Maia. Remember this mind."

———

While Keirr's wound healed and I recovered, I listened carefully whenever the dragons talked. It kept me from listening for the voice of the Edimmu.

I listened especially for the repeating patterns, like echoes added to a sound. There were a lot of those. But then there were the other noises, the whistles and chirps and barks. What did they mean? *One step at a time*, I told myself. *First find one word. A single word.*

At feeding time, I took Keirr into the storehouse, where we could be alone together. Before we ate, I sat her down and waited until I had her attention. I tried clicking or purring or rumbling to the best of my ability. Nothing seemed to prick her attention. Then one day I tried imitating Darian's whoop of joy the way she had, almost a season ago, "WHOOHOO, woohoo, woohoo, woohoo . . ."

She looked at me. Cocked her head sideways and lashed her tail in amusement. *"No,"* she said.

Then she repeated the sound as perfectly as before, multiple echoes perfectly rendered: "WHOOOHOOO hooHOOoo hooHOOoo hooHOOoo . . ."

I closed my eyes and trembled when I felt the cliffs to either side of me. "How do you do that?" I said. "You amazing creature." I tried the imitation again.

"No," she said. Then, "CLICK clCLickCK clCLick ck." She cocked her head the other way.

I shook my head. "I couldn't do that in a million years."

Keirr stared at me for several long moments. [Rumble] she said, her voice lowered. "C'n you sssay?" Then she reared up, wings spread wide, "CLICK. click. click. click."

She'd asked me to repeat a phrase. Before I could move beyond my astonishment, she dropped to her belly and tucked her wings close, forelegs stretched out in front where she could set her chin on her wrists. "TICtictictictic."

I was so bewildered I could only shake my head.

She sat up straight again, faced directly toward me with an eyebrow lifted. When did she acquire *that* mannerism? Did *I* do that?

I tried again. "CLICK. click. click. click." My weak tongue-clicks would never match the sharp noises she made deep in her throat.

"No, no." She shook her head. "CLICK. click. click. click."

"Isn't that what I said?"

She straightened her head. Her tail stopped lashing. She shuffled her front feet impatiently. "No."

Now I was frustrated. "I don't understand."

She repeated the whole pantomime—raised up again and spread her wings wide. "CLICK. click. click. click." Big CLICK, followed by diminishing clicks, like echoes. I got that. Then she hunkered down, wings drawn in, head on her paws, making herself small, and said, "TICtictictictic." Then she sat up and looked at me, head tilted to one side.

Oh, my. I understood. I rolled the storehouse door open, faced outdoors, spread my arms wide, and shouted "CLICK!" I heard my echoes: first those that rang sharply off the nearby buildings, then distant answers from the cliffs. Men on the rooftops turned to stare. "CLICK. click. click. click," I said to her. "Big space, right?" Then I closed the door again, pointed around the storehouse, and drew my arms in close. "TICtictictictic. Small space. Right? Big and small spaces!"

She tilted her head the other way. "B—bing."

"BIG," I said, arms spread wide. "And small," with my hands close together.

"B-Guh," she said, testing out this new word. "Smaw. Bi-g, smaw. Yes."

But the sounds she'd made, the ones that seemed so real, were like the *big* sounds and the *little* sounds overlapped. Layers of meaning, in a series of sounds. "You mix them, big clicks and little tics, to make—not a word, but a sound that other dragons perceive as a *picture*."

She cocked her head at me again. *Picture* was a whole new concept that might take endless explanation, but I knew this was it. It made sense. I looked at her in wonder. There were no words to be learned, only pictures to be sent and received. As if I could speak a painting. If there was a language within, it was probably beyond human comprehension.

She lashed her tail and nodded. Then, at less than a year in age, she demonstrated that she understood my language better than I would ever understand hers.

"Fish now, Maia," she demanded.

LIGHTNING CRACKLED in the sky outside when the first clutch was delivered. Rain hammered the roof of the winter stables. A year ago, our three dams together produced twenty-four eggs, our biggest number ever. Father had told me that a big clutch was a sign of troubled times ahead.

I was anxious to know the count. I didn't want it to grow.

Athys dropped eight mottled gray eggs in the fresh wood chips of her birthing nest, one more than last year. Father, Tauman, Jhem, Darian, and I took turns as they were delivered. Each was wiped dry and inspected for damage, then weighed and checked for signs that the qit inside was well. We wrote the parents' initials and the delivery-order number on it with a grease pencil. We entered the weight and number into a ledger. Then we wheeled the leathery jewel to the broodhouse where Rannu waited to provide warmth in a bed of fresh, dry straw. Athys joined him when she'd delivered the last egg. She was soon asleep, purring deeply like a gargantuan cat with Rannu watchful at her side, their new clutch between them.

We waited for the next mother to go into labor as the rain continued to pour down. At one point, Darian and Aru came in from stretching their legs. He sidled up to me. "Cairek wants to talk to you about something," he said quietly.

"What? What'd he say?"

"That he has something he wants to talk to you about."

"What?"

"How should I know? Talk to him. Find out. Something he wants to ask you."

"Oh, no." It sounded ominous. Two thoughts entered my head at the same time: *He wants me*, and *No, please*. I recalled his fantasy about a life in an aerie, and the warm feeling it had given me. The dragon he'd carved for me lived on my nightstand. I'd stared at it more than one sleepless night, wondering if it was wrong to consider a husband so soon. I barely knew him. I barely knew *myself*. I didn't want to hear this. My world was complicated enough. I shook my head to dislodge the thoughts. "When? Now?"

Darian shrugged. "Whenever."

He left me standing there, red and tingling with an infuriating blend of embarrassment, longing, and fear. It would have to wait. Coluver's labor pushed all other issues aside. The sun went down and the thunderstorm receded to a hard, steady drizzle before she finished. Ten perfect eggs would await her with Audax in the broodhouse, exceeding last year's count by two.

That left only Grus. She was larger than Athys or Coluver, and always delivered last. Father and Tauman took turns pacing the stable floor. Darian slept on his cot, but I was wide awake. I had seen it all before, of course, but Aru and Keirr would be ready to breed in another year, so I was especially interested. I sat, my arms on the back of a chair turned backward, and watched as Jhem weighed the last of Coluver's eggs.

Calm settled into me, crowding aside my disquiet, if only for the moment. Grus rumbled softly. Father hummed to himself. Tauman paused to embrace Jhem from behind, and she turned her head to receive a kiss on the cheek. He'd been more patient and loving lately.

This was where I wanted to be, right here, in the aeries, bringing little qits into the world. These broodlings would be Aru's brothers and sisters, and Keirr's by extension. A smile touched my lips for the first time in days. I wanted to hold to that fantasy as hard as I could and not think about other things.

Tired but smiling, Jhem turned a chair backward next to mine and rested her head on her arms to look at me. "You know, I think this might be my favorite time—when the eggs are newly laid, and the aeries are filled with this quiet expectation. I like all of it, but the quiet times suit me best."

Even though her ruddy hair was bedraggled and tangled, and

weary circles darkened her eyes, she glowed. Relaxed. One of those moments when she felt more like a sister to me than anything. That had been part of the fantasy, too, the idyllic picture of my life breeding dragons. Hold that fantasy, I thought. It was almost within grasp.

Her smile faded. "What's the matter?" she asked.

I didn't think it showed. Bellua. Addai. Horrors. Edimmu. Staelan's Barrage, leering soldiers everywhere. Being grounded. Where to start? I nodded at the eggs. "Look at them, Jhem. They don't know anything about the world they've entered. How many will have good lives? Most will die on a battlefield somewhere. Doesn't that make you sad?"

A strand of hair fell across her face. "Sometimes. Yes. But everyone serves the Empire in their way, don't they?"

"At least people get to choose."

"Do they?"

I looked at the cart where Coluver's last three eggs stayed warm beneath a blanket. "I suppose not. Not very often. But dragons? Never."

"We're lucky," she said. "Even with the Horrors, the Edimmu, the killing machines on the roofs of the aeries, we get to do *this*." She brushed hair back from my face. "You should take advantage of the time. Work on your dragon language some more." She smiled.

"It's real," I said. "You only have to listen for it. You'll start to hear it, too."

"I have been listening for it. I think you may be on to something." She jumped up and gave me a peck on the forehead. "I have to go. One more delivery. Keep working on it. You'll need to teach me one day." She winked, then wheeled the cart with Coluver's eggs out the door.

Bellua strode in and closed the door after her. My belly squirmed. I hadn't seen him since the day on the mountain. What was *he* doing here?

He turned to us. "If you can believe it, I have seen this part of the process only twice. I'd love to observe if I might."

Father eyed him briefly. "Stay out of the way." Then he continued pacing.

Tauman and I sat. Darian slept. Jhem returned after a stop at the manor for more blankets, hot water, and towels so warm they steamed. She eyed Bellua and made herself busy with her back to him.

Eventually, he approached me. "Maia," he said, with a brief bow. "I owe you thanks for your aid on the mountain. For my sweet Zell and myself, my deepest gratitude. She is my oldest and dearest friend. I don't know what I would have . . ." He struggled to find words.

I shrugged. "I did what I had to do."

"Oh, more than that. More than that." He let go a deep breath. "I'm not good at this sort of talk, I confess. I speak too passionately sometimes, and I know that my emotions get the better of me. But I'm not an evil man, Maia. The underlying point is this: I'm aware you could have let the monster have us. But you didn't."

I was tired. I ached. I should have been in bed. I didn't want to have this conversation. But I nodded.

Our eyes met, but he averted his gaze with a hint of embarrassment. "It might surprise you to know how much we have in common. My father was a quartermaster with the Dragonry during the subjugation of Tammuz. He was a hard man, like your father is. Long on responsibilities but short on compassion, with more expectations than time."

I didn't want to listen to this. He had my father wrong, for one thing.

His frown deepened. "Maia, like you I lost my mother when I was young."

I bit my lip to keep from speaking out.

"Tammuzi fighters stormed our village, butchered many of my neighbors before my eyes. My mother, sister, and I hid outside the warehouse as they ransacked our offices, but before they spotted us my mother took up an axe and went after them." He paused and looked at me. "I watched the Tammuzi slash her repeatedly as she struggled first to stand, then to remain upright on her knees." He swallowed. "I looked away before they took her head."

He stood motionless for a minute with his mouth turned down, staring at his fist wrapped around the back of a chair. I didn't want to know any more, didn't want one shred of sympathy to dilute my anger at him. "Why are you telling me this?"

He looked at me sideways, his brows tightly furrowed, his expression haunted. "I know you want me to leave. But we have to make the best of the situation. And so I want you to understand me."

I had no answer, so I looked away from him.

"What happened to your mother, Maia?"

I felt my face flush with suppressed anger and sorrow. I prayed he wouldn't see it in the color of my cheeks or hear it in my hesitant answer. "One of the harness straps on her saddle failed in a steep dive, and she fell to her death." Rage seethed up in me. This was not for him to know.

"I'm sorry. I didn't mean to open an old wound. I didn't mean to pry. I do understand. Truly." He bowed his head briefly. "Well, I can only thank you again," he said, and turned away. He didn't leave, but wandered about, touching nests, studying the pole-barn architecture and equipment on the walls, waiting for the clutch to deliver. Then he stopped beside Keirr and Buk Buk curled together asleep in a nest. With his nose tucked under his wing, Aru's bond mark showed. Bellua leaned toward it, frowning. Then he turned and looked at me.

Only then did I remember that I'd tied my hair back to keep it out of the way. Before I could stop myself, I'd reached back to undo my ponytail. His face lit with understanding.

Grus moaned softly, the sound trailing off into a rumble.

"She's beginning," said Father. "Tauman, hand me a towel. Darian!" He whistled through his teeth and Darian sat up abruptly.

"Time already?" He ran a hand through his hair.

Bellua wandered closer.

"Here comes one already," Father said to him. He laid his towel on the wood chips beneath Grus's arched tail. "She laid nine eggs last year. If she matches that we'll have a new aerie record." He said it grimly.

"Yes, I remember," said Bellua, but he watched me.

Grus's rumble ended, and an elongated stony tan orb with gold flecks eased onto the towel. "That's a good size," Father said as he wrapped it and passed it to Tauman, who carried it to the washbasin. Jhem took his place with another towel for Father.

The eggs appeared two or three minutes apart, just enough time for one person to wash and dry an egg. Each still needed to be weighed, registered, and recorded. Soon we had four eggs in the cart, wrapped in blankets to keep them warm on their short trip to the broodhouse where Shuja waited.

"I'll be right back," said Tauman. He checked the lantern on its hook atop the cart, then pushed the cart toward the door.

"Hurry," said Father. "They're coming faster now."

Lightning flickered outside, illuminating the Roaring across the bridge for an instant before darkness returned with a thunderclap.

Jhem took the next egg as Darian lined up. I grabbed a steaming towel from the pile. Darian lifted another egg in his arms as Jhem washed hers.

A fist pulled my hair into a tether from behind. "Hold still," said Bellua.

"Let go of me!" I reached backward, but he slapped my hand aside.

Darian shouted "Hey!" but the fist only pulled tighter.

"What do I see here?" Bellua asked. I reached backward again, but he only forced my head down and slapped my hand aside once more. His fingers brushed the bond mark on my neck. "There are two naming rings in this bond mark."

The low rumble of repeating thunder shook the doors. Bellua leaned close to me. *"What have you done?"* he whispered.

"Let go of her!" Father shouted, but he held another egg in his hands, with no one to pass it to.

Darian set his load in the straw next to him and reached for Bellua's wrist, but Bellua intercepted him with his other hand, twisting Darian's arm in an unexpected way that left him momentarily helpless. Then he released us both at the same time, pushing us away.

Jhem and Father desperately gathered another egg into a towel.

"You should have known the naming ring on Aru would emerge one day. But you expected me to be gone by now, didn't you."

"What are you talking about?" said Darian.

"Don't you know?" Bellua turned to him. "You share your dragon with your sister."

Darian's face crashed as he reached back and touched his bond mark. He looked at me with betrayal scratched in every hollow of his face. *"What?"*

"I only did it because you wanted their bond to fail."

Bellua's eyes grew wide and his brows shot up. "How can you think that?"

"It's true. You kept them apart when Darian was weak. I saved Aru's life. From *you*."

Father charged past me and grabbed two fistfuls of Bellua's coat, his hands still wet with birthing fluids, and shoved him backward until he slammed into a wall. He pinned him there and hissed, "If you ever touch my daughter like that again I will throw you off this cliff."

Bellua said nothing but waited for Father to say more or release him. Father did neither for a full minute, until Tauman returned with the empty cart and asked, "What's going on here?"

Father pushed away from Bellua, who straightened his lapels as he scanned the room. "How many of you knew?" he asked.

"Just me," I said. "No one else."

"You and Mabir, then." He looked at Jhem, then Tauman. "And who else?" He shook his head. "I warned you to stay away from Mabir and his tainted beliefs, Maia. But I see I was already too late." He looked long at Darian before he turned back to me. "You should keep your hair loose, Maia, while I decide what to do about this." He turned and marched out the door.

"What was that?" said Tauman.

No one answered. Everyone stared at me. Darian stepped up to within a foot of me, eyes narrowed. "What did you do?"

"We were afraid that Aru might die if your bond marks weren't finished, but Bellua wouldn't let us put you together. We did it so that if . . ." I swallowed my first choice of words.

"What? If what?"

"If you died from your wound, then Aru would be saved."

Anger battled with pain, gratitude, embarrassment, and confusion on his face. He looked at Aru and Keirr, both of them now alert. He turned to Father and Tauman and Jhem. Then he turned back to me and put his nose within inches of mine. "Why didn't you tell me?"

Because Mabir told me not to. Because I feared that your tongue would betray us all. Because the dhalla and I became complacent, feeling perhaps that our heresy would stay safely hidden if we remained silent. For a number of reasons, none of them good, or right.

When I failed to answer, he stalked to Aru and commanded him to his feet.

"Darian, I'm sorry. I didn't know how to tell you."

He shoved by me without a word, took the lantern from beside the door, and marched his dragon into the rain. Aru cast me a worried eye as he passed.

"No, stay here!" I shouted, and Aru stopped.

Darian stood in the rain looking back at his dragon, then glared at me with pain in his eyes. "Aru! Come! Now!"

When Aru turned at last, Darian popped him on the nose.

"Dare, please don't—"

"Leave us alone, please," he said, turning. The rain came down harder, and Aru covered Darian with a wing. I started out the door after them but Father called me back.

"I need you here," he said. "We're out of towels, and Grus is exhausted. We have a mess. Go fetch more—"

"Father, my mess is much more horrible." I waited for him to look up. When his eyes finally met mine, his expression softened, and he nodded. I headed out.

———

The thunderstorm blended everything in my eye. Sky, horizon, and aeries—a murky canvas dotted with pale lanterns and little else. I navigated by flickers of lightning across the bridge to the paddock. Men on the aerie roofs stirred at the splash of my feet on the wet paving. "Who goes now?"

"It's Maia! Where is my brother?"

"That way," said a ballista man from the darkness.

"Don't know," said another.

That was helpful.

I heard the creak of the saddle jib at the far end of the paddock and knew it was Darian. I ran to stop him. I needed to explain it to him, make him understand that I was only looking out for him. Before he did something really stupid.

But he wasn't there. Through the open tack house door, his saddle was just visible in lantern light, still in place on its rail. Puzzled, I stood and listened. Drumming rain. The occasional distant rumble. Wind shifted the jib and made it squeak again.

"Dare?"

I swiped wet hair out of my eyes and turned back toward the manor. He must be there, then. But something nagged at me.

He wasn't in his room, and Aru would have been obvious waiting outside anyway. Surely they didn't go into the forest. Perhaps the Dragonry camp, though I couldn't imagine why. I walked back to the head of the bridge, but turned toward the military camp despite my doubts. I didn't come here very often any more, so I went slowly, waiting for lightning to show me the way. All I could see were dark masses of tents and folded wings. I kicked myself for not bringing a light. Or my dragon.

"Who goes?" I hadn't even seen the man until he spoke.

"It's Maia, the broodmaster's daughter. I'm looking for my brother."

"I seen him crossin' yon bridge a short bit ago, with his dragon."

"*Gods,*" I said under my breath, but then, "Thank you."

I returned to the manor as fast as I could and grabbed a lantern from the hall. Outside again, I called for Keirr, and she met me as I rolled the stable doors aside. Father shouted something, and I answered, "Darian's leaving, and I have to stop him." Keirr and I raced across the bridge to the compound again. I cursed myself for not bringing her in the first place. Then, as I crossed the paddock, it struck me. Why were the tack house doors open? Why lantern light when it should be buttoned down tight? I ran, and Keirr trotted beside me. You could hide a young dragon in the tack house while you gathered your gear. It should have been obvious. I felt like a fool.

Darian buckled the harness across Aru's chest as I arrived. He'd strapped a knapsack across the saddle, along with his quiver and bow.

"Buk Buk!" said Keirr happily, and Aru nuzzled her.

"Dare, please listen to m—"

"I told you to leave us alone." Darian mounted into the seat as Aru shuffled anxiously. He started to unhook the saddle jib, but I reached up and grabbed his hand.

"Please, Dare. I'm sorry! Let me—"

He slapped my hand away as Aru took a step backward. He un-hooked the clasp, but I grabbed the step rung on the forward strap of his saddle. He commanded Aru back, but I clung tight.

"Darian, please listen—"

He stomped my fingers with his heel until I let go, then leaned toward me. "I have to go."

I grabbed the step rung again, now angry. "What are you talking about? Dare, what do you think you're—"

"Everything is about you now. Everything becomes yours somehow. My place in the family. My life. Getig. Even *my dragon*."

My mouth dropped open. "We were scared, Dare. We didn't know what else—"

He backed Aru up again, and my hand slipped off the rung. "I have to get away. *From you*, Maia."

The angry words left my mouth before I could stop them: "You. Selfish. Little. Shit."

He shook his head, then wheeled Aru about and galloped off the parapet into the night. I saw them briefly one more time, a silhouette against distant lightning as they lifted on a downstroke into the black sky. I saddled Keirr as fast as I could, though my hands felt slow and clumsy. Rain blinded me as we launched, but I knew which way he would go with his satchel full of gear, his coat and leggings, his bow and quiver. This wasn't simply a flight to burn off anger. I directed Keirr north, toward Mt. Zurvaan.

Lightning cracked in an arc over my head, turning the rain into bright spears. "Darian, come home," I whispered, the peal of thunder drowning my words. I'd been in such a hurry. I had no gear; no goggles, no coat, not even my bow. Soon I was soaked and shivering, but I urged Keirr higher. "Find Buk Buk."

She pressed harder, but we had little hope of catching him. I could tell the cold weakened her. Aru was a stronger flyer, but I didn't know what else to do. I could only try.

We found an updraft where wind met a sheer cliff face and rode it as high as we could, with Keirr adding wingbeats to take full advantage. A flash of lightning revealed the Crag ahead of us, and then swirling currents caught us, pushed us toward the mountain. "HAI!" I shouted, and Keirr rowed harder. It was too dark to see, but the rain and wind devoured Keirr's clicks. She roared, but I heard no echoes. Did she? I listened, thinking that Aru would have to roar as well in order to navigate, but I heard nothing. Only wind and rain, and the creak of leather.

Another bolt of lightning revealed the Crag again, but now behind us, and the peak of Zurvaan above in rain-blurred relief. We hadn't been so high since our first flight, riding the Morningtide. The gale pushed us upward, but we were far closer to the mountain than I'd imagined. Black night swallowed us again. I steered Keirr away from the peak as best I could. Swirls of wet air caught us, spun us. Keirr chirped in fear, and I clung to the harness desperately. *"Oh Gods, baby!"*

Lightning flashed again, but we saw only the nearest arm of the bolt, swallowed above and below in the fog of rain. Keirr gave out a sharp chirp, almost a honk, and I heard an echo answer only an instant later. She repeated it, and the answer came sooner still. I hunkered down and bent my legs tight against the laces, closed my eyes in fear. We hit the rock wall hard, but Keirr was ready for it. All four legs compressed to absorb the impact as her wings drew down a countering stroke. I grunted with the impact. Keirr scrabbled for a moment before her talons found purchase.

I had no idea where we were. The fog crackled with light around us but revealed no detail farther away than the span of Keirr's wings. I couldn't feel my ears or my fingertips. The wind buffeted us. Keirr pulled her wings tight, but I sensed her struggle to maintain even that tight frame. I touched my bond mark—my shared bond mark—and knew Aru wasn't far.

We clung there for what felt like an hour, until the downpour relented, and the clouds began to break apart. When dawn slit the eastern horizon like a crimson blade, Zurvaan emerged through rifts in the clouds above us, bloodied by the first light.

We saw Darian and Aru then, rising on the eastern side of the peak in the updraft Darian had told me about. Doing exactly what he said he would do. Impossibly small against that sheer pinnacle, they climbed. Their shadow indicated when they soared, when Aru ran up the face. They crawled the last few yards to the stony point, then Aru spread his wings, caught the fountain of air rising from the west, and soared higher still.

I huddled on Keirr's back with my hands in my armpits, shivering with the cold, with undeniable envy and with anger. "You did it, Dare," I said into the biting wind. "By Korruzon, you did it. Damn you, you selfish monster, you did it."

They wheeled to the north, winking bright against the dark clouds above, then glided down and beyond Zurvaan's northern limb.

Keirr shivered too, and I knew there was no way we could follow. I pressed my cheek to her neck.

"Home, Keirr. Go home."

"Buk Buk!" she said, looking back at me. "Boi!"

I sobbed and wrapped my arms around her neck.

"They're gone, baby. They're gone."

FORTY - TWO

WHEN I RETURNED to the compound, Father had Shuja under the jib, saddle in place, with large travel satchels hanging from the jib arm and more on the paving, ready to be stowed. Tauman and Jhem dropped additional bags and started my way. Rov and Cairek stood off to one side. Addai and Bellua were the last persons I wanted to see when I came home, but they were there too. Someone had raised the alarm.

When I dismounted, Jhem threw a blanket over my shoulders. She produced a cup of hot broth from somewhere and pressed it into my hands. I swallowed it eagerly.

Father put his face directly in front of mine. "Tell me what you know."

I gestured with the cup toward his gear. "What are you doing?"

"What does it look like I'm doing? Tell me what you know!"

I looked at all the expectant faces. Took a breath. I didn't want to say a word about Darian's reasons for leaving or his anger toward me. Not with Addai and Bellua standing here. So I kept to simple facts. "Darian and Aru climbed to the peak of Zurvaan and caught the updraft there. I saw him, but I wasn't able to follow. He went north as far as I could tell, but he could have gone any direction after that. I don't know."

"To the *top* of *Zurvaan*?"

I nodded.

"By the Avar, I knew that dragon was special."

"Most of his clothes are missing," said Jhem, "including his winter coat and leggings."

"His bow and gear are gone too," Tauman added.

A deep crease bent Father's brow. "Gold removed from the strongbox. Kaisi reports food missing from her larder. With that as a hint we discovered packages of meat missing from the ice vaults, too. All the fattiest cuts of meat, best suited for travel. He left a mess behind him, but he knew what to take. He'd planned this for a while."

"Why would the boy abandon his obligations here?" said Addai, hands behind his back, his chin up, his beady eyes sharp in the matrix of gravings.

My cheeks sagged, and I opened my mouth to answer, but Bellua caught my eye, looking at me with the barest shake of his head and a finger to his lips. *Don't speak, don't expose what you did.* Why would he cover for me? Why protect me now, after all the misery he'd caused? I didn't trust him, but I closed my mouth. Remembering his earlier admonishment, I pulled the tie out of my hair and let my ponytail fall out.

"He may return yet," said Tauman. "Aru is a growing dragon. He'll need feeding, and Darian didn't take enough food with him to get very far."

"Unless he knows exactly where he's going." Father's eyes were ringed with dark circles.

Tauman grimaced. "Where would that be?"

"That's what I'd like to know."

"I know who might have an idea," I said.

They both turned to me, and Father said, "Who?"

I took a deep breath, and looked at Cairek.

His face lost a shade of color as Father stepped in front of him. "Where is my son?"

"I have no idea, Broodmaster. How could I?"

"What did you say to him?"

I stepped up beside Father. "You talked to him all the time. Darian told me so."

Cairek flushed beneath his ruddy tan. "Aye, but I don't know where he went."

I pressed. "What did he talk to you about? You told me once that he always asked questions. What did he want to know?"

Cairek didn't answer immediately, but his expression betrayed him.

Father took his shirt and shook him once. "What do you know? Talk!"

Cairek raised his hands. "I'll tell you what I can, but stand down, please."

Father released him and stepped back, hands on his hips.

Cairek straightened his shirt before he spoke. "There's something you need to understand about your son, Broodmaster. Darian confided things to me, an' I wouldn't break his trust but for the circumstances. He admired you a great deal, an' spoke endlessly of your time in the Dragonry. He told me that you met his ma there. His secret wish was to join the Dragonry like you did. He wanted nothing more than to follow in your footsteps."

Father leaned toward him. "He will. He'll raise dragons."

Cairek frowned. "I didn't encourage him. I only tell you what he said."

"But his qit is bonded to Maia's," said Addai.

Cairek glanced at me and his face grew ruddier still. Then I knew the truth. I groaned. "Darian said you had a question to ask me."

He looked at me, struggling with the words he needed to say. "It wouldn't be proper now. Not under the circumstances."

"Tell me."

He hung his head. "It was a fantasy, nothing more."

"Did you encourage him?" I asked.

"No! No, I would never . . ."

Father turned to me. "What is going on? Explain."

I sighed. "Darian thought he could skip out on me and Keirr, since Cairek confided in him in that he wanted to ask for my hand in marriage. Am I right?"

All heads snapped in Cairek's direction. He said nothing, but looked at the ground.

So I continued. "Mabir would then write new bond marks, tying Keirr to Taben. The aeries would be whole, and Darian could go chase his dream."

Cairek looked up at me, cheeks red, then at Father. "I didn't encourage him."

Father growled, "What did you think would happen?"

Cairek said nothing.

"Or did you even care? Was Darian simply a means to get close to my daughter?"

Cairek's eyes went wide again, and he looked back and forth between us. "No. Of course not."

I felt sorry for him. Father's anger seemed like an overreaction, but he'd seen his world changing in ways he couldn't control. He was bound to erupt sooner or later. It wasn't really Cairek's fault at all. It was my fault, if anybody's.

I stepped in front of Father, facing Cairek. "What sort of questions did he ask? What did you tell him?"

"He asked about supply chains, the locations of Dragonry outposts, the routines of couriers an' recruitment companies, movement of troops. That sort of thing." He glanced at Rov. "I didn't give him classified information, of course. But I thought little of it. He always wanted to know everything about everything. Weaponry, tactics. *Everything.*"

Father took Cairek's shirt again. "Where did you send him? Where is my son?"

Cairek twisted free of Father's hands. "I didn't send him anywhere. I can only guess." Cairek looked at me. Then at Father again. "He asked once if there were courier posts between here and Taskis where the refugees might find aid. I told him there weren't likely any to the east, though I didn't know, but we all know there are posts between here and Cuuloda—" He stopped short when he saw Father's expression.

Father looked through Cairek as if he were a ghost. "So he went north. A courier station would give him food and see him on his way." He took Cairek again and shook him hard. "You sent my son to Cuuloda!"

When Cairek didn't reply, Father threw him on his butt. Cairek put his head in his hands. "I meant no harm," he said, but he couldn't meet our eyes.

Father stalked to Shuja, leapt up the step rungs to the saddle, and began securing one of the satchels to the saddleback as Shuja danced beneath him.

"Where are you going?" I asked, but I knew the answer.

Without looking up, he said, "I'm going to find Darian."

"I'm going with you."

He stopped working and fixed me with his haunted eyes. "No, you're not."

"Father—"

Rov stepped forward. "You can't leave, Broodmaster."

"I most certainly can." Father reached for the other satchel hanging above him.

"No, you can't," said Rov. His tone lacked its usual clipped, military tone.

Father paused. "Why not?"

Rov turned to Tauman and squinted. "Are you going to tell your Father what you told me?"

Tauman's color faded much as Cairek's had.

When Tauman didn't answer immediately, Father slid off of Shuja's back, straight to the ground. The big dragon shuffled his feet in surprise. Father walked up to Tauman much as he had Cairek, but he stood closer, eye to eye.

"What haven't you told me?"

Tauman met his gaze, swallowed, took a breath, and raised his chin. "When I was in Avigal and heard that Emperor Ahriman planned to impose charters on the aeries, I asked around. I had some time to kill, and several other aeries were represented at the capital. Without Cuuloda, resistance to the charters is weak. Three of the broodmasters had already applied. So . . ." His gaze flickered from Father to Rov and back.

"So *what*?"

"Since I had your ring, I did the only prudent thing: I applied for the charter and put your seal to it."

Father only stared at him for several pounding heartbeats.

"Captain Rov told me that he thought I'd done the right thing."

"Because he knows so much about aeries?" Father glared at Rov before turning to his son again. "You lied to me. You could have told me the moment you returned—"

"I was waiting for the right time."

"You couldn't come back and consult with me first?"

"The opportunity was there. I made a decision, and I think it was the right—"

"You understand that by applying for it, you opened the charter up to competition, don't you?"

Tauman swallowed. "Yes, but if the emperor gets his way, it will be open anyway. I was there, and who else would apply? We know this country from time before time. We underst—"

Father slapped him in the chest with both hands, pushing him back. "Foolish boy. What have you done?"

Rov cleared his throat. "That's why you can't leave. Others will make petition. Potential investors will take interest. Word of the charter's disposition could arrive by courier any given day. The broodmaster has to be here when it comes. That means *you*, with your ring—to seal the agreement and secure the charter."

Father turned to Rov, the thunderstorm brewing in his eyes.

"The world is changing, Magha. Finances are getting thinner. You're going to need investors to stay ahead of it. If you're gone, you could lose the aeries."

Father looked at each of us in turn. Bellua showed what looked like genuine surprise. Addai was unreadable. Jhem shocked, as if Tauman hadn't said a word to her about his actions. Which wouldn't surprise me. Sadness touched Father's expression when he looked at me. Then he turned back to Tauman and stared at him long. Finally he pulled the signet ring off his finger, grabbed Tauman's hand, and thrust the broodmaster's seal into it.

"Fine then. You're Broodmaster now."

Tauman looked with horror at what lay in his hand. "No, Father—"

"It's what you wanted, isn't it?" Father turned from him, shrugged into his coat, slung his bow and quiver over one shoulder and snatched the last satchel off the paving.

"No, Father, that's not—I didn't—I should go look for Darian, you should stay."

"You wouldn't begin to know where to look. You can't do it. You're in charge here now."

"Father—"

"Who else has a prayer of catching up to Darian and Aru? Listen to me: Darian is in skies he's never flown, but Broodmaster is what I've trained *you* to be. Jhem and Maia will support you. Time to take responsibility."

Tauman swallowed visibly.

"I'm coming," I said again.

"*No*. You are not. You're staying here, in this armed camp. You're safer here. The road is too dangerous."

"Father—"

"I said *no*." He mounted Shuja again, unclipped the satchel hanging from the jib, and secured it to the saddle rings. He buckled in, glaring at Tauman. "Pray to the High Ones I find Darian quickly and return before the qits hatch."

"I should come with you," said Cairek, red-faced but with his chin held high.

"I need you here," Rov said. "I can't let you go."

Cairek exhaled, his expression drawing inward. "Yes, sir."

Father snorted. "There's no way I would let you accompany me anyway."

"I'm sending a team with you," said Addai to Father. "Shuja is a brood sire. You shouldn't go alone."

"I don't want them. I'll move faster without."

"I'm sending them anyway. One dragon, one rider. You'll thank me later."

"I'll thank you *now* to keep them here, where they belong. Keep my family and my aeries safe, Addai. That's your job, and it's all I ask of you. Please."

"Regardless—"

"I won't wait for them."

He finished clipping the third satchel into place across the front of his saddle. Addai turned and sprinted to his dragon.

"Are you sure this is what you want to do, Magha?" said Rov.

Father stared at him as Shuja began to prance with anticipation. "I'm going to find my son," he said. Then he wheeled Shuja about, and with a shout they launched into the sky.

FORTY - THREE

THREE DAYS PASSED and Father didn't return.
Grus nested her eleven eggs alone. Athys and Rannu, Coluver and Audax took turns assisting so she could get off the brood platform and stretch her wings, but then she paced restlessly and moaned in quiet anguish. Clearly, she fretted over Father and Shuja. I spent as much time with her as I could, and even got Keirr to nestle her clutch of eggs for an hour each day. Keirr seemed to enjoy it, though I'm sure she sensed the disquiet, too.

"Shuja?" she asked, and made the "Poppa" honk she'd used for her own sire almost a year ago. Whether she referred to Shuja or Father, or both, I couldn't say. It warmed my heart, though it wasn't enough to silence my guilt.

This was supposed to be the easiest time of year, when the adults were least active and least in need of nourishment. Feeding them was a light chore. One person could manage it, and we had plenty of extra bodies; some of the soldiers took interest and helped in their free time. Even Bellua assisted, though I avoided him. There were no qits to wrangle. Labor was replaced with "quiet expectation," as Jhem put it.

I could only dwell on how horribly wrong everything had turned. The longer Father was away, the angrier I became, even though I understood that Darian was in danger, alone on the road. I couldn't help feeling abandoned. Again.

I'd been trying out some different language ideas with Keirr but to little avail. There weren't words to learn, only a means of *telling space* that dragons used to relate ideas that words took too long to describe.

Who needs words when you can communicate an entire landscape with all its width, depth, and height in a single sound? Frustration only compounded my guilt and worry.

Jhem found me the third afternoon in the storehouse with Keirr. She sat on the rail of the winch platform and patted the spot beside her. I plopped down. "How are you?" she asked.

I ignored the useless question. "What if Father went the wrong way? What if Darian took a different route than the obvious one, just to throw us off?"

"Why would he do that?"

"*I* did it, when I went after Keirr. Remember? I dropped the basket so it would look like I headed out after the acquisition train. I made a false trail. I keep wondering if Dare knew I would follow him. He could have gone in any direction from the top of Zurvaan. He practically said as much once."

Jhem laid her hand on my arm. "You have to stop blaming yourself, Maia. He's responsible for his own actions."

I leaned forward, my elbows on my knees. "I can't help thinking about it. What if he went east, just because no one would expect him to? Or west or even south? Why hasn't Father returned yet?"

She dropped her chin on the heel of her hand.

"So I've been thinking," I said.

"Uh, oh."

"Father went north, but we have permission to go east."

"Not very far east. And the Juza have already searched in every direction."

"Less than a day's worth."

"Addai and Rov won't allow it."

"I don't care. They're not bonded to Aru. Maybe—"

"How far can we go and really learn anything without causing a panic?"

"Not 'we.' Just me. If I leave early in the morning, take advantage of darkness, then—"

"Panic will begin at dawn. You can't do it, Maia."

"If I have an escort, and it's all logged, then the worst they can do is yell at me. I can ask Cairek. He owes me anyway, don't you think?"

"He can't, even if you make a case for it. He's a soldier. He has orders. You'd get him in trouble. And you already gave him a pretty rough time."

I frowned. It was true. I'd let him take the heat from Father when I bore at least as much blame as he did. I clamped my hands between my knees and scowled at my boots. I felt dirty. "I can't just sit here."

Jhem stared at me for a short minute, her brows pinched, her mouth disapproving. "You know that by telling me, you've already made me an accomplice."

––––––

Jhem and I launched straight off the cliff behind the winter stables. We glided without sound past the pinnacle and over Riat. The night air whistled across my cheeks and stung my wrists between coat-sleeves and gloves. The waning crescent moon served as our guide-post for the first four hours. Keirr and Audax clicked regularly, and twice we heard the roar of waterfalls in the darkness below. Other-wise we flew with silence.

The coming dawn gave shape to the horizon—soft and undulat-ing, nearly featureless. When the moon approached its zenith and the sun peeked over the distant prairie we were only five or six hours from Riat, but we'd long since passed the spot where we left Borgo-mos on his journey into exile. Our second flight ever, it had required an entire day's travel, but Keirr was a stronger flier now, more than half her adult size. Jhem left Tauman a note, detailing our agenda. He'd most likely fly after and meet us on our return.

We reasoned that if Darian went east, Taskis would be his desti-nation, the nearest major city. He would follow the Wilding river all day, until it joined the much larger river Gadia where it emptied into the sea. Then he'd fly northeast across the Daancar Peninsula until he found the Bay of Bascorel, and then simply follow the coastline to Taskis. Somewhere around the juncture of the two rivers he'd have met nightfall and made camp. We hoped to find sign of him around midday. Assuming he came this way at all, of course. We could only prove that he had if we found evidence. We couldn't prove that he hadn't.

We ate breakfast on a knoll, with the sun blinding us to the hazy plains eastward. The air smelled of dust. Behind us, Mt. Zurvaan's gray nub barely poked above a misty horizon. It felt very strange not to have mountains all around. The last of the homesteads were well behind us, too. We overlooked a broad, flat, treeless wilderness.

"Poor Borgomos," I said. Jhem looked at me in momentary surprise and then nodded sad agreement.

We took off again as soon as our mounts were fed. In late morning we spied a dugout farmhouse with a roof of logs and sod. Perhaps Darian stopped here. Perhaps they knew something of Borgomos and his people.

We sensed something wrong even before we landed. The fields contained no livestock. The patch of garden next to the house was dead, untilled and unplanted. No smoke came from the chimney to scent the brisk morning air. We landed in the yard and approached the house with arrows nocked in our bows. The door hung loose, so we peeked inside.

Dank silence greeted us. A single room, with a table and chairs, several stacked beds along one wall. A stone fireplace, an iron pot sitting sideways in cold ashes. Tools. A cupboard with stoneware dishes and cups. A chest containing clothing and blankets. In the corner, a shrine to Amrah, the Spirit of Plants, patron Avar of all farmers. But no sign of life.

"What do you suppose happened?" Jhem asked me, with a quaver in her voice.

I shook my head. What a simple existence compared to our lofty manor. I felt a twinge of guilt for every time I'd ever felt deprived. Such a hard life this would be. "I don't know. You don't suppose they joined Borgomos and his people and moved on, do you?"

She shook her head. "It doesn't look like it. There's no way to know, but if they did, they left all their belongings behind."

Without further comment we mounted up and took to the air again.

Shortly after noon we spotted an abandoned wagon with a broken wheel. A quick survey found it empty, though stains on the floor showed where trunks and barrels had sat recently.

After a hasty meal we flew on. We'd underestimated the time it would take to get to the confluence of the two rivers. Could the Juza teams that searched in this direction have come this far? Perhaps. But it seemed doubtful. We pressed harder, and a few miles on we spotted a field decorated with kites.

"What do you make of that?" I shouted to Jhem.

"I don't know. Let's have a look."

We landed and dismounted, noting wagon tracks carved into the tall grass. Just up a shallow rise twelve short poles stood above twelve mounds of fresh earth, each supporting a tattered kite.

"These are graves," said Jhem.

A lump rose in my throat. I thought of Borgomos's brave march out of Riat. He'd told the council, when he spoke of Edimmu and Utukku—Shadow and Blight—*We can face them again here or face them on the road. The difference hardly matters.* Wind rustled the grass and blew loose hairs into my eyes. I swallowed my tears.

Jhem put a hand on my shoulder. "They still had enough healthy men to bury their dead. They kept moving from here."

So did we.

The sun passed its zenith before the river Gadia emerged from the haze, glinting in the distance. Gulls' wings flickered in the strong light. The river's expanse defied belief. We could scarcely see the far bank, even from the air. Only the highlands of the Daancar Peninsula marked the horizon to the south and east.

A road emerged out of the prairie, and then farmhouses to either side. We circled but again saw no sign of habitation. The only livestock ranged through fields that should have been readied for crops. We landed only long enough to find the same strange abandonment, and no sign of Darian and Aru. Then we continued on.

A small fishing village occupied an enclosed bay in the river. Buildings and simple docks lined the banks. Hope leapt within me. If Darian had come this way he would surely have stopped, and the locals might even know something about Borgomos. The lanes were quiet, though, with no activity of any kind other than the crows and gulls that squabbled along the shores and filled the sky.

We landed in the center of the biggest cluster of buildings, dismounted, and nocked arrows to our bows. It hadn't been a big community. Not so large as Riat, certainly. Maybe a hundred people, a hundred-twenty. A mere dozen mud-brick buildings clustered along the biggest quay, where a fisherman's boat lay sideways in the mud of low tide. Jhem's wide eyes met mine. She shook her head in negation. Of what I didn't know. Disbelief. Anger. Alarm.

The first building we checked contained nets and hooks, charts and buckets and clubs and unidentifiable tools. We moved on. The second building, an accounting office, perhaps, was unoccupied too. And the third, another fisherman's hovel. When we pushed open the door to the largest building the smell nearly drove me to my knees. A murder of crows fled through open windows at our intrusion. Gulls hopped away from us in wary circles, less willing to give up their bounty. In the center of what might have been a gathering place of some sort, like a tavern or hostel, a pile of corpses rotted beneath a seething cloud of flies.

I shouted and drove the birds away, eyes tearing up at the stench. I held my hand over my nose and mouth, though it didn't help. "Gods, Jhem! What happened here?"

She ran out the door, fell to her knees outside, and emptied her stomach into the courtyard dust.

Only now did I recognize this as the local Temple of the Rasaal. Not in the least bit ostentatious, with ordinary windows rather than stained glass, a plank floor, and a simple altar made of wood carved into the semblance of a dragon. Dried blood spattered it. Blood was everywhere.

Birds and maggots had scavenged the corpses on the outside of the pile so thoroughly that injuries were difficult to make out. I wasn't about to move bodies to see what lay beneath. But here I saw blood crusted around slashes in clothing, with shattered bone beneath, and there a skull seemingly hewn in two. Finally I fled the stench.

Jhem kneeled and trembled in the sun with her face in her hands. I squatted down and patted her gently on the shoulder. When she lowered her hands I gave her my canteen so she could rinse her mouth. Afterward she nodded silent thanks and stood. Then she and our dragons followed as I walked down the center of the street toward the north end of town.

More of the same everywhere: silence and death, though it seemed that most of the townspeople had gathered in the Temple to meet their end. The smell of dust combined with the stink of carrion and brine. "They've been dead for weeks," I said.

"Horrors?" Jhem's voice was constrained and shaken.

I considered it, remembering the Horror dragon and its unholy rider in the cave. Ravenous. They tore wildly into the corpses they ate. These bodies were largely whole. We'd seen livestock from the air. Only the people were killed. I shook my head. "No, I don't think so."

"Was it disease, perhaps?"

"No." I shook my head. "No, they were murdered. Rounded into their Temple and slaughtered."

At the north end of town we found wagons—many of them, and my heart beat faster. Low fences made of rocks and driftwood surrounded several, as if they were the first pinnings of a new homestead. An entire new neighborhood made of wagons.

"Oh, Maia . . ." Jhem choked on her next words, and I looked where she pointed: Over one of the wagon doors hung a kite.

My arms and legs trembled with immediate fear and anger. I ran to the wagon, burst open the door, looked inside. On the floor lay a body, badly desiccated and swarming with flies. I couldn't even tell its gender. Despite the smell, I looked closer. A brown stain on the shirt or dress and the floor beneath indicated a possible wound. With an arrow tip I pushed the fabric aside, and studied the wound in the shriveled remains. A small puncture, like an armor-piercing arrowhead might make. The arrow had been withdrawn.

I left, stalked to the next wagon in the row, and kicked the door open. A woman and child lay in each other's arms in a puddle of dried blood, but with no obvious way to tell what had killed them.

"Maia, don't," I heard Jhem say, and realized it was me who made the unnatural sound in my own ears, a low growl of anger and despair.

The next wagon was empty, but the one after, forming a roof over a new dugout started beneath, contained an entire family of four. This time the injuries were clear. A deep gash had split the man's clavicle and opened his torso. The woman's arms and hands were mutilated as if she'd held them up in defense. The children were all but cut in two.

I shouted my anger and moved on. Keirr keened unhappily behind me as I ran. Ten more wagons. Eight murdered families, and other corpses tucked into long grass or behind fences. I shouted in rage. Felt Jhem's hands on my arm. Shrugged her off and kept moving.

Here was another kite trampled into dried mud. Here a child picked clean by scavengers. A shirt. A broken spear. A cane. A skull. A whole field full of skeletons, arrayed as if they'd been slain as they ran.

The last wagon was larger than the others, but unlike the rest had no fence around it. A large kite, slashed and broken, hung over the porch. I pushed the door open. An oddity, this wagon was appointed like a business office with a desk and chair, a broken lamp, a thick ledger book. And in the corner, a skeleton barely clothed in shriveled flesh. The robes that hung from it in tatters might have been lustrous once, trimmed in gold brocade. In the strange, detached part of my mind behind the angry screams I wondered that Borgomos's skeleton didn't have more stature, that this spare frame of bone could have carried such a large man.

I pounded the walls in fury, until Jhem came up behind me and wrapped her arms around mine. I screamed until my voice trailed off into a hoarse rattle.

"Oh, Maia, Maia—"

I pushed out of her arms and went to Borgomos's body, curled on its face. His right hand clutched the Staff of Office, with its grooves and holes where precious stones and metals had once marked his importance, now leering like the orbits in a skull.

"They killed them, Jhem. They killed all of them."

"Who?" she said, with tears in her eyes.

I didn't know. Their murderers left no evidence of any sort behind. Intentionally so; they'd removed at least one arrow. Bandits? Harodhi? *Here?* I reached out to touch his shoulder lightly, my mind a swirl of confusion. "They got only this far, but they found a place to *stay*, to settle in. These people, these ordinary fishermen, found room for them." My voice cracked. A whisper was all I could manage. "They were going to be all right."

Something peeked from beneath him, where his body would have concealed it when it was still ample and newly dead. I rolled him aside. His left hand clutched an arrow buried deep in his ribs. I pried his dry fingers loose and with some effort pulled it out into light.

"What is that?" Jhem asked, but her face told me she already knew the answer.

Long and slender with the armor-piercing head, the shaft and fletching were red as blood. I had seen those shafts nestled in their quivers for the last five months.

"Juza," I said.

"GODS, JHEM. Addai sent a Juza team with Father."
Her eyes grew wide. "You don't think they would . . ."
I shook my head, but my stomach sank. "I don't know. The Juza team wouldn't know we've found them out. Maybe Father will be safe." As the words left my mouth, I already didn't believe them.

"What is going on? Why would they . . . ? Why all of them?"

"Borgomos showed his allegiance to the old ways too willingly. Bellua . . . the Rasaal hated this situation from the very beginning, from the moment Getig appeared. They're trying to bury my story." Our eyes met and held.

She swiped a tear off her cheek. "Tauman will come looking for us. We don't want to miss him."

"Will he come alone?"

She wrapped her arms around herself. "I didn't think of that."

"He doesn't know what we found. What if Addai insists on sending Juza with him, like he did Father?" My jaw tightened at the thought. My anger spread to encompass Father, too. He'd left us at a critical hour, certain that his task would be simple. Perhaps it would have been, if he'd left alone as he intended. Instead Addai had sent one of his assassins with him.

"What do we do?" Her voice sounded small.

"We go back. Now. We tell Mabir what we found."

"What about Tauman?"

"I don't want to stay here a minute longer than we have to. It's not safe. We'll call for him as we go. Rannu will know Audax's voice. We'll find him."

"We have to tell Rov." I opened my mouth to object, but Jhem said, "No one else has authority to do anything about it."

I nodded.

She looked around unhappily. "We can't leave all these people like this."

I considered the bodies in the field, in the wagons, in the streets. "We don't have time to do anything for them."

She shook her head sadly. "Borgomos at least, then."

I nodded and swallowed the lump in my throat. Stuck the red arrow in my quiver and lashed Borgomos's staff to my saddle. Then Jhem and I piled fence posts and other loose wood under the Guildmaster's wagon. We made kindling from paper and dried grass, and doused it with oil from his broken lamp. It ignited quickly under a spark from my flint. We stood back and watched only long enough to be sure it caught.

"There's one more thing I need to do before we go," I said, turning away. Jhem watched me until she understood my intent. I located one of Cuuloda's dragon-shaped kites in good condition. It took no time at all for the breeze wafting off the sea to coax it into the sky. I tied the line to a wagon wheel and let it rise up above the murdered village, to mark the passing of Cuuloda's lost unwanted and of the people who took them in.

We followed the sun westward. Every half hour or so Audax roared in case Tauman might be within range. Twilight gave way to stars and the moon peered over the eastern horizon before we heard Rannu's answering voice. He and Audax sounded back and forth until three silhouettes appeared against the moon behind us. They had passed us by in the dark, but followed Audax's vocal beacon to find us. Jhem slowed down so they could catch up, but I kept moving. I didn't want to talk, and I wasn't sure I wanted to know who accompanied my brother.

Dawn revealed familiar terrain and gave us thermals to climb. The lower falls of the Wilding brought trees and fresh air. In the distance, Zurvaan rose above familiar peaks. The outlying farms appeared, followed by the cliffs and pinnacles of home.

I looked back over my shoulder. Jhem and Tauman followed a

couple hundred yards back. I recognized the second team now as Cairek and Taben, flanking them on the north. At first I wanted to curse, but then I felt guilt for my anger and even a bit of relief. Thank the gods for Cairek.

The third team flanking them on the south were Juza. The hairs on my bond mark rose with a shiver, and I appreciated Cairek's presence all the more. *Asha, what am I supposed to do?*

I circled the aeries once. Riders patrolled above me, and more ran to their mounts below. More Juza. I directed Keirr down below the pinnacle, past the fall of the Roaring through the mist to the Temple. We lit in the front court, away from the stable yard where the Juza kept their dragons. Keirr stood panting as I untied the staff and swung to the ground. Juza teams approached in the sky behind me. "Come on, baby. Quickly." We hurried to the Temple doors and entered together.

Morning light streaming through the stained glass lent the sanctuary a bizarre, fractured appearance. Keirr clicked and looked all about.

"Mabir!" The echoes of my voice were short and sharp. "Mabir! I have to speak with you!"

"I'm here," he said, hobbling from the chambers beyond the sanctuary. His acolyte, Tulo, came behind him and started to reach for Keirr's harness, as if to lead her out for care.

"No," I said, and his brows lifted with puzzlement. "She stays."

"What is this?" said Mabir, stopping to brace himself on a chair.

I held up Borgomos's staff, and Mabir's face sank.

"We need to talk to Rov," I said.

Mabir started toward me again, but before he took three steps, shadows filled the doorway. Jhem entered, then Tauman and Cairek. And then Addai, with four of his Juza.

Addai clasped his hands behind his back and sauntered toward me. He eyed the staff I held. "Once again you have created quite the commotion, young woman. Valuable time lost from my Juza, since they were out looking for you instead of patrolling this mountain. What have you got to say for yourself?"

I squeezed the staff so tight that I felt my pulse in my fingers. I locked his gaze. How could he pretend he didn't know what I held in my hand? "Let's wait for Rov to get here," I said.

"Indeed," said Addai, pacing a circle around me. "I'd like to know what punishment he has in mind for you. Your adventures are becoming increasingly dangerous. Not only to you, but to the aeries and everyone stationed here. You're a menace."

My ears burned and my heart pounded. "I could hardly be more dangerous than you."

He reversed his gait to circle me in the other direction. "Whatever do you mean by that?"

Bellua entered the chamber from outside, followed immediately by Rov and three more Juza.

Gods! How I wish Father was here.

Rov marched straight through the circle of onlookers and planted his feet before me, arms akimbo. "You're grounded, and your dragon will be shackled in the Temple stables until I've decided what to do with you."

In answer, I held Borgomos's staff before me, inches from his face. He considered it with mute indifference.

"Do you recognize this?" My voice rose with anger.

He looked it up and down. "It is Borgomos's Staff of Office."

I waited for some flicker of emotion to cross his face. Nothing. "Wouldn't you like to know where I found it?"

He stared at me, waiting for the answer. *Damn* his reticence. "In his right hand," I said, my voice croaking with emotion. "Where he lay dead."

Tauman looked at Jhem with worry in his eyes. She stood with her fingers over her mouth, eyes closed, forehead wrinkled in worry. Bellua stared at the staff as if it were a flayed corpse.

When Rov said nothing more, I threw the staff at Addai's feet. "Where were you for two days when Horrors attacked us on the mountain?"

"Take care, child," he said.

"No one saw you since early the day before. You didn't return until the action was over, and a Dragonry team lay dead on the mountain." I made a point of meeting Rov's eyes.

"You know perfectly well where I was," Addai said calmly. "I was on patrol."

"Where?"

His nostrils flared. "Let's *do* ask some questions, shall we?" he said. "Why did you wait until I was gone to venture onto the mountain so brazenly?"

I shook my head. "What do you suppose I found in Borgomos's rib cage?" Before anyone could answer, I pulled the red arrow from my quiver and held it up. Addai's eyes narrowed. My cheeks burned as I turned my glare to Mabir. To Tauman and Jhem. To Bellua and finally to Rov. "We found the refugees and all their wagons in a fishing village on the shores of the river Gadia. Killed, every last man, woman, and child of them, plus every villager."

I stepped past Rov, toward Addai. "Why would the Juza do that?"

Bellua looked at the arrow with alarm clouding his features. "Is this true, Prelate?"

"It's but an attempt by this headstrong young heretic to sway opinion against the Rasaal. That's all," said Addai, with absolute calm. "The cancer of heresy gnawing at the foundation of the Temple."

I trembled with fury. "Why did you do it, Addai?"

As he spoke, his chin lifted, his eyelids lowered. "It's finally time we did something about the conspiracy in this town, these aeries, and this corrupt Temple."

Mabir advanced with shock and tears in his eyes. "What in Gadia are you talking about?"

"There is a nest of Ashaani in this village, and they infiltrate every level of society, from the lowest muck scraper at the bottom of the pinnacle to the daughter of the broodmaster—or former broodmaster."

Mabir's mouth quivered before he found words. "You have no grounds for such an accusation—"

"Don't we? We have your own pronouncements based in heretical scripture concerning events in the cavern. We have this feeble effort to frame me and my warriors for something unwholesome."

There wasn't a flicker of remorse on his face. But I was in deep now; I could only press my case. "Asha scares you. And because Borgomos was open about his respect for the old ways you *silenced* him and everyone who might have been *tainted* by—"

"*Out of her own mouth*, the damning name: *Asha*." His lips twitched. "Because you can steal an arrow doesn't mean that your charges have any merit, no matter what else you found." He glanced at the staff on the floor. "However tragic it might be."

"I didn't steal this arrow."

"Of course you did. Or found it. It doesn't matter. And when you came across Borgomos's relic on the prairie you concocted this story—"

When Jhem stepped forward Tauman tried to pull her back, but she brushed his hand off her arm. "It happened exactly as she said it did. I was there. I saw it, too."

Addai leveled his gaze at her. Turned it toward me. "Did you think we wouldn't investigate thoroughly any claimed sightings of a High Dragon? That we wouldn't make certain of the people spreading the tales? Asha's is an insurgency of deceit. But then, the entire cult of Asha is a lie."

He turned to Bellua. "And it permeates this town. Is that not correct, Merihem?"

Bellua stood silent, staring at me, his brows pinching tighter and tighter.

Addai pressed, "Was it not your spies, cultivated over the last year, that unearthed this hidden church? Well? Was it not your report that drew me here?"

Bellua nodded slowly, his eyes never once leaving mine. I couldn't tell what he meant to convey, but it wouldn't have mattered. Fury throbbed in my temples. *Your spies?* All this time he laid low in our manor, making conciliatory statements to me, while buying information in Riat with Temple gold. I only wanted to kill him, to stab him in the heart with this Juza arrow.

Addai pointed at Jhem and me. "Both of you will be held here, your dragons shackled in the Temple stable. We'll begin a trial for heresy and crimes against the Rasaal at first light."

"*What?*" Tauman started forward, but two of the Juza stepped into his path, their hands on the hilts of their swords.

Keirr growled nervously behind me. I felt her breath against my cheek.

"And you, Dhalla." Addai sneered at Mabir with disgust. "You who should have exposed this cancer or converted its adherents—you accommodated them instead. You will stand trial as well."

Disbelief pulled at Tauman's face. "Rov, you can't let this happen."

Rov crossed his arms and turned a scowl toward Addai before he answered. "I swore my oath to the Dragonry. The Dragonry serves Korruzon. Addai is the ranking Juza official here—the highest authority in this *military* installation. You should have kept these volatile children in check, Broodmaster."

Jhem's face drained of all color. "I don't believe what I'm hearing. He murdered the refugees from Cuuloda! How can you not—"

"Matters of heresy are his battlefield, not mine," Rov said.

No one spoke for several seconds. Astonishment marked every face. Cairek looked at me with concern creasing his brow.

"Send a team to the village and see for yourself," I said. "Then you'll know that he's lying."

Rov only stared back at me, the gravings on his face like a cage written to contain his emotions. The icy demeanor was all wrong. It tickled at the back of my neck and down my spine. Realization struck me. "You knew about it," I said.

He didn't even blink. "My task here is clear: protect the aeries. The continued defiance of the *children* here makes it all but impossible. I've been tempted to lock the bunch of you up myself."

I was stunned to silence. Was this the same man who defended Keirr and me against Bellua's threats so many long months ago?

Addai stalked an arc around the four of us—Jhem, Tauman, Mabir, and me—breathing heavily, staring at me. "Which brings up the final issue I was sent here to adjudicate." He stopped in front of Tauman. "The disposition of these aeries."

Tauman startled. "What are you saying?"

"The Ministry of Dragons tasked me with making the decisive opinion on your Petition for Charter."

"What?"

"You heard me. One of my duties here is to determine your worthiness for the charter created for these aeries."

"The aeries are ours."

"Don't be a fool. You own nothing, except at the indulgence of the emperor. Certainly you understood that others might apply for your charter."

Tauman's face whitened. "What? Who?"

Addai glanced at Rov, but the Captain showed no emotion.

Incredulity drained Tauman's face, and he stepped toward Rov, shaking visibly. "Rov? You can't be serious."

The Dragonry Captain faced him.

"*When?*" said Tauman. "When did you apply?"

"Two couriers ago, after the incident on the mountain. I showed the petition to Addai before I sent it. I only look out for the Empire's interests, Tauman." He turned to Addai and Bellua in turn. Then to me. Then back to Tauman. "I do what I must to protect this facility."

Finally, I understood: Rov had a stake in the decision, some degree of ownership in our aeries. *Our aeries.* All the Dragonry teams that arrived late with the engineers were friends of his. Rov wanted our aeries. Addai knew that, used it as leverage, and Rov supported him with silence. I thought of the road Captain Rov was building across Cinvat to the cliffs. What else was in his plans? Expansion? A broodmaster of his own choosing?

Tauman stood trembling with anger. Addai brushed something off his armor, then folded his hands behind his back once more. "It's my duty to make certain the aeries are in the best possible hands, Broodmaster. There is too much at stake here, and at this moment you're on very shaky footing. Very shaky footing indeed. I expect your full cooperation."

I advanced toward Addai with rage burning in my cheeks, my fists. "You're unfit to judge us," I snarled. "Murderer! And you buy the silence of a thief with bribery—" Two more of Addai's Juza intercepted me, each grabbing an arm. I struggled but couldn't break their hold. Cairek started toward them, but Rov grabbed his arm. Addai stepped between us.

Keirr growled and moved tentatively in our direction. I shouted, "*No!* Keirr, No!" The remaining three Juza nocked arrows and drew bead on her. "Oh, gods, baby, No . . . Whoa! Please!" Keirr hesitated, circling slowly, growling low in her throat. The archers fanned out to track her.

I let the red arrow fall to the floor, struggling against the fingers digging into my arms. "Please don't shoot her," I cried. "Damn it, let me go."

"Prelate," said Rov with a reprimanding tone, "That's a valuable animal. I want her in this stable."

Addai nodded, and the soldiers released me. I ran to Keirr, took her by the ear frills and purred for her, saying "Shhh, baby. Please." She stopped, backed up a step, looked at me with confusion. A low rumble still filled her throat. The soldiers kept their arrows targeted. I hung on her neck to keep her head low and myself in the line of fire.

Addai picked the arrow up off the floor. "We will begin by rounding up the rest of the cult leaders, starting with Kaisi the cook and the woodsman Fren."

Kaisi? *And* Fren? My chest ached and my temples pounded. My throat tightened. "They're innocent. They haven't hurt anyone. Leave them alone."

"They're no more innocent than you are." He handed the arrow to one of his lieutenants, who poked it into his quiver, now one arrow among many.

Bellua tore his eyes away from me at last and turned to Addai. "This is not a proper quorum. You and I alone can't decide their innocence or guilt. There is protocol—"

"This isn't a court," snapped Addai. "It's a battlefield. I won't brook heresy when the interests of Korruzon are threatened. These aeries are all but falling apart from lack of discipline, from a culture of disobedience and arrogant self-interest."

He approached me, stood with his black eyes mere inches from mine even though Keirr rumbled a warning. "And here I stand accused by *this* one, who brings disaster with her every move, and summons demons out of the mountain. No monsters appeared except when you were there."

"You're insane," I said.

"What pact did you make in the dark in exchange for your animal? What did you offer to your unholy Asha? What depths will you sink to in your quest to undermine the aeries and the Rasaal? I see nothing but calamity in your wake."

He leaned closer and whispered, "Witch, in service to darkness." Then he turned from me with his hands clasped behind him. "I must do what you failed to do, Bellua: stamp out this dangerous cult before it gets any greater foothold than it has. Before it destroys this important asset of Korruzon and Gurvaan. I will finally have order in this compound."

TAUMAN WAS FORCED at arrow-point to return to the aeries. With Juza bows trained on us, Jhem and I led our mounts to the Temple stables to be unsaddled and shackled. To keep them from rearing, a chain connected the manacles on their forelimbs through an eyebolt set in the stone floor. There were eyebolts like these in any aerie stable, but we never used ours. We never had need.

Neither Audax nor Keirr understood what the shackles meant until the lock went through the hasp. First they tested them, then they pulled and stamped. Audax growled and bit at the chain. Keirr tugged until I feared she would cut her wrists. "No, Maia!" she said. "Off!"

"Shh, baby! Shh." I took her ear frills and pulled her head down, wrapped my arms around her snout, and covered her eyes with my hands. "Calm, sweetheart. Be patient. I'll get us out of this somehow." Next to us Audax roared and made the chain ring with the force he exerted.

"Calm that animal," said Addai, silhouetted in the doorway. Jhem shot him a withering glance.

"This isn't necessary," she growled. "They're no threat."

"Calm him down, or I'll *put* him down."

Jhem's face turned pale. "You wouldn't dare."

"Oh, I will if he becomes dangerous."

"What threat could they be with us locked in the Temple?" I snapped. "Are you insane?"

Addai pointed at Audax, still shaking his manacles and growling. "Gentlemen, prepare." His Juza archers nocked blood-red arrows to their bows.

I couldn't tell if he was serious or bluffing. The square runes covering his face made his beady eyes impossible to read. He couldn't possibly mean it. It would truly be insane. But he had murdered an entire village of innocents to further his dogma, whatever it was.

Jhem's eyes on mine were terrified. In desperation I started the calming tune that we used during the writing of the bond marks. Jhem joined in, and Addai raised his hand to stay his men. Soon Audax ceased his struggles. His growls subsided to a low harmonic rumble—still annoyed, but in control of himself. Jhem embraced Audax's head, trembling. Tears streamed down her cheeks.

With some further coaxing we got both our dragons to lay down, and finally gave them the water and food they needed after our long flight home.

As we left the stable I passed close to Addai. "Is that how you would protect the aeries? By killing the broodsires?"

"I do nothing lightly, witch. But sires can be found for dams—"

"You know nothing about raising dragons—"

"And any pair of dragons can raise a brood," he clipped.

That shocked me to silence. It was true. He could steal the entire brood and replace our dragons with breeding pairs of his choosing, with an aerie and supporting community ready-made. In so doing, he would spare his own animals from combat, so why not? Once hatched, the qits would identify with whichever dragons cared for them. It didn't have to be their true parents. He could even keep some qits to preserve the bloodline. They might lose an entire season of breeding, but they'd gain everything that we and our ancestors before us had worked for, refined, and made sustainable. Stripped from us by fiat, and given to *investors*. Sense be damned when there was profit to be made, or power to be gained.

"You're a monster," I hissed before I could stop myself.

His only answer was a gesture to the Juza warriors whose bows targeted us still. They directed us back to the Temple and into the chambers beyond the Sanctuary. We watched with Mabir and Tulo as two Juza warriors and their dragons took guard positions in the outer chamber. Then they closed and barred the doors—something I'd never witnessed in my entire life.

"**S**top pacing," said Jhem. "Sit down. Try to rest."

"Rest? How can you even suggest—"

"We need to be sharp tomorrow if we're going to defend ourselves."

"There's not going to be a trial! What do you think is happening here? The verdict is already decided."

Jhem turned to Mabir, who put a comforting arm around Tulo's thin shoulders. "Maia is right, I fear. In a fair tribunal, at least one of the ordained would act in defense of the accused. But Addai will dismiss protocol because the aeries are in danger. He is a true believer. He'll stop at nothing to protect the truth as he sees it."

"And what is the sentence for heresy?" I asked.

His sad eyes looked up at me. "If we're lucky, excommunication and exile. But I doubt that Addai has that in mind for us."

"So what, then?"

He shook his head. "You know what he'll do. The facts will be made to conform with the outcome he's decided on."

Fear shot through me and left me trembling. The lives of an entire fishing village and the lost exiles of Cuuloda weren't enough to appease Addai's "truth." I bent down to look Mabir in the eye. "Then we have to get out of here somehow. Is there another way out?"

"There's a tunnel, but it leads to the stables—which are also guarded. Unless young Tulo here has found a secret way of his own."

Mabir's acolyte shook his head. The poor boy looked gray.

I resumed pacing back and forth, as my mind rushed through everything that had happened, every possible scenario.

"Are there weapons here of any sort?"

"Nothing I am strong enough to wield or have been trained to use." Mabir shook his head. "A flail, some spears. A pair of crossbows, but they're in the Sanctuary with our guards."

I cursed, frowning at my feet as I paced. "The sun is down. Why does he draw this out?"

"Addai needs a spectacle," said Mabir. "He's setting the stage for his little charade. He'll want all his Juza present, once he's gathered as many Ashaani as he thinks he needs to make the right impact. He'll want Rov and his men visible to bolster his accusations, since Rov is part of his strategy. And I suspect he'll want Cairek and his teams away on patrol. Somebody has to be, and Cairek showed sympathy for you. Better to remove him."

"They haven't found Fren. Or Kaisi. They'd have brought them here immediately if they had."

"They may be locked up somewhere else," said Mabir.

True enough. We were on our own, no matter what else happened. I suddenly wished I hadn't been so hard on Cairek. For a moment I fantasized that he might attempt a rescue. I imagined Father returning, his fury setting things aright, with Darian beside him. But I dismissed the thoughts with sorrow. Addai had sent one of his Juza assassins with Father. We were on our own.

I moved a table under the stained glass windows and jumped up on it, where I could touch the colored panes. The depictions of Korruzon in his many guises were dark without the light of day behind them, like shadows of the stories they were meant to convey. "We can break a window."

"The Juza make their camp in the Temple yard," said Mabir. "They'll hear it."

I clutched my head with my trembling hands. "We can't stay here."

"What would you do?" said Jhem, anger tainting her voice. "Get out and do what?"

"Find Father."

"Without our dragons? We are *days* behind him, even if we knew which trails he might have found and followed."

"Escape."

"To where?"

I was angry, too. "I don't know! But we can't just sit here. What do *you* propose?"

Jhem didn't answer. I turned back to see her huddled close to herself, shaking her head. "First we have to clear ourselves of heresy," she muttered at last.

"We have to fight them."

"How? With our *fists*?" Her voice cracked.

"I don't know. I don't care."

"Damn it, Maia! You and your stubbornness. If you hadn't . . ."

The sting of her words rendered me mute for several seconds. "If I hadn't *what*?"

She shook her head. "No. I'm sorry. I didn't mean that. I didn't mean to imply—"

"But you did. If only I hadn't run off and found my dragon, proved Bellua wrong, and brought the Juza into Riat. Is that what you meant? Or flown to the coast to discover that the Juza murder civilians? Or do you wish I had never seen the Summer Dragon at all?"

"No! No. I'm sorry."

"And so is everyone else, I suppose." I inhaled. Mabir didn't meet my eyes.

Suddenly I was with Darian again, hiding in a dragon's nest on the cliffs, with Mother's curse whispering at the corners of my mind. My cheeks burned at the memory, and at the imperative that pushed me into the mountain to begin with—to prove that the Summer Dragon hadn't come to curse me, but to lift me up. I *had* proved it.

But Jhem's words filled me with doubt, and I grabbed my head to silence it. I'd already faced this demon more than once. I'd put lie to Bellua's accusations, found a qit of my own, and strengthened the aeries. For the last several months my bond of love for Keirr helped me suppress my night terrors, calm my anger, and make peace with Mother's words. Had it not? It couldn't end like this. It had nothing to do with fate or preordination, only Addai and his narrow interpretation of "Truth," whatever that really meant. I was little more than a paper boat on a river, carrying the candle of my life, but I could bob along helplessly or do what I'd done before. Something. Anything.

I swallowed my anger. "Whatever it was, I did it. I can't undo it. So the question remains: What do we do now?"

Mabir looked up. "We trust the Avar to—"

"Oh, for the love of Truth, what are the Avar going to do? Sit on a hill and look at us? What is Asha going to do? I'm done praying for miracles, Mabir. If I've learned anything in the last six, eight months, it's that Korruzon, Asha, and the rest of them are fantasies. There are no miracles—"

"Only in action is prayer answered," said Mabir.

Fren had said the same thing to me in my delirium following the ordeal on the mountain. *Prayer is Work. Prayer is Action.* Hollow platitudes that revealed nothing. It angered me again. "And so I look for action, while you tell me why it won't work. You contradict yourselves as you contradict me."

"That's not what I meant. Don't lose faith, Maia."

"For months demons and theologies have competed in my head. To what end? For what good? The Rasaal is a tyrant and Getig a mystery, but Asha is a silent . . . *promise* and little more. What am I to do with that? Right now we need a plan. What are we going to do?"

I was interrupted by the sound of the bar lifting, and the door latches turning. Jhem looked at me in surprise, Mabir in confusion, and he hugged Tulo closer. The doors opened.

The last three people I expected to see together stood in the chamber beyond. Cairek dressed in full Dragonry regalia—armor, sword, spear. Beside him Fren with a pair of quivers over one shoulder, his bow over the other, and a long hunting knife stuck in his belt. He also wore a dragon rider's harness. Standing before them, with an uncharacteristic sword at his hip, a crossbow and quiver slung on his back, was Bellua.

"What is this?" I said, when my wits caught up to me at last.

Bellua stepped into the room. "I served your guards their evening meals an hour ago, laced with sedatives to knock them out. I did the same to the guards in the stables. We must go now, while Addai and the rest of his Juza are out on patrol. There isn't much time."

"What?" I heard myself, and I sounded more than a little bit dumbfounded. "Why? Why would you do that?"

"You have one chance to prove your innocence, Maia, in a way that even Addai can't dismiss. You need my testimony in the trial to come. But it can't be hearsay or opinion. It must be the experience of another ordained in the Rasaal. You need me."

"Explain."

"We should go," said Cairek.

"We can hear his answer first," I said.

Bellua took a deep breath and studied me for several long seconds, then turned his gaze downward. "This has been a long time coming, Maia, but it's not easy to convey in the little time we have. My experience here in Riat has challenged my beliefs to the core. I've witnessed things that shook me. I've seen ancient ruins that I don't understand. I was challenged in no small part by you, Maia. Not just your words, but also your actions. You saved my life, and Zell's." He met my gaze with his head ever so slightly bowed. "I know you're not a witch, but now I have to know the truth about Asha and the Rasaal. And the Summer Dragon."

I couldn't speak. Was this for real? Or another ploy? But what *ploy* would involve Cairek and *Fren*? Bellua had seen my bond mark, but he'd told me to continue wearing my hair down; he hadn't betrayed me to Addai. In fact, something changed in him the day Addai arrived.

"Why should we trust you?" said Jhem, as if she read my mind.

"I can't blame you if you don't. I've treated you terribly."

Mabir stood slowly and took several steps toward Bellua. "There's more here than doubt alone. Something pushed you. What was it?"

Bellua looked to each of us as he replied. "My orders from the Rasaal were the first indication to me that something wasn't right. Addai was put in charge, with the clear command that we were to discredit you, Maia, by whatever means possible. But I had seen too much. I felt that the Temple disregarded truth in favor of convenience. I didn't know how far it would go until this morning, when Addai revealed the lengths he would follow in pursuit of that end."

"So you believe me? Addai killed Borgomos and the last of Cuuloda's refugees."

The familiar stern facade returned to his face, but now it looked careworn. "I do."

"You sabotaged the aeries with words and actions. You've been ruthless, too. You could have said something, but now Borgomos and his people are *dead*. And worst of all, you may be right that Getig is an aspect of Korruzon. In the end, what scared you—and what Addai killed for—is a dispute over which way to tell the *story*."

He lowered his eyes again, but nodded agreement. When he looked up his face was haggard. "I'm compelled to know what's true, and what isn't. For the sake of my soul."

"*We have to go*," said Cairek.

Mabir reached out and put a hand on Bellua's shoulder. "I believe

I understand what you are saying. You have brought Fren because his well of knowledge is deep, and Cairek because he is a sympathetic force."

Bellua nodded. "There is only one way to answer my doubts and to end Addai's inquest. That's why we must go. All of us. You too, Mabir."

"Go where?" I knew what he would say before he answered, and my knees went weak.

Fear shadowed his gaze. "The key to your freedom and mine are monuments deep in the mountain."

———

We walked past the drugged Juza guards, their dragons resting complacently beside them. Tauman waited in the courtyard, with Rannu, Audax, and Keirr fully saddled, our gear stowed—including our bows and multiple quivers of ammunition. Five of Cairek's men waited as well, including Marad, one of the talon leaders he'd introduced to us when they first arrived in Riat.

Keirr danced on her forefeet, nodding happily. "Maia!" she said. I kissed her nose and hugged her head.

Cairek's eyes caught mine as I mounted. His grim face showed relief, but also fear. Affection, but also sadness. He averted his gaze with embarrassed haste. He knew that I didn't want his courtship, but he'd come with Bellua anyway. I felt guilt for all I'd put him through. He was a good man. I might do far worse. My heart pounded with emotion as I realized what he risked. "You could be court-martialed."

"M'lady, I can't abide what's happening here. As I see it, my duty is to protect the aeries, which includes you an' your kin. I let you down once. I won't do it again."

My throat tightened, and I nodded my thanks. "Cairek, I'm sorry that Father was so hard on you. I'm sorry that I'm so much like him. I get angry. You didn't deserve it."

He nodded in return, then mounted his dragon, Taben, and strapped in, cartridges of arrows secured to the saddle behind him.

Bellua and Fren combined to get Mabir onto Zell's back. He wore his old harness—left over from a time before his bonded dragon died of age—and strapped himself efficiently into the secondary spot behind Bellua. Fren climbed up behind Tauman and with some assistance fastened his harness. He looked at me with mixed determination and terror, and managed a weak smile. He'd never been on the back of a dragon in his life. I returned what I hoped was a reassuring nod. I was glad for his presence.

Jhem and Tauman buckled in, but Cairek positioned Taben in their path. "You should take Jhem an' Maia into hiding until we return an' get this issue with Addai resolved."

A deep, frightened part of me liked Cairek's suggestion quite a bit, but I shook my head. "I'm going. I need to know the truth too, and I'm not about to let others fight my battle for me."

"And I won't let her go in without me," said Jhem.

Cairek frowned. "You and Tauman put your breeding pair at risk."

"They're already at risk," I said. "From Addai himself. He made it clear that he would happily claim the entire brood for the Rasaal and replace as many breeding pairs as it took."

Tauman took that news with clouded anger, and the look he turned to Cairek might have melted stone. "This is as much my mess as anyone's. And I'm with Maia—this is our fight. Let us fight it. What we *should* do is ambush Addai and end his inquest. Now."

"You'd never overcome his Juza," said Bellua. "They are elite fighters. You'd lose."

"Somehow I like those chances more than I like going back into the mountain," I said.

Cairek leaned toward me. "Believe me, I weighed those options. I've seen the Juza in action, an' I do not want to tangle with them."

"And you don't want to forget about Rov," said Bellua.

Cairek shifted uncomfortably in his saddle. "I've arranged for my own men to be on duty in the cavern. We won't encounter any of Rov's teams going in."

"This is crazy," I said.

He nodded. "Yes, it is."

"Where's Tulo?" said Mabir.

"I'm here," said a small voice.

Tulo stood in the doorway of the Temple, wearing an ancient and oversized harness, his quiver of drawing implements clutched tight.

"If these monuments are important, then they need to be recorded, don't they?"

Mabir's chin quivered for a moment. "By the High Ones. It's true. Bellua?"

The merihem studied the acolyte—his thin arms, tousled dark hair, eyes wide but mouth firmly set—and nodded. "I've seen your drawings, young man, and I agree."

"He can ride with me." Jhem urged Audax to lower himself, leaned down and took Tulo's quiver, then offered him a hand up the step rungs. He slipped in behind her and together they secured his harness.

I arranged my weapons for easy access. We all met each other's eyes with a look of shared resolve.

Bellua said, "We're ready."

When we launched, the waning moon sat on the eastern plains, a pale bowl, half full of light. The stars barely twinkled in air crisp and clear and still. Cairek led us on a path that clung to the cover of shadowed canyons, around Zurvaan to the far entrance, where Darian and I had made our stand against the Harodhi and their Horrors.

I couldn't dismiss the thought that Bellua might have laid a trap for us. Every muscle in my body tightened, and the skin on my neck and arms prickled. My jaw clenched so tight my teeth hurt. I became aware of every sound, every smell. But what else could I do? It was true that we needed an advocate. For better or worse, he was it. I would watch him like a cat.

———

When we landed, the redolence of ash and soot still lingered all these months later, even though they'd cleared the bone and wood from the porch of the cave. Lanterns inside revealed a new masonry wall, erected about thirty feet in. It spanned the cave from side to side, floor to ceiling, with large double doors in the center barred against anything that might come up from the depths.

Two more of Cairek's men awaited us—one of them Ajhe, his other talon leader. Once we all landed safely, they each gave their mounts a command, and the dragons reached up with their forefeet to take rings at the end of two ropes suspended from the shadows above either side of the doors. As they pulled them down, pulleys squeaked and groaned in the darkness, and the heavy bar lifted out of its braces with a grating rattle. Once it cleared the lintel, they slipped the rings onto hooks set in the stone floor.

Cairek trotted in front of us on Taben and turned him around. "Listen! Here's the marching order: me in front, then Darid an' Skot." Two names I'd not heard before. "Tauman with Fren, Bellua an' Mabir. Maia. Jhem an' Tulo. Then Marad, Ansin, an' Teff." Two more. "We'll stay mounted at all times. Only Bellua and I have been to the deep chambers we're going to visit. We'll do what we came t' do as quick as possible, then turn around in exact reverse order an' beat it back out. Understood?"

Some nodded. Some said "yes" or "aye." I only swallowed the bile in my throat and wiped my sweaty hands on my pants.

"Okay then." He nodded to his talon leaders. Ajhe and Marad's dragons took a ring in the center of each door with their teeth and pulled them outward. The hinges moaned and chattered. Lantern light flickered in the long hall beyond. Cairek wheeled Taben around again and trotted into the passage. We followed in silence. Ajhe and one of his teams remained outside to swing the doors closed again behind us. We heard the grate and rattle of the bar dropping on the far side. The thump as it settled into its braces again echoed with unsettling finality.

We proceeded down the corridor and the first short set of steps. The flicker of torches animated the friezes on the walls. People and dragons engaged in happy pursuits—marches, festivals, banquets—were made somehow morbid by stark shadows, the dank air, the hollow echoes of talons on stone, and Keirr's nervous clicks. We descended the long stair toward the green glow of the Chamber of the Seasons, where Malik had given me my Keirr.

The Chamber welcomed us with a floor cleared of debris. All the fallen stone and bones and even Poppa dragon's bloody footprints were gone. As we skirted the crystal fountain, I looked to the eastern entrance, now closed off with a new door and braces of steel. Above it the Summer Dragon seemed to ripple with life in the strange light. I marveled once more at the detail and precision of the sculpture. I shivered. Took a deep breath.

Keirr's head raised up, and she clicked repeatedly, looking all around. She made her Poppa-honk, but not as if she called him. She *said* it to me, looking over her shoulder. She recognized this room, and remembered what happened here.

I patted her neck. "That's right, baby."

I wanted to mutter a prayer, but I didn't know what name to choose. It was here that Mabir had explained the philosophy of the Ashaani to Father and me. It struck me now that it was that and no more—a philosophy. Not a religion. Certainly not a god. Asha was nothing so simple as that, no. *Truth* was far more complicated and difficult to grasp. It could *contain* gods. The philosophy of Asha invited doubt for reasons it considered noble. How could you pray to that? Doubt could invite fear. I listened for the Edimmu but felt nothing and pushed the thought down for fear that thought alone might summon it. I didn't remember drawing the arrow nocked to my bowstring.

Four more of Cairek's wing met us as he headed toward the door surmounted by the carving of Waeges, the Autumn Dragon in her leafy mien. A new door of steel also blocked this passage. When last we'd been here, Harodhi fighters and the Edimmu poured through it from the depths.

Keirr sensed my fear and faltered. Before I could urge her forward again, Cairek halted the whole procession. He spoke quietly with the riders at the door, their muted voices lost in the confusion of whispering echoes, smothered by the splash and hiss of the fountain. His men brought lanterns; one each for Cairek, Bellua, Jhem, and me. I shook my head *no*. I didn't want it—it would make me a target. The soldier shrugged and gave it to Marad instead.

Then two of the riders grasped either side of a wheel set in the door and began to turn it. Gears ratcheted on the face of the door, sound reverberating and multiplying throughout the chamber like echoes in a fever dream. Two fat bars of steel withdrew from holes in the metal casing. It finished with a resounding clank. I cringed at the volume of noise. Could we have knocked any louder? A bead of sweat tickled the side of my face.

Cairek turned to us, Taben prancing nervously. "Listen! There's a metal knocker on the other side of this door. On our return, three

424

short raps followed by three long ones will signal my men to open it again. Rapraprap. Rap . . . rap . . . rap. Got it?"

"Smaw, bi-g," said Keirr quietly.

Again, a chorus of *aye* and *yes*. I looked back at Jhem. Her face was ashen, but she too had nocked an arrow to her bowstring.

At a nod, Cairek's men swung the door inward on groaning hinges. One by one we started forward into the black heart of Mt. Zurvaan.

FORTY-SIX

A STRANGE CALM FILLED ME. Not calm, a bizarre suspension of fear. Or integration of fear. I'd been in these caverns before, faced the Harodhi twice now, the Horrors twice, and even the Edimmu twice. Every sensation was heightened. My bow in my hands, arrow nocked. Harness tight. Keirr alert, clicking and stepping lightly, her talons retracted in order to walk silently on the pads of her feet. The temperature of the air, the scents of stone and water, the tension in my companions. I was taut as a bowstring. Calm wasn't the word.

Ready.

Ahead of me, Cairek's lantern lit a narrow swath of melted stone, the sort of terrain that Dare and I passed through on our run from the Harodhi. Bellua kept his lantern mostly shuttered, but he couldn't resist opening it briefly to illuminate this statue or that chasm. The clicking of dragons reverberated in my ears. They all sought an image of the terrain; they saw it with echoes, heard their own voices resounded back to them. They saw their world more perfectly this way than with sight alone, so who could blame them?

I urged Keirr forward, past Bellua and Mabir, past Tauman, past Darid and Skot. Alongside Cairek I slowed her again and said as quietly as possible, "We have to silence our dragons, Cairek."

"What? Why?"

"Their clicking and sounding will alert any other dragon who might be listening."

In the dim light of various half-shuttered lanterns I saw him turn my way, head cocked. His eyes lit as he heard what I heard: a dense weave of susurrate echoes vibrating off the unseen walls and ceilings around us, like the whispers of ghostly music in the darkness. He nodded, perhaps hearing and understanding it for the first time in his life.

"Listen everyone," he said with quiet urgency. "Dragons silent. No more clicking or sounding of any sort."

There were murmurs behind us as riders gave commands to their mounts. Cairek shuttered his lantern to nothing, and darkness enveloped us completely. Only when silence followed suit did he part the shutters on his lamp enough to see the way forward again.

I remained just behind Cairek as we proceeded. I heard only the rustle of leather and cloth, the distant echoing drip of water on stone or into pools. I wondered if even those tiny sounds could create an image in a dragon's mind.

We descended a long staircase, flanked on the left by friezes similar to the ones behind us—people at work, at play, at war—and on the right by a deep chasm. After what seemed to be an hour spent in silence, we entered a tight passage with friezes on either side, and lanterns were opened again partway. Carvings of animals in a forest peered out between buttressing trees that arched up and over to texture the ceiling above with an intricate pattern of branches and leaves. A label in ancient runes accompanied each, as if this were a glossary of the outside world.

Light grew from behind, along with scratching noises. I turned back to see that Jhem had opened her lantern a sliver so Tulo could make quick drawings as we passed. He'd clearly never been this far on his previous trips.

We came out of the passage into another chamber, circular, with only one other doorway on the opposite side. Bellua whispered to Cairek, "Here lies my first question. Let us stop." He opened his lantern shutters a little wider to reveal the scope of the room. It wasn't as large as the Chamber of the Seasons, but a domed ceiling soared above and the far wall nearly disappeared into shadow. A relief of a city decorated the walls, the viewpoint of a person standing in the center of a public square, looking out at streets, avenues, mountains, and towering clouds. Tiny people scattered about and dragons dotting the sky gave it scale, but the focus of the work was the buildings.

They were magnificent. Taller than anything I'd ever seen, though

I'd never been to any of the big cities of the Empire. The impression was of a vast landscape of stone, streets at the bottom of canyons, gardens on terraces complete with giant trees. On our left, a dome commanded the center of attention. Atop it like a symbol stood a circle—a simple ring. The doors carved at its base gave the impression of huge scale. On the adjacent walls, it seemed that palisades might be glimpsed between the buildings, surrounding this city captured in stone.

The image on the wall opposite astounded me. Mt. Zurvaan, its summit partially obscured by stylized clouds, loomed over the landscape. With shock I realized that I knew this city, but as it appeared at its height, alive and vital. "It's Cinvat," I said aloud.

"That's right," said Fren, and Bellua stared at me with surprise and confusion on his face.

Buildings marched up the slopes where I'd found only the barest remnants of roads. An amphitheater sat to the right where I'd seen a bowl in the forest. I looked for the giant head sculpture covered with moss, but perhaps something obscured it from this vantage. It didn't matter. I felt as if the ghosts of Cinvat inhabited this hall and spoke to me excitedly of their time in the world. Tears of wonder clung to my lashes. I'd imagined many times what Cinvat might have looked like in its day, but here it was, depicted in stunning detail. Were these my ancestors? I felt them in my bones.

On the left a plateau met the mountain's lower slopes where I had entered a crack in the mountain in search of Keirr. But there was no cave in this representation. Instead I saw structures that could only be one thing. Ranks of brood platforms stacked one atop another lined the cliff's edge, with suggestions of more buildings behind. "Look, where the caves should be—an aerie. A huge one."

"And look at the floor," said Fren. "It's a map of the city, street for street."

"Please let me get down and draw this," said Tulo in a whisper that barely contained his excitement. "I need room to open my scrolls."

Cairek gave Bellua a questioning glance. "Do we dare spend the time?"

Bellua considered only a moment. "Yes. A record would be wise, but keep your drawing spare, boy, and be quick."

Tulo scrambled down from Audax and moved to the center of the room as if pulled there. "Look," he said. "From this spot"—he pointed to a star chiseled into the stone at his feet—"the perspective is perfect. It's like you're standing in the square. The illusion is exactly right."

"I wish we had more time," said Mabir. "Promise me that if all turns out well with Addai we can return and record it properly."

Bellua hesitated, as if he could guarantee no such thing. But he said, "I promise."

"Be sure you draw that." Fren pointed across to the image of the dome. "That is the temple of Asha, topped with the symbol of Truth."

"A circle?" said Bellua.

Fren turned in the saddle to face him directly. "Of course a circle. The endless turning of the Evertide in simplest form."

Bellua's face sagged. A few months ago he'd have said something about Korruzon representing the end of Cycles, or some such. But now he held his tongue.

Mabir shuffled in the seat behind him. "I have a question for you, Bellua," he said. "Why did you keep this secret?"

He didn't answer for a long span of time. "Pride, I suppose. I hoped to figure it out for myself. Now time makes understanding urgent."

"Has Rov seen this?"

"Yes."

"And he never mentioned it either," Mabir pressed. "The secrets you kept from us, about our own mountain, our own home and history."

Bellua's chin grew firm, and he nodded.

"And now Rov and Addai act to take the aeries for themselves," I said. "That explains the massive road Rov built between the aeries and the cliffs. He saw these pictures, and it gave him ideas."

Bellua nodded at me but said nothing.

Jhem and Tauman looked all around with big-eyed wonder.

"Why would they create such a monument?" said Cairek. "And deep in a cave, no less."

"Indeed," said Bellua. "That is my exact question."

In answer, Mabir pointed at Tulo, who sat drawing frantically on a scroll of parchment. "Perhaps it's a record of something they feared to lose. Or had already lost."

———

Bellua urged Tulo to complete his sketch quickly. The boy scribbled a few more lines, then took a sheet of blank parchment and used a stick of chalk to make a rubbing from a block of ancient text beside the depiction of the dome. He rolled his parchments and put his tools away only reluctantly, then with a hand up from Jhem clambered onto Audax's back again. We crossed to the far door and left the record of Cinvat behind.

Once more we descended into inky darkness, lit only with glimpses by lantern light, unaided by the questing clicks of our dragons. At one point we seemed to cross a bridge as a dark void fell away on either side. I heard only the faintest of echoes.

"Bi-g," said Keirr, in a whisper. Even without clicks, incidental sound painted a picture for her.

Then we found ourselves in another close passageway, adorned with images of a library. Ranks and ranks of books on shelves but carved out of the root of the mountain. I could barely imagine why anyone would create a library you couldn't read, full of books that were nothing more than spine and empty promise. "I wish I could take rubbings of all of it," whispered Tulo, but we didn't stop.

The tunnel opened to a snaking trail through natural terrain of hanging stalactites and the spires that rose to meet them. From the dark beyond the reach of our lanterns came a rushing sound. Cairek closed his lantern entirely, and I realized that we could see by a pale blue glow through a crack in the distance. As my night vision adapted I saw glimmers from far-off walls.

"We're almost there," he whispered.

The first waterfall spouted from a fissure to our left and tumbled into a narrow ravine. Our trail descended by twists and stairs to meander alongside its swift torrent. It fell twice more before I realized that the luminescence had grown around us, outlining our surroundings in light. The air grew markedly colder as we descended. At last the way opened into misty radiance, blue and ethereal, so bright that it took several seconds for my eyes to adjust. We gathered together on a broad ledge overlooking a strange vista.

"Holy Avar," said Mabir. I heard gasps from several of the soldiers as well.

The blue glistened on the watercourse as it leapt down a series of falls into a vast chamber, long and narrow, incredibly tall, ending in a lake so still it scarcely shimmered. In that distant end of the cavern, a beam of light came from somewhere out of sight far above, its source hidden by the intervening ceiling of stone.

"What is it?" said Jhem, looking up.

"Daylight," said Bellua, "filtered through the glacier nestled between the Crag and the mountain's pinnacle."

"Gods, is it morning already?" said Tauman.

"Oh my," Mabir whispered. "I see. Old legends tell that Zurvaan is an ancient, sleeping volcano, and spewed fire in ages past. This chamber is an empty lava shaft. See the boulders and rubble that cover the floor? The plug that once formed the ceiling crumbled away over the ages to reveal the glacier above, like a skylight."

"That's only half correct," said Bellua. "I flew to the top of this chamber to see for myself. It is indeed the glacier, but there's a thick ceiling of glass supporting it, buttressed with steel arches. The glacier is man-made. The stone around it has decayed and the glass has fallen away in places, but the glacier has its own integrity. The people who lived here created the skylight as a light source, disguised by its very nature from the outside."

"Why would they do that?" said Jhem.

"The people who *lived here*?" said Mabir.

Bellua nodded. "Look closer. I believe this was a secret home, a sanctuary, hidden from the outside world."

Not all the irregular forms that littered the floor were boulders or rubble. Square shapes tottered with age, their upper margins broken, piles of debris at their feet. A subtle pattern of streets and avenues was clear once I looked for it. The ethereal blue limned a city—an actual city of buildings and courtyards and avenues—crumbling and covered with black moss, but clearly the product of human hands.

"Astounding," said Tauman.

Tulo's pencils scratched on paper somewhere to my right.

"I've been through this city," said Bellua. "Many of the structures are homes, still containing furniture and personal items of stone or metal. The mountain was the home of an entire race. It seems that the Harodhi shaman Maia killed occupied one of the buildings, along with several lieutenants or servants. What happened to them all we can only guess. But what I want you to see is beyond the city and across the lake." He turned Zell in Cairek's direction. "Sergeant?"

Cairek launched Taben over the azure chasm, settling into a low spiral above the secret city by the lake. I followed, then Bellua with Mabir, then the rest in order. A tremor swept me as we passed over the dead buildings, as black and fractured as a long-forgotten grave-yard. Huge chunks of melting ice littered the long-ago streets, sug-gesting that the integrity of the glacier so incredibly far above was compromised. We emerged into the shaft of light. Peering up, I saw a latticework of dark lines like the veins of a leaf against the pale blue ceiling. Here and there, thin trickles of water sparkled as they fell. Cairek sped over the city, across the lake toward the opposite wall, led us beneath an overhanging slab of ancient stone and into a cleared space. We alit beside him.

An amphitheater surrounded us, broad and open, hidden from the view of the skylight above by the ledge stone. Here and there fallen boulders broke the sweeping arcs of stone seats and stairs, all iced with hardened liquid stone. Spires climbed up from the perimeter to meet pinnacles hanging from the lip above, a colonnade self-made over the course of an age.

Bellua pointed toward the focus of all those seats, and upward. "Here is the image I could not decipher. This is the mystery that chal-lenged me."

A wall stood behind the fractured stage, just as broad and several stories tall. Smooth and flat, subdivided into two dozen or more tall, narrow panels. As our eyes grew accustomed to the gloom, carved scenes emerged, each stranger than the one beside it. Some were easy to make out—animals and forests—but others were bizarre depictions of strange architecture, odd ships of the sky like bloated whales fes-tooned with sails, or machinery crawling amongst ruins, or buildings in the air spewing men and constructs above landscapes impossible to fathom. They reminded me of the carvings in the Hall of the Seasons.

Without asking permission, Tulo scrambled down from Audax and opened his quiver of drawing tools. We all followed suit as if that had been the signal. Even Cairek. Only his Dragonry remained mounted.

Fren dropped to his knees, looking up with tearful reverence. Jhem and Tauman took note and turned to each other, then to me. Cairek and Bellua watched Mabir. The dhalla stood transfixed, studying the giant frieze intently, his posture straightening as if a few inches of additional height would help him to see it better. Cairek opened his lantern fully to accommodate him as Tulo's pencil began to scratch. Mabir hobbled closer to the left-most image, signaling Cairek to follow with his light.

Men in primitive skins and rags huddled around a cookfire. Cleverly sculpted knobs of stone suggested the eyes of wild animals, peering from the low forest. Above it all, in upright pose two stories tall, loomed a bear against a night sky, where an arc of moons progressed from sliver, to half, to full and back again.

Without comment, Mabir moved to the next panel, and Cairek followed. A carved sky contained orbs like our moon, but in great numbers, one with a ring like a flattened hoop encircling it, others with lesser orbs arranged around them. Small raised spots shaped like stars were scattered in the spaces between, connected by grooved lines, perhaps denoting constellations, though none were familiar to me. On the ground below, surrounded by plants bearing unfamiliar fruits, sat a strange idol, a woman with pendulous breasts, her belly swollen as if with child. A serpent crawled over her knees.

In the next panel a circle surrounded by flames rode in the sky above stylized clouds and a plain cut by a river. A strange building, triangular in shape, with two smaller triangles behind it, stood above a lush landscape that gave it impressive scale.

Two-wheeled carts pulled by horses filled the next, the occupants armed with bows and spears. A mountain dominated the background, its peak circled with cloud and surrounded by rays of light.

A man stood upon a mountain in the next, but the panel was badly damaged by cracks and a hard casing of mineral deposits. The next few were also in bad shape, but I made out a bird's wing with long pinfeathers, like those of a hawk or an eagle. The next revealed the snarling face of a lion. Then came a sky filled with arrows in flight, armies on the ground clashing with sword and shield in frozen terror.

The following images were harder to comprehend, more like those in the chamber of the seasons behind us. Impossible towers, beneath swollen, whale-like craft adorned with sails. Horseless wagons arrayed with strange ballistae. Depictions of flames and ruin. Men holding books, balance-scales, sextants, and other tools of indescribable function. Men in anger shouting and holding up scrolls, atop a mountain built of people, those at the bottom crying and starved, cradling their dead. Bizarre constructs of odd geometry, shaped like blunt cylinders or disks or wings, again in a sky of stars and planets with no ground at all below them.

Panel after panel of warfare and destruction, in which the machinery grew ever more strange. Only in the last few most severely damaged friezes did I see dragons at all.

The final image sent a shiver down my spine—a gigantic dragon carved in such a way that it seemed to fall back into the stone, like a shadow, even though it stood in the foreground of everything. The artist had somehow made the creature seem like a negative space, an absence more than a presence, and I couldn't help but think of the Edimmu. Other dragons filled the sky. Tilting on its foundation below was the temple of Asha that we had seen in the room recalling the long-dead city of Cinvat. I'd seen that monster somewhere else though, too, and when I realized where, my spine shivered into a frozen rail: the statue in our temple ruins, the black dragon battling with the white. The Dahak.

After several minutes of silence, Mabir said, "It's a history, whether real or mythical I cannot say."

"Myth can spring from truths long forgotten," said Fren, from his knees.

Mabir nodded. "My knowledge of history goes only as far back as the beginning of our own age, with the fall of Cinvat." He pointed at the last image, in which the shadow monster towered over the Temple of Asha. "This is far more ancient, and of course the Rasaal doesn't really want it remembered."

Bellua turned a cold eye on him but said nothing.

Mabir continued. "Given the record we've seen already, and adding this testament to their beliefs, I believe this hidden city is the last hiding place of the people of Cinvat, who fell at the end of an age and created this monument to memory. Perhaps they died here. Or perhaps they emerged and became our own ancestors. It's impossible to say."

"That is my guess also," said Bellua. "But I want to know what these panels mean."

Fren stood. "I believe I can explain."

Bellua took a step toward him. "Please. It's why we're here."

Fren took a deep breath. "It *is* a history. It's a history of the Avar."

Bellua frowned. "How? How is this a history of the Avar?"

"The oldest scriptures from the Ashaani say that whatever the people hold in highest reverence, they will see in the Avar. Over the ages the Avar have appeared in many forms, for their true form would be incomprehensible to us."

Bellua seemed horrified. "How is that possible? That reduces them to little more than"—he hesitated, searched for words—"than reflections of our ignorance."

Fren shrugged. "Does it? Or perhaps messengers must appear in an understandable guise. I can't explain it. I am only a vessel for the old words and the old ways. A man should add no interpretation to something he does not understand. He should only ask questions that may lead him to an answer."

He pointed at the friezes and began to recite as if from rote memory. "There was a time of the Bear and the Dark Night. Then of the Mother and the Heavenly Spheres that spanned many ages, when life shed its skin like a serpent to be reborn again and again. Then a time of the Horse, a time of Mountains and God Kings. Then followed the Eagle, the Lamb, and the Lion. A time of Arrows. A time of Exploration and Ships of the Sea, of Machines and Great Cities. A time of Philosophies. A time of Gold and of Great Deceptions. A time of Storms. A time of Deserts and a time of Ice. A time of Stars, of Falling Heavens and a Rain of Death. A time of the Created, the eras of the Dragon Wars. An age of Starvation and Cannibals. A long darkness when there were no stories." He turned back to us. "This telling ends before the age of Cannibals. Perhaps the people of Cinvat escaped that dark time, for the last panel can only be the Dahak bringing ruin down on their fair city in the first of the Dragon Wars. Always there is War, and the Avar change."

We listened to the distant rush of the waterfalls for several moments before Fren continued. "We still live in an age of Dragons. Notice there are no dragons in most of the previous ages. They appear late in the chronicle, at the end of the time of Stars, but they've survived many cycles. They are among the 'Created' that scripture speaks of. Somehow, in a time of greater science, men *made* them, bringing together the most useful qualities of many creatures."

"That's impossible," said Bellua. His eyes were wide, not with anger or conviction but with something else that teetered between fear and madness. "Did men create the Avar, then, too?"

Fren shook his head. "No, the Avar only manifest as that which we revere most, whether it is beast or machine or even something imagined."

"How do you know that's true?" Bellua asked.

I cleared my throat. "Father told me once of a mercenary he knew during his time in the Dragonry. The desert he lived in wouldn't support dragons, and so the Avar appeared to his people as great horses."

Bellua looked up again at the panel on which horses drew the odd two-wheeled carts filled with warriors. "But it doesn't put lie to the teachings of the Rasaal that Korruzon is the Original Flame, the ultimate expression of the First, who pushed the mountains up with his writhing . . ." His words trailed off as he took in the contradiction before him: a vast series of ages in which there were no dragons at all. He fell to his knees, still gazing up at this ancient rebuttal to the beliefs his life was built upon, written in stone by a dead people.

"The things we hold in reverence reflect our nature," said Fren. "Warlike people worship jealous gods and build their altars of steel. Those who love wealth build their altars of gold. Content people build their altars of love."

The sight of tears in Bellua's eyes shocked me. "Then what are the Avar really?" he asked.

The very question I'd asked Father an age ago. The thought of him filled me with worry.

Fren answered with measured deference to Bellua's pain. "If the

Ashaani knew, they left no record of it, which only suggests that it's among the questions they couldn't answer."

I shivered in the cold air, looking across those many panels, the very last of which showed an event older than the statue in our ruins, the Dahak destroying Cinvat. It seemed impossible, yet here was silent testimony, chipped out of the heart of a mountain and overlaid with stone, surrounded by a tomb-like city.

"The world is older than you can imagine," said Fren.

Cairek signaled Taben to his feet. "We need to go. We've been gone too long."

"I need more time!" Tulo knelt with several parchments spread out in a fan before him, his hands skipping like stones across the surfaces with chalk and pencil—now scribing, now rubbing tone out of the chalk dust, now punching in darks that might define a shadow or edge.

Bellua remained on his knees. "I've been a fool."

Mabir gripped his shoulder. "No, good Bellua. It's not so simple as that."

"I thought I might find some way of arguing leniency for Maia and the rest of you. But if the Rasaal learns of this place, they will bury it. It puts lie to everything they expect us to believe."

"Not everything," said Mabir. "Surely if Addai sees it too he would—"

"His job is to defend the Rasaal, not to question its teachings." Bellua stood and turned to me. "You don't realize, Maia, that it's not me or even Addai, but the entire structure of the Temple that stands against you. I knew in the beginning that I should silence the story of Getig until I could tease truth out of it. But I thought it would be Korruzon's truth. Addai's orders instructed me to discredit you entirely or, failing that, to kill you and have your dragon destroyed."

The distant rumble of waterfalls combined with the throbbing of blood in my ears. "Why?"

"Because you threaten the order of things. You represent a heresy that cannot be allowed to return—that Korruzon and His temple are temporary things. There is too much to lose. The Rasaal will never forgive you, never acknowledge you. You are poison to them. You must be eliminated. For the Rasaal, there is no other choice. They will hunt you until you die."

My heart thudded in my chest. "Then what kind of Avar is Korruzon?"

Bellua shook his head slowly.

"If the Avar are but reflections of our faith, then what is the *Edimmu*?" I could only whisper the name of the shadow creature for fear of awakening it. "What is *its* nature? What does *it* reflect? And what of the *Utukku*?" I looked to Fren and Mabir for some sort of answer, but they stood mute. "And what is *that*?" I pointed to the carving of the Dahak. "It also looks like a dragon, but is it?" No one answered me.

From far above us came a crack and a hiss. We turned in time to see a chunk of ice from the distant ceiling hit the still lake in an explosion of water. Its echoes boomed around us as shards of ice fell like snow, glittering in the wintery light.

"Addai has surely discovered our absence by now," said Cairek. "We need to go."

"Let the boy draw!" urged Mabir. "As long as he possibly can. Nothing now is more important than this record."

"There is one hope." Bellua's face was a frozen mask. "That Korruzon uses this incident to clean His Temple, to drive out the iniquitous forces within it. Perhaps the viewing of these relics was the ultimate aim of His appearance in the guise of Getig."

Fren and Mabir exchanged a look.

"That is possible," said Mabir. "Or perhaps you seek a rationalization that allows you to cling to your belief."

Bellua pressed the heels of his hands over his eyes. "I don't know what to do, or what to believe."

"You must make your case," said Mabir. "Either this was Korruzon's will, and it will come to good, or it was not. And then you will have your answer. For good or ill, the Truth of this cave must be shared."

Bellua stared long at Mabir, his eyes full of sorrow and anger, until the old dhalla stepped closer and gripped his shoulders. "Don't lose all faith, Bellua. You've embraced Truth, even though you're unsure what Truth is. That's faith of a higher sort. Your better nature comes forth, even in the face of uncertainty." Bellua gripped the dhalla's forearm as if he might fall otherwise, but it was my face he sought.

His eyes searched mine, as if I knew anything about anything. Too many points of view collided in my head. Uncertainties. The teachings of the Rasaal. Mabir's turmoil. The puzzles Fren tossed at me. Bellua's machinations. Addai's blatant, unyielding belief. Father's doubts. Even Mother's curse, lurking still, so deeply rooted that I half expected the Edimmu's voice to evoke it again. Gods! I thought I'd silenced the curse.

Finally, the only word I could summon, the only thing that made any sense at all. "Truth," I said aloud, to Bellua. To myself.

Fren nodded. "Asha has known many names, among them Obedience, Love, and Submission. But Truth above all."

Bellua stared at me, and he nodded.

"*Maia,*" whispered Keirr. I realized that all our dragons were utterly silent, listening with breaths held. Another loud crack came from far above, and again we turned in time to see a chunk of ice crash into the lake in a geyser of white spray.

"Are you sure that roof is stable?" Cairek said to Bellua.

"It's held for thousands of years—"

"Listen!" I said, and we all fell silent.

The last echoes of the splash continued to resound, until I was certain we heard new sounds, not echoes, not the waterfalls. The echoing beat of many wings far overhead. I saw shadowbeams— flitting columns of shadow like the boles of manic trees dancing in a forest of light. I walked toward the edge of the amphitheater, into the light, so I could hazard a peek at the ceiling.

"Avar, help us," I whispered.

Dozens of dark, tattered shapes massed inside the skylight, swarming against the glacial haze, thick as bats in a twilight sky.

Horrors.

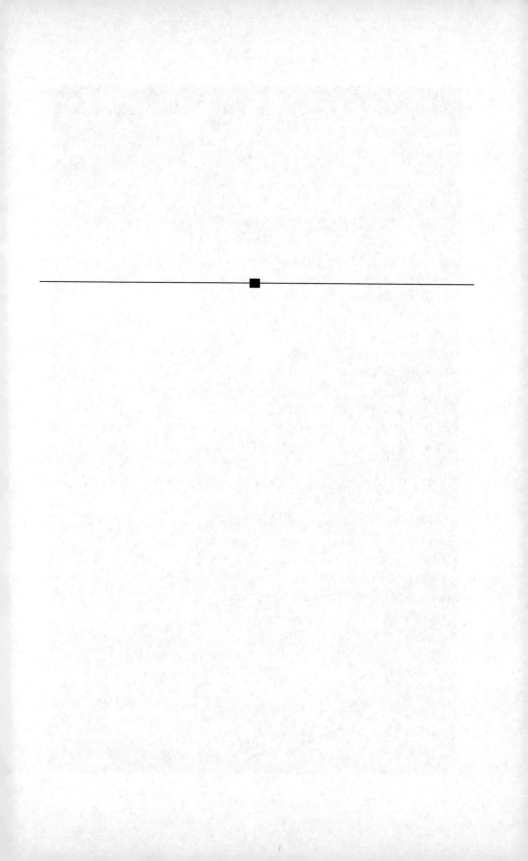

F O R T Y - S E V E N

"**D**O YOU THINK they saw us?" Cairek whispered.
"No, I don't. They're tearing at the ceiling."
"Why? What are they after?"
A tremor passed through me. "They want *out*."
"How can they not know the way out already? Why now?"
"They're mindless without something to direct them. They've been out of food. Dormant. But now something has awakened them, and I don't think it was us."
Cairek backed away into shadow. "Like what?"
I turned to see his eyes wide and glittering with fear. I couldn't bring myself to say *Edimmu*.
"*Mount up*," Cairek whispered again, but with all the force of a command. He scrambled onto Taben. His Dragonry had been in their saddles and ready all along. I climbed onto Keirr, looked to see Cairek helping Fren into the saddle.
"Dhalla. Merihem," said Cairek. "Quickly, please."
Mabir and Bellua hovered over Tulo, urging him to haste as he frantically rolled up his drawings, scooped up his tools, and thrust them into the quiver. Jhem hauled him up and harnessed him in behind her. Bellua and Tauman assisted Mabir into place, then Tauman ran to Rannu and leapt up the step rungs.
Cairek scanned the company. "Full retreat. Reverse order, back the way we came. Quietly as possible."
Marad was first to gallop up the ranked seats of stone and launch into the air. His men followed in order. "Those drawings are impor-

tant," I said to Cairek. "Tulo should be in the center of the formation." He nodded and waved me ahead of Jhem and Tulo.

The insistent beat of wings from above grew more pronounced. Suddenly there came a stupendous *crack* and rumbling from the top of the vault. Chunks of ice so large they seemed to fall slowly crushed the structures below. Others hit the lake in a sluggish geyser that doused us with spray. Thunderous booms followed, rebounding back and forth across the chasms. I cried out, my voice lost in the din.

Ice and snow drifted down as the wingsnap and screech of the Horrors grew louder. They continued their assault on the ceiling. Tore at the metal struts and clawed into the glacier above.

"They'll bring down the ceiling," I shouted, scarcely able to hear myself.

Ansin barked something to his men. He stayed close to the wall as he led us toward the city. We passed over the lake, out from beneath the skylight of ice and groaning steel, into the cave proper. Climbed toward the ledge beside the waterfalls, where the passage would take us back through the long darkness to a barred metal door. Sweet Avar, we'd be hours getting out.

Marad landed on the ledge and started toward the passage, but halted abruptly when he spied the sickly green lights within.

A hybrid Horror croaked and stepped out of the shadows. The head and upper torso of a creature once human, stitched to the shoulders of a juvenile dragon less than half Keirr's size. The dragon's mouth snapped from where the human's belly should have been. Another Horror followed: two men sewn together, sharing legs woven into the harness and flesh of their dragon. Green light spilled through the haphazard seam binding their three torsos. Another Horror emerged beyond them, and another, little more than flickers in a confused abstract of moving shadows. Our way out was blocked. They cried out with one voice and charged.

Marad launched off the ledge again. Ansin, Teff, and I aborted our landings. More Horrors squeezed through the passage. The ledge swarmed with them.

Keirr cried out in fear, turned, bolted out of formation. "*No*, baby—calm." But I gave her her head to catch up to Cairek as he began to turn.

"There's another way out!" I called to him. "There has to be. We know that."

Upward and to the east. Three Horrors used it once before, while the Edimmu crouched on a ledge outside. Why didn't they use it again? Or now? Was it blocked somehow?

"How will we find it?" he shouted.

"Keirr, find me a small tunnel, baby. A small cave, up high. Tictictic! HAI."

She clicked twice and listened, climbed a beat higher and did it again. Clicked twice more, then cocked her head at me.

"Hurry. They're coming," said Cairek.

"*A tunnel*," I said to Keirr. How in the world would she draw a sound-picture of a tunnel? What would a space that was small but also long sound like? Close echoes but also distant ones? "Tictictic . . . Tic . . . Tic," I said, hoping that might be a tunnel in her ears. She cocked her head at me again. Rose higher, with a purpose.

"Ttttic . . . tttc . . . ttc . . . ttc . . ." she said. It almost sounded right.

I patted her on the neck, then turned back to Cairek. "Follow us!"

He pulled Taben into a hover and waved everyone past him with a windmilling arm.

I laid forward in the saddle, legs tight against the laces. Keirr's muscles bunched and stretched beneath me. She rowed hard, clicking and listening. Tried several ledges, clicking into shadows. Launched again.

I glanced back. The Horrors below climbed after us slowly. Cairek covered our retreat with his topbow; Taben rearming it with his elbows, Cairek cranking hard to reload. He paused once to discard an empty cartridge, pull another one from his gear and slap it into place. I heard the thump of other bows.

Out over the city, shadowbeams danced in the light of the glacier, to the music of screeching metal and cracking ice. Several of the shafts peeled out of the climbing spiral. The monsters atop them descended into view. At least three of them headed toward us, beneath the stone ceiling at this end of the cave. Behind them, a sudden ripple in the column of light. It flashed downward, as wide as the shaft of the lava tube, at lightning speed. A titanic boom sounded from above. The vaulted ceiling of Zurvaan failed all at once and the glacier poured in. Air displaced from below surged upward, pushing us higher on a whirlwind. It smashed the Horrors approaching us into the ceiling. Darkness swallowed us briefly. I clung tightly to Keirr's saddle grips, waiting for an impact that didn't come. Light returned in all the colors of afternoon to reveal the plummeting mass of the glacier. It swept Horrors down with it, cascading into the lake and burying the lost city with an impact that shook the very atmosphere. An avalanche of glass and ice and stone covered the city. I ducked as rocks chattered down around me, as the cleanest light to fall through that shaft in an epoch glittered off the spume of ice and snow. Beneath it was ruin. The lake, the city, and the amphitheater were buried in a mountain of ice. I screamed at the loss.

Horrors milled about or clung to perches until, few by few, they peeled off the walls or rose out of the fog to seek the top of the mountain once more. They curled upward in a twisted column. The shaft was filled with Horrors. There'd be no escape that way.

Keirr clicked twice and resumed searching. Found a ledge canting back toward a manmade arch above an inky black hole. "Ttttic . . . tttc . . . ttc . . . ttc . . . Yes!" she said.

"Here! This way!" I shouted.

Marad and Teff landed first. As they turned to take up a defensive stance, Cairek arrived too. "Marad—into the tunnel. Keep moving. Reverse order. Go!"

They sped through the arch. I paused and waved Jhem and Tulo past again. I wanted them away from the Horrors.

I watched the air behind us.

A Horror flapped up onto the landing and snatched at one of Cairek's teams—Skot. The man ducked low, presenting the spiked backplate of his armor. His dragon lunged to one side. The monster grabbed at Skot, but momentum took it past. It rebounded off the cavern wall to land on the ledge. I still had an arrow nocked in my bowstring. I drew and released at the creature's maw. Saw my arrow disappear into its hellish furnace. Fren's bow thumped, then Darid's and Tauman's. Skot frantically backed up his mount. The *chunk chunk chunk* of Cairek's top bow, the singing of the cables as Taben rearmed it with motions of his elbows. Fren loosed shafts from behind him. The Dragonry and Tauman and I rained arrows on it. Finally, the beast charged.

Bellua and Mabir passed me, under the arch and into the cave. Cairek shouted, "Go! Maia, Tauman, go!"

I backed Keirr into the cave, shooting as I had opportunity until Tauman and Rannu blocked the way. From outside came angry shouts, the roar of a dragon. Savage scuffling and snarling. A scream of terror.

Darid and then Cairek with Fren backed in next, all pale as ghosts even in the scant light.

"Keep moving," gasped Cairek to me. His Taben was bloodied, with stripes across his shoulders. "Go. Skot is gone."

The ceiling hung too low for flight. Keirr galloped up a rising scrabble of broken debris. The way widened even as the ceiling dropped. From ahead I heard curses and orders to "*Dismount*." I soon understood why.

The passage was chopped up by stout columns of accreted stone, barring the way with colonnades of the mountain's own making. Jhem dismounted and Tulo with her. Keirr was still small. By crouching low to her neck I was able to stay mounted. Everyone else walked beside their mounts, even Mabir. He struggled with the uneven terrain, though Bellua had his arm. I called him and stopped Keirr by his side. "You ride. I'll walk."

"No, child. No, I will manage."

I dismounted, and Keirr lay down so he could climb up easily. "Thank you," he said.

"Don't worry—she'll take good care of you."

"I know she will." He smiled.

Bellua and I helped him onto Keirr's back, and I scratched her under the chin briefly. "Be good."

From behind—screeching and fluttering.

"Cairek?" I called back.

"The crispies follow," he said, "but they don't like this restricted path. They fall behind."

"Then let us gain ground."

Jhem and Marad's lanterns ahead showed as a horizontal sliver of pale light. Keirr crawled on her belly. Mabir clung tightly to her neck, me at her side. We inched toward the light through a maze of stone columns.

I tumbled down a short slope into a landscape of bones. Shadows careened as Jhem and Marad's lanterns swung ahead of us. Keirr slid down carefully. When Bellua paused at the lip of the basin, his light revealed the scale of the room.

Dragon skeletons filled a broad, shallow cavern—cupped rib cages, gnarled wings, coiled spines. Some were bleached white, others mummified in skins of leather. Columns of stone swallowed and preserved the oldest of them, a twisted architecture of bone and glass.

"Holy Avar," hissed Darid. "What a sight."

"It's a good sign," I said. "A dragon boneyard. Dragons came here to die. It means there's an exit to the outside nearby."

"Let's find it," said Cairek. "Many of these bones are partially eaten. Only two things I know of'll eat bone, if bone's all there is. One is rats, but there's no rats here."

Across the boneyard, Marad found a natural tunnel, just tall enough for our dragons to stand fully but not with a rider. Only Keirr was small enough that Mabir could stay in the saddle, lying forward on her neck and clutching the lower grips. We hurried through in order. I slowed just long enough to see that Cairek followed safely.

———

The passage rose steadily. The floor became smoother, then paved with huge flat stones. We entered a natural vault bigger than lantern light could reveal. Marad, Teff, Ansin, and Darid mounted up again. We spread out, instinctively separating ourselves as targets, but a new spectacle on the floor kept us to a narrow path. The acrid stench of rotting meat overpowered that of stone or water.

"Oh Gods," said Mabir beside me. "Please . . . open your lanterns that we might bear witness."

First Bellua, then Jhem, Cairek, and Marad opened the shutters on their lamps.

In every direction fading into shadow, we saw bones. Human bones. And dragon bones. The nightmare had a pattern. Manacles linked to spikes hammered into the stone filled the chamber. Black stains runneled into troughs or low spots. Here and there a shackle held the bones or mummified remains of a foot, possibly a leg bone or wing bone as well. What remained was small—finger bones, wrist bones, an occasional rib. The distinctive fragment of pelvis or skull. Morsels fallen by the wayside.

The spotlight of Marad's lantern traced up the clear trail to a workbench hung with spikes and chains. Tongs, needles. Saws and hammers. On a rack beyond it hung an abomination.

Jhem gasped aloud, and Tauman cursed under his breath. Cairek said, "Dear sweet Avar."

Wrists, legs, wings, torso were strapped to the rack. The man-portion above still glowed with horrible nonlife, the green light dim and failing in its hollows. The head lolled back, demonic eyes staring. The dragon below sagged as dead weight, pulling at the unfinished stitches where the two were joined. Dark as char, the dragon crumbled at the extremities and around the deep scars, exposing blackened skeleton. Clotted piles of cold cinder lay beneath it.

"Its maker never returned to finish what he started," I said.

"What?" said Bellua.

"The leader of the Harodhi, I killed him. He controlled the Horror that chased Darian and me. Look—don't you see? He was making Horrors."

"Sweet Korruzon," Bellua said. "One man made all those nightmares?"

"And how many more? We've seen dozens already." I tore my eyes from the carnage, turned to him and Cairek. "I thought he was their leader, and they were his soldiers, but these men weren't willing. They were shackled to the floor. Prisoners or even slaves. Meant to bond with dragons and become an army."

"An army of Horrors," said Cairek.

"And when the Harodhi leader died, there was no one to finish this monster. Without their shaman, or priest, or whatever he was, there was no one to control them, no one to stop the dozens of Horrors already made from"—I swallowed my gorge—"from killing and eating all these prisoners."

"How in this good world do you make a Horror?" asked Bellua.

"He may have brought many of them with him," I said. "But why steal qits? I'm missing something."

"It solves one mystery," said Cairek. "What happened to the Harodhi leader's lieutenants in the city by the lake."

"And begs another," I answered. "Who or what controls the Horrors now?"

The monster's mouth opened in a hiss like sand on glass. The head jerked upright. As it struggled against its shackles, a bow thumped. An arrow rocked its head back. The hiss became a screech. A second arrow pinned the head to the wall. The third shattered the neck below. It ceased moving. The screech died. The sick light faded. As it sagged, a chunk of dragon flesh fell away with a dry thud.

The last echoes died. Fren lowered his bow, staring at the thing.

From the belly of the tunnel behind us came a rasping shriek. Horrors still followed. Not close—not yet. But too near. "It's time to go," said Cairek.

From the other direction, blocking the way ahead, came the soft crunch of pads on bone. Almost immediately the images penetrated my head—pain, vertigo, sorrow, haunted memories in an overlapping crescendo. I doubled over in pain. Gasped.

"Edimmu," I said.

"Lady?" said Cairek.

"Oh dhalla, it's here."

"Sweet Asha," said Mabir.

"*It's here.*" I winced against phantom pain—the sting of an evil word, the cut of a blade, the cold touch of a Horror. "I know you now, Edimmu. Show yourself, monster!"

Instead it showed me the angry scowl of my mother. Darian's spite and scorn as he stomped on my fingers. Father's contorted face before he turned and left in search of his son. It drew on my guilt and shame and anger, turned it on me.

"I said show yourself, monster!"

We heard it before we saw it—bone snapping, rustle of wing. Then it stepped within range of our lanterns.

The Edimmu had changed. More substantial now, the thing once made of little more than mist and shadow had a core, like a blackened skeleton strung together with sinew inside a smoky bottle. I loosed two arrows at it faster than thought. Both struck it in what might have been the head, pierced it without sound, and emerged from the back like quills.

Rooting around in my head, pulling things from my memory to throw back at me like arrows. A fly on an eyeball. Vomit in clean water. The dead in the fishing village. Borgomos's desiccated corpse. Addai's threats. Father's absence.

"*I know you now, Edimmu,*" I shouted again.

We liked that one, it said angrily, shocking me. Did I hear that? Or only remember hearing it?

"One? What one?" I countered with memories of mother's smiles, of her attempts to speak with dragons, of Keirr teaching me about Bi-g and Smaw. Felt the trickle of blood on my lip.

That one, on the wall—its suffering was music. Interesting creations, these Horrors. We like them.

"Who are you?" I loosed another arrow. It vanished into the smoky body.

Us, in all our many names.

"What are you? Are you Dahak?"

The thing paused in its assault, as if intrigued by the idea of conversation. A respite, then images in my head of swarming darkness. Stone. A cavern full of colorless people and yearling dragons chained to the floor. Horrors standing motionless. The Harodhi shaman working over his table.

Not my memories. Its.

They awakened us. We came to see what they were doing. We knew that we belonged to it.

"I don't understand."

In answer, the assault resumed in a deluge. Horrors descended on the screaming prisoners. Tearing, swallowing, blood spraying. Screams extinguished, horrible pain. Delicious fear. I cried out and fell to my knees. Beneath it all, the Edimmu's pleasure in their torment. Its pleasure at pouring sick memories into my head.

I vaguely heard the beat of our bows. More barbs pierced its head to protrude from the back like spines. It showed no response.

I sought another remembrance: sunshine, qits at play, the joyous vertigo of flight. But the Edimmu clawed deeper into my mind. The meaty sound when an arrow pierces flesh—again and again. Stabbing at the face of a Horror. Screams, flames. The images built to a rapid-fire pace, then subsided all at once.

We learned much from watching them die. All of them.

I heard movement behind me. Mabir hobbled past. How did he get down from Keirr? I failed to grab the hem of his robe or a dangling harness strap. He placed himself between the Edimmu and me, squaring his shoulders. "Leave the girl alone."

The assault on my head ceased as the monster turned what might have been a face in Mabir's direction. The old man took another step forward. The Edimmu raised its head. Mabir tensed in pain, went rigid, fingers curled in agony. "We all know you, foul Edimmu!" he rasped.

Our bows thumped without pause. Arrows blossomed from its neck and chest. It didn't care.

Mabir stiffened even more, drawn straighter than I'd ever seen him. "You're but a phantom, a shadow," he croaked.

Oh, but you're wrong, said the creature. *We were a shadow, but we become.*

Mabir sucked in a deep breath. "The Harodhi shaman summoned you, didn't he?"

The Edimmu fell silent for several breaths, the cascade of imagery in my head slowing to a trickle.

I vaguely heard the beat of our bows resume. More barbs pierced its head to protrude from the back like spines. I realized that Mabir's intervention had distracted it, if only for a moment.

Marad and Teff on their dragons charged in from my right. Talons raked, teeth slashed. Dragons growled in surprise and pain. Stumbled. Retreated, shook their heads.

"The congregation of the Edimmu is the fearful, the desperate," Mabir said, between gasps. "It takes root in ignorance and grows in its own filth." He groaned and dropped to his knees. "You don't scare me, monster." He straightened and spread his arms wide. "Your presence gives me great joy, because you vindicate me—"

Mabir went rigid. Spittle foamed on his lips. Blood ran from his nose.

Do you fear us now? said the beast.

Somewhere, sobbing. Tulo.

"You always fail," whispered Mabir. "The Circle always turns." Then he moaned and fell to the floor.

I shouted and tried to stand. The Edimmu turned to me again. Knives sliced across my body, image of Keirr hanging from a scaffold, splayed open like—

I rejected it with the sound of Keirr's echoes in high places, the sight of sunlight sparkling on water, the smell of spring rain.

It showed me images of the time it followed three Horrors out into sunlight, just to observe. I saw myself in the Edimmu's memory, riding Keirr.

We learn from you, too.

Images pelted me. I crouched down against the pain. Things I'd shown it without meaning to: the aeries, Riat. Darian and Father. Everything this coalescing nightmare knew about the world outside came from its victims. From *me*. Every image I'd ever shown it, willingly or not, had a story, and I'd shown it everything I loved in an effort to turn back its madness. Cold terror curled down my spine. It had used my defenses to unlock my mind. But at the same time, I understood something it didn't mean for me to know.

Whether the Edimmu was ancient or not, its memories were new. Much as Mabir had once said—with a potential released or achieved, or some arcane line crossed, it *became*. It emerged into existence. It came to be. More than that, it remembered becoming. It recalled being drawn to the Harodhi shaman at work and to the carnage that followed when he no longer kept his Horrors contained. Something new to it: memories of its own. It seemed eager to share them with me.

I summoned one of mine. Of Cheien and Shuja tearing it to smoky tatters at our first encounter. At the same moment a volley of arrows from half a dozen bows struck. The Edimmu released me. I sagged onto my hands, crawled to Mabir, lay with my arm around his shoulders, gasping for breath.

The Edimmu reared up, and smoky wings spread wide. *You misread us, girl*, said the apparition. *We are new, but we are also ancient. We are timeless. And now we give direction to the monsters. We show them what you showed us. Your village, Riat. Your aeries. Your love for them.*

A screech sounded from behind us, and the first of the Horrors appeared. The Dragonry teams rained arrows on it. Marad and Teff seemed unsure what to do until the Edimmu stepped back into shadows.

I pushed to my feet. The Horrors charged.

"Go!" cried Cairek, backing up.

Yes, go! said the Edimmu.

Fren appeared beside me. Together we hauled Mabir onto Keirr. I got us both strapped in, gathered the dhalla's arms around my waist. I clung to his sleeves, to hold his unconscious body against my back. Fren loosed arrows, backing up, until Tauman called, *"Here,* Fren!" and he scrambled onto Rannu's back.

With everyone mounted again, we left the room of shackles, dashing into the tunnel. Jhem's lantern lit the way ahead, bobbing, careening. Screeches, roars, and shouts came from behind. A scream of terror. I peered over my shoulder to see Marad, then Cairek and Teff behind him in full retreat. The other Dragonry team was missing, but I'd lost their names. Ansin? Who was with Jhem? Keirr clicked and sounded, moving with amazing efficiency through black passages scarcely lit.

We hunger for what will come, said the monster.

"No more," I groaned. "Get out of my head."

The cascade of images changed. Memories stripped from other victims, their guilt and injuries and private torments. I cried out at the unexpected avalanche of pain, pulled tight to the saddle grips, fighting to keep my sanity. Light ahead. A crack. Late day in an eastern sky. That seemed right if this opened where I expected. Jhem and Tulo's silhouette, then a Dragonry team, then Bellua. Mabir's additional weight didn't slow Keirr at all, so I urged her onward. *"Faster!"*

The Edimmu faded behind me—thank the High Ones. Sky broadened before us, then opened all around. We galloped through the crack and into a golden evening, on a high, narrow ledge of Mt. Zurvaan. Jhem paused in front of me, and Bellua beside her. She looked back, Tulo wide-eyed over her shoulder. Darid just beyond set an arrow. I turned.

Cairek and Teff stood their mounts side-by-side across the opening of the cave, Marad behind them. A dragon Horror and rider fought them arrow, tooth, and talon. Dragons snarling, glowing chunks flying. Arrows rained into the monster. Taben rearmed Cairek's topbow with every swipe at the thing; the cables in the mechanism sang, the pulleys squealed. Cairek loosed just as fast. I couldn't shoot without letting go of Mabir's arms, but there was too much activity for a clean shot anyway. In frustration, Jhem, Tauman, and Fren held their arrows nocked.

The monster faltered, stumbled, then its entire front spilled out in a cascade. It fell into its fading embers like spent logs collapsing in a fire. Immediately another stepped up to claw through its wings and past its body.

"Hold the line!" Cairek fell back as Marad took his place. He yanked the magazine from his topbow and tossed it, slapped another in. Shouted back at us, "*Go*. Get back to the aeries. We'll hold—"

Screams and roars of pain and terror erupted from the mouth of the cave as a blackened monster bowled Teff and his dragon over. The Horror enveloped them, its wing obscuring savagery that ended in screams. Another Horror bulled out of the cave to join it in a frenzy of tearing. A third scrambled to get past them as they fed.

"*Go now!*" shouted Cairek.

I turned, saw Tauman spin, too. Jhem and Darid launched from the brink of the ledge. I pulled Mabir's arms tight and shouted, "*Go, Keirr*, catch Audax. Hurry!"

We dived off the precipice. Keirr rowed hard twice, spotted Audax, and pulled her wings tight, gliding on just the fingers of her wings and the fan of her tail, shooting like an arrow. "Jhem," I called as we pulled up alongside.

Her face snapped up to me.

"You have to take Tulo back to the Chamber of the Seasons and warn the rest of Cairek's men: The aeries are under attack. Keep Tulo safe. Hurry, before Horrors spot you."

"But Maia—"

"*You* have to do it, because you have to keep Tulo and his drawings safe."

"I'll go with them," shouted Darid, gliding on my left.

Jhem nodded and hunkered close to her saddle. Tulo clung to her, though his wide eyes stuck to me for as long as he could crane his neck my way. Then Audax, his charges, and his escort faded down into the mountain's shadow, out of sight.

I looked around me. Tauman, Bellua, and I remained, carrying Fren and Mabir.

"We go home!" I shouted, but I stole one last glance back at the mountain.

Two dragon teams stood out against the failing sky. At this distance I couldn't tell Cairek or any of his men from the Horrors.

Behind them appeared another winged shape, and another. Then four more. Then too many to count.

FORTY-EIGHT

W E   C A M E   I N   F A S T over the last ridge, spotted the aeries. A dragon and rider rose up to greet us. Addai.

He rode high, then turned to come in from above and behind. Gods, but his Torchbearer was fast. "What have you done?" he yelled. "Witch, what have you done?" But for Mabir on my back and the eyes of Staelan and his barrage, I didn't doubt Addai would rip me out of the sky.

I ignored him. Keirr opened her wings to brake in for a landing. "Staelan—Horrors come," I called. "Prepare your men!"

Keirr's head was high, ear frills deployed in alarm. Her eyes snapped to every loud or unfamiliar noise as Staelan's men ratcheted their machines into readiness. Spears clattered. Crossbowmen dashed into the log palisades. I patted her on the bond mark. "You're good, baby. You're fine. Shhh." She nodded, her left eye turned back to me, but her feet shuffled uncertainly. I dismounted and pulled her head down, wrapped my arms over her eyes. She laid down.

Addai landed a few yards away, and with fury in his eyes turned his mount toward us. Bellua and Zell dropped into the space between us, blocking his way. I heard Addai above the clatter and shouts. "What have you done? What is the meaning of this insubordination?"

Bellua's voice; words indiscernible, but the tones calmer, more measured. Tauman warning that Horrors were on their way, Addai snarling, "Stand aside."

As I undid the first buckle in the dhalla's harness, I saw Tauman in the corner of my eye and called to him. "We need to get the eggs and broodmothers into the ice vaults."

"Right." He grabbed one of Staelan's soldiers as he hurried past. "Give me your help."

"Sir?"

"Help me with these doors." He ran to the brood platform and unlatched one of the big rolling doors. All the buildings on the aerie had trapdoors leading to the old, original aeries, below the paddock in what was now the ice vaults. That's where I needed to take Mabir, as well. The doors to the broodhouse were but the first line of defense.

The ice vaults were our only sanctuary.

Bellua appeared at my side. "Are you hurt?"

I ignored him. He reached for a buckle on Mabir's harness but I pushed his hands away. "Leave him," I said. "I'll do it."

Bellua frowned and reached again, but I took hold of his elbow. With a single move, he twisted my grip around, and had me by my wrist. "Let me help," he said.

I wrenched my hand free. "Haven't you done enough?"

Addai's voice sliced into my hearing, but Bellua turned and stood between us again.

I released the last buckle and allowed Mabir to slump down onto my shoulder. As I stepped away from Keirr, his legs slid onto my other arm.

I'd never realized how frail he really was. A bundle of sticks covered in parchment. Wisps of hair. I started toward the broodhouse cradling him like a child. "Come along, Keirr," I said, and she jumped to her feet.

Staelan barked orders in the background. Latches clanked, men shouted. The rattle of a war machine turning on its gimbal. Another flurry of wings and a team landed, Marad with them. I looked to the sky for Cairek but saw only a terrifying mass of silhouettes against the deepening twilight. The broodhouse door stood partway open. Inside, Tauman cranked the windlass that opened the trapdoor to the ice vault. The two sides folded back like shutters in the floor.

Addai grabbed my arm, one of his Juza fighters behind him. "You're under arrest. Give the dhalla over and surrender."

I struggled to keep Mabir steady in my arms, but I wouldn't let Addai take him. I leaned against Keirr to keep my balance. "Go fall off a cliff," I said, my voice cracking. "You don't know what's happening here."

He looked startled for a moment, and then Bellua imposed himself again, breaking Addai's grip on me.

"You're under arrest, too." Addai snapped.

I stepped past Bellua, and faced Addai directly, my arms burning with the strain. "We're under attack," I rasped. "We have to get the eggs and broodparents into the ice vaults. We have about thirty seconds to do it. Do you really want to have this fight now?"

He tapped his Juza warrior's arm, then pointed at Mabir in my arms. "Take the priest." Before the man could act, Rov intervened.

"We don't have time for this, Prelate. Get your teams assembled, *now*."

Addai's mouth snapped shut. I turned and headed to the broodhouse before he could regain momentum. Cairek rushed up to greet me. Cairek—thank the Avar.

"You're safe," he said.

"For now. We've got to get eggs and mothers downstairs." I started toward the broodhouse again, but stumbled under the weight of Mabir. Cairek caught him and lifted him up.

"You lot," he said, to six of Staelan's men passing by, "come with us." The metal-clad step of soldiers followed us into the broodhouse.

The trapdoors lay open in the floor behind Athys's nest. Grus huddled on her eggs to the right, wings open wide in a threat display. Coluver keened in fear on our left. Athys picked up an egg gently with her teeth and passed it to one of Staelan's men. Another soldier carried an egg down the stair. I followed. "This way," I said to Cairek, and he followed me with Mabir in his arms.

Tauman had lamps lit already. He directed the soldier to place the eggs carefully in piles of straw arranged in the rearmost chamber of the vaults. When he saw Cairek carrying Mabir, Tauman broke open another bundle of straw and laid it in a corner. Cairek kneeled and let Mabir slide off his arms into the bedding, where Tauman covered him with his jacket.

I pushed past Cairek and felt for a pulse in Mabir's neck. His eyes fluttered open. He scanned the room with alarm, then confusion before finding my face. "Maia?" he rasped.

"You're in the aeries, in the ice vault. You're safe."

"Thank the Avar you're alive." He raised a hand and touched my upper lip. I felt the crust of blood there crumble under his fingertips. "Are you hurt, girl?"

"Yes."

"How badly?"

"I don't know. I have to leave you. Horrors are coming."

He groaned and let his hand fall. "I'm sorry. I meant only to take its attention so you could escape. You should have left me."

"You bought us time. You saved my life, dhalla. All our lives."

"Oh, sweet Asha," he whispered, staring blindly with rheumy eyes. "It invaded my mind. Such truths for a monster to show an old man in his last hours."

I swallowed a lump, bit back tears. "I have to leave you now, dhalla. But I'll be back for you. I promise."

He closed his eyes and nodded.

———

I bounded up the stair to the broodhouse. Keirr nuzzled me at the top, shivering with fear. I patted her on the neck. Bellua followed me with a crossbow in his hands, and Zell met him. A soldier passed me in the opposite direction with another egg. We didn't have half of them secured yet.

"We need to move faster," I shouted, and another soldier jumped to help. I grabbed the handle on the last paddock-side door to roll it closed. Fren stopped me with one hand. With the other he waved several of Staelan's foot soldiers in the paddock toward us, shouting, "This way. Hurry!"

The spectacle unfolding outside froze me in place. I watched from behind the door.

Roaring watchfires lit the paddock. Rov and his talon of eleven teams waited at the ready, along with Cairek and Marad, Addai and his seven remaining Juza. We had twenty-two teams, against how many? All six lancers, including Rov, took up positions on the perimeter. At his command, the mounts sat up on their haunches. Each rider attached a lance from a cache on their dragons' backs to the lance mechanism, then cranked it forward, butt first. It flipped up and around as it crawled over the dragon's shoulder and down to a stop on his belly. Guided by the dragons' forepaws, they made a fence of tall spikes pointing outward.

"Let them come," shouted Addai. "Draw them in!"

"Hurry!" I called out to Staelan's men in the paddock. Behind me I heard the broodmothers keening in fear, heard footsteps on the stair to the ice vaults.

Horrors descended on the paddock, charcoal black with portals glowing green. In the flutter of wing and failing light it became difficult to tell one from another. They hovered for an instant above the fighters below, and Staelan bellowed, "Loose!"

Half the crossbows released. Ballistae rocked from the top of the broodhouse, the storehouse, the tack house. A cloud of arrows, and two dozen bolts the length of tent poles, caught the Horrors in crossfire. Two of the beasts tumbled into the paddock. A lancer jumped up to meet the first, impaling it before it hit the ground. The lance released as the thing fell to the paving. The Dragonry rider immediately readied another spear. Topbows met the other Horror as it struggled against several bolts through wing and torso. The remaining monsters coiled above in a confused knot.

"Loose!" bellowed Staelan again. The rest of the archers released. Even the soldiers running toward our door paused long enough to let fly. The monsters scattered, screeching in anger, circled once, then descended on the ballistae crews. Passengers that had once been men dismounted, dropping through the log cages with swords and crossbows. Addai launched with his Juza. Cairek and Marad followed. Rov's teams sprang as one.

A Horror dragon clawed at the cage surrounding one ballista crew, on the storehouse roof across from me. A Dragonry team landed atop the Horrors, the dragon raking the monster's wings and shoulders, the rider shooting arrows. Another monster dropped out of the darkness and ripped the rider from his saddle with a horrible snap. It clutched the body close as it savaged the dragon's neck with its teeth. The dragon still struggled as the two Horrors ripped bites out of it.

I waved the soldiers to greater speed. "Don't look up. *Run!*"

Other monsters fell on the palisades. The men inside leveled oversized crossbows between the logs. Nightmares reached inside to claw at them. A man howled in terror as a Horror dragged him out to the paddock. Two other monsters joined it in a manic feeding squabble that lasted only seconds.

I heaved with all my strength to start the big door moving. Fren and the last soldier backed through, but the door was heavy and only inched toward closed. I could still see, as a Juza team landed near the squabbling Horrors and did something astounding. The Torchbearer took a breath, convulsed as if choking, then spat a thick gout of blazing liquid on the Horrors. They burst into flame where it clung, splashed fire where they stomped in puddles.

I felt a moment's hope. It struck me as a weapon that had to be directed carefully, since the blazing liquid clung to everything and burned white hot. Would it injure a Torchbearer too?

From the roof above came a loud crunch, tearing noises and screams, breaking timber. The clacking of many crossbows, the ring of swords. The body of a ballistaman fell to the paddock, missing an arm. A thud on the broodhouse roof shook the building. Shouts became screams as ripping and tearing commenced above.

Fren joined me and together we rolled the door closed at last. I threw the latch and set the bolt in the floor.

Sounds of battle raged outside. We heard the heavy *thud* of a ballistae firing, but the bolt casters still thunked and crossbows sang. Shouts and screams of pain cut the air. Heavy impacts shook the roof and the doors to the paddock. Something crashed against the doors on the cliff side of the broodhouse opposite, then crashed again. Scraping. Another blow. Athys growled restlessly, Rannu beside her. Coluver moaned in fear, wings spread in threat display, unsure which set of doors to defend, cliff or paddock? There were still eggs in the nests.

"Keep moving eggs!" I yelled. One of the soldiers snapped off orders to his men. Two of them grabbed up eggs and ran down the stairs to the ice vault, even as a third returned for another egg. The rest spread out down the length of the broodhouse with their oversized crossbows lowered.

I ran to Coluver's nest, but the cliffside door next to it boomed and shuddered. Scrabbling and scratching. Metal shrieked as a strap was torn off outside. Splinters flew into the chamber, pelting Coluver. She roared in anger. Talons wrapped around the edge of the door.

"*This way,*" I shouted, pulling my bow off my shoulder. Two of the soldiers came running with Tauman right behind. Fren nocked an arrow as the cliffside assault intensified.

The door flexed outward. I saw a rear leg pushing on the door next to it, causing it to buckle inward. It snapped and bounced out of its track, swung inward and swept Tauman and the soldiers off their feet. The door in front of me ripped off its track at the same time, wheels exploding from the overhead rail. It twisted aside and fell away into the night.

The dragon Horror hovered outside, recovering its balance. With each downbeat of its wings, glowing dust puffed out of the cavities in its body, along its neck and shoulders, up the arms of the wings. The rider on its back aimed a crossbow our way. Fren's arrow appeared in his ribs. I nocked, released, hit the rider as he shot. His bolt went wide, but struck Coluver in the wing. The monster pushed toward us, sculled to a landing. I shot two arrows into its body.

Tauman jumped up and released into the beast's maw, causing it to lurch. The rider fumbled reloading his bow. In the same time, Fren shot twice into the creature's head. I put arrows into its neck. More bolts struck from out of sight above—a topbow repeating. The beast veered aside and dropped out of view. A Dragonry team flashed by in pursuit. Another Horror swept in to the doorway before us.

"Damn it!" said Tauman.

I loosed, striking the monster's face between nostril and eye. Fren put an arrow through its cheeks as two soldiers flanked him, spears at the ready. The dragon turned and lurched toward them. Fren fell back, shooting, as the soldiers set their spears against it. The beast swatted one of them aside—off the cliff into darkness with a cry. More of our arrows sprouted from its neck and head. The other soldier plunged his spear into the beast's open mouth as it snapped at him. He pushed forward until its death throes ripped the weapon from his grasp. The rider failed to escape its harness before the dragon spilled off the edge.

The next cliffside door in line already hung broken and loose. A Horror swept it aside as if it were a curtain of paper, exposing Rannu, Athys, and their clutch.

Rannu launched into the monster before it could regain its balance, took it by the throat, and drove it backward. They tumbled out of sight below the lip of the platform. "Rannu!" Tauman cried, and stepped toward the precipice to see. Fren grabbed him by the belt and pulled him back. Another Horror wheeled into the doorway.

We loosed arrows as rapidly as we could. Athys roared by Tauman's side, Keirr keened beside me. A blizzard of arrows came down from the aerie roof above as well. The creature flinched backward as a score of barbs struck home. Its rider slumped in his harness with arrows sticking up from shoulders and helmet. The dragon turned and dropped from sight.

The assault paused for a brief moment. Horrors dived and veered in and out of firelight. Sounds of battle came from above and behind. Tauman turned my way. "Maia?"

"I'm fine," I said, though my voice trembled. My arms shook as I nocked another arrow. I made a quick scan of the situation: all three broodmothers remained in their nests, to defend eggs still waiting to be moved downstairs.

The onslaught began again. A new beast lit in front of me and surveyed the platform as it clung to the lip. Almost as quickly, a lancer dropped from above, impaling it. The lance broke away and the dragon crashed onto the monster's haunches, driving it to the paving. He took a wing in each forepaw, chomped down on the rider. Snapped his head from side to side like a terrier on a rat. The Horror came apart in his harness, stumps glowing like coals, fading as they scattered. The dragon spat the thing's torso aside with a roar of pain.

Another monster dropped down on them from above. The lancer's experienced mount twisted over on his back, breaking one Horror's wings against his body, grappling mouth to mouth with the second. The entire mass of three snarling, struggling dragons fell away from the lip.

The onslaught paused again, though we heard combat on the roof and in the paddock. Logs tumbling, masonry breaking. We all looked at each other—fear and grim determination on each face.

"Eggs," I said.

Four soldiers stood ready. I passed eggs to them from Athys's nest as quickly as I could, and they hurried down the stair.

I started after them with my arms full, when the paddock-side door next to Coluver's nest shook from a heavy blow. She roared in terror. The door shattered and two burnt dragon Horrors lunged through. Before we could react they grappled Coluver, tearing and biting. I put Athys's eggs back in her nest. Fren and Tauman shot without effect as the soldiers tried to reload their crossbows. The Horrors pushed Coluver off the precipice and out of sight.

"*No no!*" I cried, and Keirr moaned in fear.

Man-Horrors followed them in from the paddock, five or more bearing curved swords.

Soldiers lined up on either side of us. "Lead crispy," shouted one of them. "Loose!" They all released at the Horror in the front. I added two arrows of my own, as did Tauman and Fren. Only when the ninth and tenth arrows pierced torso and skull did it finally collapse. We reloaded, retreating toward the stair, as two soldiers closed on the monsters with swords drawn. One swung at a neck, but failed to penetrate the armor. The Horror chopped the man's arm off with a downward stroke. The soldier shrieked, but the man-thing grabbed him by the throat and silenced him with a crushing grip. The second soldier hacked at the creature, lopping off its arm in turn. Green glowing pieces fell from the wound.

I'd seen this once before, in the caves; wounds that would fell an ordinary man didn't faze the Horrors at all.

The monster turned to the man without pause and struck, one-armed, at his shield, parried another strike at its neck with the stump of its arm. The next Horror in line pushed past the reach of the soldier's sword in a rush and grappled him. He screamed at the icy burning touch as the things bore him down.

From the paddock, a Dragonry team charged through the creatures, the mount sweeping them up in its forelimbs, roaring at the freezing pain of contact. It pushed them through the broodhouse and off the precipice on the other side.

The team turned to face the paddock again. Cairek! My heart lifted. Then a pair of dragon Horrors charged. Taben sat up on his haunches, cocking Cairek's topbow with his elbows, and Cairek cut loose. Taben danced a rhythm that kept the topbow fed while nimbly sidestepping the creatures' attacks. He lured them sideways, then around. They followed him when he took off again. We had time for a few deep breaths.

Fires burned everywhere. Some of the palisades still stood, but were under assault. Bodies and pieces of bodies littered the paddock, dragon and human alike. Among them one of the Torchbearers lay crumpled face down with only half a rider in the saddle.

The door to the paddock beside me boomed and rattled. Claws reached around the edge and ripped it out of its tracks. As the Horror steadied its momentum to attack, a Torchbearer dropped on it from above and broke the Horror's wings efficiently before ripping the rider apart. With the monster pinned beneath, the Torchbearer bit down and snapped its neck behind the skull.

Addai again. He turned, spotted me. Galloped to my side and turned to face the paddock. "There are too many of them, and they double up on the Juza. Their burning touch makes melee dangerous, but arrows are ineffectual. We can't hold out. Get your eggs moved, and we'll follow you in."

I nodded, but suddenly the cliffside door before Grus rolled violently aside. A Horror filled the space beyond, screeching. Grus spread her wings to guard her nest, roaring defiance. The monster landed, lunged at her. She met it with claws and teeth.

Addai charged on his Torchbearer, but another creature burst in, blocking his path. They broke into furious battle, obstructing my view of Grus. I dashed to my right to see her in full grapple with the monster. I targeted its body, afraid to aim for a more critical spot for fear of hitting our dam. They wrestled in huge sweeps and lunges. I ducked under Grus's wing, made for her nest to use it as cover and guard her eggs.

It took that little time for the Horror to drag Grus off the platform into darkness. The beast battling with Addai broke away from him and leapt into the darkness as well. Only Keirr's whimpers kept me from falling to my knees in grief. I took her head in my arms. "Oh gods, baby."

Bellua directed Zell down the stair, following beside her with an egg under each arm. I didn't see Cairek. Fren and the soldiers sent arrow after arrow into the paddock.

Horrors everywhere—on the storehouse roof, dismantling war

machines in search of flesh. Fighting over scraps by the water trough. Men in the palisades between broodhouse and tack house battled still. Dragonry yet flew; I spotted Rov once, and Marad. And others. But we lost ground even inside the broodhouse. A soldier ran up to me with two eggs in his arms. "We'll never get them all," he said, and dashed down the steps. Behind him, Coluver's nest and her remaining eggs vanished under a swarm of man-Horrors.

"I'm out of arrows!" shouted Fren, lowering his bow and pulling his long knife. He backed toward the stair as man-things charged across the paddock.

Two Horrors landed on the broodhouse platform. Addai directed his mount into a defensive retreat, dismounted and collected two eggs from Grus's nest. He passed them to me. "Everybody downstairs!" he called.

Keirr tailed me into the stairwell. A short string of soldiers followed, then Fren. Addai backed down, his Torchbearer trading swipes with something out of sight above. Fren cranked on the windlass for the trapdoors above, but a dragon Horror crawled down the stairs, its face slashed to glowing green tatters. Bows snapped and arrows sprouted from its head, neck, shoulders. Vulnerable in the stairwell, unable to bring its foreclaws into play, Staelan's men stabbed it with spears. Finally the Torchbearer locked its teeth on the monster's face and shook. The thing collapsed, blocking the stairwell. On its back the stump of a rider crumbled into cinders.

Shrieks sounded from above. Five or six of Staelan's men were up there yet. A heavy boom. A hiss. Scrabbling. Steel clashed. A war machine shook the aeries with its heavy release. Roars and screeches opposed each other. Shouts bled into screams. The thud of the big machines dwindled. A few moments' silence. A topbow cranking. A roar.

The screams ended.

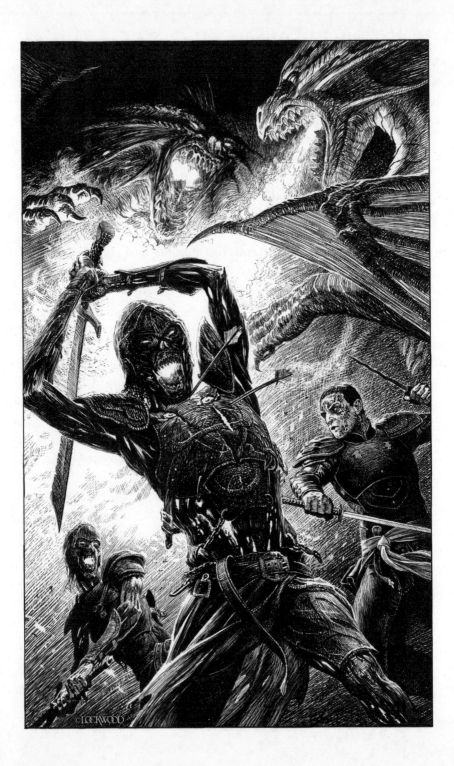

Tauman met Fren with two quivers of arrows. Athys stayed close by him, keening with fear and concern.

"Rannu?" I said.

Tauman shook his head. "I don't know. Grus or Coluver either." He wouldn't let his eyes linger on mine. He handed me a quiver. "This is all we have, the entire cache in the ice vault. There's two more like it in the winter stable and the Manor, but they might as well be in Avigal."

Then he turned to Addai. Hesitated for a moment, and finally held the last quiver out to him. He didn't take it immediately, and when he did, Tauman didn't let go until their eyes had met. "You still have a full quiver. I give this to you for one reason: You are Juza, and your duty is to defend us."

Father wouldn't have made the offer, I thought to myself.

Tauman turned away before Addai could respond. "Bellua, and the rest of you—I'm sorry. I have no crossbow ammunition."

Bellua nodded, touching his quiver. He had three quarrels left. Staelan's men checked their count.

Addai scowled at Tauman for a moment before he turned to Staelan's men, pointing. "All the crossbow ammunition to you four. Divide it evenly. You'll alternate shooting and reloading by pairs at my command until you're out. You three on spear."

"Yessir."

Addai pointed at the big rolling doors at the north end of the vaults. "The original brood platform. This is where we're most vulnerable."

"They've not been opened in decades," said Tauman. "And the space between the inside and outside doors is filled with straw. They're nailed shut. It will slow them down, at least—we'll get that much warning."

The sound of a repeating topbow rang down the stairs, then faded. Something shook the broodhouse. Pebbles chattered down onto the dead thing in the stairwell.

I felt Addai's burning gaze before I turned. He stared at me for several seconds, his face unreadable. Then he glanced at Tauman. My brother watched him. So did Fren and Bellua. With expectant faces, Staelan's soldiers looked back and forth between the lot of us.

"Now's not the time, Addai," I said.

"Now is always the time."

Bellua started toward us.

From the direction of the old brood platform came a muffled thud, then scratching and splintering, hushed by the barricade of straw.

"Gods," said Tauman. "There go the outer doors."

A pair of topbows chattered. Voices rang out. Crushing noises. Roars.

"We have some friends out there yet," said Fren.

Addai finally turned away from me. "Be ready to target all shots on the first breach of the inner doors," he said. "If we have to retreat, use the ice shelves as cover. If we're lucky, they'll stop for the easy meal of frozen meat."

We lined up, arrows nocked. Arms and legs drawn as tight as crossbows. Athys, Keirr, Zell, and Addai's Torchbearer spaced themselves evenly along the expanse of doors—wings tucked tight, teeth bared, each by his or her bonded rider. Staelan's archers watched the stair. Fren stood at my side.

The sounds grew clearer, closer. Ripping. Fighting. The inner doors shook once. Scraping and clawing. Keirr growled low, a menacing threat I'd never heard from her before.

Crossbows snapped. "The stair!" shouted one of the soldiers. A man-thing pinioned with crossbow quarrels fought its way past the dead dragon Horror in the stairwell.

"Don't let them close," said Addai. "Aim!" Two bowmen stepped back to reload as their counterparts stepped forward. "Release!" he shouted, and they shot in turn. The Horror jerked at the impacts but came on.

"Aim! Release!" A soldier with a spear stabbed the thing in the chest and pushed, held it at bay long enough for Addai to repeat the rotation again. *Aim! Release!* Two more arrows struck it, but it chopped at the spear with its sword. I didn't have an angle for a shot. *Aim! Release!* Another man-thing crawled down the stairwell behind it.

A thunderous *boom* rattled the inner door to my left. Splinters pelted me. The door split vertically, bolts flying. A dragon-Horror's face and forearm started to push through, but the straps on the door held it in place. A soldier dashed up to hack ineffectually at its armored neck. Arrows bloomed on cheek and snout, and it shook its head, screeching in anger. The wheels ripped out of their track and the heavy door became a trap for the monster, dragging it face-first to the floor, crushing the soldier beneath it. It struggled to free itself while the rider slid down from the saddle, drawing a black sword. An extra skirmisher dropped down from behind him.

Addai's Torchbearer leapt to the attack. It crushed the rider like an insect, assailed the exposed neck of the creature. Addai shot the skirmisher, dropped his bow, then met the thing with sword and dagger.

The next door to the ancient broodhouse shook and cracked.

Aim! Release! from my right—one of Staelan's soldiers had taken up the litany. Fren's bow sang. A howl. Addai fought in slow retreat. His sword and dagger flashed with terrifying efficiency. I kept my attention on the broodhouse door, bow drawn, waiting for a target of opportunity. The charred head of a dragon came around the edge. I pinned it. Tauman and Bellua loosed as well. The door shattered, and the monster charged in.

Athys met it, slashing and biting. Cried out in pain at the Horror's icy touch. Zell joined her. Bellua's crossbow snapped. Tauman's bow sang. A staccato rhythm punctuated the noise from somewhere behind the monsters—a topbow. Could it be Cairek?

Aim! Release! I wouldn't risk a look at the stair, but the repetition of the order lifted me—Staelan's men still fought.

Addai dropped his opponent at last only when, armless, legs mangled, it stumbled to its knees and presented its neck. Bellua released his final quarrel, dropped his crossbow, drew his sword. Addai's Torchbearer ripped through the neck of the trapped Horror, and it ceased struggling.

Another dragon-beast loomed out of the shadows behind it, but stopped in its tracks, dragged backward. It freed itself, turned, and backed into the ice vault to face Cairek and Taben before it. Cairek aimed for the monster's head with his topbow as Taben slashed and grappled. Addai's Torchbearer attacked it from the rear. Addai released arrows into it at incredible speed.

Tauman and Fren targeted the monster facing Athys and Zell. Chunks of cinder fell away from its chest, but it battled on as yet another Horror pushed past it into the vault.

The Torchbearer redirected his attack to face it. The rider, already free of harness, jumped down to the platform and charged Addai. A skirmisher slid down as well, and came at me.

I shot, and shot again. Torso, neck—but it came on, raising a dark curved sword over its head. With the impossible inferno glowing out of the chasms in its flesh, it seemed that it ought to burst into flames. I put an arrow through its forehead. On it came. I ran into the shelves and fell over a fallen package. The man-thing opened its horrid, lipless mouth in a rasping scream, and drew back to hack me in two.

But Keirr chomped down on its hands, the sword flew aside, and she shook it until both arms ripped free. She struck at its head, crunching down on the helmet and shaking the thing again. She screamed in agony, but refused to let go until the head separated and the thing finally dropped lifeless to the floor. She positioned herself over me and roared defiance, anger, pain, fear—all at once.

I crawled to my feet in time to see Addai's Torchbearer crush the skull of the dragon Horror in its jaws. Cairek and Taben took down the last, crushing the fallen door to splinters in the process. Addai, covered in his own blood, dispatched the rider.

Silence followed briefly, then two more Dragonry teams landed on the ancient platform and made their way in: Rov and one of his men, then Marad and a pair of Juza. All of them, man and beast alike, bled from multiple gashes.

"How many are left?" asked Addai.

"We're it," said Rov. "In even numbers we're overmatched. They've slaughtered us. We're out of lances and down to the last of the topbow ammunition. This is where we make our stand."

I paused only long enough for a single deep breath, then started pulling arrows from dead things to be reused. The Horrors' burnt flesh gave up the arrows more easily than I expected. Fren and Staelan's men did likewise, while Tauman and Bellua looked to their dragons' wounds.

Zell bled profusely from chest and shoulders, neck and face. She lowered her cheek to Bellua's, and he held her head close. "I'm so sorry, my poor faithful girl," he said quietly. She licked his face.

Taben stepped in front of me, and Cairek leaned down. "Are you hurt, Mai—my lady?" His eyes were wide.

I shook my head no, and put my arm around Keirr's neck.

"Thank the Avar. Stay behind me." He turned Taben around to face the shattered doors.

Enough twilight remained to reveal the far side of the old broodhouse, opened through to the outside for the first time in generations. The awakening stars struck me like they never had before. This might be the last time I ever saw them. I smelled the ancient straw and dust, sweat and blood, the carrion char of the Horrors. Felt the air in my lungs and the beat of my heart.

Silhouettes obscured the view almost immediately, overlapping each other. Cold light burning in deep hollows of corrupted flesh made it hard to tell each creature from the next. Hisses and growls rang off the stone.

Rov, his man, and the Juza dismounted and took up positions behind their mounts. They faced the Horrors with nocked arrows or leveled spears. Marad and Cairek stayed mounted to use their topbows.

I made a quick count—I had eight arrows. "Get behind me, Keirr."

The monsters advanced, and we pelted them with arrows until Addai shouted, "Hai!" The military dragons—Juza and Dragonry alike—leapt to the attack. A display of power and ferocity erupted before us. Dragons met Horrors with teeth and claws. Cheien was a fury, seemingly immune to the monsters' icy touch. Cairek shot the last of his ammunition, unholstered a spear to fend off a creature as Taben slashed in measured retreat. A pair of screeching Horrors overpowered Marad and his mount. They vanished with a cry behind a curtain of torn wings. One of the Juza Torchbearers attempted to spit fire as it grappled, but it was spent. Two Horrors bore it down.

We were all nearly finished. I had three arrows left. Addai turned to me, glancing at Tauman and Fren and Bellua. His eyes were wide, his mouth hardened with resolve. He seized his sword and dagger—a wicked, serpentine thing—and turned his back on the battle. His lips parted as his breath quickened. He started toward me.

I nocked an arrow and drew. "Don't do it, Addai." He didn't slow.

Bellua stepped between us with his sword drawn. "Don't do it, brother. You're wrong."

Addai halted, looked up at him. "She's seduced you, Bellua. Don't try to stop me."

I sensed the Edimmu, on the outskirts of awareness.

Bellua kept his sword lowered, but his shoulders were squared. "There's more going on than you comprehend. Don't—"

"Stand aside," Addai said. "This ends now. Can't you see what's happening right before your eyes?"

Fren ran to my side, an arrow nocked in his bow. One of Addai's Juza warriors drew on Bellua. Fren aimed at the Juza. I targeted Addai.

The Edimmu intruded on the edge of thought. *How interesting,* it said.

The din of battle filled the next few seconds—snarls and roars, shouts of fear and snapping crossbows. Thud, crack, and moan.

"Stand aside," Addai repeated. "Or I will come through you."

We like this one.

"Edimmu," I gasped, my heart pounding.

Addai feinted at Bellua, knocked his sword aside, then stabbed him full in the ribs with his dagger. An instant later, an arrowhead burst out of Bellua's back in a gout of blood, buried to the red fletching under his heart. He slid off Addai's blade with a moan and crumpled to the paving. Addai's Juza companion whipped another arrow into his bow. Fren's arrow thunked square into his chest, dropping him. I released and struck Addai shallow in the ribs under his left arm. Fren and I reloaded. Addai came at me.

Keirr jumped in his path, blocking our shots. She lowered her head and hissed with anger. Addai hesitated an instant. I took half a step to my right and let loose. With unnatural speed, Addai knocked my arrow aside with his sword. He spun, took a step toward Keirr with blade leveled shoulder high.

From where he lay, Bellua lunged at Addai and stabbed him in the meat of his left hamstring. Addai cried out, stumbled, turned. Raised his dagger for a second strike at Bellua.

His Torchbearer screamed with pain. He looked up to see his dragon stumbling backward, overborn by a monstrous Horror with its teeth locked on the dragon's neck, shaking and tearing.

Looming beyond was a smoky ruin, a shadowy semblance of a dragon's rotting corpse. The Edimmu. It was here.

I drew, aiming for Addai's heart while he stood entranced, but the Edimmu's assault cascaded into me like a dam bursting. Every death of the last hour played in my head in a torrent. All the terror and pain, fear and rage and regret. The cold sting of every blade, the rip and shear of tooth and talon. I fumbled my last arrow, dropped my bow. Fell to my knees with a shout of anger and pain. I heard Cairek call my name.

Addai dropped to his knees, facing the Edimmu. His weapons slipped from fingers contorted with agony.

Through the haze I saw Cairek and Taben charge the Edimmu, only to be intercepted by a dragon Horror of immense size, with a man, howling like a damned thing, grafted to its chest. Cairek leveled his spear. "Maia—take cover!" he cried through teeth clenched with pain.

I couldn't move. The Edimmu turned its head to me. *If you see the Avar as that which you revere, why do you see us?*

The bizarre conversational tone of the question underlay images of disembowelment, decapitation, and other sick pleasures I scarcely understood. Visceral. Sexual. Sensations stripped from other minds, thrown at me out of context.

Blinded by red. Runnel of blood on my lip. "I also saw the Summer Dragon," I gasped, trying in vain to remember how that felt, to see that majesty clearly.

It ignored me. *We know you now. We know your scars. They run deep.*

The Edimmu released me. Turned its misty head to Addai. I collapsed onto my hands, breathless.

Look at this one. Addai groaned and spasmed, as if the Edimmu shook him by his soul. *He has seen many things. His scars are profound. But his knowledge runs deep. We use the first to acquire the second, you see. What a vessel full of hatred, distrust, and fear this one is. But so wise in the ways of death.*

Addai's Torchbearer crumpled beneath the onslaught. The Prelate cried out in anguish, powerless to move.

The Edimmu's unrestrained joy at Addai's torment washed through me like fire. Like needles. Like acid. Scouring my nerves.

I saw Fren in the corner of my right eye, his face distorted with agony, but shooting, advancing. He fumbled an arrow, reached for another. Did the Edimmu attack him as well? Cheien wrestled with a monster, crashed into the shelving. Blocks of ice and packages of meat flew. Shouts and cries.

A scream from Cairek turned my head. The Horror struck at him with its teeth. He stabbed it in the mouth with his spear. It recoiled, ripping the spear from his hands, spat it aside. Then it took him in its teeth, and with a snap of its head, ended his cry. Taben roared in fury as the monster ripped his bondmate from the saddle and leapt off the precipice. Taben howled in anguish and followed it into the night.

I fell to my side, scream drawn out into a sob.

There, you see? Another scar for you.

I tried again to picture Getig, the Summer Dragon, in my head. Blood and death blunted his presence. Fiery cold and exhaustion blurred his image. But I reached for it. Needed it. The Edimmu showed me my need, mocking. Showed me Cairek's death again. And again.

I had to answer, somehow. I showed it the Dahak, in the last panel of the frieze in the hidden amphitheater, testament to the failure of its kind.

The Edimmu countered with the collapse of the glacier, burying the frieze and with it my hopes against the Rasaal. *This much is true: only change is constant. Anything can happen.*

It dragged images through me like barbed strands of cattle-wire.

Mabir held in rictus, Bellua sliding from Addai's rippled dagger. Cairek torn from his saddle again and again. All of them victims of the Edimmu.

Yet the apparition never touched any of them. Not even me. Not physically. It only ever poured malignance directly into our heads. That's all it did. All it was. The Avar of Fear. Despair. Desolation. Dark emotions. It wanted my fear, *needed* my fear. Fed and guided my fear.

I would give it my anger instead. I found the rage beneath my tears and showed the Edimmu the statue in our ruins of the White Dragon defeating the Dahak. The Edimmu paused for the space of a blink.

"Mabir was right," I gasped, clinging to that moment of hesitation. "You always fail."

Do we?

Cheien backed away from a ferocious onslaught, deeper into the shelving. A Horror had one of the Torchbearers cornered against the straw, wings in tatters, no longer able to produce its cough of flame. Tauman knelt with head clutched in hands as Athys and Zell traded swipes with a monster. The Edimmu showed me snippets of history it had gleaned from every mind it violated. A landscape of war, endless.

You will see your age of dragons give way to an age of Horrors. The world will be changed forever.

I sobbed but pushed up to my knees. "When you were nothing but ripples of shadow, Shuja and Cheien tore you apart. You're little more than smoke now."

The creature drew its head back, cocked it at me. Two colorless lights glimmered out of the smoke, like the first representation of eyes.

And yet we become stronger.

I grabbed the arrow I'd dropped, panting, nocked it to my string. "Mabir said you were but a phantasm. A shadow."

Oh, but we are so much more.

I shot the Edimmu in the neck. The arrow emerged out the back, one of many. The thing had a mane of arrows. It stepped toward me. But then the tenor of battle shifted abruptly.

The Horrors that had advanced on us spun to face the slash and tear of new opponents behind them. Topbows sounded from outside.

The creature devouring Addai's Torchbearer went down suddenly, as a riderless dragon attacked it from behind. "Rannu!" wheezed Tauman. Alive still. Our broodsire ripped at the monster's flanks with claws and teeth. Ajhe, Darid, and the remaining four of Cairek's talon from the caverns burst into the lamplight with topbows cranking. Jhem and Darid had brought reinforcements.

The Edimmu released me. Addai collapsed face-first to the floor. The Horrors all hesitated, dancing for an instant in confusion. Rov and Ajhe and all their teams sprang forward. I pushed to my feet, saw Fren on his hands and knees nearby. I took a fistful of arrows from his quiver. He shook his head and started to rise.

Our dragons brought the last of the monsters down. Tauman staggered to his feet. Fren shot at the Edimmu from his knees, and the Edimmu retreated a step as our dragons advanced.

I nocked an arrow. Turned to locate Addai's Juza. One down already, with Fren's barb in his chest. I spotted the other even as he pulled an arrow. For me? I wouldn't take the chance. I shot him in the ribcage. As he staggered and fought to raise his bow I let loose again. His arrow dropped to the paving and he fell.

Then I turned to where Addai struggled to his knees. He picked up his sword and dagger. Turned his head and looked at me with nostrils flared. I shot him, point blank. He tried to stand. I shot him again. When he toppled I shot him a third time.

Our dragons closed on the Edimmu, shaking their heads and growling but pressing forward. The apparition looked back at me with its new eyes.

You are young and strong. Resilient. But you are tied to another, and another through that one. Images of Aru and Darian, their bond marks.

I shot an arrow into the monster. Another. Where before it had seemed futile, now it jerked with each impact.

You draw on them. But they are your weakness. And your deepest scar. We will find them and open that wound again. You'll acquire more scars. We'll rip at them until one day you won't be able to resist us.

As our dragons tore into the apparition with claws and teeth, forcing it to act in its own defense at last, I showed it the Summer

Dragon, recalling the moment when Darian and I stood in wonder, our world rocked off its center by His very presence. It hurt to think of Darian, but we shared that moment at least. That amazing moment.

"My scars give me strength," I said.

The roars and growls of our dragons grew in confidence. The nightmare retreated to the precipice, howled in our minds. It stumbled, then seemed to crumble and break apart before it fell from sight.

F I F T Y

KEIRR LICKED MY FACE ONCE before I threw my arms around her. I sobbed into her neck for several minutes, shaking with exhaustion and spent fury.

Other voices drew me back. Tauman hugged me briefly, then ran to Athys and Rannu. Fren knelt beside Bellua, propping his head up with a hand. I stumbled to his side too, and kneeled. Blood ran from his mouth and nose, stark red against the deathly blue-white of his flesh. He looked at me through slitted eyes. "*Maia,*" he whispered.

"I'm here."

"I'm sorry," he said, and stiffened against pain, grimaced as he labored to take a rattling breath. "Forgive me. Please forgive—"

He would be dead soon. He knew it. There was nothing any of us could do. And now at his end, after all he'd done, he wanted forgiveness. I wouldn't speak words to absolve him of the horrible mess he made. Two days ago, I'd have saved an arrow for him.

He closed his eyes, as if he understood my hesitation. "Faith," he rasped, "was a cage I could not see." He shook, and blood bubbled from his lips. He collapsed, any other words coming only as the sigh of a final breath.

My opportunity to give him solace had passed. I met Fren's eyes. Hard. Sad. Weary beyond words. He dried my cheek with a thumb.

"I have to check on Mabir," I said, and he nodded.

As I stood, I caught sight of Addai's face, one cheek pressed into the floor, blood congealing under his lips. His small eyes stared with frozen terror into an abyss. I staggered, then ran to the back of the vaults, to the corner where Mabir lay. Darkness. Thin light approached—Tauman with a lantern. Someone followed in his shadow, and another beyond.

The dhalla lay as we'd left him, beneath Tauman's jacket, hands folded across his chest.

"Mabir," I said, reaching out to touch his cheek.

His flesh was cold and dry, like the skin on cooling candlewax. Eyes stared calmly at nothing at all.

"Is he gone?" asked Jhem.

I turned in surprise, took in her face. Grabbed her in my arms and squeezed her tight. *"Yes,"* I whispered.

She held me close and wept. Shortly, I felt Tauman's hand on my shoulder and heard Tulo's muffled sobs.

We found Coluver's body at the base of the pinnacle. Nearby, Taben stood guard over Cairek and would allow no one near. Jhem wanted only to tend to her beloved dam, but Taben chased her back. We knew a rider's death could sometimes make it necessary to put the mount down before it became crazed and dangerous, but we scarcely had the manpower to put Taben down. Or the will. Eventually, Taben curled up beside his bondmate and succumbed to his own wounds. Only then were we able to retrieve Cairek's body.

Jhem cradled Coluver's head in her lap and wept for hours.

Zell stood vigil over Bellua, though she let us remove the arrow and lay him out straight. She keened sadly as we packed his body in ice and led her back to the winter stable. She allowed Tauman and me to tend her wounds once we had treated Rannu and Athys. Then she folded her head under her wing and keened through the night.

Grus disappeared. We searched far and wide, but found no body. With Father and Shuja gone, her brood almost entirely demolished, and the aeries in ruin, perhaps she had snapped like a strained bowstring and fled. I hoped so, because it would mean she was alive and might return.

Local craftsmen collected the bodies of the dragons. Their leather was not a resource to be wasted. The meat, organs, and bones all had value, too. We knew that, but we couldn't watch when they came for Coluver and Taben.

Jhem with Audax. Tauman with Athys and Rannu. Keirr and me. Rov and Cheien and one of his teams. Ajhe, Darid, and four others from Cairek's talon. Fren. Seven of Staelan's thirty-two men, but not Staelan himself. Not one of the Juza. That was it. We were the survivors.

The village went largely unscathed, as did the manor house and the winter stable. We gathered the charred remains of the Horrors in an empty field and burned them. It was impossible to make a proper count, but there were at least thirty dragon skulls in the mix.

The Edimmu left a corpse as well. The rotting skeleton of a very large dragon lay at the bottom of the pinnacle, crusted with dried sinew and tatters of leather. It might once have lain in the boneyard hidden in the mountain. After some debate, we burned it and buried the ashes in a deep hole, far from the farms and aeries, then capped the grave with a slab of stone and left it unmarked.

Fren and Tauman started repairs to the broodhouse. In the meantime, we placed the remaining eggs in the winter stable nests. Out of twenty-nine eggs, sixteen survived.

Rannu's wounds kept him out of the brood nest. He fell ill and spent several days in a feverish state. We bound his wings to his side with netting and shackled his legs to the floor, for his own protection—and ours. We'd never done that before, but in his delirium he might well be dangerous.

Tulo hadn't yet begun to learn the graving arts, but Mabir had taught him well, and his knowledge of medicine was deep. He applied poultices to the strange cold-burns sustained from contact with the Horrors. Mouths had to heal before dragons could eat well again. He set up a large iron pot in the paddock and made gallons of herbal broths for all the wounded. He helped the riders dress their dragons' wounds, even assisting as they closed gashes with needle and sinew. He was tireless.

Rannu recovered after a week and lapped up Tulo's broth eagerly until he was strong enough to stand again. Audax took Coluver's death hard; Jhem had her hands full even as she grieved. Every time I saw her, there were tears in her eyes. She and Audax spent hours alone together in the air. She slept by his side.

I watched the skies for Shuja's familiar silhouette, angry at the same time that Father had left us to face monsters—Horrors and Juza alike—without him. And I worried about the Juza companion Addai had sent with him. Was Father still alive?

Meanwhile, Keirr took to egg-sitting, happy to nestle the remaining eggs in Coluver's nest.

All around the paddock was activity—repair work especially—which meant tradesmen and wagons and noise. But in the winter stable Jhem's time of "quiet expectation" returned. Even Zell responded. She started to eat again and observed the order of each day as if she saw it for the first time.

Rov sent Darid to Avigal as courier with a report. "If the Ministry acts quickly—and they will—" he said, "we should expect reinforcements by Brood Day."

———

I hadn't shed a tear since the end of the battle, not even when Mabir and Cairek were cremated. I began to wonder what was wrong with me.

I felt burned out. Hollow. Like a Horror. The comparison made me shudder with fear. I might have slid into a darker place but for Keirr. She always greeted me with licks and happy purrs, shielded me with her wing when we walked together, allowed me to hug her constantly. She keened unhappily if I left her alone for more than a few minutes.

The sky was our greatest solace. The caress of the wind, the rhythm of breath and muscle, the boundless, rushing silence. I would lay forward on her neck, close my eyes, and simply feel the moment. Wrap myself in it. Use it as armor against sudden memory.

———

Rov gathered us all together for debriefing—Tauman, Jhem, and me. Fren, Tulo, and Ajhe. We sat in the courtyard of the manor and told him, in simple terms, the tale of our journey through the mountain. Afterward I expected a lecture or threat of arrest or something more horrible. But Rov only sat silently for minutes on end, elbows on the table, his chin on his clasped hands. "You realize that we only beat the Horrors because they paused to squabble over fresh kill," he said. "They were unguided. If they'd been under proper command, they'd have slaughtered us."

"You can thank Maia for that," said Jhem. "She killed the shaman who controlled them."

Rov leaned toward her, placing his hands on the table. "You can thank sixteen Dragonry teams and over two dozen of Staelan's soldiers." He looked at me. "And you can thank the Juza, too. They all died in your defense. All of them."

I felt my pulse quicken.

He looked to Jhem and Tauman, then back to me. "You know I only acted to protect the aeries. I was prepared to take ownership, yes, but I think the point is moot now. We have only one breeding pair—Tauman's—a handful of war animals and a nurse dragon. My candidates are all dead." He folded his hands together.

"More than that, Addai is dead, and as far as I'm concerned his decision died with him. I didn't invite the Juza—that was Bellua's doing. My petition for the charter remains, but circumstances have changed. My standing has changed. I'll abide by whatever decision is made. I only want what's best for the aeries."

"You expect to get the charter anyway," I said.

He squirmed. Nodded. "I'll need your expertise."

The stunned silence drew out until I couldn't stand it any longer. "I think yours is a special kind of cowardice."

His eyes snapped to mine, but he stayed silent.

"You were willing to let that monster Addai kill me so you could have the aeries."

He squinted. "I followed orders."

"Convenient orders. You gave all moral authority to a madman."

Rov clenched his fists unconsciously. Opened them and laid his hands flat. "I won't hold you responsible for his death. I'm honestly relieved that he's gone."

I now saw that all this time—nearly a year now—Rov said and did only what he needed to, in pursuit of his own goals. I should have shot him too, but that had been Addai's solution for Keirr and me—murder at the height of battle.

I shook my head. Whatever else was true, with Father missing, the aeries needed the expertise of men like Rov now. It didn't matter whether I approved.

"There are two things you need to think about, Captain Rov. First, a shaman summoned the Edimmu, whether he meant to or not. It's possible another shaman could rouse a monster like it."

Rov waited for me to continue.

"Secondly, the Edimmu likely stripped from Addai many closely held secrets. It did so to me."

"And me," said Fren.

"Me, too," said Tauman.

"It likely did the same to you," I finished.

When he realized that all eyes watched for his response, Rov nodded grim assent.

"We should assume that it knows everything you know," I said.

"But the Edimmu is dead."

"Is it?"

"We buried its corpse."

I shook my head at him. "We called it 'Edimmu.' It called itself '*us*.'"

Rov's face grew pale. "What does that mean?"

"I don't know. But if another like it appears, how much will it know as it *becomes*? Will it also be one of 'them'? What are 'they'? Do they share thoughts? Memories? *Knowledge*?"

And whoever *they* were, whatever body the Edimmu was *of*, were they drawn to *me* or to the aeries? What did my experience with the Summer Dragon say about that? Though Addai's assertions were wrong, it felt true to me that the Edimmu was connected to me somehow. Why? Would any future spawn or relative be any different?

Rov stared blindly at his clenched fists.

I scanned the table. "If Mabir's warnings were true, this is only the beginning."

———

The brood hatched right on time in the newly repaired broodhouse, four weeks after the festival of Oestara and the dawn of spring.

Keirr watched, happier than I'd seen her in weeks. She bounced from foot to foot.

"Qit!" as a window opened in each shell.

"Smaw," in wonder, as mewing qits tumbled into the straw to be cleaned and weighed.

Nine boys and seven girls, all healthy and active. Eight wore the dun and tan markings typical of Athys and Rannu's broods. Six were white and gray, like Coluver and Audax. Only two carried Shuja's black or Grus's copper. I remembered Addai handing me two eggs from Grus's nest as we prepared to abandon the broodhouse to the Horrors.

The qits drew Athys and Rannu out of their depression, too. They relaxed. Even Zell took part, her nurse instincts awakened. Her health improved.

Keirr stayed by the qits for the next eight weeks, played with them when they grew big enough to crawl out of the nests. Shepherded them. We'd not had a yearling in the aeries since Audax and Coluver were young. She was a wonder—curious and engaged as a wilding of her age would be. Like a big sister.

Darid returned in advance of the reinforcements. He sought me out the moment he landed in the paddock. Jhem had seen him approaching and ran to join us in the storehouse.

"Where's Rov?" he asked.

"On patrol."

"Good." He frowned as he clawed his gloves off and unbuckled his helmet. "Has your da' returned?"

I shook my head *no*, swallowing the pain.

"I'm sorry for that. I have news for you, Miss Maia. I wish it was good news, but it's not. There's a new Prelate in charge of the acquisition. His name is Poritor. Bellua reported to him." He looked at Jhem and me, the corners of his mouth turned down. "He's Juza, like Addai was."

"What manner of force does he bring?" I asked.

"One talon of Dragonry—"

"That's it?"

"And two entire wings of Juza."

Jhem groaned and sat down on a barrel.

"More engineers and masons travel with the acquisition train," Darid added. "More barrage machines too."

I sighed, looked at my feet, and nodded.

"There's worse news, m'lady. I have here his orders to Captain Rov. May the Avar protect me, but I broke the seal and peeked at them. As soon as he arrives, Poritor expects to arrest you, confiscate your dragon, and take you to Avigal for a hearing of some sort."

Jhem and I looked at each other. "Here we go again," she said.

"Bellua warned us it would be this way. The entirety of the Rasaal in opposition to us. To me."

"I'm sorry, young ma'am, but I knew . . . well, I knew that Cairek would have wanted you to know. I can only delay giving this to Rov for so long, but I'll give you as much time as I can."

"How long before Poritor arrives?"

"Not more than two weeks, ma'am. He may arrive sooner than that. But I can't give you more than a day."

Darid was young. Why hadn't I noticed that before? Perhaps twenty-two. Though his eyes were harrowed, though sun and wind had already marked his face, he had a boyish earnestness.

"Thank you, Darid. I appreciate the warning. Do what you must." A stone settled in my gut. I knew what I had to do.

———

I made my way to the broodhouse. The cliffside doors were opened, and qits bounced with excitement on the precipice. Athys and Rannu, Audax, Zell, and Keirr drew them back deftly from the edge with paws and wingtips, while allowing them enough leeway to see over the lip and *feel* the altitude. It was an age-old dance. We'd never lost a qit to the fall. It was their way; dragons loved and understood heights.

Keirr engaged in mock combat with an ornery little male, black like Shuja, with stripes of Grus's copper. He would be gorgeous one day. One of only two who survived out of their brood. Mews and chirps and high-pitched growls of kittenish threat filled the air. Athys and Zell chattered to each other in low clicks and purrs. The unknowable gossip of dragons.

Here was my entire life before me, everything I'd ever known—

the life cycle of dragons. I missed Father and Shuja, Darian and Aru terribly in that moment, and worry for them burned in my chest.

This was normally the most joyous time of year, when the aeries overflowed with cheerful, playful, mowping qits. Keirr was so happy. She didn't understand that we couldn't stay.

I wept, at last, for everything taken from me.

FIFTY - ONE

TULO PREPARED THREE packages for me, made of paper. They contained herbs and seeds and the ashes of Mabir, Cairek, and Bellua. I kept them, waiting for the right weather to manifest.

Darid delivered Poritor's orders to Rov, but the Dragonry Captain chose not to arrest me. "You understand I can't assist you in any way," he said, "but I won't hold you for them either."

It was more than I'd hoped for. I wondered, not for the first time, what drove him. Just when I thought I understood Rov's motivations, he surprised or infuriated me. It seemed to bounce from altruism to duty to greed and back again. I wished I had the time to figure him out. It wasn't to be.

Jhem and I prepared satchels so we'd be able to leave at a moment's notice—but I couldn't muster the will to go. We had qits to feed and clean up after, and while Staelan's men were happy to pitch in, they lacked the native instincts. Tauman would have his hands full managing the workload when we'd left.

Several more dawns came and went. I spoiled Keirr with extra fish and fatty treats; she'd benefit from built-in reserves. She and I spent every minute we could on the brood platform with Rannu, Athys, and the qits. Keirr chased the babies back from the lip with mock growls and gentle swats. They swarmed around her, bouncing off her feet and battling with her tail.

Tauman stood by while I said my goodbyes to his broodparents. Athys's face was striped with pink scars, though only a few minor scabs remained. I stroked her chin. She nuzzled me. "F-ly safe," she said, struggling with the difficult "L." "Come back."

"I'll see you again," I said. "I promise," though I could promise no such thing. I kissed her on the nose, then turned to Rannu. He sat with his head held high, his chest and shoulders a mass of bright red wounds only now beginning to form scar tissue.

"Father would be proud of you, old boy. Shuja too. You were wonderful."

He nodded and rumbled something in dragon speech, then added, "Maia: bi-g." Exactly as if Keirr had coached him on the word. He cocked his head at me, then lowered it for a pat. I'd have hugged him but for the many lacerations. A kiss would have to suffice.

Babies swarmed at my feet. I knelt down and let them brush against my fingers as they bounced and chased each other. Softly pebbled skin, like fine leather.

"Maia," said Tauman. "You know you shouldn't touch—"

"I want them to know me. I want them to remember me."

He nodded and said nothing.

On the sixth day I smelled something different in the wind. Crisp and cold, blooming but not yet ripe. Familiar. Keirr and I sought Fren, feeling an unspeakable urgency. We found him on the clifftop, raking wood chips and sawdust into bins in preparation for Brood Day.

"How's your shadow doing, Fren?"

He looked up in surprise. "My shadow is well. How is yours?"

"It's been almost a year since I caused your injuries, Fren."

"One year since the Summer Dragon," he countered with a smile.

The words constricted in my throat. "I don't want to leave you."

He set aside his rake. "I understand. I have to go into hiding myself. But tell me what's in your heart, young ma'am."

I hung my head, unsure how to reply, decided that direct was best. I looked him in the eye. "I don't know how my shadow is doing. I'm confused. I have so much to learn, to understand. I don't know what to believe, or where to begin."

He pursed his lips and puckered his brow for a moment. "Old Ashaani saying: 'The things we hold in reverence reflect our own nature. Warlike people worship jealous gods and build their altars of steel. Those who love wealth build their altars of gold. Content people honor loving gods and build their altars of love.'"

"You said that before, in the caves. But I don't understand."

"Your religion is revealed in the way you live your life. It doesn't matter what you claim to believe. You have to decide what your altar is made of."

I frowned. Walked up to him and put my arms around him. He embraced me. Gods, how I missed Father.

"And what of my curse, Fren? Did Getig come to lift my curse, or to cast it in stone?"

"What curse?"

I shrugged and shook my head. "Darian knew about it. It's hard to explain."

He stroked my hair. "There's no such thing as a curse."

"That's what Darian always said to me. But look around!"

"You can't think in those terms, daughter of my heart. Curse or blessing, we contend with it. Neither arrives without the other close behind. It's all part of the Evertide."

In my mind's eye I saw wheels inside of wheels, turning. "Why did the Summer Dragon choose me?"

Fren thought for a moment. "*Did* he choose you? That's not what I think. No, I suspect he was *drawn* to you, like the Edimmu was drawn to you."

"That's even less comforting."

He smiled. "Your story will be told, Maia. I know you don't want to be a story, but you saved the aeries from the Horrors. More than that, you saved the story of Getig from Addai. He lost, Maia. You beat him. If you're cursed, then your curse was our blessing."

I closed my eyes. "Poritor will arrest you if you spread tales of Asha."

"I am but a ripple on a wave of sound. Poritor may think he can smother this story yet. But we've already heard its echoes."

———

The seventh day broke with fire, and we hustled into the yard to witness a Morningtide billowing up. A broad, roiling cliff face of cloud reflected the first light, climbing skyward. At the height of summer it shouldn't happen, but it was tall and magnificent, and growing taller. The air was sweet and crisp.

I'd felt it coming. "This is it, Jhem," I said.

She swallowed and nodded.

We sprang into action. Tauman and I swung the saddle jib over Audax, with Jhem riding the saddle.

Fren ran up to us. "Darid sighted dragons on the horizon, Miss Maia. Ajhe has gone to meet them, but it's Poritor for certain. He'll be here today."

Tauman and I ran to the parapet to see for ourselves. A cloud of bright glints sparkled where the breaking sun skimmed over a multitude of wings.

"What timing they have," I said. "I guess they get a show, then."

"What do they think they're protecting?" Tauman asked. "The aeries are all but ruined."

I looked at him sideways. "The community, Tauman. That's the real heart of the aeries. Father understood that even if you never did."

"What do you mean?" He glared at me.

"Any two bonded dragons can make babies. Even Addai knew that. Yes, you have to know how to care for them, and you want your broodparents to be well matched. But the system that supports them— the network of farms and craftsmen and wilderness. That's still here. That's what we saved."

He frowned and hung his head. Jhem called us back to the saddle-jib. She climbed into the seat, and Tauman returned to help her with the straps and buckles.

They finished in silence, then he reached up and grabbed her hand. "I wish you could lie to them. Tell them what they want to hear. And stay."

"You know that won't work."

"I should go with you then. You're my wife."

She bent down and laid her head on their joined hands. "You know I can't let her go alone, and you know you can't leave. You're the broodmaster until Father returns or Poritor says otherwise."

"I know."

"You have to hold this together. You're Magha's son."

His chin bunched up. "I've treated you so poorly," he said. Then he climbed onto the harness so he could kiss her. They clung to each other's necks for a long time.

"We'll be back when we've found Darian and Father," I said. It sounded like a daunting task after so much time. A fool's mission at best. It was more pretense than plan. But Tauman agreed with a simple nod.

We saddled Keirr quickly. She and Audax danced on their nerves, sensing something different as Tauman, Fren, Jhem, and I hugged and held each other by turns.

Then I climbed into the saddle and strapped in. Jhem's eyes held mine, and she raised her chin. We had our weapons. We had food. We had gold and silver. We had our bondmates and each other.

"*Hai!*" I shouted, and Keirr launched into the rising dawn. Jhem shouted Audax into the air behind us.

We lifted on the Morningtide without effort. The spire of the aeries stood out of swirling mist that hid all but the tallest rooftops in the village below. The Roaring tumbled into a gray oblivion. I couldn't see the Temple at all.

Jhem rose behind me, called to me, looking to the east and pointing. Four or five dragon shapes broke off from the main mass to flap in our direction. I took note of them, but I wasn't worried.

I removed the three paper packages from my satchel, each about the size of a melon and tied with string. I held them close, remembering the day I collected them from Tulo. "I prepared these in the old ways," he said, "with herbs to confer our blessings on the departed and seeds to encourage the next cycle of life."

I untied each of the packages in turn and lifted them into the currents. The gentle maelstrom drew out their contents of herbs and seed and ash, dispersing them into the sky.

"It's not much, but it's what I had," Tulo had explained.

"For Mabir: sage and pine, for wisdom and humility; hyssop for sacrifice and cleansing.

"For Cairek: white jasmine for innocent love, mint for virtue, sweet willim for gallantry.

"For Bellua: willow for sadness, coriander for hidden worth."

"Who taught you this?" I asked him, stunned.

"Mabir. A long time ago. It's of the old ways, of the Ashaani."

I'd been unable to speak, touched by his thoughtfulness. Finally, I said, "Thank you, Tulo. Keep the drawings safe."

"I wish they could do some good."

"Someday. But right now they would only get you in trouble. Keep them hidden."

His voice cracked. "I wish you could stay."

I'd found myself wanting desperately to explain to him why I couldn't. I'd become exactly what Bellua and Addai and even my mother said I would: A curse. A weight. A hindrance at best. If I stayed, Riat would only suffer more. The Rasaal or the Edimmu or something worse would come, seeking me. I knew that. Or was I merely damaged by self-doubt? Scarred by invasions into my head?

How would I ever know? How did anyone know?

I heard my two mothers in my head—the one who cursed me before she died, and the one who spoke to dragons.

What did Fren say? *Curse or blessing, we contend with it. Neither arrives without the other close behind. It's all part of the Evertide.*

In the end I'd only kissed Tulo's forehead, and left him standing red-cheeked.

Jhem called again and pointed. The Juza outriders drew nearer. They didn't concern me. But that's not where she was pointing.

Two kites lifted from the aeries—the kites Borgomos had given Father so long ago. Only Tauman could have launched them. Within a few minutes, others rose above Riat to bob gently in the dawn.

I raised my goggles long enough to wipe the tears from my eyes. "Thank you," I whispered, though to who I wasn't sure. Asha, perhaps.

We mounted higher, while the Juza riders took an angle to intercept us. We slid northward along the wave front, high above the Crag. The crest of the Morningtide curled over the tip of Mt. Zurvaan, hiding the new cavity where a glacier once nestled.

The only way past the Crag was over the peak of the mountain. The Juza never had a chance of following us, only a slim hope of escaping the torrent I'd led them into. The currents around the Crag sucked them in and pulled them down. Perhaps some of them would survive.

Jhem and Audax, Keirr and I rode the wave all the way to the top. Higher than Zurvaan, higher even than Darian and Aru when they leapt from its point. The horizon stretched as we climbed, drawn into finer and finer slivers of distance until it vanished altogether.